ALSO, BY BRYAN WEMPEN

Fiction:
Mystery & Suspense
Unbound Ambitions: The Candidate (2025)
In New Mexico and Washington, D.C., rival campaigns collide over truth, power, and redemption. As secrets unravel, one idealistic team must confront corruption's cost to reclaim democracy—or lose the nation's soul.

Sumner Whispers, A Wyoming Murder Mystery of Secrets, Shadows, and Cursed Legacies (The Wyoming Murder Mysteries Series, 2024)
Secrets lurk beneath the surface in the quiet town of Sumner, Wyoming. Sheriff Grace Thompson must uncover the truth behind a shocking murder that ties the town's dark past to a chilling new crime.

Non-Fiction:
F**K My Demons: Redefining Normal (2024)
Personal Transformation – An honest and bold exploration of overcoming personal demons and rediscovering spirit and purpose in life, blending personal stories with powerful personal growth messages.

Sober Is Better: My Note to Self (2019)
Memoir & Addiction Recovery – A raw and personal account of Bryan's journey through addiction and recovery, offering hope and lessons learned along the way.

Note to Self: A Collection of 99 Life Lessons (2015)
Self-Improvement – An inspirational collection of personal reflections and lessons learned throughout life, offering practical advice and insights on growth, resilience, and mindfulness.

Dancing with Big Data (2015)
Technology & Business – A thought-provoking exploration of how big data is transforming industries and reshaping decision-making, featuring insights from leading experts on the future of data in business.

ADOPTION, INC.
A FAMILY AFFAIR

BRYAN WEMPEN

A NOVEL

Published by Red Yarrow Books
Santa Fe, New Mexico

Published by Red Yarrow Books,
an imprint of Cerrillos Road Holdings. Santa Fe, New Mexico

Red Yarrow Books are available at special discounts for events,
promotions, fundraising, or educational purposes when purchased in bulk.
For details, please get in touch with us at
redyarrowbooks@cerrillosroad.com

Copyright © 2025 by Bryan Wempen

Adoption, Inc. — A Family Affair is a work of fiction. Names,
characters, businesses, events, and dramatic incidents are the product of the
author's imagination. Any resemblance to actual people, living or dead, or
events is purely coincidental.

Cover design — Sherwin Emmanuel Minhas
Bio photo — Michella Wempen
Editor — ChatGPT

Library of Congress Control Number: 2025934455
ISBN: 979-8-9887219-6-3
eISBN: 979-8-9887219-7-0

Printed in the United States of America
Published in the City of Santa Fe, New Mexico

*This is for Dad and Max Evans and John Elroy Sanford
and Steve King.*

"Families are messy. Immortal families are eternally messy. Sometimes the best we can do is to remind each other that we're related for better or for worse...and try to keep the maiming and killing to a minimum."

— Rick Riordan, The Sea of Monsters

"This place is already shaping up to be a disaster movie. And we're the poor suckers who get eaten first."

— Marge Trenton

"At the root of every great fortune there was a crime."

— Honoré de Balzac (more or less)

ADOPTION, INC.
A FAMILY AFFAIR

INTRODUCTION TO THE SERIES

Families don't always come together the way they're supposed to. Sometimes, they don't come together at all. And sometimes—against all odds, better judgment, and the occasional court order—they form out of sheer stubbornness and a refusal to let the world win.

Ron and Marge Trenton never planned on raising a house full of kids, let alone ones the system had in some way written off. They could barely keep their own lives together, bouncing between overdue bills, half-baked business ideas, and a junkyard that functioned as much as a home as it did a money pit. But when Ron, a fast-talking dreamer with a talent for stretching versions of the truth, stumbled onto an opportunity to take in foster kids through a very creative interpretation of the rules, Marge found herself in the one role she'd never take— Mom.

Adoption Inc.: A Family Affair is a story about a different kind of family—the kind built on bad decisions, good intentions, hard work, and just enough dysfunction to keep things interesting. It's about kids who weren't wanted, parents who weren't prepared, and a system that often fails both. But more than anything, it's about survival—not just the kind that keeps you alive, but the kind that makes life worth living.

In this world, love isn't perfect. Hell, half the time, it's barely understandable. But you might see something real if you squint hard enough through the cigarette smoke and red chile fumes.

Welcome to the Trenton family; hydrate and buckle up; the story might get bumpy.

CHAPTER 1

The bathroom in Trenton's rented house was the kind of place that made you reconsider every life choice that had led you there. The walls were yellowed—whether from age, cigarette smoke, or something worse, Marge didn't want to know. The faucet leaked. The floor tiles were cracked. And the toilet took **exactly** two and a half flushes to get the job done—three if you were particularly unlucky.

Marge stood at the sink, squeezing the last sad inch of toothpaste from the tube. The dim overhead light flickered, buzzing like it was working overtime just to stay on. She spat into the sink, watching the water swirl slowly, like even the plumbing in this place was too tired to keep up.

Behind her, the toilet **groaned** as Ron finished up his morning routine.

Silence.

Then, Ron's voice, flat and resigned: "Marge. It's doing the thing again."

Marge closed her eyes. Took a breath. "Try jiggling the handle."

"Already did."

She turned to find Ron standing over the toilet, staring at it like a man who had fought this battle too many times before. He hit the handle again—one, two, three times—then sighed in defeat.

"I think it's time," he said solemnly.

"For what?"

"For a plunger funeral."

Marge rolled her eyes, grabbed the old plunger from the corner—where it had seen **far too much action**—and muttered a few choice words under her breath as she went to work. The toilet **gurgled, resisted, and finally gave in**, swallowing the water like a reluctant kid forced to eat vegetables.

Ron clapped his hands together. "That's my girl."

Marge shot him a look, tossing the plunger back in the corner. "Not your girl, asshole. Your wife, life partner, or better half—pick one."

Ron smirked. "Duly noted, sweetheart."

Marge exhaled, stepping out of the **too-small, too-hot** bathroom and into the rest of their **too-small, too-hot** rental house. "We need to move."

Ron leaned against the doorframe, rubbing his jaw. "We need money first." Marge sighed.

She walked into the kitchen, flicking open her cigarette lighter with one hand while absentmindedly stirring a pot of macaroni with the other. The **ceiling fan's click-click** overhead blended with the soft simmer of overcooked pasta. It did **jack all** to cut through the stifling air, but at least it made an effort—unlike certain household members.

Ron sat at the kitchen table with a mug of coffee and a spread of papers—some newspapers, some of his own half-baked ideas scrawled on the back of overdue bill envelopes. His brow furrowed like the secret to turning their lives around was hidden somewhere between the classifieds and the cartoons.

"Goddamn bullshit," he muttered, stabbing a finger at the paper.

Marge didn't even turn around. "What now?"

"'Junkyard King Strikes Gold,'" he read aloud, voice dripping with disdain. "This asshole's getting rich off piles of scrap metal, and here I am, sitting on my ass, trying to make sense of this godforsaken economy."

Marge smirked. "Maybe if you spent less time reading about other people's success and more time finding a job..."

Ron shot her a look. "Very funny. You want me to go bag groceries for minimum wage? Or maybe I could sell Avon door-to-door. Is that what you want, Marge? A husband who folds like a goddamn lawn chair?"

"I want a husband who can pay the electric bill," she shot back, but there was no malice in her voice. She set the spoon down, turned off the burner, and faced him, arms crossed. "Look, Ron, I'm not saying you gotta be a stockbroker. I'm just saying you can't keep sitting around dreaming up schemes. It's not like any of them ever worked."

Ron's eyes lit up with mock indignation. "Hey now, I've had plenty of good ideas!"

"Name one."

He paused, tapping a finger on the table. "The calculators!"

Marge snorted. "You mean the fifty crates of broken calculators you bought off that shady guy in Las Cruces? The one who also tried to sell you 'genuine Rolexes' out of his trunk?" The ones we couldn't even give away at the swap meet?"

Ron waved her off. "That was a fluke. Those calculators had potential."

"They had potential as paperweights, Ron. And now they're taking up half the garage."

"Alright, fine," he grumbled, leaning back in his chair. "But you gotta admit, I'm trying. I've been thinking a lot lately, Marge. About what we're doing. About what we're not doing. And you know what I've realized? We're spinning our wheels. We've got no direction, no... purpose."

"Speak for yourself," Marge said, lighting a fresh Marlboro and exhaling a plume of smoke. "My purpose is keeping this whole damn family from falling apart while you sit there philosophizing like some half-drunk high school dropout."

Ron ignored the jab. "No, seriously. What do we want, Marge? What's the big picture? Ron slapped a letter onto the table. "Final notice," it read in bold red letters. Marge felt her stomach sink. "And what's your grand plan for fixing this?" she asked. He grinned, the kind of grin that always meant trouble. "I've got an idea," he said. "A real winner this time."

She exhaled a plume of smoke and tilted her head. "You're working up to something. Just spit it out already."

Ron hesitated, his fingers drumming on the table. "Okay. What if—just hear me out—we stop waiting for the world to cut us a break and make our own luck?"

Marge arched an eyebrow. "Ron, I swear to God, if you're about to pitch me another sure thing or pyramid scheme—"

"It's not a scheme!" he interrupted, holding up his hands. "It's about family, Marge. You've been talking about how much you want kids, right? We've tried going through the adoption agencies, but those stuck-up pricks won't give us the time of day. So why don't we just... skip 'em?"

Marge stared at him. "Skip them? What the hell does that mean?"

"It means we take a different route," Ron said, leaning forward like a salesman about to close a deal. "Private adoptions, fostering. I've been looking into it, and let me tell you, it's a hell of a lot easier if you're creative. We get one kid, maybe two, and show everyone we're good at this. Then they'll have to take us seriously."

"There are tons of kids in New Mexico who need parents—tons!" Ron said with a warm smile.

"Creative, huh?" Marge took another drag of her cigarette. "And where's this sudden passion for kids coming from? Last time we babysat your cousin's kids, you locked yourself in the garage to 'fix the mower' for three hours."

"That was different!" Ron protested. "Those little bastards were hellspawn. But I'm talking about kids who need us, Marge. Ones who'd be better off with parents like us instead of stuck in some shitty state system."

Marge tapped her cigarette ash into the sink, her expression unreadable. She wanted to dismiss him, to scoff at his half-baked idea like she had so many times before. But something in his voice—earnestness, maybe, or desperation—gave her pause. Flawed as he was, she loved him dearly.

"And how exactly are we supposed to pay for all this?" she asked finally. "Raising kids isn't cheap, Ron. Last I checked, our bank account has less padding than a diner seat—and about as much as a church pew."

"Well..." Ron rubbed the back of his neck, a sheepish grin creeping onto his face. "Maybe we get a little creative with that, too."

Marge groaned. "Jesus Christ. You want to make money off this?"

"No! Not... not like that," he said quickly. "I just mean... we offset the costs a little. You know, balance the books. Some of these private adoption places are already making a killing. If they can do it, why can't we?"

"You are unbelievable."

"Unbelievably smart," Ron countered, his grin widening. "Look, I know it sounds crazy, but think about it. We get to build the family we've always wanted. We give these kids a good home. And if we happen to break even in the process, what's the harm?"

Marge sighed, stubbing out her cigarette in the sink. "Alright, let's say I entertain this lunacy for a second. Where do we even start?"

Ron sat up straight, his confidence growing. "We start small. Find a kid who needs a home, work out the kinks, and take it from there. We'll be naturals, Marge. Trust me."

"Oh, trust you? That's interesting," she said, but the corners of her mouth twitched into a reluctant smile.

"C'mon," Ron pressed. "You know this could work. You and me? We've always been good at making shit happen. This'll be no different."

Marge shook her head, half in disbelief and half in resignation. She let out a long breath, staring at the peeling wallpaper. Maybe he was full of it, but maybe a tiny part of her wanted to believe in something bigger than this crumbling house, this dead-end life. "Fine," she said, her voice softer. "But if this goes south, you're sleeping in the car."

"Deal!" Ron declared, slapping the table. "You won't regret this, Marge. We're gonna do something amazing."

She turned back to the stove, muttering under her breath, "Amazing, my ass."

Ron beamed as he returned to his papers, already dreaming up the future. Marge knew better than to trust his visions of grandeur, but deep down, she couldn't shake the thought that maybe—just maybe-this one wasn't entirely doomed.

CHAPTER 2

The **Morales Junkyard** sat on the outskirts of Albuquerque, a sprawling maze of rusted cars, forgotten appliances, and enough scrap metal to build a small battleship. The air smelled of hot metal and oil, and a feral cat yowled like a ghost caught between gears somewhere in the distance. Marge stepped out of the car first, taking a deep breath of the New Mexico air. It smelled like dust and potential disaster.

"This place looks like a tetanus shot waiting to happen," she muttered.

Ron climbed out from the driver's seat, squinting against the sun as he surveyed the junkyard like a man appraising his future empire. "You gotta see the vision, Marge. This isn't a junkyard. This is an opportunity, baby, a big opportunity!"

"I see a **hubcap graveyard**," Marge replied, shading her eyes with one hand. "And you're the one and only one dumb enough to want to buy it."

"Not buy it," Ron corrected, patting the side of their aging sedan, which groaned under the abuse. "Lease it. Big difference. We're not sinking money into this—just renting until the goldmine reveals itself."

Marge gave him a long, measured look. "I feel like I'm married to a fortune cookie that spits out bad advice."

Ron laughed. He had to admit that was pretty funny.

Then before Ron could find something clever to fire back, the sound of a chain-link gate screeching open caught their attention. A wiry old man with a cowboy hat perched precariously on his head emerged from the entrance. His boots clanked against the gravel, and his grin revealed a set of teeth as uneven as the junkyard's terrain.

"Hector Morales," he said, extending a hand toward Ron. "You the fella who called about the yard?"

"That's me," Ron said, puffing out his chest as if he were shaking hands with destiny.

Hector's gaze shifted to Marge, who raised an eyebrow. "And you must be the wife. God bless you, ma'am. Takes a lot of patience to keep up with a man who wants to lease a junkyard."

"I'm not patient," Marge said dryly. "I'm resigned—and complicit."

Hector let out a raspy laugh that turned into a cough. "Fair enough. Come on, let me show you around. And watch your step—there's a nest of feral cats somewhere near the south lot. They ain't friendly."

As Hector led them deeper into the junkyard, Marge and Ron exchanged glances. The place was a chaotic sprawl, with rusted car frames stacked precariously like the world's worst Jenga tower. Random scrap piles gleamed under the sun, and a trio of vultures loitered on an old washing machine like they were waiting for something to keel over.

A rustling noise came from behind a pile of scrap metal. A wiry kid, maybe ten or twelve, emerged, wiping his hands on a torn hoodie. He glanced at them, quickly looking away, stuffing something into his pocket.

"Nico!" Hector barked. "I told you—no digging through the lot without asking."

"I wasn't stealing," the kid shot back, chin raised. "Just seeing if there's anything I can use."

"Use for what?" Marge asked, eyeing the kid's scuffed sneakers and the duct tape holding the sole together.

"Fixing my bike," Nico muttered, nudging a rusted frame with his foot. "Or selling parts. I need cash."

Hector sighed. "Marge, Ron—this here's Nico. Sticks around, helps out now and then."

Jesus appeared from behind a workbench, arms crossed. "Helps out when he's not sneaking off or getting into trouble."

"I don't get in trouble," Nico muttered.

Ron squinted at him. "You got folks, kid?"

Nico frowned. "What are folks?"

"Parents," Ron said. "Folks is an old-time word, I guess."

"Nah. Foster homes." The words were clipped, practiced—like he'd answered that question a thousand times. "Don't stick around long."

Marge and Ron exchanged a look. For a fleeting second, something unreadable crossed Marge's face—sympathy, maybe, or recognition. But then she exhaled and looked away.

"C'mon, Nico," Jesus said, nodding toward the office. "Get washed up and stop messing with the scrap."

As the boy slouched away, Ron watched him go, a strange expression creeping onto his face.

"So," Ron began, sidestepping an ominous puddle, "what made you decide to sell this... uh, fine establishment?"

Hector shrugged. "Been runnin' it for thirty years, give or take. Figured it's time for me and the missus to retire. She wants to move to Las Cruces, buy a little house, maybe do some gardening. Me, I just want to sit in a chair and not think about catalytic converters for the rest of my days."

"Sounds like a dream," Marge said. "Why not sell it outright?"

Hector stopped and turned to them, his face suddenly serious. "Because this place isn't just a business. It's a legacy. And I ain't sellin' it to just anybody. I want someone who'll respect the yard. Someone who understands its... value."

Ron nodded solemnly, though Marge could see his fingers twitching with suppressed excitement. "Oh, I get it," he said. "This isn't just scrap metal. This is history."

"Exactly," Hector said, his grin returning.

As Hector led them deeper into the junkyard, he suddenly clapped his hands together. "Before we get to business, there's someone you gotta meet. PALOMA!"

The name rang out across the junkyard, echoing off the rusted car frames. A moment later, a stout woman in a floral blouse appeared, carrying a clipboard and radiating an aura of no-nonsense authority.

"This them?" Paloma asked, eyeing Marge and Ron like she was sizing them up for a fight.

"They're interested in the yard," Hector said. "And speaking of things that should interest you—did I ever tell you my wife here holds a world record?"

Paloma stiffened. "**Hector—**"

"A world record?" Ron perked up. "For what?"

Marge crossed her arms. "Yeah, what are we talking about here? Hot dog eating? Staring contests? Something involving a motorcycle jump?"

Paloma shot Hector a glare that could have dented steel. "It's nothing. It's ancient history."

"Ancient history?" Hector scoffed. "Woman, you still got the damn certificate framed in the office!" He turned back to Ron and Marge, clearly enjoying himself. "Get this—Paloma here holds the record for **stacking the most tires in under three minutes.** Fifty-three, back in '98."

Ron let out a low whistle. "That's a hell of a lot of tires."

Paloma shook her head, pressing her fingers to her temple. "I was young, I was foolish, damn good, and I was dared. That's all there is to it."

Hector grinned widely. "Dared by a radio station for a county fair stunt, and she didn't just win—she **demolished** the competition! Some guy from Arizona thought he had it in the bag with forty-two. Then boom—Paloma shows up and stacks 'em like she was **born for it.**"

"God help me," Paloma muttered under her breath.

Marge looked her up and down, smiling and shaking her head. "I goddamn, respect that."

Ron nodded solemnly. "You ever get the itch to stack again?"

Paloma sighed, crossing her arms over her clipboard. "Only when Hector runs his mouth too much. I think about stacking him under fifty-three tires."

Hector let out another laugh, unfazed. "See? Ain't she amazing?"

Paloma huffed but couldn't quite hide the twitch of a smile at the corner of her mouth.

Ron clapped his hands together. "Well, damn. I don't know if we're cut out for this business, but I like you two already."

"Good," she said. "Now, let's talk about this deal before my husband shares my high school GPA or my last medical test too."

Paloma narrowed her eyes, getting serious and looking at Ron. "You a mechanic?"

"Not exactly," Ron said, shifting uncomfortably.

"Good," Paloma snapped. "Last thing we need is some grease monkey ruining the inventory." She turned to Marge, her gaze sharp enough to cut through sheet metal. "And you? What's your deal, Mrs.?"

Marge met her stare without flinching. "I'm the one who keeps this guy from setting himself on fire."

Paloma cracked a small smile. "Good. He'll need lots of that."

With the introductions over, Hector led them into the office, which was crammed with filing cabinets, faded Polaroids, and a coffee machine that looked like it hadn't worked since the Reagan administration. Paloma sat behind the desk, gesturing for Marge and Ron to sit across from her.

"So," she began, folding her hands neatly on the desk, "why the hell do you want a junkyard?"

Marge opened her mouth, but Ron beat her to it. "Because it's not just a junkyard," he said, leaning forward like a man pitching the next big invention on *Shark Tank*. "It's a foundation. A hub. A place where dreams can grow."

Hector blinked. "What the hell does that mean?"

"It means I see potential," Ron said, warming up now. "People see junk, but I see opportunity. Cars, appliances, scrap—it's all waiting to be turned into something better. And I want to be the guy who makes that happen."

"Uh-huh," Paloma said, unimpressed. "And do you have any experience running a business?"

Ron hesitated, and Marge jumped in. "He's great with numbers. Quick on his feet. And he's got more ideas than most people have sense."

"I believe that," Paloma muttered under her breath.

"What my wife means," Ron said, glaring at Marge, "is that I'm resourceful. This yard needs someone who can think outside the box, and that's me. I'm not afraid to get my hands dirty, and I'm not afraid to take risks."

Paloma and Hector exchanged a glance. Finally, Hector shrugged. "Well, he's got the enthusiasm, I'll give him that. What do you think, Paloma?"

Paloma leaned back in her chair, tapping the clipboard with one finger. ""I think it's a goddamn miracle this guy hasn't talked himself into bankruptcy already. But…" She tapped the clipboard, her lips tightening. "I like her. Reminds me of my sister—tough, no-nonsense. We need more women like that in charge of things."

"Our niece Jen is running for Secretary of State. Not sure which side of the family she got that political ambition from, but she's smart and a good kid. So, make sure you give her a vote—whether we do this deal or not!" Hector smiled, then glared, as serious as a heart attack.

Ron leaned his head back, desperately craving a cigarette. "I'll take it," he said.

"You don't even know the terms yet," Paloma said, arching an eyebrow.

"Doesn't matter," Ron replied. "If you're willing to give me a chance, I'll make it work."

Paloma shook her head, muttering something in Spanish that Marge suspected wasn't complimentary. But then she handed Ron the clipboard. "Fine. It's a month-to-month lease. You break it, you pay for it. And if you screw this up, don't come crying to me."

Ron grabbed the clipboard like it was the Holy Grail. "You won't regret this. I promise."

"We'll see," Paloma said without hesitation.

As they left the office, Marge couldn't help but feel like they'd just signed a deal with the devil. The junkyard loomed around them, its twisted metal casting long shadows in the afternoon sun.

"Are you sure about this?" she asked.

"Sure? Hell, Marge, I've never been more sure of anything in my life," Ron said, beaming.

Marge sighed. "That's what I was afraid of."

And as they climbed back into the car, Hector and Paloma watched them go, shaking their heads.

"You think they'll make it?" Hector asked.

Paloma snorted. "Not a chance. But hey, we'll get some free help for a couple of months."

CHAPTER 3

The junkyard was a symphony of chaos. The groan of rusted metal, the shriek of a blowtorch, and the occasional bang of a car door falling off its hinges blended into an orchestra of questionable productivity. It was exactly the kind of mess Ron Trenton thrived on.

He stood atop a stack of scrapped car hoods, barking orders like a general surveying his troops. "Joey! Stop hammering the air and hit the damn nail! And Beth, for Christ's sake, don't stack the bumpers like that—you're building a death trap!"

Joey, their youngest, waved his hammer in a vague circle. "I'm making it sturdy!"

"You're making a lawsuit!" Ron yelled back. "Goddamn, I thought kids had common sense. Was I wrong? I was wrong, wasn't I?"

Beth, arms crossed, glared up at him. "You want to come down here and do it yourself, Dad?"

"Don't tempt me, missy. I could do it faster with one hand tied behind my back!"

Leaning against the doorway of their newly acquired office-slash-storage closet, Marge took a slow drag from her cigarette and shook her head. She'd seen enough of Ron's "motivational communication" to know it usually ended in someone bleeding or cursing—or both.

"You're gonna blow a gasket if you keep yelling like that," she called out, her voice steady but tinged with amusement.

"It's not yelling!" Ron hollered, arms outstretched in mock indignation. "It's *motivational communication.*"

"Sure it is," Marge said, exhaling a plume of smoke. "And those aren't vultures circling the yard—they're just big fans of your management style."

Sure enough, three vultures sat perched on an old refrigerator at the yard's edge, watching Ron with the focus usually reserved for roadkill.

"Ignore them," Ron grumbled. "They're freeloaders."

The office, which Marge had claimed as her domain, wasn't much better than the yard. It was crammed with relics the Morales's had left behind: ancient filing cabinets that groaned when opened, a coffee pot that smelled faintly of mold, and a wall calendar from 1979 featuring a pinup girl leaning suggestively against a tractor. Marge had cleared just enough space for a desk, a chair, and a permanent spot for her ashtray.

The kids had scattered into their assigned roles—or, more accurately, the roles Ron had arbitrarily bestowed on them. Beth, the eldest, was the "inventory manager," which mostly meant jotting down notes in a notebook she never let anyone else read. Joey, the youngest, had been declared the "construction foreman," despite his main qualification being an ability to wave a hammer around without hitting himself (most of the time). Danny, the middle child, was the "mechanic," a title he'd earned by successfully changing a tire once.

Danny trudged over to Marge, wiping grease-streaked hands on his jeans. "Mom, the Honda's engine is making this sound like... like a dying walrus or something. Should I hit it with a wrench?"

Marge raised an eyebrow, flicking ash into a tin can on her desk. "Don't hit anything until I come look at it. And stop wiping your hands on your pants—you look like you just lost a wrestling match with an oil slick."

Danny shrugged, muttering something about "work clothes," and wandered back to the wreck in question.

Marge stepped out into the yard, surveying the scene. It was equal parts disaster and... well, mostly disaster. But there was a rhythm to it, a kind of chaotic harmony that, if not exactly promising, at least felt survivable.

"All right," she said, clapping her hands to get everyone's attention. "Everybody take five. Joey, put the hammer down before you nail yourself to something."

The kids scattered, grateful for the break. Marge made her way over to Ron, who was now inspecting a pile of old mufflers as if they held the universe's secrets.

"You know," she said, crossing her arms, "this place is already shaping up to be a disaster movie. And we're the poor suckers who get eaten first."

Ron grinned, brushing a streak of dirt off his shirt. "You say that now, but wait till we've got this place humming. People will come from miles around with money to see what we've built here."

"People already come from miles around," Marge said dryly. "Mostly to dump their crap. And then there's the other crowd."

"What other crowd?" Ron asked, frowning.

"The nosy crowd," Marge replied. "That social worker's been sniffing around again. Donna something."

Ron groaned. "Not her. She's got it out for us, Marge. I can feel it. Probably heard about Joey playing hide-and-seek in the junked RV."

"Or maybe she's just doing her job," Marge said. "God forbid someone checks in on a bunch of kids living in a junkyard."

Ron waved her off. "The kids are fine. Happy as clams. Joey's got room to run, Beth's got her notebook, and Danny's elbow-deep in grease. What more could they want?"

Marge tapped her cigarette, ash tumbling onto the ground. "I don't know... school, maybe? Friends? Stability? Fewer opportunities to contract tetanus?"

"Details," Ron said, brushing off her concerns with a dramatic sweep of his hand. "We'll handle it if it comes up. Trust me, Marge, this place will be the heart of the operation."

Marge raised an eyebrow. "**What operation?**"

Ron hesitated, then gave her his best attempt at an innocent smile. "You know... the operation."

"That's not an answer."

"It's a... flexible business model," Ron said, gesturing vaguely to the yard. "Scrap, salvage, maybe some refurbished parts—*creatively acquired,*" he added, his voice dropping to a mumble. "The point is, it's ours. And we're in control."

Marge lit another cigarette, blowing out a plume of smoke as she stared at him. "I swear, if you get us shut down because you can't resist 'hustling,' I'm throwing you to the vultures."

Ron clapped her on the shoulder. "Relax, Marge, love you. We've got this."

Just then, a beat-up truck rattled into the yard, kicking up a cloud of dust. A man in a black pork-pie hat climbed out, squinting at them from beneath the brim.

"You, Ron Trenton?" he called out, his voice carrying across the yard.

"Depends who's asking," Ron replied, his grin faltering slightly.

The man sauntered closer, hands resting on his hips. "Name's Earl. I'm with the county."

Marge and Ron exchanged a glance.

"Great," Marge muttered under her breath.

Earl pulled a clipboard from under his arm and flipped through it. "Looks like you folks didn't file all the permits you need to operate a salvage yard. That's a problem."

Ron's grin turned into a strained grimace. "A problem? No, no, Earl, you must be mistaken. We're fully above board here. Just a little... startup hiccup, you know?"

Earl didn't look convinced. "Hiccup or not, you're missing about half a dozen signatures. We'll have to shut you down if you don't get this sorted."

Marge stepped forward, her tone calm but firm. "Earl, honey, is there a way we can, I don't know, work this out? A little extra paperwork? Some clarification?" She could be extra convincing when necessary.

Earl scratched his chin, oblivious to Marge's charms, eyeing her warily. "I'll give you four weeks. After that, if I don't see those permits, we're shutting this whole place down." With that, he climbed back into his truck and drove off just as quickly as he arrived, leaving a trail of dust and concern behind him.

Ron let out a string of expletives, most starting with F, pacing in agitated circles. Marge just sighed, flicking ash to the ground.

"So," she said finally, her voice **dripping with sarcasm**, "about that 'flexible business model' of yours..."

CHAPTER 4

The office was exactly what Marge expected: the air smelled like stale coffee, the walls were stained from decades of cigarette smoke, and the ceiling fan wobbled like it was ready to give up.

It fit **Philip "Phil" Grayson** perfectly.

He sat behind a cluttered desk, his suit straining against a stomach at odds with both shirt and belt—yet far too nice for a lawyer renting a second-floor office above *Big Joe's Pawn & Loans*. He wasn't nervous, but he wasn't exactly comfortable either. He was the kind of man who lived in the middle of deals—always one signature away from easy money, always one misunderstanding away from a *Fredo-style* fishing trip.

Across from him, Ron lounged in his chair like he was catching up with an old friend, while Marge sat stiff-backed, arms crossed—unimpressed.

Phil leaned forward, tapping a thick manila folder against the table. "Alright, let's make this official." He slid it across the desk.

Ron picked it up, whistling as he flipped through the pages.

"Damn. This looks real."

Phil smirked. "Because it *is* real, Trenton. Just a little… untraditional."

Marge plucked the papers from Ron's hands, scanning the fine print. Independent Foster Placement Agreement. The words looked official, but the signature lines were what caught her eye.

"And who exactly is signing off on this?" she asked.

Phil shrugged, sipping his coffee. "Depends on the county. Some caseworkers push these through when the system gets clogged. Some judges have their own reasons for approving things fast. And some…" He trailed off, smirking. "Some just don't ask questions when the right people tell them not to."

Marge shot a look at Ron. This stinks.

Ron grinned. "So what you're saying is, we're working the angles?"

Phil laughed. "Jesus, Trenton. You act like you discovered high treason."

Ron chuckled, flipping through more pages. "It's not about discovery, pal. It's about execution."

Marge resisted the urge to smack him.

"And what exactly does the 'special case committee' do?" she pressed, focusing back on Phil.

Phil waved a hand lazily. "They sign off on cases that don't go through the normal state channels. It's less used, but it happens." He smiled, taking another sip of coffee. "And let's just say someone upstairs is ensuring this happens for you."

Marge narrowed her eyes. "Someone upstairs?"

"God?" Ron shouted.

Phil leaned back in his chair, arms crossed. "You don't want to know."

A heavy silence settled over the room, broken only by the creak of the ceiling fan. Each turn seemed louder, more insistent.

Phil exhaled sharply. "Damn fan. Replace that someday."

Ron grinned, as if that was the best news he'd heard all week.

Marge felt something cold settle in her gut. It seemed too easy.

She didn't like how it felt—too neat, too convenient. And she sure as hell didn't trust good ole Phil.

Phil watched them for a second, then sighed and leaned forward.

"Look, I get it. Feels too good to be true. But here's the deal—nothing we're doing is illegal. Gray? Sure. But illegal? No. You get the kid, you get the stipend or not, and the paperwork clears. General rule, no stipend, less reporting and paperwork, and you're just not sitting on a five-year waiting list like the suckers doing it the *typical* way."

Ron nodded. "That's what I like to hear."

Marge rolled her eyes. "Of course it is."

Phil grinned. "You think you're the first guy to work an angle in this town? The only difference between you and the rich folks adopting straight out of private agencies is that you don't have a lawyer charging you a hundred grand to 'expedite' things."

Marge took a slow breath. She hated that he had a point.

Ron, enjoying himself, leaned forward. "You know, you talk a good game, Grayson. Almost too good. Starting to think you might be my type."

Phil grinned at her. "Marge, I like you. You've got a good head on your shoulders."

"Yeah? That's why you're handing me a contract signed by people you won't name?"

Phil's smirk didn't waver, but his eyes flicked toward the paperwork—just for a second.

He didn't know who was behind this either.

Phil sighed. "Look, if you're worried, walk away. But you won't. You wanna know why?"

Marge stared, "enlighten me."

"Because you want this. Maybe not for the same reasons as Ron, maybe not for money, but you *want* it. And someone out there wants you in it. That's a rare thing in life—when what you want lines up with what the system's giving you."

Ron tapped the table, looking amused. "So what you're saying is, don't look a gift horse in the mouth."

Phil smiled. "I'm saying—if the horse shows up with gold-plated horseshoes, maybe don't ask who paid for 'em."

Marge shook her head. This is a mistake.

Ron started to sign the contract.

Marge stopped him. "Damnit, wait."

Ron frowned. "What now, Babe?"

Marge turned to Phil. "What happens if we say no?"

Phil stared, unblinking. "Then someone else gets the call. Maybe they're worse than you. Maybe they're better." He tapped the file, slow and deliberate. "But the opportunity?" His voice sharpened. "It's not yours anymore."

Ron hesitated—just for a second. Then, with a sharp breath, he signed the paperwork.

Phil slid the folder back into his briefcase, sealing the deal.

"Pleasure doing business, Trenton. Marge, it has been a delight."

Marge frowned but said nothing.

Phil stood, straightening his suit, his stomach pressing against the strained belt. At the door, he hesitated. The usual smirk was gone.

"One last thing. If I were you, I wouldn't ask too many questions about the kids that end up on your doorstep."

Marge's stomach twisted. "Doorstep?"

"Not the doorstep, literally, Marge," Phil said.

He gave them a long, unreadable look. Fewer questions. Better for you. Then he walked out.

Ron smiled. "He's fun."

Marge was pissed and not laughing. She picked up the contract, flipping through it again. And at the very bottom, in tiny, near-invisible text, a detail sent her pulse racing:

Placement Approved by: **[REDACTED]**

Someone had already signed it—before they ever agreed.

CHAPTER 5

Junkyard's chaos had peaked by mid-morning—a cacophony of clanging metal, barking dogs next door, and shouted expletives echoing across the dusty lot. To an outsider, it might have looked like a scene from a post-apocalyptic survival movie. To the Trentons, it was just another Tuesday.

Ron stood in the middle of it all, shouting over the noise like a man who thought volume was the key to authority.

"Joey, **I swear to God,** if you keep throwing rocks at the crow, it's gonna start throwing 'em back!" he hollered.

Joey, perched precariously on top of a rusted washing machine, glared at the bird. "He started it!"

"You're six! Damn near a grown man, ACT like it!"

This made Joey puff out his chest; all he heard was "grown man."

Nearby, Danny was neck-deep in the engine of a wrecked Ford, grunting with effort as he tried to loosen a bolt. He looked up, grease smudged across his face like war paint. "Pop! This thing's stuck!"

"Then hit it with something heavier!" Ron bellowed.

"I already hit it with a wrench!"

"Then hit it with two wrenches! Goddamnit."

"Two wrenches?" Danny muttered to himself. "That's not how tools work..."

Beth, 15, the only one in the family who seemed to possess a shred of common sense, stood at the edge of the chaos with a clipboard. Her official title was *inventory manager*, but in reality, she had become the *keeper of the family's questionable decisions.*

When she wasn't trying to impose order on the mayhem, Beth could be found alone, either writing in her notebook or lost in another book—her two favorite pastimes.

"Dad, we've got a problem," she said, approaching Ron.

Ron let out a weary chuckle, waving a hand toward the yard. "Kiddo, we've got *lots* of problems. You'll have to be more specific."

Beth held up the clipboard. "The social worker's coming back for a visit tomorrow, and half the yard looks like it's been hit by a tornado."

Marge appeared at Ron's side, arms crossed and cigarette firmly in place. "Half the yard? That's generous, Beth."

Ron groaned, running a hand through his hair. "Why can't these people just leave us alone? Don't they have better things to do than harass a family trying to make an honest living?"

"Honest living?" Marge raised an eyebrow. "You're teaching Joey to hotwire a lawnmower for 'salvage purposes.'"

"That's a life skill!" Ron shot back. "And don't act like you weren't impressed when it worked!"

Beth waved the clipboard in his face. "Focus, Ron! What are we gonna do about the yard? If Ms. Donna shows up and sees this mess, she's gonna cause us lots more problems for sure."

Ron sighed, his eyes scanning the junkyard like a captain surveying a sinking ship. "Alright, here's the plan: We clean up. We make this place look... presentable."

"Presentable how?" Beth asked. "There's a dead squirrel in the engine Danny's working on."

"Not dead!" Danny yelled. "It just moved!"

Joey shrieked from his perch. "It's alive? Cool!"

"Alright, new plan," Ron said quickly. "We're skipping 'presentable' and going straight for 'distract and deflect.'"

"That's not a plan!" Beth protested.

"It's an approach, and barely that, geesh!"

Marge sighed, dragging a hand down her face. "Jesus Christ, Ron. If this is your idea of parenting, I'm amazed none of them have run away yet."

"They're too busy learning to run the business to run away," Ron said, grinning. "Right, team?"

The kids groaned in unison, rolling their eyes and sighing dramatically. But beneath the theatrics, they couldn't deny it—they were part of something. And despite the complaints, they were pretty happy about it.

Later that afternoon. To say the junkyard cleanup was a disaster would be an insult to disasters. Joey had taken the directive to "organize" the scrap pile as an invitation to build a fort out of old car doors, which promptly collapsed and sent him running for cover. Still a bit traumatized by the squirrel incident, Danny locked himself in the shed and refused to come out until someone else "handled it."

Beth, meanwhile, was trying to re-label the inventory, a task made significantly harder by Ron's constant walking past and yelling, "No, don't write it down as a muffler—call it a 'dual-purpose exhaust device'! It sounds fancier, so we can charge more!"

"Do you even know what a muffler is, Ron?" Beth snapped.

"I know it muffles!" Ron replied.

Watching all of this unfold from the office doorway, Marge lit another cigarette and muttered to herself, "One of these days, this place is gonna make it into the news. And not in a good way."

Her prediction seemed eerily prophetic when a loud crash echoed across the yard. Everyone turned to see Joey standing in front of a shattered windshield, a baseball bat dangling from his hand.

"It slipped!" he shouted defensively.

Ron pinched the bridge of his nose. "That's it. I'm calling a meeting."

The "meeting" took place around the rusted picnic table near the center of the yard. Marge sat at one end, already halfway through her third cigarette of the hour. Ron stood at the other, pacing like a motivational speaker about to deliver the keynote at a scrapyard convention.

"Alright, listen up!" he barked. "Tomorrow's visit from the social worker is make-or-break. If she doesn't buy what we're selling, this whole operation goes up in smoke. We don't want that."

"What exactly are we selling, Pop?" Danny asked.

"Stability!" Ron declared.

Joey raised his hand. "What does that mean?" A fair question for a six-year-old.

"It means we act like a normal family," Ron explained, though he wasn't entirely sure what that looked like either.

"We're not a normal family," Beth pointed out, arms crossed.

"Then we fake it!" Ron declared. "You ever heard the saying, 'fake it until you make it'? Alcoholics say that one a lot."

Joey wrinkled his nose. "What's an alholic?"

Everyone ignored him.

Marge leaned back in her chair, exhaling a long plume of smoke. "Ron, that's not helpful," she said, her voice dry as the New Mexico air. "And faking it's gonna take a hell of a lot more than a fresh coat of paint."

"Don't you worry about paint," Ron replied. "I've got a plan."

Beth groaned. "Every time you say that, something catches fire."

"That's not always true!" Ron protested.

Beth stared at him.

"Okay, it's happened once or twice. But this time, it's foolproof." He turned to Joey. "You're gonna clean up the scrap pile."

Joey's face lit up. "Can I build another fort?"

"No, damnit!" Ron snapped.

He turned to Danny. "You're on engine duty. Make sure everything that looks broken gets shoved out of sight."

Danny frowned. "What if it still smells like squirrel?"

"Air freshener!" Ron barked.

"And what am I supposed to do?" Beth asked.

"You're the face of the operation," Ron said, pointing at her. "You talk to the social worker. Be polite. Smile. Act responsibly and normally!"

Beth rolled her eyes. "Why don't *you* do that?"

Before Ron could answer, she shook her head, already losing interest. *Never mind. I'm going to start a new book—a murder mystery this time.* Anything was better than dealing with *this* mess.

"Because I'll be too busy managing!"

"Managing what?" Marge asked, smirking.

Ron grinned. "The **illusion of success and normality**," he said, then bowed exaggeratedly.

CHAPTER 6

Among the Yard's most familiar faces was a man named Anthony Redmoon, a Jemez Pueblo artist whose quiet presence made a lasting impression. Every few weeks, Anthony would arrive in his battered turquoise truck, weaving slowly through the maze of rusted cars, discarded appliances, and tangled wire, eyes keenly scanning for hidden treasures. He wasn't looking for spare parts or scrap for profit—he was searching for inspiration.

Anthony's art was rooted in the traditions of his people but infused with the raw, weathered beauty of salvaged metal, wood, and stone. To him, the Yard wasn't a junkheap; it was a living spirit of forgotten things waiting to be reborn. Hector Morales always greeted him warmly, often setting aside particularly interesting scraps he thought Anthony might want. Paloma pretended to grumble about "giving away the good stuff," but everyone knew she had a soft spot for him.

Sometimes Anthony would pay in full, other times he'd barter with a small sculpture or a hand-forged wind chime, which Paloma hung proudly in the office. His visits were a balm amid the daily chaos—a reminder that not everything discarded was worthless. His finished pieces, displayed in small galleries and roadside shows across New Mexico, carried a spirit of endurance and reclamation that reflected both the land and the people who lived close to it.

In a place built on second chances, Anthony's presence made everyone quietly believe that beauty could grow from even the most broken beginnings.

CHAPTER 7

The morning of the social worker's visit dawned with a fiery sunrise, but the Trentons were too busy panicking to enjoy it. The junkyard was its usual disaster zone, and Donna Lujan, their assigned social worker, was scheduled to arrive in less than an hour.

Ron stood in the middle of the yard, wearing a Hawaiian shirt he'd uncovered from a clearance bin at Goodwill. A combination of panic and delusion was plastered across his face. "Alright, team! This is it! This is our chance to prove we're a well-oiled machine of responsible parenting!"

"More like a dumpster fire with good intentions," Marge muttered, leaning against the side of a rusted van.

Ron ignored her, clapping his hands for attention. "Joey! Get your ass down from that refrigerator! Today, we're not running a goddamn circus, kiddo!"

Joey, perched on top of an ancient fridge in his underwear and a pirate hat, waved a foam sword in the air. "I'm not coming down till you call me Captain Joey!"

"For the love of shit," Ron groaned. "**Fine. Captain Joey**, get your pirate ass down!"

Joey grinned triumphantly and slid down the side of the fridge, landing in a pile of hubcaps with a loud crash.

Danny poked his head out of the garage, his face streaked with fresh grease. "Pop, the lawnmower's stuck in reverse, and I think I accidentally shaved half the cactus garden with it."

"Leave it!" Ron barked. "Priorities, Danny boy!"

Marge, smoking her second morning cigarette, squinted at him through the smoke. "You know this will blow up in your face, right?"

"Not if we stick to the plan!" Ron declared.

"Plan? You mean that half-assed list of demands you barked at the kids last night?"

"It's called delegation, Marge."

"It's called desperation," she shot back with a scowl.

Carrying a box of spray paint, Beth joined the group with a scowl. "Who thought painting the 'welcome' sign pink was a good idea? Now it just says 'elcom.'"

Ron grimaced. "Goddammit, Beth, why didn't you fix it?"

Beth held up the can of white spray paint. "Because somebody"—she shot a pointed look at Joey—"used the rest of the paint to draw dicks on the side of the van."

Joey puffed out his chest proudly. "I am a pirate and artist!"

Ron turned a shade of red that nearly matched the hibiscus flowers on his Hawaiian shirt. "You drew dicks?! Donna's gonna take one look at us and think we're running a nudist colony for graffiti perverts!"

"Technically, it's *abstract* dicks," Marge corrected, barely suppressing a smirk.

"I'll abstract all of you if you don't grab a rag and clean it off!" Ron snapped, his voice climbing in frustration. Then, taking a deep breath, he steadied himself and got rarely serious for a moment.

"Look, everyone," he said, his tone unusually serious. "We need to impress the social worker to stay a family. Do you all understand?"

Sensing the shift in his mood, the kids nodded quietly, even Joey, who had been snickering moments ago.

Marge exhaled a long plume of smoke, watching Ron closely. "Well, that's the first sensible thing you've said all day," she muttered. "But if you think scrubbing off some art's gonna fool Donna Lujan, you've got another thing coming."

Ron glanced at the kids, then back at Marge. "Maybe not, but we're gonna try anyway! Now grab a rag and get scrubbing!"

By the time Donna Lujan's car pulled up to the junkyard, the Trentons had slapped a thin veneer of stability over their chaos. The spray-painted van had been parked strategically behind a wall of tires, the cactus carnage was hidden under a tarp, and Joey had been bribed with a Snickers bar to wear pants.

Ms. Lujan stepped out of her car, clipboard in hand, her sharp eyes sweeping over the yard like a hawk searching for prey. She was a no-nonsense woman in her late forties, her hair pulled into a tight bun.

Her look practically screamed, I'm not here to fuck around. Yet... fairly attractive, Ron mused unsaid to himself.

Plastering on his best salesman's smile, he strode forward with his arms outstretched. "Donna! Welcome to our humble little family enterprise!"

Donna's eyes narrowed. "Is that a shirt or a cry for help?"

"It's both festive and reasonably priced," Ron shot back, trying not to sound defensive. Not that it mattered—he couldn't wipe the grin off his face if he tried.

Marge snorted from the office doorway, muttering, "Festive like a drunk uncle at a wedding—the kind you definitely cross the room to avoid."

Donna approached the picnic table they'd set up for the meeting, her heels clicking against the gravel. She sat down without invitation, scanning her clipboard. "Alright, Mr. and Mrs. Trenton. Let's get to it. How are things going with the kids?"

"Great!" Ron said a little too loudly. "Things are fantastic! Joey's thriving. Danny's practically a certified mechanic. And Beth—well, Beth's basically running the place. Right, honey?"

Beth, standing nearby with her arms crossed, shot him a look. "Sure, Dadddddddd." Then she turned to Donna with a smirk. "Just kidding, Ms. Donna. Doing well over here."

Donna made a note on her clipboard, her expression unreadable. "And how's the home life? Stable?"

"Stable as hell!" Ron exclaimed, gesturing around the junkyard. "Just look at this place. You'd be hard-pressed to find a more harmonious environment!"

At that exact moment, a loud crash echoed from the garage, followed by Danny's voice yelling, "Oh shit! Oh shit!"

Donna arched an eyebrow. "What was that?"

"Uh... innovation? Uh…maybe inspiration?" Ron said weakly.

Marge, sensing disaster, stepped in. "You know how kids are. Always experimenting. Keeps 'em sharp."

"Mm-hmm," Donna said, unimpressed.

Joey chose that moment to streak across the yard, **stark naked except for** his pirate hat, yelling, "The treasure's mine, you scallywags!"

"Oh, for fuck's sake!" Ron bellowed, taking off after him.

Donna blinked, her pen hovering over the clipboard. "Is he... always this spirited, acting out, and naked?"

"Every damn day," Marge replied, deadpan. She paused for effect, "Well, minus the naked part—that's definately new and improved."

While Ron wrestled Joey into a pair of shorts behind the shed, Donna continued her inspection, her keen eyes missing nothing. She spotted the pink not completely fixed "elcome" sign but said nothing, her lips twitching ever so slightly.

In the garage, Danny tried explaining how the lawnmower had somehow launched a tire into the air and lodged it in the side of the shed. "It's, uh, kinetic energy," he said.

Sensing the visit was spiraling out of control, Marge stepped in to salvage what she could. "Look, Ms. Lujan, we're not perfect, but we're doing our best. The kids are learning skills. We're giving them a home. It's not polished, but it's real."

Donna studied her for a long moment, her expression softening just slightly. "I can respect that," she said finally. "And, for what it's worth, they do seem happy enough."

"Unfortunately, in this job, I see a lot of unhappy and at-risk kids," Donna said, her tone heavy. "It's the part that gets me up every day—the part that makes me work hard to try and make a difference."

At that moment, Joey burst into the yard, fully clothed, and tripped over a pile of hubcaps, landing face-first in the dirt.

Donna sighed. "I'll be honest. I've seen worse—a lot worse, unfortunately."

"You hear that, Marge?" Ron called from across the yard. "We're not the worst!"

Marge lit another cigarette, shaking her head. "Both amazing and a low bar, Ron. I repeat, low bar."

Marge sighed, taking a long drag before flicking the cigarette away. "Alright, enough of this circus. Let's go to the Taco Shack."

Ron perked up. "**Taco Shack**?"

"Yeah," Marge said, exhaling smoke. "The local, family-owned Mexican place, a hole-in-the-wall off Cesar Chavez. Good tacos, carne adovada burritos, tamales—hell, even menudo on the weekends."

Ron's face lit up. He and Marge had been coming to the Taco Shack since before they were married. It was one of the few places that had remained a constant in their chaotic lives. The little restaurant was nothing fancy—just a small stucco building with a faded sign, a few wobbly picnic tables outside, and the kind of neon "OPEN" sign that flickered unpredictably. But what it lacked in aesthetics, it more than made up for in flavor.

The moment they walked in, the air hit them like a warm embrace—thick with the smell of slow-simmered red chile, fresh masa, and grilled carne asada. The sizzle of meat on the flat-top, the rhythmic chop of cleavers against wooden boards, and the bubbling of deep-fried chips in hot oil were a symphony to anyone who appreciated good food.

Marge swore they had the best carne adovada burritos in town—thick flour tortillas wrapped around tender, marinated pork that had been stewed for hours until it practically melted in your mouth. The red chile sauce had just the right balance of heat and depth, making every bite an experience. On the other hand, Ron lived for their street tacos—grilled carne asada or carnitas, piled high on fresh corn tortillas, topped with diced onions, cilantro, and a squeeze of lime. He drowned his in salsa verde, swearing that the little kick of heat made them perfect.

Then there were the tamales—Max's downfall. Fluffy, homemade masa wrapped around shredded pork or green chile cheese, steamed to perfection in corn husks, they were soft, rich, and ridiculously addictive. It was easy to lose track of how many you'd eaten until you found yourself in Max's predicament. Every time he has the opportunity, he overindulges and then spends hours on the toilet.

If you came on the weekend, the menudo was legendary. It was a deep, rich broth filled with tender hominy and tripe, spiced with red chile, and served with a side of fresh tortillas for dipping. Some swore by it as the ultimate cure for a hangover. Others just loved the tradition of it, a dish that took time and care to make right.

Ron clapped his hands together. "Now we're talkin'," he said, already heading for the truck. "And Max, maybe don't eat *too* many tamales this time."

Max groaned, fake clutching his stomach. "No promises."

Marge just shook her head with a smirk as they all piled in. No matter how wild things got, at least there was always good food waiting for them at the Taco Shack.

CHAPTER 8

By the time Donna Lujan's car disappeared down the dirt road, leaving a trail of dust in its wake, Ron was pacing the junkyard like a caged animal, muttering under his breath. Joey sat in a bucket, sulking, while Danny poked at the busted lawnmower with a screwdriver. Beth stood near Marge, arms crossed and jaw clenched.

"Well?" Beth said, breaking the silence. "How do you think it went?"

"It went fine," Ron snapped, spinning on his heel to face her. "You're all still here, and she didn't shut us down, did she?"

"Yet," Marge added, lighting another cigarette. "She didn't shut us down *yet*. Big difference."

"Oh, ye of little faith," Ron said, throwing up his arms. "We're fine. The kids are fine—Donna's fine. Everything is *fine*! Love, peace, and joy, family!"

"Yeah, except for the part where Joey streaked through the yard," Beth said. "Or the part where Danny's 'kinetic energy' explanation sounded like a stoned high schooler's science project. Or—"

"**Okay, *fine*! It wasn't perfect!" Ron bellowed.

Joey raised his hand from the bucket. "I thought it was fun."

"No one asked you, Captain Underpants," Ron snapped.

"I was wearing the pirate hat," Joey muttered.

Danny tossed the screwdriver onto the lawnmower and stood, brushing his hands on his jeans. "Pops, can we talk about how this whole junkyard thing being a *terrible* idea?"

Ron turned to him, incredulous. "What? Terrible? This is the best idea I've ever had!"

"Do you not like working in the yard with stuff, Danny?" Ron asked, his expression genuinely perplexed.

Danny paused, clearly unsure how to answer. He didn't say a word, but Ron didn't miss a beat and moved on.

"Your *best* idea was buying fifty special calculators we couldn't sell," Marge shot back without missing a beat.

"That was a supply chain issue, Marge! We've *established* that," Ron protested, pointing a finger for emphasis.

"No," Marge muttered, lighting a fresh cigarette. "That was you being a shortsighted, optimistic idiot."

Ron spun on her, pointing a finger, his agitation bubbling over. "You're supposed to be on my side!"

"I am on your side," she said. "But that doesn't mean I'm gonna sit here and pretend this place isn't one bad inspection away from having our family condemned."

Ron let out a long, exasperated sigh. "You people have no vision. None! You can't see the potential here!"

"Potential for what?" Danny asked, throwing up his hands. "A tetanus outbreak?" he added, echoing what his mother had said a hundred times before.

"How the hell do you know about tetanus, Danny?" Ron bellowed.

"For greatness and success!" he barked. **"This junkyard is a diamond in the rough, a blank canvas.** *And I—your fearless father—am the goddamn artist!"*

"You're about as artistic as a drunk raccoon," Marge muttered.

Joey giggled. "Drunk raccoons are funny I bet."

Ron ran a hand through his hair, clearly on the edge of losing it. "Alright, fine. You want to know the *real* problem here? It's not the junkyard. It's you kids!"

Beth's eyes narrowed. "Us?"

"Yeah, you!" Ron said, pointing a finger at her. "And you!" He turned the finger on Danny. "And *you!*" Finally, the finger landed on Joey, who was still sitting in the bucket.

"Me? What did I do?" Joey asked, looking genuinely confused.

"Everything! You're all whining and bitching and moaning instead of pulling together like a goddamn family!" Ron shouted. "This isn't just a junkyard, okay? This is our *home*. And if we don't make it work, we're all screwed. So instead of nitpicking every goddamn thing I do, maybe try *helping* for once!"

The silence that followed was deafening. Even the crows seemed to stop talking to watch the fallout.

Finally, Beth broke the silence. "You know what, Ron? Screw this." She tossed the clipboard onto the ground and started walking toward the house.

Ron blinked. "What the hell does that mean?"

"It means I'm done," Beth said, not looking back. "You want to play junkyard king? Fine. But I'm not wasting another second pretending this is a good idea."

"Beth, get back here!" Ron shouted.

But she didn't.

Marge sighed, tossing her cigarette onto the ground and stomping it out. "Good job, Ron. You pissed off the only person who was halfway on your side."

"She'll come around," Ron said, waving it off. "She's just being dramatic."

"Right," Marge sighed. "Because *you're* the picture of calm, rational behavior."

Later that night the junkyard was quiet, save for the occasional creak of metal as the wind rolled through. Marge sat on the steps of the office, sipping beer and staring at the stars. Ron was pacing nearby, still muttering to himself.

"Beth'll come around," he said for the tenth time.

"She's fifteen, Ron," Marge replied, not looking at him. "She'll come around when she feels like it. Which, if you keep acting like this, might be never."

"She doesn't get it," Ron said, throwing up his hands. "None of them do. This is for them, Marge. I'm doing this for them!"

Marge raised an eyebrow. "You sure about that? Because it feels an awful lot like you're doing it for you."

Ron stopped, staring at her. "What's that supposed to mean?"

"It means you've been chasing one crazy idea after another since the day I met you," she said. "And most of them? They're about proving something. Not to me. Not to the kids. To yourself."

Ron opened his mouth to argue but quickly shut it again. For once, he didn't have a snappy comeback. Deep down, he knew she was right.

Marge sighed, taking another sip. "Look, I'm not saying you're wrong about the yard. I get it—you see something here. But you can't force everyone else to see it just because you're convinced you're right. That's not how families work."

Ron sat down beside her, rubbing his face with his hands. "I just… I want to give them something, you know? Something better than what I had—and make us good money in the process."

Marge nodded, her tone softening just a touch. "I know, Ron. But maybe try listening to them instead of yelling at them. They're not just tools in your toolbox—they're people. *Our* people now."

Ron snorted. "Since when did you get so wise?"

"Since I married an idiot, wisdom is required," she replied with a smirk. "Keeps the world in balance."

Ron chuckled despite himself, shaking his head. "Fair enough, Babe."

The next morning, things were tense. Beth avoided everyone, holing up in her room with a notebook and refusing to come out. Danny was still poking at the lawnmower, muttering curses under his breath. Apparently unaffected by the drama, Joey was busy building a "fort" out of discarded tires and door panels.

Marge looked at the scene and decided she needed a break. She grabbed her keys and headed for the car.

"Where are you going?" Ron asked, watching her from the porch.

"To the store," she said. "We're out of coffee."

"We have coffee," he said.

"No, we don't," she replied, climbing into the car.

Ron frowned, but he knew better than to argue.

Marge lingered in the coffee aisle at the store longer than necessary, enjoying the quiet. As much as she was falling in love with her acquired family, they could be a lot. And sometimes, a woman just needed five minutes to herself.

She heard a familiar voice behind her as she reached for a can of coffee.

"Mrs. Trenton?"

Marge turned to see Donna standing there, a basket of groceries in her hand.

"Ms. Lujan," Marge said, trying to sound casual. "Fancy meeting you here." Donna smiled faintly. "Small town I suppose."

The two women stood there for a moment, the silence awkward. Finally, Donna spoke.

"You know," Donna said, "your family's... unconventional. But I've seen so much worse."

"Gee, thanks," Marge replied dryly. Then, softening, she added, "They're good kids. And, well... we're trying to be good parents." Her tone was genuine, even if her words were understated.

"**I mean it**," Donna said. "You've got your work cut out for you, but I can tell you care about those kids. That counts for something."

Marge nodded slowly and forced a smile. "Thanks. I think."

Donna hesitated, then added, "But if you want to keep this arrangement going, you might want to rein in the chaos a bit. Just a suggestion."

Marge smirked. "What's life without a little chaos?"

Marge leaned toward Donna with a spontaneous question. "You wanna go across the street for something delicious and not super healthy?"

Donna smirked. "I could eat, Marge."

A few minutes later, Marge tore open a small bag of Fritos and dumped a ladle of steaming red chile and ground beef right inside. The scent of spice and melted cheese filled the air as Donna raised an eyebrow. "You're really doing that?"

Marge shrugged. "Saves dishes."

"You know, some people actually put it in a bowl. Like civilized human beings."

"Yeah, and those people have to wash that bowl," Marge

countered, shaking on a handful of shredded cheese. "This is the proper way—the way."

Donna sighed. "I'm not saying it doesn't taste good. Just feel it's a bit, well… feral."

Marge took a bite, licking chile off her thumb. "**Feral tastes better**."

CHAPTER 9

Marge's presence made people take notice, even if she wasn't trying to. Her auburn hair, streaked with strands of gray she refused to dye, was usually pulled back in a loose bun or ponytail, though a few stubborn wisps always escaped to frame her face. Her sharp hazel eyes seemed to see straight through nonsense, softened only by the faint crow's feet etched at their corners. She had a **wiry build**, lean from years of hard work and little patience for sitting still, and her hands carried the calluses of someone unafraid to get them dirty.

Most days, she wore a denim jacket over a threadbare T-shirt, jeans scuffed at the knees, and old, ankle-high boots that had seen better decades—boots so worn they looked like they might crumble if anyone else tried to wear them. A lit cigarette was her most frequent accessory, the faint smell of smoke clinging to her like a signature, but there was a warmth to her—gritty and no-nonsense—that made her feel like the anchor of the family, whether or not she realized it.

The sun was barely over the horizon when Ron announced his latest plan with the kind of manic energy usually reserved for late-night infomercials.

"Alright, team!" he said, banging an old hubcap against the side of a rusted pickup truck to get everyone's attention. "Today's the day we turn this junkyard into a money-making machine!"

Still clutching her coffee like a lifeline, Marge gave him a long, deadpan stare. "You said that yesterday. And the day before that. And the day before that."

"Yeah, but this time it's different," Ron insisted. "I've got a plan!"

"You've *always* got a plan," Beth muttered from the office doorway.

"This one's foolproof," Ron said, ignoring her. "We're going to branch out. Diversify."

Danny, still half-asleep, scratched his head. "Branch out?"

Ron gestured dramatically toward the junkyard. "Scrap art."

"Scrap *what?*" Marge asked.

"Art, Marge! Art made from scrap metal! People pay big bucks for that kind of thing. I saw it on TV. Some guy turned an old muffler into a lamp and sold it for $500!"

Beth raised an eyebrow. "And you think we can do that?"

"Of course we can! We've got plenty of junk, and I've got creativity coming out of my ears," Ron said, tapping his temple.

"Pretty sure that's hot air," Marge muttered, sipping her coffee.

Undeterred, Ron marched to the middle of the yard, clapping his hands like a coach rallying his team. "Joey, you're in charge of finding interesting pieces. Danny, you're on welding duty. Beth, you're—"

"Nope," Beth interrupted, holding up a hand. "Not doing it."

"You're managing inventory," Ron continued, undeterred. "And Marge, you're..."

"Watching this train wreck from a safe distance," she supplied.

"Exactly!" Ron said, clearly not listening.

An hour later, the junkyard was somehow even more chaotic than usual. Joey had embraced his role as "chief materials scout" with wild enthusiasm, dragging random pieces of metal to the center of the yard.

"Look, Dad!" he shouted, holding up what appeared to be part of a bicycle frame. "This could be a giraffe!"

"Perfect!" Ron said. "Put it in the 'animals' pile!"

"There's a pile for animals?" Danny asked, looking up from the welding torch he held with visible apprehension.

"There is now!" Ron declared.

Meanwhile, Beth was sitting on a stack of tires, scribbling in her notebook with a sour expression. "This is ridiculous," she muttered. "We're not artists. We're just a bunch of lunatics playing with junk."

"Sounds like art to me," Marge said, leaning against the office doorframe and lighting a cigarette.

As the hours wore on, the so-called art project began to take shape—a series of vaguely recognizable shapes. Danny's attempt at welding a "tree" looked more like an octopus having a bad day. Joey's giraffe was missing a leg, but he insisted it was "abstract—just like Marge described. Several times."

Ron, for his part, was focused on his pièce de résistance: a "modern art masterpiece" made entirely of hubcaps.

"This is gonna be our moneymaker," he said, admiring his creation. "I call it **Hubcap Symphony.**"

"It looks like a metal porcupine," Marge said.

"Art is subjective," Ron shot back.

"Yeah? And subjectively, it's roadkill," Beth muttered, barely stifling a laugh.

A surprise visitor arrives. As the family argued over whether or not *Hubcap Symphony* was a work of genius or an abomination, the sound of a car engine broke through the commotion. Everyone turned to see an unfamiliar SUV pulling into the yard.

"Who the hell is that?" Marge asked, narrowing her eyes.

The car came to a stop, and a man stepped out. He was tall, dressed in a crisp suit that looked absurdly out of place among the rust and grease of the junkyard. His polished shoes clicked against the gravel.

"Mr. Trenton?" the man asked, his voice smooth and businesslike.

"That's me," Ron said, stepping forward with a grin. "You are?"

"Michael Donahue," the man said, extending a hand. "I represent a... group that's interested in your operation."

Marge's eyes narrowed further. "What kind of group?"

Michael smiled, but it didn't reach his eyes. "Let's just say we specialize in... unconventional ventures. We've heard about your unique approach to business, and we think there's potential here."

"And your name, Ma'am?" Donahue smiled.

Beth snorted. "Ma'am? Huh. Nothing says 'potential' quite like a rusty hubcap porcupine."

Ron, however, was intrigued. "Unconventional, huh? What exactly are you offering, investment, purchase, marketing, or something else?"

Donahue pulled a business card from his pocket and handed it to Ron. "Why don't we discuss it over dinner? My treat."

Marge stepped forward, arms crossed. "I'm Marge Trention, co-owner. And hold on a second—we don't even know who you are. What kind of 'ventures' are we talking about here?"

Donahue's smile widened. "The kind that could make you a lot of money."

Ron's eyes lit up. "I'm listening."

Marge groaned. "Of course you are."

That evening, Ron and Marge found themselves sitting in a fancy steakhouse in Nob Hill, across from Michael, who had a knack for saying a lot without actually revealing anything.

"So," Ron said, cutting into his steak. "What exactly are you proposing?"

Donahue leaned back in his chair, steepling his fingers. "Let's just say we're interested in expanding your... capabilities. Turning your junkyard into a hub for a different kind of business."

Marge bristled. "What kind of business?"

Donahue's smile didn't falter. "Transportation. Storage. Distribution. The specifics aren't important right now. What matters is the profit."

Ron's eyes gleamed. "How much profit are we talking?"

"A lot," Donahue said.

Marge wasn't buying it. "And what's the catch?"

"No catch," Donahue said. "Just an opportunity. Of course, if you're not interested..."

"Oh, we're interested," Ron said quickly.

Marge kicked him under the table while simultaneously grabbing his shirt. "Can we have a minute?"

Donahue nodded. "Take all the time you need."

As he stepped away, Marge glared at Ron. "Are you out of your goddamn mind? This guy screams 'shady, jail time, and creepy.'"

"Shady or not, he's offering us a chance to make some real money," Ron whispered. "Do you know how much we could do with this place if we had some cash to work with?"

"And what happens when the cops show up asking questions?" Marge said. "You really want to risk everything for some mystery deal?"

Ron hesitated, but his greed was outweighing his common sense. "We'll be fine. The cops owe us. Trust me—if it gets too shady or, you know, *super illegal,* we'll step away and be done with it."

Marge sighed, tilting her head as she gave Ron a knowing look. "You know, this reminds me of when we first met—back when you were sweet-talking your way out of trouble for selling lumber that wasn't yours. What was it you said to the sheriff? Something about 'creative redistribution of resources'?" She shook her head. "I should've known then that life with you would be one long, questionable business venture."

"Famous last words," Marge muttered, lighting another cigarette. "Dammit, the cops owe us."

When Ron and Marge returned, the kids roasted marshmallows around the fire pit. Joey skewered them with a bent piece of rebar.

"How'd it go?" Beth asked, her tone dripping with sarcasm.

"Great!" Ron said.

"Terrible," Marge said at the same time.

Beth sighed. "So, business as usual."

Ron clapped his hands, grinning widely. "Don't worry, team. Big things are coming. Mark my words! Print that and take it to the bank!"

Beth raised an eyebrow. "Pretty sure the bank doesn't take optimism as currency, Dad."

The group paused, looking at Beth.

You never called me… Dad," Ron said, his voice catching.

Beth smiled softly. "I've forgiven you for all the ranting and raving. I get it—you've been trying your best."

Ron hesitated for a moment before stepping in for a side-hug. Beth hadn't expected to feel emotional, but seeing how much it meant to him caught her off guard.

"I'm hungry," Joey yelled.

Danny poked at the fire with a stick, a smirk tugging at his lips. "That's what you said about the calculators," he said, enthusiastically echoing one of Marge's favorite stories.

Joey grinned. "And the scooters."

Beth smirked. "And the time you tried selling lawn ornaments made of plungers."

Marge lit a cigarette, blowing a plume of smoke as she eyed Ron. "Here's hoping this one doesn't end in flames, turning our life into one big fire pit, Ron 'Sure Thing' Trenton!"

Ron stared into the flames as the fire crackled, his mind spinning with possibilities. He didn't know exactly what he'd just gotten them into, but life at the junkyard was about to get a hell of a lot more complicated and profitable.

CHAPTER 10

It was supposed to be a quick stop.

Marge just needed a few things—milk, eggs, coffee—the essentials, plus a few bribes to keep the kids from tearing the house apart. There were four of them now, and some days, it felt like more.

Ron stood beside the car in the grocery store parking lot, lighting a cigarette while the kids fought in the backseat. Marge could already hear Beth threatening to "tell Mom," and Joey calling her a liar.

She sighed, rubbing her temples. "If one of you so much as breathes wrong when I come back, you're all eating vegetables for a week."

That got them quiet.

Marge shut the car door and turned toward the store—then stopped.

A small figure sat on the curb near the shopping carts, hunched over like he was trying to disappear.

Her stomach sank.

Nico.

The hoodie was different this time—newer, but still too big. He sat cross-legged on the concrete, poking a straw into a half-empty soda cup. He wasn't begging, wasn't talking to anyone. Just sitting. Waiting.

Marge looked over her shoulder. Ron had seen him too.

"Hell," Ron muttered, exhaling smoke. "That kid's got the worst luck."

Marge didn't say anything. Just started walking.

Nico looked up when her boots scuffed against the pavement. His face hadn't changed much—still small, still sharp. But there was something different in his eyes this time. Something that made Marge's chest feel tight.

"Nico," she said, stopping in front of him. "What are you doing out here?"

The boy shrugged. "Just waitin'."

"For what?"

He tapped the side of his soda cup. "For this not to be empty."

Marge exhaled, crossing her arms. "Where you staying?"

Nico hesitated.

Marge's stomach twisted.

Ron walked up beside her, hands shoved in his pockets. "You still in a foster home?"

Nico shook his head. "Not anymore. They're sending me to Utah."

Marge frowned. "Utah?"

Nico shrugged like it didn't matter. "Some people there got legal rights to me. Distant family, I guess. Never met 'em."

Marge felt her stomach tighten.

"That don't seem right," Ron muttered. "What about the home you were in?"

"They said it wasn't up to them. Paperwork stuff. I gotta go where they send me."

Marge knelt so they were eye level. "Do you want to go?"

Nico didn't answer. But he didn't have to.

Ron let out a long breath, rubbing his jaw. "There's gotta be a way—"

"There's not."

Nico's voice was quiet. Matter-of-fact. Like he'd already run through every option and knew how this ended.

Marge swallowed hard. "We could talk to someone, maybe—"

"I already asked." He looked away, his fingers tightening around his cup. "They said it's done."

Marge felt a lump in her throat.

She and Ron had gotten used to doing something when they saw a kid in trouble: figuring it out and making it work.

But this time? This time, there was nothing they could do.

Ron dug into his pocket, pulling out a crumpled twenty. He held it out, but Nico didn't take it right away.

"Nico," Marge said softly.

The boy finally looked at her.

"You remember where we live, right?"

He nodded.

"If you ever need something—" She stopped herself. What was she even saying? That he could show up at their door? That she'd turn him away?

Nico studied her for a long moment, as if trying to memorize her face.

Then he took the twenty.

"Thanks," he mumbled.

Marge felt her chest ache. "When do you leave?"

"Tomorrow." He looked down at his shoes. "Early."

Ron let out a slow exhale. "Damn kid."

Nico smirked, but it didn't reach his eyes. "Yeah."

Marge reached out, hesitated, then ruffled his hair the way she had the first time they met.

Nico didn't pull away.

Then, without another word, he turned and walked off.

Marge stood there, arms wrapped tight around herself.

Ron watched until the boy disappeared into the fading light. Then he shook his head, letting out a breath.

"I hate this," he muttered.

Marge didn't answer. Just flicked her cigarette into the dirt, watching the embers die.

She wasn't sure why, but she felt they wouldn't see Nico again.

And she hated that too.

Marge barely spoke that night, and neither did Ron. She knew he was feeling it, too, the same helplessness and frustration.

"We woulda taken him," Ron muttered finally, staring at the ceiling in bed.

"I know."

The next morning seemed to come quickly. Another day to wrestle with life and the Yard.

Marge flipped the last of the breakfast burritos onto a plate and slid it toward Beth. "Here, eat."

Beth eyed it skeptically. "Red or green?" "Red."

Beth sighed. "Why do you always pick red?"

"Because it's better," Marge said matter-of-factly, biting into her burrito. "It's got depth. It's got history. It clings to the tortilla like it belongs there."

Beth smirked. "So does green. Green chile is fresh, vibrant, and actually has some kick."

"Red's got heat too," Marge countered. "And it doesn't need to prove itself."

Beth took a bite, thoughtful. "Alright, fair. But next time, we're doing green."

Marge waved her off. "Next time, make your own damn burrito."

"Someone's here," Beth said, looking up from her plate.

"Who the hell visits a junkyard at 9 a.m.?" Marge muttered, heading toward the gate.

When she reached it, she found an old van idling just outside. Its faded paint and duct-taped bumper gave it the kind of charm only desperation could buy. Marge's sharp eyes immediately clocked two figures inside: a woman in the driver's seat and a young girl in the passenger seat.

The driver rolled down her window. "Hi," she said, her voice tight and uncertain. "Are you Marge Trenton?"

Marge nodded. "It definitely depends on who's asking."

The woman glanced nervously toward the girl, who looked about 12. Her curly hair was pulled back into a ponytail that had seen better days. The girl stared intently at the dashboard, clearly trying to avoid eye contact.

"My name's Carla," the woman said, her grip tightening on the steering wheel. "**This is my daughter, Grace**. Look, I'm not gonna beat around the bush—I heard from someone in town that you, uh, take kids in."

Marge blinked, caught off guard. "What exactly do you mean by 'take kids in'?"

Carla shifted in her seat, clearly uncomfortable. "I... I can't do this anymore," she admitted, her voice cracking. "I'm sick, and things are falling apart. Grace deserves more than I can give her right now. Someone told me you and your husband... well, you might be able to help."

Marge stared at her, unsure whether to laugh, cry, or light another cigarette. "This isn't exactly an adoption agency," she said finally.

"I'm not looking for an agency," Carla said quickly. "Just... someone who can keep her safe. Someone who won't let her get lost in the shit family system."

By this point, Ron had wandered over, his curiosity piqued. "What's going on?" he asked, peering into the van.

Carla glanced at him, then back at Marge. "Please," she said, her voice barely above a whisper.

Marge looked at Grace, who still hadn't said a word. The girl's wide brown eyes briefly flicked up to meet hers before darting away again.

"You wanna come inside?" Marge asked after a long pause.

Carla nodded.

Inside the office, the air was tense. Marge had offered Carla a cup of coffee, which she held with shaking hands. Grace sat on the worn-out couch, her backpack hugged tightly to her chest.

"This is kind of sudden," Ron said, breaking the silence.

"No kidding," Marge muttered, taking a long drag from her cigarette.

Carla took a shaky sip of her coffee. "I know. Believe me, I know." Her voice broke as tears welled up. "But I don't have any other options. Grace is smart, she's kind... she deserves a shot at something better."

Ron leaned back in his chair, scratching his chin. "This isn't exactly how we planned to expand the family," he said, half-joking.

Marge shot him a look. "Not the time. Would get her a glass of water, please, Ron."

Grace finally spoke, her voice soft but steady. "You don't have to take me if you don't want to."

Marge's heart twinged at the quiet resignation in her tone. "We're not saying that, sweetheart," she said gently.

"We'll figure something out," Ron added as he walked back into the room. "It's what we do."

Tears flowed down Carla's face as she set down her coffee. "Thank you," she whispered.

Grace watched her mom, her expression unreadable, before turning to Marge. "What's it like here?" she asked.

Marge laughed. "Messy. Loud. A little nuts. But it's home, and think everyone is happy most days."

"Does everyone have a job?" Grace asked.

"Damn right, everyone pulls their weight," Ron said. "You'll get one   too." (excited and grinning)

Grace hesitated, then nodded slowly.

"Well, that's settled," Marge said, standing. "Ron, get her set up in Joey's old room. And Joey—if he's still alive—can sleep on the couch."

"What about Carla?" Ron asked.

Marge looked at the woman, who was wiping her eyes. "Do you need a place to stay?"

Carla shook her head. "I'll be okay. I just needed to know she'd be safe."

"She definitely will be," Marge said, placing a hand on Carla's back in an attempt to reassure her about Grace.

As Carla drove away, dust swirling around the old van's tires, a heavy stillness settled over the junkyard. Grace stood by the office, no real expression. She was scanning her new surroundings with a blend of curiosity and sadness, unsure of what came next.

Joey popped up next to her, his face streaked with dirt. "You wanna see my fort?"

Grace blinked at him, then smiled faintly. "Sure." Joey's innocent timing and good intentions made the moment a little easier.

Before Grace could walk away, Marge stepped closer and murmured, "We'll check on your mom in a couple of days, sweetheart."

Marge watched them go, then turned to Ron. "Well, there's one more," she said. "Four more to go."

Ron cracked a smile and groaned. "You're gonna hold me to that, aren't you?"

"Damn right I am," Marge replied, finishing her cigarette.

Ron shouted, "Marge! The first payment is in the bank, just like Donahue said—**$11,500** for a month's storage!" He hesitated, then thought to himself, *I hope there are a lot more months like that.*

CHAPTER 11

Grace had been with the Trentons for a week, and the adjustment was... rocky, to say the least. She was quiet, almost unnervingly so, and seemed content to fade into the background while chaos erupted around her. But Marge noticed the girl's sharp eyes constantly scanning the junkyard, cataloging every scrap of metal and every strange habit of her new "family."

"Are they always like this?" Grace asked one morning as Joey tried to duct-tape a broom handle to his "scrap throne."

"Like what?" Marge replied, her tone carefully neutral.

"Loud. And... weird," Grace said, glancing at Joey as he declared himself "King of the Junk."

Marge smirked. "Loud and weird is our normal, sweetheart. You'll get used to it."

Grace didn't look convinced, but she didn't argue either.

Ron's booming voice cut through the yard. "Alright, everyone! Family meeting! Assemble at the picnic table!"

Beth rolled her eyes as she stepped out of the office. "What now, Dad? Another 'big idea' to save the junkyard?"

"Damn right," Ron said, clapping his hands together.

Danny groaned, wiping grease from his hands as he emerged from the garage. "I swear, if this involves more spray paint, I'm out. I might take a holiday."

"Holiday, huh? It's not spray paint," Ron said, grinning. "It's a partnership!"

Marge lit a cigarette, eyeing him warily. "A partnership?"

"Actually, it's more of an expansion," Ron said, gesturing vaguely toward the gate.

It was as if a car pulled up on cue, its engine rattling like it might give out at any second. The vehicle was a relic from the early '90s, held together by duct tape and a combination of hope and panic.

The driver stepped out—a grizzled man in his 60s with a baseball cap pulled low over his eyes. He opened the back door, and out climbed a boy who looked about eight, with dark skin, short-cropped hair, and a scowl that could curdle milk.

"This is Lewis," the man said, his voice gruff. "I'm his uncle, Jimmy. Heard you folks are good with kids who need a place to land."

Marge blinked. "What is this, a junkyard or an orphan..." She stopped herself midsentence, her voice catching in her throat.

Her thoughts seemed heavier now, the weight of her sentence pressing down like the rusty iron piles stacked haphazardly around the yard. She stuffed her hands into her coat pockets and looked away, feigning sudden interest in the wreckage.

"Sorry," she said, more to herself than anyone else. "I didn't mean..."

The boy standing beside her—grimy-faced, no older than ten—didn't flinch. He just stared at her, his too-large shirt flapping like a flag in the wind. His silence was louder than any protest could have been, cutting sharper than any sarcastic remark.

"It's not like I don't know what it is," he finally said, his voice steady but quiet.

Marge opened her mouth, then stopped. She had no comeback, no quick remark to patch over her blunder. Instead, she nodded, just once, and crouched down to the boy's level.

"You're right," she said softly. "I'm sorry."

The boy held her gaze for a long moment, then shrugged. "It's fine. I hear worse." He turned away and walked deeper into the maze of broken machinery and forgotten parts, his small figure swallowed by the shadows.

Marge stood frozen for a moment, staring after him, the echo of her words—her mistake—bouncing around in her chest like loose screws in a tin can.

Jimmy shrugged. "Kid's been through a lot. He's struggling—his mom, my sister, died a year ago, and I've been looking after him since. But I'm on the road too much. He needs stability, school, the same people around him. A chance to just be a kid."

Ron stepped forward, his grin wide and welcoming. "Well, you've come to the right place. We're big on stability here. Right, Marge?"

Marge shot him a look that could peel paint. "Sure, Ron. Stable."

Jimmy didn't seem to notice the sarcasm. He turned to Lewis. "Go on, kid. Say hello."

Lewis crossed his arms, his glare sweeping over the family like a spotlight. "This place sucks," he muttered.

Joey's head popped up from behind the scrap pile. "No, it doesn't! We have a fort!"

Lewis rolled his eyes. "Big deal, that's little kid stuff."

"You can be in my pirate crew if you want," Joey offered,

undeterred.

Lewis ignored him and turned back to his uncle. "Can we please go home now?"

Jimmy sighed, rubbing the back of his neck. "Look, he's… a handful. But he's a good kid, who will need a bit of time to adjust and get into a routine."

Marge studied the boy for a moment, then nodded. "We'll take him."

Ron blinked in surprise. "Really?" He hadn't expected that.

Marge raised an eyebrow. "You wanted expansion. Here it is."

Jimmy looked relieved as he handed over a small duffel bag. "Thank you, I know he'll do better. I'll come visit when I can, but… well, you know how it is."

Marge nodded. "We'll take it from here."

As Jimmy drove away, the family turned to face their newest addition.

"So, Lewis," Ron said, clapping his hands together. "What do you like to do for fun?"

Lewis stared at him like he'd just asked the dumbest question in the world. "I don't know. Whatever."

"Great! You'll fit right in!" Ron declared, giving him a firm pat on the back.

"Come on," Joey said, grabbing Lewis's arm. "I'll show you the fort! And the pile of weird metal! Oh, and the place where **I saw a rat** once!"

Lewis hesitated but eventually let Joey drag him away—once again, Joey to the rescue of an awkward moment.

Marge sighed, lighting another cigarette. "Three down, four to go."

Ron turned to her, his grin faltering. "Wait, what?"

"You wanted more kids," Marge said, blowing out an extra-large plume of smoke. "That's the deal, isn't it?"

Ron groaned. "My math isn't always great but didn't three go to four?"

"Damn right," Marge replied with a smirk. *She thought one more won't hurt,* teasing as she nudged her husband with the idea.

Beth crossed her arms, watching Lewis and Joey disappear behind a stack of tires. "This is going to be a disaster. How many strays are you going to take in?"

"Probably 10 or 15 more," Marge said, straining not to be irritated by Beth's comment. "But it's our disaster—and it'll be more fun than you know what to do with."

CHAPTER 12

Ron stood in the junkyard, staring at the tarp-covered trailer Michael Donahue had dropped off. His hands were on his hips, his brow furrowed as if deep contemplation alone could solve the mystery of its contents.

"What are you doing?" Marge's voice cut through his thoughts. She leaned against the office doorway, a cigarette in one hand and a coffee mug in the other.

"Thinking," Ron said.

Marge smirked. "Careful. You don't want to pull something."

Before Ron could fire back, Beth appeared from behind the garage, her clipboard in hand. "What's the plan with this thing?" she asked, gesturing to the trailer.

"The plan," Ron began, puffing out his chest, "is to make it look like it belongs here. Blend it in. No one's gonna suspect a thing."

Beth raised an eyebrow jumping in. "It's a **giant trailer covered with a tarp**. In what universe does that 'blend in'?"

"Don't you have inventory to count? Ron clearly flustered, shot back.

"Don't you have smarter decisions to make?" Beth retorted, walking off.

Marge chuckled, taking a drag of her cigarette. "She's not wrong, you know."

Before Ron could respond, Grace and Lewis emerged from the scrap pile, their conversation carried on the breeze.

"It's not a fort," Lewis said, his tone dripping with disdain. "It's a pile of trash."

"It's not trash! It's a castle!" Joey's voice yelled from somewhere behind the stack.

Marge shook her head. "Those kids are gonna put in an early grave."

Ron turned to her, his expression unusually serious. "Speaking of kids, we need to talk about this whole trailer situation."

Marge gave him a wary look. "What about it?"

"Donahue said this could be big for us," Ron said, his voice dropping conspiratorially. "A real chance to turn things around."

"And what exactly is 'this'?" Marge asked, nodding toward the trailer. "Because unless you know what's under that tarp, I'm not convinced it's anything but trouble."

Ron hesitated. "He said it's mostly legal."

Marge snorted. "Yeah, because people always tell the truth when handing you a mystery trailer full of who-knows-what."

Ron ran a hand through his hair. "Look, I get it. You're skeptical. But we need the money, Marge. We're stretched thin as it is, and now we've got two more mouths to feed."

Marge's sharp hazel eyes locked onto his. "And whose bright idea was it to take in more kids, Trenton?"

He winced. "That's beside the point. It will all work out."

"No, it's exactly the point," she said, jabbing a finger at him. "You want to play junkyard king and family man? Fine. But you don't get to gamble everything—including our lives."

Marge could feel herself heating up, ready for a full-blown fight.

Ron opened his mouth to argue but was interrupted by the rumble of an approaching vehicle. A sleek black SUV rolled into the yard, its polished exterior contrasting with the rusted chaos surrounding it.

Marge sighed. "And there's your shady partner now."

Donahue stepped out of the SUV, his tailored suit immaculate despite the dust swirling in the air. He adjusted his sunglasses as he approached, flashing his too-perfect smile.

"Good morning, Mr. and Mrs. Trenton," he said smoothly. "I trust everything is going well with our little arrangement?"

Marge crossed her arms. "Define 'well.'"

Donahue chuckled, ignoring the jab. "No unexpected visitors, I hope?"

"Just you," Marge glared.

Donahue turned to Ron. "Have you considered my offer? There's a lot more where this came from, Mr. Trenton. All you have to do is prove you're up to the task."

Ron hesitated, glancing at Marge, who practically dared him to say yes.

"What exactly does 'proving ourselves' involve?" Marge asked, her tone sharp.

Donahue's smile didn't falter. "Simple. Storage, transportation, discretion. You handle the logistics, and we pay. It's a mutually beneficial arrangement."

"And if we say no?" Marge pressed.

Donahue's smile cooled ever so slightly. "You won't because I see potential here. And I know you'll make the right decision."

"Potential for what, exactly?" Beth's voice rang out as she reappeared, her arms crossed, book under her arm. She gestured to the junkyard around them. "You really think this is the kind of operation that screams 'trustworthy'?"

Donahue turned to her, his smile returning. "Young lady, some of the most successful businesses in the world started in garages. Don't underestimate what your family can accomplish with the right support."

Beth rolled her eyes. "Right. Support."

Donahue turned on the charm. "What book are you reading?"

The genuine question caught Beth off guard for a moment. "Uh, it's *Sumner Whispers*, a cozy murder mystery set in a small Wyoming town. The sheriff and a local doctor team up to solve a murder that ties into the town's past. They also track down and prosecute criminals for their illegal activities," she added, narrowing her eyes at Donahue.

"Huh." He held her gaze for a beat, then smirked. "Sounds like a good read. Hope you enjoy it."

Beth snapped the book shut. "Well, this conversation made me need to pee. Excuse me."

Donahue chuckled, his smile effortlessly charming as he watched her go.

Marge stepped forward, her patience clearly wearing thin. "Alright, slick, let's cut the crap. We're not agreeing to anything without knowing exactly what we're getting into."

"My mom **called me Slick** growing up," Donahue reminisced.

Donahue nodded, as if expecting this. "I admire your caution, Mrs. Trenton. Here's what I can tell you: the work is straightforward. Legal. And lucrative. Beyond that, the less you know, the safer you are."

"That's not reassuring," Marge said flatly.

Ron, however, was already nodding. "We'll talk it through, but we like it so far."

Marge spun on him. "Ron—"

"We need the money," Ron said, his voice firm. "We can handle this."

Donahue clapped him on the shoulder. "That's the spirit. I'll be in touch with the next steps."

As Donahue returned to his SUV and drove off, Marge turned to

Ron, her eyes blazing. "You're out of your goddamn mind. Seriously, what the fuck?"

Ron shrugged. "Maybe. But if this works, we could finally catch a break."

Marge sighed, lighting another cigarette. "Or we could end up in jail. Great plan. Just great."

"Ron, they paid us a lot of money for a month—to not look or ask any questions about what we're storing for them," Marge said. "I'm really nervous. I don't think I want to do this."

CHAPTER 13

The tarp-covered trailer sat like an elephant in the junkyard, an unspoken presence no one wanted to acknowledge. Ron avoided eye contact with Marge as he tinkered with an old truck, whistling a more nervous than cheerful tune.

Beth was perched on a stack of tires, flipping through her notebook and muttering under her breath. Grace sat nearby, organizing a pile of bolts by size, her quiet efficiency contrasting with the chaos around her.

"Stop whistling, Ron," Marge said, leaving the office. "You sound like you're trying to summon a tornado."

"I'm just in a good mood," Ron replied, tightening a bolt that didn't need tightening. "Big things are coming, Marge. Mark my words."

"They better be the kind of big things that don't involve lawyers or bail money," she muttered, dragging on a cigarette.

The sound of gravel crunching under tires interrupted their bickering. A police cruiser rolled into the yard, its lights off but its presence ominous. Everyone froze, their heads snapping toward the approaching car like deer caught in headlights.

"Crap," Danny muttered, peeking out from the garage. "What did we do now?"

"Nothing," Ron said quickly, wiping his hands on a rag. **"We've done nothing…….. recently."**

Marge shot him a glare. "Relax. They're probably just here to harass us like usual."

The cruiser came to a stop, and the door opened. Out stepped a woman in uniform—tall, broad-shouldered, and with a no-nonsense expression that rivaled Marge's.

"Ron and Marge Trenton?" she asked, her voice carrying over the yard.

"That's us," Marge said, stepping forward. "What's this about? We're busy?"

The officer glanced back toward the car, where a young boy sat in the backseat, his face partially obscured by a hoodie. He looked eight or nine, his dark eyes beneath a mop of jet black hair.

"This is Max," the officer said. "We picked him up last night. He's been sleeping in alleys and sneaking into warehouses in the South Valley. Says he's got nowhere to go."

Marge's eyes narrowed. "And you're bringing him here because...?"

"Because the social worker says you're good with kids like him," the officer replied. "You've got space, right?"

Marge scoffed. "Space? Sure. Sanity? That's another question."

The officer didn't laugh. "We've already called the department, but placements are full. He needs somewhere fast and safe, at least for now. We really need your help, please, we won't forget that you helped us and this kid out."

Ron stepped forward, his usual grin faltering slightly. "Well, uh, we've got a couch. And some extra cereal. That counts, right?"

The officer didn't wait for a better offer. She opened the back door and gestured for Max to get out. The boy reluctantly slid out of the car, his hands stuffed deep into his hoodie pockets.

"This isn't permanent," the officer said firmly. "Just until something opens up. We'll be back in the morning to check on things."

Marge sighed, her hands on her hips. "Yeah, that's what they all say."

Max shuffled forward, glancing up at Marge with wary eyes. She studied him for a moment, then softened.

"**You hungry, kid?**" she asked.

He shrugged. "A little."

"Beth, get him something to eat," Marge said. "And Joey, get down from the roof before you kill yourself!"

"I'm fine!" Joey yelled from the top of a stack of scrap.

"Now!" Marge barked, and Joey scrambled down, muttering under his breath.

As Beth led Max toward the office, Ron turned to the officer. "So, uh, what's his story?"

The officer shrugged. "Says he's been on his own for a few months.

Parents are out of the picture, drugs or booze. He doesn't trust adults much, so... good luck with that."

"Great," Marge said dryly. "Just what we needed. Another independent thinker."

The officer gave a curt nod, handed Marge a card, and climbed back into her car. Ron sighed as the cruiser drove off, rubbing the back of his neck.

"That should earn us some goodwill with the ABQ PD—at least for a little while," Ron shouted.

"Well," he said, trying to muster some optimism, "welcome to the family, I guess."

Marge shot him a look. "You're enjoying this, aren't you?"

"Not enjoying," Ron replied, holding up his hands. "I'm just... embracing the chaos and opportunity."

"Yeah, well, if this chaos bites us in the ass, I'm blaming you," Marge muttered, heading back to the office.

Inside, Max sat at the small living room desk and table, cautiously eating Beth's sandwich. He barely looked up as Grace hovered nearby, her curiosity obvious but unspoken.

"What's your deal?" Joey asked, plopping into a chair across from Max.

Max didn't answer.

"It's okay," Grace said softly. "Joey's annoying, but he means well."

Max glanced at her, then back at his sandwich. "You all live here?" he asked finally.

"Yup," Joey said proudly. "It's the best junkyard in the world!"

"Seems like a dump," Max muttered.

Joey gasped, clutching his chest like he'd been mortally wounded. "Take it back!" He held the dramatic pose for a second, then dropped his hands to his growling stomach. "Okay, but also—I'm starving."

Danny popped his head in the door. "Hey, new kid, have they given you your number yet?"

Max spun around. "What number? Like... jail? What?"

Beth rolled her eyes from the corner. "Ignore him. He's messing with you."

Marge appeared in the doorway, her hands on her hips. "Alright, Max. Here's the deal: you stay out of trouble, follow the rules, and help when possible. Think you can handle that?"

Max shrugged. "Maybe."

"Good," Marge said, nodding. "And if you've got any smart-ass comments, save them for Ron. He deserves it."

Back in the other room, Joey sat at the kitchen table, staring at the golden, puffed-up sopaipilla in front of him. "So... am I supposed to eat this with honey or what?"

Ron gasped like the kid had just insulted his entire ancestry. "*With honey?* You don't just *eat* a sopaipilla with honey, kid. You *baptize* it. You *drown* it. Every bite should perfectly balance crispy, chewy, and sweet—*divine perfection* in food form."

Joey hesitated, squeezing a little honey onto the corner.

"More," Ron instructed.

Joey drizzled a little more.

"*More,*" Ron said, voice low and deadly serious.

Joey sighed and practically flooded the sopapilla with honey. "Happy?"

Ron took a satisfied bite of his own, nodding. "Now you're getting it."

CHAPTER 14

"**Y**ou've been staring at that trailer for ten minutes," Beth said.

She tucked her notebook under her arm, her expression unreadable. "Are you waiting for it to explode or something?"

The tarp on Donahue's trailer flapped ominously in the wind, a fitting metaphor for the uneasy sense of foreboding Marge couldn't shake. She stood at the edge of the junkyard, smoking her third morning cigarette, her sharp eyes scanning the horizon as if expecting trouble to arrive in a shiny black SUV.

It wasn't paranoia if you knew trouble was coming.

"Wouldn't be the first time," Marge muttered, exhaling smoke.

Beth smirked. "You know, most people deal with their midlife crisis by buying a sports car. Not agreeing to store questionable cargo in their backyard."

"Yeah, well," Marge said, "most people don't marry Ron Trenton." **(dryly delivered)**

As if summoned, Ron's voice boomed from across the yard. "Joey! I said **organize** the bolts, not throw them at the chickens!"

"They started it!" Joey yelled back.

Beth raised an eyebrow. "What's the over-under on us surviving this latest scheme?"

"Not great," Marge admitted.

The sound of tires crunching on gravel interrupted their conversation. Marge stiffened, her cigarette frozen halfway to her lips.

"Is it him?" Beth asked, craning her neck.

"Let's find out," Marge said, stubbing out her cigarette as a familiar black SUV rolled to a stop in front of the office.

Donahue stepped out, his suit immaculate as always, his smile a little too wide to be genuine.

"Mr. and Mrs. Trenton!" he said, spreading his arms like a salesman at a used car lot. "How's my favorite entrepreneurial family?"

"We're surviving," Marge said extra loud, arms crossed, her expression unreadable.

Donahue laughed. "Surviving? Let's aim higher than that, shall we? Thriving—that's the goal."

Ron stood beside Marge and crossed his arms. "Get to it, Donahue, we're busy. What do you want? It's only been two days since the last visit. I am not a fan of babysitting."

Donahue's smile didn't fade, but his eyes hardened slightly. "I just came to check on my investment. And reiterate discretion is key."

"Define 'discretion,'" Marge said, her face twisting like she'd just smelled something rotten.

Donahue gestured to the trailer. "That stays exactly as it is— untouched, unexamined, and unquestioned. You're just the middlemen here. Anything else, and... well, let's just say it's better if you don't find out."

Marge's jaw tightened, but a loud crash echoed from the other side of the yard before she could react.

"So what happens if the wind blows the tarp off your discreet trailer?" Marge asked.

Without hesitation, Donahue answered, "You call me immediately, 24/7. Someone will come fix it, and you don't touch it."

BOOM! CRASH!

"What now?" Ron groaned. He already dreaded the answer.

Jogging toward the commotion, they found Joey standing amid a scrap pile, gripping a baseball bat and grinning like he'd just discovered a new sport. Nearby, Grace stood with her hands on her hips, looking like she'd rather be elsewhere.

"Joey," Ron said slowly, "what did you do?"

"I was testing it," Joey said proudly, gesturing to the now-destroyed refrigerator.

"By beating on it with a bat?" Ron asked, his voice rising.

Joey nodded. "It failed."

Donahue watched the scene unfold with mild amusement. "Charming operation you've got here," he said to Marge.

She shot him a look that could peel paint—one that clearly translated to *Fuck you.*

"What do you want, Donahue? Really," Marge said.

Donahue's look sharpened. "Just a friendly reminder. This opportunity is a test. Pass it, and there are bigger things ahead. Fail it, and... well, let's not think about that."

"Sounds like a threat," Marge said.

"Not a threat," Donahue replied, his tone deceptively light. "Just encouragement."

Before Marge could respond, Max appeared, his expression unusually serious. "There's a guy at the gate," he said. "He looks... police like."

Donahue's tone changed. "What kind of police?"

Max shrugged. "The kind with a badge."

Marge felt her stomach drop. "Damn it, Ron."

Ron held up his hands. "What did I do?"

"You fucking idiot," Marge snapped.

Donahue straightened his tie, his calm demeanor cracking ever so slightly. "I'll handle it," he said, moving toward the gate.

"Handle it how?" Marge called after him.

Donahue didn't answer.

They watched as he approached the man at the gate, their conversation too far away to hear but tense enough to be palpable. After a few minutes, Donahue returned, his expression carefully neutral.

"Who was that?" Marge demanded.

"Just a routine check," Donahue said smoothly. "Nothing to worry about."

"Funny," Marge said, her tone dripping with sarcasm. "I'm worried."

He glanced at his watch. "I'd love to stay and chat, but I currently have other matters to attend to. **Remember: DISCRETION**," said Donahue.

With that, he climbed into his SUV and drove off, leaving a cloud of dust in his wake.

Marge turned to Ron. "You do realize he's going to get us killed, right?"

Ron scratched his head. "No, you think? I thought just jail?"

"Ron," Marge said, lighting one cigarette with another, "I'm being serious, asshole. I can feel trouble."

Beth walked up, holding her notebook. "So what's the plan? Because if this goes sideways, I'm not going down with the idiotic idea."

"Thanks for the support," Ron muttered.

"I'm serious," Beth said. "This feels like the kind of thing that ends up in a 'true crime' documentary."

"Not helping, Beth," Marge said.

Danny appeared, wiping grease from his hands. "What's going on now?"

"Just another day in paradise," Marge said, exhaling smoke.

Danny glanced at the trailer, then at Marge. "You want me to check what's inside?"

"Absolutely not," Ron said quickly.

Danny smirked. "That's what I thought."

As the kids scattered, Marge stood beside Ron, staring at the trailer. "We're in deep already," she said quietly.

"I know," Ron admitted.

"You better hope this pays off," Marge said, her tone cold. "Because if it doesn't, Donahue won't be the only one coming after you. Goddamnit, Ron, I am really worried."

Ron swallowed hard, and tried to keep smiling, suddenly feeling the weight of the mess he'd gotten them into.

CHAPTER 15

The sun beat down on the mismatched scrap piles like a relentless interrogation. Ron sat at the picnic table with his head in his hands, staring at the faded wood as if it held the answer to all his problems.

"Okay," Marge said, dropping a thick folder onto the table before him. "Here's where we're at: a few overdue bills, a half-empty fridge now that all the kids are home, and a shady guy with perfect teeth expecting us to play along with whatever nonsense he's dragging us into. **Any bright ideas, Ron?**"

"Fake our deaths and move to Canada?" Ron muttered.

Marge gave him a look. "One, I don't think Canada will take us. And two, try again—a little harder this time."

Before Ron could respond, the sound of yelling drifted over from the far side of the yard.

"I told you to stay out of my stuff!" Lewis's voice rang out.

"You don't own stuff," Joey shot back. "It's a junkyard. Everything's junk."

The argument escalated into a flurry of insults, punctuated by the occasional clang of metal.

Marge sighed, pulling out a cigarette. "I'll deal with this one."

"Good luck," Ron said, slumping further into his chair.

Marge made her way to the source of the commotion, finding Lewis holding a rusted bike frame above his head like a weapon. Joey stood a few feet away, clutching an old hubcap like a shield.

"Enough!" Marge barked, her voice cutting through the chaos.

The boys froze, their makeshift weapons still raised.

"What the hell is going on here?" Marge demanded.

"He stole my spot!" Lewis yelled, pointing at Joey.

"It's not your spot!" Joey retorted. "I was here first!"

"Both of you, knock it off," Marge said sharply. "We don't have time for this crap. Joey, find another pile of junk to play with. Lewis, put the damn bike down before you hurt yourself."

Grumbling, the boys complied, casting each other dirty looks as they went their separate ways.

"Don't push me today, boys." Marge said.

Marge rubbed her temple, cigarette hanging from the side of her mouth. "Kids," she muttered. *(shaking her head)*

When she returned to the table, Ron was staring at the trailer, his expression unreadable.

"You thinking about opening it?" Marge asked, sitting down across from him.

"No," Ron said quickly. "Absolutely fucking not."

"Good," Marge said. "Because if you did, I'd have to kill you, before anyone did."

Ron chuckled weakly. "You think it's drugs or guns?"

"Or stolen art. Or dead bodies. Does it matter?" Marge replied. "Whatever it is, it's trouble; we're in a lot of trouble."

Before Ron could respond, a car pulled into the yard. But this wasn't Michael Donahue's sleek SUV—it was an old station wagon, the kind you'd expect to see in a '90s sitcom, held together by Bondo and sheer determination.

The car door creaked open, and a man with a nervous smile stepped out. He was tall and lanky, with slightly crooked glasses on his nose.

"Uh, hi," he said, waving awkwardly.

"Great," Marge muttered under her breath. "What now?"

The man approached, holding a manila envelope like it might explode if handled too roughly.

"**Trentons?**" he asked.

"That's us," Ron said cautiously.

The man extended the envelope. "I'm from Family Services. I've got a temporary placement for you."

Marge groaned. "Of course you do, and a bucket of money to feed them all?"

The man paused awkwardly, not sure how to respond.

He glanced back at the station wagon. "She's been in and out of foster homes for years. We're hoping this will be more... stable even if only temporary for her."

The car door opened, and a teenage girl stepped out. She was about sixteen, with dark brown skin and braided hair pulled back into a bun. She carried a worn-out backpack slung over one shoulder, her posture rigid and her expression carefully neutral.

"This is Ivy," the man said. "She's... well, she's been through a lot."

"Who hasn't?" Marge said, lighting yet another cigarette, regretting as soon as she said it.

Ivy's eyes flicked to Marge, her brow furrowing slightly at the cigarette, but she didn't say anything.

"Hi, Ivy," Ron said, offering his best attempt at a warm smile. "Welcome to the madhouse."

Ivy didn't respond immediately, her gaze drifting from the trailer to the scrap piles before settling back on Marge. "This place is... interesting," she said, her tone dismissive.

"That's one word for it," Marge replied.

The man cleared his throat. "I'll leave you to settle in. If you need anything, my number's in the envelope."

Marge watched him drive away before turning to Ivy. "Alright, kid. Ground rules: no sneaking out, help with the work, no picking fights with the other inmates—and I'd say no stealing, but there's not much worth swiping in the Yard."

"Inmates?" Ivy asked, raising an eyebrow.

"Welcome to the junkyard, sweetheart" Marge said, smirking.

As Beth led Ivy inside to get something to drink, Ron turned to Marge. "You think she'll stick around?"

Marge shrugged. "If she's smart, she'll run for the hills."

"Not exactly a vote of confidence," Ron said.

"I'm just saying," Marge replied, exhaling smoke, "we're not exactly showcasing stability here."

Ron glanced at the trailer again, his jaw tightening. "We'll make it work. We always do."

Marge didn't respond, her head spinning as her gaze lingered on the trailer. *A gust of wind sent the tarp flapping again.*

Marge and Ron stood silently, thinking the same thing—how poetic...

CHAPTER 16

The morning at the junkyard started like any other—with yelling.

"Joey, I swear, if I catch you throwing bolts at the chickens one more   time—"
"They like it!" Joey yelled back, darting behind a stack of old tires.

Marge, coffee in one hand and a cigarette in the other, leaned against the office door, watching the chaos with a look of practiced indifference. Ron was perched atop a half-disassembled tractor, his Hawaiian shirt flapping in the breeze as he scribbled furiously in a notebook.

"Uh-oh," Marge muttered, blowing out smoke.

"What?" Beth asked, emerging from the office with her ever-present notebook.

"*Dad* is thinking again," Marge said.

Beth followed her gaze. "That's never good."

Ron hopped down from the tractor, his grin wide and manic. "Alright, everyone, gather up! Family meeting!"

Beth groaned. "Can't we just skip the part where we pretend to listen to Dad's terrible ideas?"

"Nope," Marge said, taking a sip of her coffee. "It's the price of admission."

The family reluctantly assembled at the picnic table. Grace and Lewis wandered over, looking like they'd rather be elsewhere. Ivy hung back, leaning against a nearby scrap pile with her arms crossed, her expression skeptical.

"First things first—everyone, say your name and one thing that makes you laugh!" Ron shouted.

"What are you doing?" the group asked almost in unison.

Ron smiled. "I watched a video on YouTube about setting the tone for the day. This was one of the questions." He clapped his hands. "Okay, Lewis, go!"

Lewis blinked. "Uh... whatever. Lewis, and... I guess bad lip-reading videos always get me laughing."

"Solid choice," Ron said with an approving nod. "Next!"

Grace sighed, arms crossed. "Grace. And watching people trip— but only if they don't get hurt."

Danny grinned. "Danny. Fart noises. Any kind, any time."

Beth rolled her eyes. "Of course."

Ron pointed at her. "Your turn, Beth."

She shrugged. "Fine. I'm Beth, and I laugh when Dad tries to fix anything and makes it ten times worse."

"Hey!" Ron protested. "That's slander. I am very handy."

"Sure you are," Beth smirked.

Marge shook her head but played along. "Marge. Honestly? Watching you all try to function before my first cup of coffee."

The group chuckled, and Ron spread his arms. "See? Look at us bonding already. Team morale is sky-high!"

Beth smirked. "Yeah, yeah. Your YouTube guru would be proud."

"Damn right," Ron said. He clapped his hands again. "Now, let's get to work!"

A beat of silence. Then Ron grinned.

"Alright, folks," he began, clapping his hands together. "Big news! I've got a plan to bring in some real cash."

"Here we go," Danny muttered, leaning on his elbow.

Ron ignored him, pulling a hand-drawn flyer from his pocket and slapping it on the table. "Behold: the Trenton Family Junkyard Treasure Hunt!"

The kids stared at the flyer, which featured a crudely drawn treasure chest surrounded by stick-figure people holding wrenches.

"Let me get this straight," Marge said, lighting another cigarette. "You want to turn this place into a... what? A theme park?"

"Not a theme park," Ron said defensively. "An *experience*. People love treasure hunts! We hide stuff around the yard, charge an entry fee, and let folks dig for buried treasure. It's genius!"

"Genius?" Beth said, raising an eyebrow. "You mean like when you bought fifty calculators to resell at the flea market?"

"That was a *logistical hiccup,*" Ron shot back. "This is different."

"What exactly are we hiding as treasure?" Ivy asked, her tone dripping with skepticism.

"Scrap," Ron said, gesturing grandly to the piles of junk around them. "Stuff we don't need. We slap some paint on it, call it 'vintage,' and boom—instant profit!"

"Ron, that's not treasure," Marge said, exhaling smoke. "That's fraud."

"Not fraud," Ron corrected. "Creative marketing."

"Creative is one word for it," Danny said.

Joey, however, was fully onboard. "Can I be the pirate captain? Please? I'll wear the hat and everything!"

"See? Joey gets it," Ron said, pointing at him. "It's about the *experience.*"

Beth shook her head. "This is going to be a disaster."

"It's not a disaster," Ron said, puffing out his chest. "It's innovation."

Grace, who had been quiet until now, finally spoke up. "What if someone gets hurt? Like, they step on a rusty nail or something."

"Waivers," Ron said confidently. "Everyone signs a waiver. Problem solved."

"That's not how liability works," Beth muttered.

Before Marge could respond, a loud honk came from the gate. A beat-up truck pulled in, its bed piled high with mismatched furniture and boxes. A wiry man with a scruffy beard climbed out, waving cheerfully.

"Hey there, Trentons!" he called out.

"Who's this?" Ivy asked, frowning.

"Meet Carl," Ron said, walking toward the truck. "He's the key to our next big idea."

"Another scheme?" Marge muttered.

"Come on, Marge, have a little faith!" Ron called over his shoulder.

Carl hopped down from the truck and shook Ron's hand. "Brought the first load, just like you asked."

"First load of what?" Marge asked, approaching with narrowed eyes.

"Furniture," Ron said proudly.

Marge blinked. "Furniture."

"Yeah! People love refurbished furniture," Ron explained. "We take these old pieces, fix them up, and sell them as *vintage chic*. It's a goldmine!"

"Or a termite infestation," Marge said dryly.

Beth peered into the truck bed. "This stuff is falling apart. That chair's missing a leg."

"Easy fix," Ron said, waving her off. "A little glue, a little paint—it'll be good as new."

"Or it'll collapse and sue us," Danny said.

"Glass half full, people!" Ron said, clapping his hands.

"Ron, we've got a mystery trailer in the yard, five kids to feed, and now you're starting a furniture empire?" Marge said, her voice rising.

"It's called diversifying," Ron said.

"It's called nuttery," Marge replied.

Carl cleared his throat. "So, uh, where do you want this stuff?"

Ron gestured toward an empty corner of the yard. "Just stack it there for now. We'll get started tomorrow."

The first mishap came less than an hour later, when Joey declared himself in charge of "furniture restoration." Armed with a can of bright pink spray paint and zero supervision, he managed to cover half a wooden chair—and most of himself—before Beth caught him.

"What are you doing?!" she yelled, grabbing the spray paint can out of his hand.

"I'm making it better!" Joey declared proudly, standing in a growing puddle of pink paint.

Beth stared at the dripping chair, her hands twitching. "Dad is going to kill you. Or Mom. Probably Mom."

Meanwhile, Ron had decided to test his treasure hunt idea by burying an old toolbox in the yard's far corner. Unfortunately, he underestimated just how much Joey had used the shovel last week for "excavation practice."

"I swear, it was here yesterday," Ron muttered, digging through a pile of dirt with growing frustration.

Marge appeared, arms crossed. "You lost the treasure before the hunt even started?"

"It's a minor setback," Ron said, wiping sweat off his brow. "We'll find it."

"Yeah," Marge said, lighting a cigarette. "You and Indiana Jones over here are doing great."

The chaos peaked when Carl's furniture stack tipped over, narrowly missing Grace and Lewis, who had been arguing about whether or not the chairs were salvageable.

"I told you this was a bad idea!" Lewis shouted, glaring at Ron.

"It's not the *idea* that's bad," Ron said defensively. "It's the execution!"

"Execution is what we're headed for," Marge muttered under her breath.

As the sun began to set, the yard looked more like a war zone than ever—pink paint streaked on the gravel, broken furniture scattered everywhere, and Ron still digging futilely for the lost toolbox.

Marge surveyed the mess, hands on her hips. "Well, Ron, you wanted big ideas. Congratulations. You've officially got yourself a big mess."

CHAPTER 17

The junkyard felt eerily quiet the next morning—a stark contrast to the usual symphony of yelling, clanging metal, and Joey's attempts to reenact action movies with varying degrees of success. Marge stepped out of the office, her coffee steaming and her cigarette trailing smoke, her sharp eyes scanning the yard for signs of trouble.

Trouble, as always, was not far behind.

"Ron," Marge called, her voice cutting through the stillness like a knife.

Ron appeared from behind a stack of hubcaps, looking suspiciously sheepish. "Morning, Sweetheart!" he said with forced cheer, brushing dirt off his hands.

"What are you up to?" she asked, narrowing her eyes.

"Nothing!" he said quickly, making her more suspicious.

Before Marge could interrogate him further, a rusted delivery van rumbled into the yard, its muffler barely clinging to life. The driver, a wiry man with a cigarette dangling from his lips, climbed out and waved at Ron like they were old friends.

"Christ sake, who's this?" Marge asked, crossing her arms.

"Uh... new business partner," Ron said. He purposefully avoided her gaze.

The driver opened the back of the van, revealing boxes stacked precariously high. "You said you needed bulk inventory, right?" he said to Ron.

Marge raised an eyebrow. "Bulk inventory for what?"

"Distribution," Ron mumbled.

"Distribution of what?" Marge said.

Ron sighed, rubbing the back of his neck. "Candy."

Marge blinked, not smiling. "Candy."

"Technically gum," Ron clarified.

Marge's guard shot up. "Why does this feel like a lie?"

"It's not a lie!" Ron said, his voice climbing. "It's... entrepreneurial innovation."

Marge lit her fourth cigarette of the morning, exhaling slowly. "Trenton, if I find out you're smuggling drugs, I'm calling the cops myself. Then possibly kill you, slowly, just so we're clear."

"It's not drugs!" Ron said, clearly offended. "It's gum. Specialty gum. Like, high-end."

"High-end gum," Marge repeated, deadpan.

"Yup," Ron said, nodding enthusiastically, clearly all in on this new business plan.

The driver handed Ron an invoice, which he quickly stuffed into his pocket before Marge could grab it. "Pleasure doing business with you," the man said, climbing back into the van and driving off in a cloud of white exhaust and dust.

Marge turned to Ron, her patience gone. "Alright, spill. What's the deal?"

Ron sighed, gesturing for her to follow him. He led her to the office, where a table was piled high with boxes labeled in bold, cartoonish letters: "**CHEW CHAMPS—The Gum That Keeps You Going**!"

Marge stared at the boxes, Ron, and the boxes again. "You bought a warehouse's worth of bootleg gum?"

"It's not bootleg!" Ron said. "It's perfectly legal... most likely, probably. And it's got caffeine!"

"Caffeine," Marge repeated.

Ron grinned. "Think about it. People love coffee, right? This is like coffee, but in gum form. It's genius!"

"It's goddamn idiotic," Marge said. "What are you planning to do with it?"

"Sell it, babe," Ron said. "We set up shop, build a brand, maybe even expand into energy drinks—"

Marge held up a hand. "Let me stop you right there. You don't even know if this stuff is safe. It might kill someone!"

"Of course it's safe," Ron said, opening a box and popping a piece of gum into his mouth. He chewed for a moment, then grimaced. "Okay, it tastes a little weird."

"Define 'weird,'" Marge said, already regretting asking.

"Like burnt tires," Ron admitted. "But the energy kick is real!"

Before Marge could respond, Joey burst into the office, clutching a handful of gum packets. "This stuff is awesome! I gave some to the chickens, and now they're running laps around the yard!"

Marge stared at him, her eye twitching. "You fed it to the chickens?"

"They seemed curious!" Joey said defensively.

Ron looked delighted. "See? It's effective!"

Marge pinched the bridge of her nose. "Ron, you've officially lost your mind."

Danny appeared in the doorway, holding a box of gum. "So what's the plan, Pop? Selling to the locals, or are we going full black market with this?"

"NO, it's not black market!" Ron shouted.

Ron mused. *That kid's a prodigy—already thinking about business and making sales at his age. Makes me proud.*

Beth wandered in, flipping through a packet. "The ingredients list just says 'proprietary blend.' That's not sketchy at all, Dad!"

"It's perfectly fine!" Ron insisted. "This is a golden opportunity, guys. We could be sitting on a good money!"

Marge gave him a long, hard look. *Ron, if you get us shut down over this, you're sleeping in the trailer in a different town, goddamn it.*

Ron waved her off. "You worry too much. Everything's gonna be fine."

Ron's idea of selling gum turned out to be a family affair. Beth and Ivy were tasked with "marketing," which mostly involved taping handmade flyers to telephone poles around town. Joey volunteered to "test" the product, chewing gum nonstop until he started vibrating like a wind-up toy.

"Joey, stop bouncing!" Marge snapped, watching him zip around the yard.

"I can't!" Joey yelled, his voice several octaves higher than usual. "This gum works!"

"NO MORE GUM, JOEY!" Marge shouted.

"But Pop said…" Joey trailed off when he caught the look on Marge's face.

"I don't care what that man said. Understood?" Marge demanded.

Grace and Lewis, meanwhile, were tasked with setting up a makeshift "storefront" in the junkyard. They dragged out an old card table, decorated it with scraps of ribbon, and set up the gum boxes like they were selling luxury goods.

"This is so dumb," Lewis muttered, folding his arms.

"It's not dumb," Grace said. "It's... weirdly charming, and we get part of the sales!"

"Charming?" Lewis snorted. "It's a card table in a junkyard."

"It has a certain allure," Grace said with a smirk, trying to put the best spin on it.

"What does 'allure' even mean?" Lewis asked. He was completely ignored, his voice drowned out after all his complaining.

Their first customer was a teenager from down the road, who approached the table with the caution of someone expecting a trap.

"How much?" he asked, eyeing the gum.

"Two bucks a pack," Grace said.

The teenager handed over a crumpled bill, grabbed a pack, and walked off chewing.

"See?" Ron said, clapping his hands. "We're already making moolah!"

"It's one sale," Marge said, lighting yet another cigarette before breaking into a fit of coughing. "Don't pop the champagne yet."
(cough, cough, cough)

By the end of the day, they'd sold a dozen packs, mostly to curious locals who had no idea what they were getting into. The chickens, meanwhile, had worn themselves out and were now passed out in a pile near the coop.

As the sun set over the Yard, Ron stood proudly by the table, his grin wider than ever.

"This is the start of something big," he said.

Marge shook her head, muttering under her breath. "It's the start of something, alright."

CHAPTER 18

Ron had more than a few run-ins with the police when he met Marge—mostly for what he liked to call *misunderstandings* and what the law called *theft, fraud,* and *trespassing.* When their paths crossed, he had just gotten off probation for selling lumber that technically wasn't his. In Ron's mind, none of it was real crime; it was *investment capital* for whatever half-baked deal he was working on at the time. If a pile of wood was left unattended, it meant someone didn't need it. And if they didn't need it, why shouldn't he sell it?

By age six, Ron had already developed a knack for spotting opportunity where others saw nothing. He grew up in a town made of dust and regret, where tumbleweeds were more common than good luck. His mother, Loretta, did her best to keep them afloat, humming when she worked and stretching every dollar until it screamed. His father, Hank, spent more time cursing life at the bottom of a whiskey glass in between railroad jobs.

Ron's first business venture came on a blistering summer afternoon when he decided **painted tumbleweeds** could turn a profit at the local market. His father scoffed, but Loretta helped him scrounge up leftover paint from the neighbors. He sold three before a gust of wind sent the rest rolling across the parking lot. Even Hank cracked a rare smile that day, and Ron learned a valuable lesson—success wasn't about luck; it was about persistence.

By sixteen, Ron had taken over as man of the house, working nights at the gas station, fixing bikes for extra cash, and dreaming of something bigger. But dreams didn't pay rent. Reality had a way of yanking him back down.

His twenties were a whirlwind of schemes, failed ventures, and just enough success to keep him going. He flipped cars, hustled scrap metal, and spent more time convincing himself he was *this close* to making it big than actually making it big. Then came the lumber incident—his most "profitable" disaster yet. Before anyone figured out it had originally belonged to the county, he'd sold a whole truckload. The judge wasn't impressed with his *creative acquisition* defense, and Ron spent the next few months on probation, swearing he'd find a way to do things *legally.*

That's when he met Marge.

She was a waitress at a roadside diner, sharp-tongued and unimpressed by nonsense. Ron walked in looking for coffee and walked out smitten. She handed him a steaming cup and said, "Drink up, cowboy. You look like you've been rode hard and put away wet."

Marge had a way of grounding Ron without killing his fire. She saw his potential even when he was neck-deep in another doomed scheme.

When they married, she became his partner in every way—his anchor, his equal, the only person who could call him an idiot and make him want to be better.

Years later, standing in the middle of the junkyard they now called home, Ron couldn't help but think of the long road that had led him there.

"You're staring at that pile of rust like it's the **Mona Lisa**," Marge said, lighting a cigarette. "What's going on in that unique brain of yours?"

Ron grinned. "Just thinking about something a guy at the gas station told me years ago."

Marge smirked. "Oh yeah? What'd he say?"

"To look for the gold in what other people throw away."

Marge exhaled a plume of smoke, glancing around at the sea of broken-down cars and twisted metal. "And you still think there's gold in this junkyard?"

"I *know* there is," Ron said. "We just have to keep digging."

Marge shook her head, but a small smile tugged at her lips. "You're impossible, you know that?"

Ron laughed. "Maybe. But I am your impossible, and that is always where the fun starts."

CHAPTER 19

The morning at the junkyard started off quietly—a suspicious kind of quiet. Marge was the first to notice, leaning against the office doorframe with her coffee. Joey wasn't shouting about his "pirate fort," Beth and Ivy weren't scribbling in their notebooks, and Max and Danny weren't fighting over a broken engine. Even the crows perched on the rusted-out Ford seemed unusually still.

"Something's off this morning. I can feel it," Marge muttered with an anxious tone, taking a slow drag from her cigarette.

Ron came around the corner, wiping his hands onto a rag. "What are you talking about? It's peaceful. For once, the kids aren't trying to kill or out-yell each other."

"Exactly," Marge said, narrowing her eyes. "They're plotting something. Mark my words."

Before Ron could respond, Joey came sprinting around the corner, his face streaked with dirt and a wild grin plastered across his face. "Pop! Mom! Gotta see this! It's awesome!"

Ron perked up. "See? Not plotting. Just being a kid."

Marge squinted at Joey. "What kind of 'awesome' are we talking about here? 'Look, I found a cool rock' awesome, or 'Oops, I accidentally set something on fire' awesome?"

Joey grinned wider. "Both!"

The source of Joey's excitement turned out to be a makeshift slingshot fashioned from old bungee cords and the frame of a rusted lawn chair. Danny stood nearby, looking smug, while Beth leaned against a stack of tires, rolling her eyes. The contraption was aimed at a pile of scrap metal, and judging by the scorch marks on the ground, it had already been tested.

"This," Joey announced proudly, "is the **Scrap Blaster 3000!**"

"Patent pending," Danny added with a smirk.

Ron's face lit up with a mix of pride and disbelief. "You built this? From the junk around here? And you actually know what 'patent pending' means?"

"Yeah!" Joey said, bouncing on his heels. "It's for launching stuff! Like rocks. Or cans. Or—"

"Stop," Marge interrupted, raising a hand. "Just... stop. I don't even want to know what else you've launched."

Beth snorted. "Pretty sure the social worker would love to hear about this."

Ron ignored her, walking up to the slingshot and inspecting it with the critical eye of a man who knew good chaos when he saw it. "This is impressive," he said, shaking the frame. "Sturdy. Functional. Hell, you kids might've just invented something."

"Something dangerous," Marge muttered, taking another drag of her cigarette.

"Not dangerous, Mom, it works!" Joey said. "Wanna see?"

"No!" Marge and Beth said in unison.

"Yes!" Ron said, his eyes gleaming.

Danny stepped forward, holding a dented hubcap. "Check this out." He loaded it into the slingshot, pulled back the bungee cords, and released. The hubcap sailed through the air with a high-pitched *whiiizzz* before crashing into a distant scrap pile, sending a dust and rust cloud into the air.

Joey whooped, jumping up and down. "Did you see that?!"

Marge shook her head. "Congratulations. You've officially created the world's least practical weapon. But your ambition is commendable."

"Or the most fun," Ron countered with a grin. "Think people would pay to launch stuff?"

Later that day, as the kids continued to "test" their invention, Marge and Ron sat in the office, going over the week's bills. The numbers, as usual, weren't adding up.

"This place is a money pit," Marge said, slamming the ledger shut. "We're one bad month away from eating no label beans straight out of the can."

Ron leaned back in his chair, rubbing his chin, thinking hard. "We just need to diversify. Add another revenue stream or three."

"Like what? Renting out the Scrap Blaster 3000 for birthday parties?"

Ron chuckled. "Don't knock it. Kids love destruction."

Before Marge could respond, the sound of an engine revving outside interrupted their conversation. They exchanged a glance before heading out to investigate.

A beat-up pickup truck had pulled into the yard, its exhaust belching black smoke and one almost flat tire. The driver was a wiry man with a crooked smile and a black cowboy hat tilted low over his eyes. He climbed out, giving the place a once-over before slowing and making his way toward Ron and Marge.

"Nice setup you got here," he drawled, his voice as slick as oil on pavement.

"And you are?" Marge asked, crossing her arms.

"Name's Clyde," the man said, tipping his hat. "Heard you folks might be lookin' for a business opportunity."

Ron's eyes lit up. "What kind of opportunity, Clyde?"

Marge groaned. "Oh, god help us, here we go."

Clyde leaned against the truck, pulling a toothpick from his pocket and sticking it between his teeth. "Let's just say I've got a line on some... specialty scrap. Stuff that could fetch a pretty penny if you know the right buyers."

"Specialty scrap?" Marge repeated, her tone dripping with skepticism. "Sounds shady."

"Shady?" Clyde feigned offense, clutching his chest. "Ma'am, I assure you, everything I deal in is perfectly legal... enough."

Ron grinned. "I'm listening."

Marge threw up her hands. "Of course you are. He said

'opportunity,' and now you're all in."

Clyde's pitch turned out to involve "repurposing" parts from abandoned vehicles parked in lots that may or may not have been public property. Marge wanted no part of it, but Ron, ever the rationalized optimist, was already imagining dollar signs.

"This could be the break we've been waiting for!" he said as Clyde drove off.

"This could also be prison time," Marge shot back.

"Come on, Marge," Ron said, throwing an arm around her shoulders. "Where's your sense of adventure?"

"Adventure doesn't pay the bills," she muttered. "And it sure as hell doesn't keep the cops off our backs."

"Marge, the cops are our friends right now—our partners, really—because we take in tough kid cases and help them out. That's earned us at least one or two strikes we can use. But this… this sounds big for us," Ron said.

"Look, babe, think of it like a cat getting a couple of extra lives." He flashed a big, somewhat insincere smile.

That evening, weird tension hung around the Yard. Beth holed up in her room, reading a new novel. Danny searched for just the right part with Lewis. Meanwhile, Joey, Max, and Grace were busy rigging the Scrap Blaster 3000, trying to make it shoot even farther.

Marge feeling a little blue, watched it all from the doorway, her cigarette glowing in the fading light. She felt the weight of it all pressing down on her—the bills, the chaos, the constant tug-of-war between Ron's big dreams and reality.

Ron joined her, a cold beer in hand. "You're quiet tonight," he said, cracking open the bottle before pulling her hand into his.

"Just thinking," Marge replied.

"About?"

"How we're one step away from this whole thing blowing up in our faces," she said, exhaling a plume of smoke. "Literally, if Joey gets his hands on any fireworks."

Ron chuckled. "You worry too much."

"And you don't worry enough."

They stood in silence for a moment, the sounds of the junkyard filling the space between them. Finally, Ron spoke.

"You know, Marge, for all the mess and madness... I think we're doing okay."

Marge glanced at him. "You think?"

Ron nodded. "Yeah. The kids are happy—well, mostly—and we've got a roof over our heads... well, *mostly*. That's more than I had growing up."

Marge softened, just a little. "You're a dreamer, Ron. Always have been, and honestly I am just feeling a little down tonight."

"Babe, you're the realist," Ron said with a smile. "That's why we work. Maybe a good night's sleep will help."

"**I love you** more than yesterday—and a lot more than last week." He didn't say it enough, but Marge was his soulmate.

"Sometimes I wonder," Marge muttered, but there was a hint of a smile on her lips.

As the night wore on, the junkyard settled into its usual rhythm of rust, ruin, and resilience. Somewhere in the distance, Grace proudly fired the Scrap Blaster 3000 one last time, sending a hubcap soaring into the night sky. It gleamed briefly in the moonlight before crashing into the darkness.

Ron raised his beer. "Here's to making it work—one way or another."

Marge rolled her eyes, but she clinked her coffee mug against his bottle anyway. "Here's to surviving another day."

CHAPTER 20

The morning sun painted everything in a dusty orange glow, so serene until Joey started shouting about his "kingdom," and Ivy, a newer addition to the family, stood off to the side, arms crossed, observing the chaos like a scientist studying a particularly unhinged experiment.

Marge leaned against the office doorway, coffee in hand, watching them with a blend of amusement and exasperation. Each of these kids was a puzzle piece—rough-edged, mismatched, and impossibly stubborn—but somehow, together, they fit. Not perfectly, not neatly, but in a way that made its own kind of chaotic sense.

She took a slow sip of coffee, suppressing the urge to cough. Damn cigarettes. She told herself she'd lay off them for a week, maybe more, to give her lungs a break. **Not that she was quitting—hell no**. Just... pausing. A temporary truce with her own body.

Joey, at six, was the youngest and, in many ways, the loudest. A ball of energy, constantly in motion, today he wore a pirate hat he'd found buried in one of the junk piles, his face streaked with dirt, and his hands clutched a long stick he'd declared his "scepter."

"Behold!" he shouted, climbing onto a stack of old washing machines. "I am the King of Scrap! Bow before me, peasants!"

"Joey, get down from there before you break your damn neck!" Marge barked, her voice sharper than usual. The kid had pulled plenty of reckless stunts before, but today, her patience was running thinner than a gas station burrito.

She exhaled through her nose, fighting the itch for a cigarette. No nicotine, no buffer. Just raw nerves and the slow burn of withdrawal making everything—and everyone—twice as irritating.

"I'm fine!" Joey called back, striking a dramatic pose. "The King fears nothing!"

"He should fear himself," Beth muttered.

Joey's imagination was as boundless as his energy. One day, he was a pirate. The next, an astronaut. The day after that, a treasure hunter. His adventures often ended in disaster—broken tools, mysterious stains, and occasionally something catching on fire—but he was always ready for the next one.

Danny, at nine, was Joey's complete opposite—quiet, methodical, and fiercely independent. While Joey climbed anything that would hold his weight (and plenty that wouldn't), Danny kept to the garage, sleeves rolled up, hands deep in the guts of an old engine. He had a knack for fixing things, a skill Ron was quick to both exploit and encourage.

Ron watched him work, a hint of pride tugging at the corners of his mouth. The kid reminded him of himself at that age—focused, stubborn, always trying to make something run just a little better. Difference was, Danny actually had a chance to do something with it.

"Danny, can you take a look at this carburetor?" Ron would ask, holding up some greasy hunk of metal.

"C'mon, Pop, that's a starter," Danny said, shaking his head with a laugh. **"You're being ridiculous."**

Ron narrowed his eyes, folding his arms as he loomed over the open hood. "Boy, I've been fixing cars since before you were even a thought. You sure you wanna school me on this?"

Danny just grinned, wiping grease off his hands. "Yeah, actually."

For Danny, the junkyard was both a sanctuary and a proving ground. He didn't talk much about his past, but Marge suspected it was difficult. There was a hardness to him, a guardedness that only softened when he was deep into a project. **He loved the *Yard*.**

One afternoon, Marge found him crouched over an old lawnmower, his hands black with grease. "What are you working on?" she asked, leaning against the doorframe.

"Trying to get this piece of crap running," Danny muttered, not looking up. "Pop said it might be worth something if we can fix it."

"And?" Marge prompted.

"And it's a piece of crap," Danny said, sitting back on his heels, wiping his hands on an already grease-stained rag. "But I'll figure it out."

Marge leaned against the doorframe, arms crossed, watching the exchange with a smirk. "Pop always thinks things are worth something, bless his heart," she laughed.

Ron came around the corner, waving a hand both dismissively and dramatically. "Hey now, one man's junk is another man's gold—just gotta know where to look."

Danny snorted, tapping the rusted metal with his wrench. "Yeah? Well, this 'gold' looks like it hasn't run since the dinosaurs were around."

Marge chuckled, taking a sip of coffee. "Keep telling yourself that, Ron. Meanwhile, Danny's the only one around here actually making things work."

Ron clapped his hands over his ears. "Lalalala, can't hear you, babe," he sang-songed, grinning. Then he dropped his hands with a dramatic sigh. "Where's the faith?"

Danny smirked, wiping his hands on his jeans. "Probably rusted out—just like this thing."

That was Danny in a nutshell: determined to make things work, even when they seemed impossible. He was well beyond his years.

Beth, at fifteen, was already tired of the world. Sharp-tongued and sarcastic, she had little patience for nonsense—which, unfortunately for her, made her the perfect foil for Ron's endless schemes.

"You're the brains of this operation," Ron liked to tell her, usually when he needed help with paperwork or inventory. "Without you, this place would fall apart."

"That's because you keep building it out of duct tape and bailing wire," Beth chimed in, rolling her eyes as she leaned against the workbench.

Her notebook was her constant companion, filled with sketches and notes, and what Marge suspected were biting observations about her family. Beth didn't share much about what she wrote, but one evening, Marge caught a glimpse of a half-finished poem.

"Rust and ruin, chaos and charm,
We build our lives with broken parts.
A family of misfits, flawed and true,
Finding hope in what we do."

Marge didn't say anything, but the words stayed with her.

Max, at eight, was a whirlwind of curiosity and mischief. He had the kind of grin that usually meant trouble, and if Joey was the king of chaos, Max was his second-in-command. He was fascinated with taking things apart, but putting them back together. That was a work in progress.

He was hovering around Danny's workbench, watching him fiddle with the lawnmower.

"You sure you know what you're doing?" Max asked, squinting at the engine.

Danny sighed. "Yes."

"Because last time, you set something on fire."

"That was Joey."

Max shrugged. "Oh yeah."

Lewis, at eleven, was the observer of the group. He wasn't as wild as Joey or as hands-on as Danny, but he had a sharp mind and a knack for reading people. He wasn't a leader or a follower—he existed on his own terms, slipping between conversations with a quiet confidence.

Marge often found him sitting on the hood of an old car, sketching something in a notebook.

"What are you drawing?" she asked one evening.

Lewis flipped the notebook shut. "Nothing."

"Doesn't look like nothing."

Lewis smirked. "Guess it's something, then, but I don't want to show you."

He was like that—private, but not unfriendly. A puzzle Marge hadn't quite figured out yet. He didn't push people away, not exactly, but he kept just enough distance that no one ever got too close.

"You don't talk much," Ron observed one day.

"You talk enough for both of us," Lewis replied without looking up.

Ron grinned. "Fair enough, kiddo."

By mid-afternoon, the yard pulsed with energy, a tangle of voices, laughter, and the occasional *clang* of metal. Joey's shouts rang out as he tore across the lot, a makeshift sword in hand, locked in a dramatic battle only he understood—a stray cat, clearly uninterested in piracy, shot under the porch in search of quieter company.

From beneath the hood of a truck, Danny muttered a curse, his tools clattering against the engine as he worked. Nearby, Beth flipped a page in her notebook, her pencil moving in sharp, deliberate strokes, though she still found time to sigh dramatically whenever Joey got too loud. Ivy sat cross-legged beside her, absently braiding wildflowers into a chain, her fingers quick and practiced as if she'd done it a hundred times before.

A sudden *snap* cut through the air—Max and his slingshot, taking aim at a row of soda cans lined up on the fence. Grace, ever the diplomat, stood with arms crossed, watching him like a teacher waiting to confiscate a toy before it inevitably caused trouble.

And then there was Lewis, perched on a stack of tires, silent as always, his faint smirk suggesting he was in on a joke no one else had quite figured out yet.

Marge stood with Ron, taking it all in. "This is our life," she said, her tone equal parts wonder and disbelief.

"Kinda beautiful, isn't it?" Ron said, surveying the chaos with a satisfied grin.

Marge shook her head, exhaling through her nose. "You're insane," she muttered. Then, after a beat, she added, "And... it's turned out okay."

"Maybe," Ron admitted, slinging an arm around her shoulders, his grip warm and easy. "But we've got something good here."

Marge glanced at him, then back at the yard—at the mismatched group of kids, at the noise, the mess, the life filling every corner. She sighed, but there was no real weight behind it.

"Yeah," she said softly. "We really do."

Marge couldn't argue. For all its chaos and occasional dysfunction, the yard had become more than just a business. It was home—a place where broken things got a second chance, where misfits found a place to belong.

Them included.

"Hey, Mom!" Joey shouted, waving a hubcap over his head. "Can we keep the cat?"

Marge sighed. "No, Joey. We're not eating the cat."

"NO, KEEP THE CAT!" Joey yelled as the cat bolted over a pile of scrap.

"He stays because you keep feeding it," Beth said.

"It's called being nice!" Joey replied.

"It's called being dumb," Beth retorted. "I'm going back to my new book—another cozy murder mystery, this time by a lady who wrote like a hundred of them."

Ron laughed, squeezing Marge's shoulder. "Never a dull moment, huh?"

Marge groaned, rolling her eyes. "Never." But the smile tugging at her lips gave her away.

As the day crawled closer to the end, Ron could tell Danny had a bad day—shoulders slumped, that tired, distant look in his eyes. No words were needed. Instead, Ron grabbed his keys, clapped a hand on Danny's back, and said, "C'mon, kid. Burgers."

Now, sitting at their favorite hole-in-the-wall diner, Ron took a huge bite of his green chile cheeseburger, then pointed at Danny's. "Why'd you get yours without chile?"

Danny shrugged. "Not in the mood."

Ron froze mid-chew. "Not in the—" He set his burger down like he needed both hands to process this. "You live in New Mexico. You don't just 'not feel like' green chile."

Danny picked at his fries. "I just wanted a regular burger."

"Regular? You mean *bland*." Ron exhaled dramatically. "You're breaking my heart, kid."

Danny sighed, dipping a fry into the melted cheese that had dripped onto his plate. "I like chile. Just… not every time."

Ron stared at him like he was some alien. "We're gonna have to work on that."

CHAPTER 21

The sun was almost always out—320 days a year, to be exact—baking Albuquerque in its relentless glow. A city vehicle—a white pickup with a faded municipal seal peeling on the door—rumbled into the junkyard, kicking up a haze of dust.

Marge spotted it first from the office porch, piping hot black coffee in hand. She squinted against the glare, let out a low groan, and muttered, "Not this guy again," as a familiar figure climbed out of the driver's seat.

"Well, if it isn't our favorite bureaucrat," she muttered. "What do you think he wants now?"

Ron emerged from the garage, wiping his hands on a stark white, new work rag—formerly known as a T-shirt. "It's Sam," he said, glancing toward the driveway. "He probably needs something moved. Or 'repurposed.'"

Marge snorted. "Uh-huh. And by 'repurposed,' you mean 'disappear without questions'?"

Ron shrugged, tossing the rag over his shoulder. "Details, babe. Details."

"Or he's here to collect," Marge said, her tone dry.

Ron grinned. "That's the beauty of our arrangement. We collect *for them*, remember?"

Sam Gutierrez was a city waste coordinator, though *"coordinator"* was a generous term. Most days, he looked more like a man trying to keep a dozen spinning plates from crashing to the ground. Wiry and perpetually sleep-deprived, he carried the air of someone who'd seen too much and cared just enough to stay out of trouble—but not enough to avoid it entirely.

He was also impossible to miss, thanks to the cloud of cologne that clung to him like a bad decision.

Sam liked Ron and Marge well enough, but he never let them forget that their arrangement with the city was more of a handshake than a contract—not exactly official and definitely not foolproof.

"Ron. Marge," Sam greeted as he approached. "How's business?"

"Booming," Ron replied, raising his arms to gesture at the scrap piles around them. "Got a little of everything—cars, bikes, washing machines. You name it, we've got it."

"And most of it legal, I'm sure," Sam said, arching an eyebrow.

Marge snorted. "We're on the up-and-up, Sam."

Sam gave her a weary smile. "That's what I like about you two— your honesty. Now, listen, we've got a little situation downtown."

"What kind of situation?" Ron asked, leaning in like a kid being let in on a secret.

Sam sighed, rubbing the back of his neck. "You know the old strip mall on Central? The one that's been empty since, like, 2003?"

A Deal with **Albuquerque**.

"Yeah, I know it," Ron said, rubbing his chin. "Been an eyesore forever."

"Well, the city finally got funding to tear it down," Sam replied. "Problem is, there's a ton of metal in there—gutters, shelving, HVAC units—and we don't want it all going to the landfill. Figured you might want to take it off our hands."

Ron's face lit up. "You kidding? That's a goldmine!"

"Not quite," Sam said, already dampening Ron's excitement. "You'll have to haul it yourself, and you'll need to sign a waiver. Liability and all that."

Marge crossed her arms, unimpressed. "So, let me get this straight: you want us to clear your junk for free, take on all the risk, and call it a favor?"

Sam smiled faintly. "Pretty much."

"Sounds about right, Albuquerque," Marge muttered, taking a drag of her cigarette.

Ron and Marge's unofficial partnership with the City of Albuquerque had begun a year earlier when Ron's endless optimism collided with one of Sam's many bureaucratic headaches.

The city had been grappling with a problem: what to do with the growing piles of scrap and salvageable materials from condemned buildings, abandoned lots, and illegal dumping sites. The official channels were slow and expensive, and the cops were constantly chasing after rogue scrappers who stripped everything of value, with piles of needles and bottles left as a gift.

Enter Ron—always thinking about shortcuts and opportunities in the same breath, as if one couldn't exist without the other.

A year ago, when Ron first stumbled into Sam's office at **City Working for Citizens**, he had been looking for "business opportunities," a term that made Marge roll her eyes so hard she swore she saw another dimension. Sam had been buried under complaints about illegal scavengers tearing apart abandoned properties, city crews overwhelmed with hauling costs, and local businesses frustrated with rising disposal fees.

Ron had listened, nodding along, pretending to care about the city's problems. Then, ever the opportunist, he grinned and asked, "So… what if I just took all that junk off your hands?"

Sam had squinted at him. "What do you mean?"

"I mean, you guys don't want to deal with it. I *do*. You give me a call when you've got scrap, I haul it out, no questions asked. You don't have to pay a dime, and I get first pick at the good stuff."

Marge, who had tagged along purely to make sure Ron didn't sign them up for something *really* illegal, had cleared her throat. "And if someone gets hurt?"

Ron waved her off. "Details, Love of mine!"

Sam had leaned back in his chair, considering. He was a man who had spent too many years wading through red tape and budget constraints. On paper, Ron's offer was absurd. In reality? It was the kind of off-the-books solution that could make a few headaches disappear.

So, after a handshake, a half-hearted waiver, and a test run hauling scrap from an abandoned motel, Ron's "partnership" with the city had been born.

A year later, Sam had learned an important lesson: Ron *would* take the city's junk, no matter how ridiculous. But Marge *would* make him suffer for it.

Marge exhaled slowly, the glow of her cigarette illuminating the skepticism on her face. "Let me guess, Sam—this is one of those buildings full of old wiring and rusted beams held together by a prayer, right?"

Sam didn't even try to lie. "It's not *that* bad."

Marge glanced at Ron. "Do you hear that? That's the sound of a man who's covering his ass."

Ron, already mentally counting the salvage value, grinned. "Come on, Marge. HVAC units alone could be worth a small fortune. Copper wiring? Aluminum gutters? This is easy money."

"Well, you've got me thinking— with metal and aluminum prices skyrocketing thanks to all those poorly thought-out tariffs, maybe we do have some of that 'gold' you've been talking about for years," Marge mused.

Sam coughed. "Well… about that. Some of the wiring's already gone."

Marge's eyes narrowed. "Gone, huh? And how much is 'some'?"

"Yeah," Sam admitted, rubbing the back of his neck. "Some… *unofficial* goddamn scrappers got to it first."

"Fantastic," Marge deadpanned. "So now we get to clear out what's left while dodging rust, roaches, needles, shit piles, and whatever structural failure is waiting to happen."

Ron, ever the optimist, clapped his hands together. "Marge, we've done worse."

"Oh yeah?" She flicked ash from her cigarette. "Name one time."

"The motel."

"The motel where you fell through the second floor?"

Ron winced. "Okay, bad example."

Sam cleared his throat. "Look, if it makes you feel better, the building isn't condemned *yet*. It's just… in transition."

Marge let out a forced laugh. "In transition… into piles of rubble?"

Ron turned to Sam, ignoring Marge's sarcasm. "How long do we have?"

Sam checked his watch. "Demo crew starts in two weeks."

Ron nodded. "Then we're in."

Marge sighed. "Of course we are." She turned to Sam. "What's the catch?"

Sam smirked. "No catch. Just don't sue the city if a beam falls on your head."

"Great," Marge muttered. "Add it to the list of ways Ron's gonna get himself killed."

Two days later, Ron and Marge stood outside the old mall. It was even uglier in person—damn ugly, and more than a little foreboding.

The faded brown block was streaked with grime, the windows were either boarded up or shattered, and the main entrance looked like it had been kicked in more than once. **No Trespassing** sign hung crookedly from a chain-link fence, as if the city had given up enforcing it.

Beth, standing beside them, adjusted her backpack. "So, uh… do we have, like, hard hats or anything?"

Marge shot Ron a look.

"Safety equipment?" she asked, voice dripping with sarcasm. "Oh, no, honey. We throw ourselves into dangerous situations and *hope for the best*."

Beth rolled her eyes. "God, Mom, I was just asking."

Joey, who had been staring up at the building with a mix of fascination and horror, frowned. "Are there ghosts?"

Ron grinned. "Only one way to find out, buddy."

Joey did *not* like that answer.

Marge shook her head. "Let's just get this over with."

Max came around the corner, groaning, holding his stomach. "I think I ate too many tamales."

Beth didn't even look up from her next careful step. "That's what you said last time."

"I know, but this time I *really* mean it."

Beth shook her head. "You always really mean it."

Max groaned again. "Why didn't you stop me?"

Beth finally looked at him. "You really think I have the power to stop you when there's tamales in front of you?"

Max frowned. "No… but please try harder next time."

With that, they all proceeded into the unknown project.

Inside, the place smelled like dust, mold, faint sewage, and bad decisions. Old metal shelving stretched from floor to ceiling, most of it empty. A few broken chairs and forgotten crates lay scattered across the concrete floor. The air was thick—stale and heavy with the weight of years of neglect, as if the building itself had given up on being useful.

Max, who had snuck ahead, called out from behind a shelf. "Guys! I found something!"

Marge sighed. "If it's a dead rat, I'm out. Period. Not fucking around!"

Max emerged, grinning, holding up a metal pipe. "Weapons!"

Beth groaned. "Oh my God, Max."

Ron, however, looked thoughtful. "Actually… we could use that."

Marge buried her face in her hands. "For the love of all things holy, tell me you're not about to encourage this child to start piping rats, shelves, and whatever else he can get his hands on?"

Ron grinned. "No, no. I was thinking… some of this shelving could be repurposed for the Yard."

Marge sighed. "Fantastic. So not only are we looting a condemned building, we're also bringing home *more* junk."

"Okay, everyone—kids, and Ron, listen up! Please be careful, wear your limited safety equipment (gloves), and watch out for needles, like we explained before," Marge yelled.

Ron clapped his hands. "Exactly! Now, let's get to work."

Marge took a long drag of her cigarette and muttered something about "bad choices and fucking Ron."

When this endeavor started, it was Ron's straightforward and smart initiative. He'd approached Sam after overhearing him complain about a dumpster fire—both literal and figurative—at a city council meeting. Ron's pitch was simple: let the junkyard handle the overflow. They'd haul away the scrap, salvage what they could, and keep the rest out of the city's hair.

"You get a cleaner city," Ron had said, flashing his best salesman smile. "And we get inventory, and our permits to operate all signed. It's a win-win-win."

Sam had been skeptical, and a hard "no" at first. "And how do I know you won't just take the good stuff and dump the rest? How will I get your permits signed?"

"Because we're not idiots, nor are you." Marge had chimed in, lighting a cigarette. "We live here too, you know. We're all part of this community, and a small business trying to make some sales."

Against his better judgment, Sam had agreed to a trial run; if that worked, he would get the permits all signed off on for the junkyard operation. It had worked better than expected, and soon, the junkyard became the city's unofficial cleanup crew. The arrangement wasn't without its hiccups, but it kept the cops off their backs, and Sam got a half dozen Yard permit signatures over lunch and drinks with friends at the city. As long as Ron and Marge played by the city's loose rules, they had a free pass to operate in the gray areas of legality.

"Today's Job," Ron shouted. Alright," Ron said, clapping his hands together. "We'll take the strip mall job. When do we start?"

"Demolition begins Monday," Sam said. "You've got until then to clear out whatever you can use. After that, the contractors move in, and anything left gets bulldozed."

Ron's grin widened. "Plenty of time."

"Sure," Marge muttered. "Plenty of time to break something-or someone."

Sam handed Ron the waiver and a set of keys to the site. "One more thing," he said. "Keep it clean, okay? Last thing I need is a phone call about you guys tearing up the place or, God forbid, finding something you're not supposed to."

"Define 'not supposed to,'" Ron said, grinning.

Sam groaned. "Just... don't make my life harder than it already is."

"No promises," Marge said, smirking as Sam climbed back into his truck and drove off.

Now, a day into the mall scrapping project, it didn't seem like such a bad idea after all. They had two shipping bins loaded with copper, aluminum, appliance and electrical parts, and shelving.

Later that evening, as Ron and Marge sat on the porch watching the kids chase each other through the yard, Marge lit another cigarette and glanced at Ron. "Have you ever thought about how close we are to getting shut down?"

One thing they didn't skimp on was beer. Ron took a sip of his ice-cold Mexican lager. "All the time."

"And it doesn't bother you?"

"Nah," Ron said, leaning back in his chair. "Sam's got our back. If we keep doing the city's dirty work, they'll keep looking the other way."

Marge shook her head. "It's not just Sam. People are watching us—social workers, neighbors, that nosy bastard from the zoning office."

Ron grinned. "Let them watch. We're not doing anything wrong, much."

The tone and atmosphere of the meeting shattered as Max yelled in the background, "I need to go number two—so bad! I ate too many tamales. Ouch!"

Much—a large and conveniently vague word," Marge said, exhaling a plume of smoke as she sipped her beer.

Ron laughed. "You worry too much."

"And you don't worry enough," Marge shot back.

But for all her grumbling, Marge knew Ron was right. Their arrangement with the city was a balancing act—one misstep, and the whole thing could come crashing down. But for now, it was working, and all they had to work with. And in a town like Albuquerque, that was more than most people could say.

It had been an epically long day stripping junk from the strip mall. That night, after the kids had collapsed into bed, Marge found Ron in the garage, tinkering with an old generator, his gaze lost in the haze of exhaustion.

"You think this'll last?" she asked, leaning against the doorframe.

"What, the generator?"

"No, babe," she said. "This. The junkyard and the business. The deal with the city. We're staying one step ahead of everyone with authority."

Ron paused, wiping his forehead. "I don't know. Maybe. Maybe not."

Marge sighed. "That's comforting. Shit."

Ron smiled, walking over to her. "Hey, we're making it work, aren't we? As long as we keep doing that, we'll be fine. **By the way, I love you. You're my partner in crime.**"

"You asshole," Marge said, but her tone was softer. "I love you too."

Ron wrapped an arm around her shoulders, pulling her close. "That's all we need. One day at a time."

"Are we having sex tonight?" Ron asked.

Marge rested her head against his shoulder, listening to the mysteries of the distant city sounds. For all its flaws, Albuquerque was their home—and for now, that was enough.

"No, asshole, I'm exhausted—but you can watch my boobs while I brush my teeth," Marge smirked.

CHAPTER 22

The old four-seater truck rumbled down the highway, the junkyard shrinking in the rearview mirror.

Marge kept one hand on the wheel and the other wrapped around her gas station coffee, sipping it like it was her last. The early morning sun wasn't as intense today, and the highway stretched ahead—an endless ribbon of cracked asphalt.

Despite Marge's earlier warning, Beth rode shotgun, legs propped up on the dashboard.

"You keep doing that, and the first time I have to hit the brakes, you're gonna be eating kneecaps."

Beth didn't move. "I'll take my chances."

In the backseat, Grace sat with her earphones in—not playing anything, just wearing them like armor, a silent excuse to ignore the world. She stared out the window, her gaze searching, as if scanning for fractures in the surface of the earth.

For a while, the only sounds were the tires against the pavement and the occasional slurp from Marge's coffee. She let the silence sit, let them settle. Then she spoke.

"Alright, girls. Two rules for this trip." She held up a finger. "One—don't wander off. I do not have the time, or patience to deal with a kidnapping today."

Beth smirked. "Today?"

Marge shot her a look.

"Second rule—if a man over thirty tells you you're mature for your age, you kick him in the balls and run."

Grace snorted, and Beth and Ivy nodded in approval.

"Good life advice in general," Beth said.

"Damn right it is." Marge took another sip of coffee, shifting gears as the road curved through a stretch of dusty hills. "I don't care if we're in a gas station, a rest stop, or a damn Walmart—if I yell your name, you show up in under ten seconds, or I'm assuming you got snatched by a serial killer."

Beth rolled her eyes. "A little dramatic, don't you think?"

Marge gave her a flat look. "Do I look like someone who underestimates the stupidity of men?"

Beth considered that. "Fair point, Mom."

Grace finally spoke, her voice dry. "Why does it sound like a serial killer has personally hunted you?"

Ivy stayed quiet, and Marge let her be. Still, she couldn't help but wonder what Ivy had been through. There was a decent chance it wasn't good—men, violence—hopefully not, but Marge didn't know.

Marge shrugged. "It's a long life, sweetheart. You pick up some wisdom along the way."

Grace lifted an eyebrow. "Like what? Other than serial killer prevention."

Marge tapped the side of her coffee cup. "Always carry cash. Never trust a man in snakeskin boots. And if you ever get a bad feeling about a place, you listen to your gut."

Beth raised a skeptical eyebrow. "Okay, but what about, like… fun road trip rules?"

Marge scoffed. "***Fun* road trip rules?** We're driving six hours to pick up a salvaged water pump from some dude named Bobby in a town that barely exists. This ain't exactly spring break in Ft. Lauderdale."

Beth grinned. "Then I call DJ privileges, if we're pretending it's spring break."

Ivy finally smiled and spoke up. "I'll be in charge of drinks!"

Marge groaned. "Not if you're playing whatever noise you and Joey call music."

"Noise?" Beth gasped, clutching her chest in mock offense. "Mom, that *noise* is the soundtrack of our generation."

"Well, your generation sounds like a car crash."

Beth ignored her and reached for the radio. A moment later, a heavy bass line filled the truck, vibrating the dashboard.

Marge winced. "Jesus Christ. Turn it down before my organs rupture."

Beth smirked, lowering it just a notch. Beth and Grace exchanged amused glances, but neither objected.

They drove like that for a while—Marge grumbling about the music, Beth flipping through stations, Ivy quietly absorbing the landscape as the truck powered forward.

Two hours later, Marge pulled into a gas station that looked like it had last been renovated during the Cold War.

"Alright," she said, throwing the truck into park. "Bathroom break. Stretch your legs. But remember rule number one—nobody wanders off."

Beth was already unbuckling. "Yeah, yeah, don't get kidnapped. Got it."

Marge watched as they piled out, stretching stiff limbs and blinking against the harsh sunlight. The station was one of those half-abandoned places with flickering fluorescent lights, a single gas pump, and a dusty vending machine that might have been older than Marge.

Inside, the air smelled like burnt coffee and something vaguely fried.

Beth beelined for the snack aisle, while Grace and Ivy hovered near the drinks, scanning the options like they were making a life-altering decision.

Marge grabbed a new coffee and stood by the counter, eyeing the lone cashier—a guy who looked like he'd given up on life about twenty years ago.

"Morning," she said, handing him a few crumpled bills.

He grunted in response, barely looking up.

Marge turned to check on the girls just in time to see Beth staring down a guy near the candy rack. He was older—maybe twenty-one—wearing a faded Metallica shirt and too much confidence.

Marge's stomach tightened.

Beth had that look—the one she got when she knew she was being watched and debated whether to ignore it or start a fight.

The guy smirked. "You from around here?"

Beth gave him a deadpan stare. "Do I look like I'm from around here?"

Marge was already moving.

Metallica Guy leaned in. "What's your name?"

Before Beth could answer, Marge stepped between them, coffee in hand, smile razor-sharp. "Her name is *none of your fucking business.*"

The guy blinked. "Uh—"

"And if you're about to say she looks *mature for her age,*" Marge added, voice pleasant but dangerous, "you might wanna start running now, before I remove your balls, the hard way."

The guy hesitated, then wisely decided to exit the conversation. He muttered something under his breath and wandered toward the door, shoving his hands in his pockets.

Marge turned to Beth. "You okay?"

Beth rolled her eyes. "I had it handled."

Marge sighed. "I know, kid. But just because you *can* handle something doesn't mean you *should* have to."

Beth didn't reply, but the tension in her shoulders eased just a bit.

By the time they left the gas station, the mood had shifted.

Beth was uncharacteristically quiet. Grace shoved her hands in her hoodie pockets, flicking her gaze between Beth and Ivy. Marge, meanwhile, wished she were watching a movie with a beer and zero responsibilities.

Ivy finally broke the silence. "**That guy was a creep**."

Beth snorted. "No kidding."

Marge kept her eyes on the road as they pulled back onto the highway. "Men like that don't expect girls to bite back. That's why they do it."

Looking out the window, Grace murmured, "That's why they think they can."

Marge glanced at her in the rearview mirror. Something about the way Grace said it—quiet, knowing—made her heart ache.

She took a slow breath. "Well. That's why I carry a tire iron."

Beth chuckled, Grace shook her head with a small smile, and Ivy just nodded in agreement.

The truck rolled on, the desert stretching endlessly around them.

Beth reached for the radio, turning it up—but not all the way. She didn't want to stress Marge out. At this point, she knew Marge was there to protect them, and she appreciated that.

And just like that, the tension eased.

But Marge kept one hand tight on the wheel, eyes scanning the road, already thinking about the next stop.

Because trouble had a way of finding them.

And Marge had a way of making sure it ***regretted*** it.

Marge took another sip of coffee and finally lit a cigarette. She'd held off because of the girls but couldn't wait another minute.

"You pick up a few things when you've been around. Now, let's get this shopping done before one of you starts whining about starving— like we don't have a pantry full of food at home."

Beth crossed her arms. "We have a *pantry* full of *canned horrors.* There's a difference."

Marge gave a one-shouldered shrug. "When the apocalypse comes, you'll be thanking me."

Beth made a dramatic shudder. "I'd rather be taken out in the first wave than live off expired mystery soup."

Grace, who had been quiet again, spoke up. "Are we going to the good store or the cheap store?"

"Wow, are you smoking the whole rest of the trip? Ivy asked.

Marge tried to smile. "Smoking, yes. Or maybe, I'm just dealing with some stress. We will see."

"As for stores—both. First stop is the cheap one, because I refuse to pay highway robbery prices for things like dish soap and toilet paper. Then we'll go somewhere nice, so you don't all act like I'm committing war crimes in the kitchen."

Grace raised an eyebrow. "You mean when you *do* commit war crimes in the kitchen?"

Marge let out a dramatic gasp. "Grace. Wounding. Right to the heart."

"I mean, I appreciate the effort," Grace smirking.

"Uh-huh. You just lost snack privileges," Marge deadpanned.

Beth turned to Grace and Ivy, serious. "You gotta learn. Marge plays nice, but food-related treason will get you put on rations."

Grace held up her hands. "No insults about the chef."

"Damn right," Marge muttered.

The truck bumped over a pothole, making Beth swear under her breath as her knee smacked the dash.

"Hmmmm.......Told you," Marge said without looking over.

Beth groaned but dropped her feet. "You scare me sometimes, you know that?"

"Good," Marge said.

Grace, still looking out the window, tilted her head. "You don't trust people much, do you?"

Marge was quiet for a beat before answering. "Not until they prove I should."

The girls seemed to think on that, letting it sit between them.

Beth was the first to break the silence. "Alright, enough life lessons. Let's get this shopping over with."

Marge snorted. "That's the spirit. Now, let's see if we can get through one trip without any of you getting into trouble."

Beth smirked. "Where's the fun in that?"

Marge just shook her head and pulled into the parking lot.

The store was exactly what Marge expected—too bright, vaguely depressing, and full of bargain-hunting grandmothers who could *and would* throw hands over the last discounted bag of rice.

Marge grabbed a cart and turned to the girls. "Alright, split up. Grace, you're on canned goods—nothing dented or bulging, for the love of God. Ivy, take this list. Beth, you're with me."

Beth sighed. "Why do I get stuck with you?"

Marge chuckled. "Because I'm fun."

"That's somewhat debatable at times."

"And because you know how to do math quickly, and I refuse to pay full price for anything."

Beth groaned. "I knew there was a catch. I'm being used."

Marge stopped. "And your point is… oh, never mind. Let's go."

Grace and Ivy wandered off in different directions, leaving Marge and Beth to tackle the essentials. It was mostly smooth sailing until Marge turned a corner and nearly ran into a man blocking the aisle.

He was tall, mid-forties, and had the distinct look of someone who thought he was charming. "Well, hello there," he said, flashing a too-white smile. "Didn't expect to see someone as lovely as you in a place like this."

Beth made a face. "Oh, no."

Marge barely blinked. "You hit your head this morning, or do you just have terrible taste?"

The man chuckled. "Feisty. I like that."

Beth took a step back. "I'm so uncomfortable."

Marge grabbed a family-sized can of beans off the shelf and held it up. "You know what's funny? This can is about the same weight as a human skull. Pretty sure I could knock someone into next week with it."

The man blinked. "Uh—you hitting on me? Get it, hitting."

Marge smiled. "Want to find out, slick?"

The man cleared his throat, let out a forced laugh, and backed away. "No, ma'am. Sorry—my humor's a bit dated."

Beth watched him go. "You are terrifying."

Marge dropped the can into the cart. "And effective."

"Remember, Beth—don't take any shit. You're a smart young lady, so act like it. That means making people earn your trust."

They walked side by side in silence, each processing the scene in their own way.

The good store was practically a palace compared to the first store. Grace immediately found the bakery section and started eyeing the fresh bread. Then, she inspected the produce as if searching for classified information.

Marge handed Beth a list. "Pick out whatever's freshest. I'll grab the meat."

Beth scanned the list. "You trust me not to screw this up?"

Marge clapped a hand on her shoulder. "Kiddo, if something ever happens to me, you're the one running the show. Might as well start training you now."

Beth blinked. "Wow. That's... a lot of pressure."

"You'll handle it. You're smart. And stubborn. Good survival traits."

Beth hesitated, then nodded. "Yeah. Okay."

She turned toward the produce section with a little more confidence.

By the time they loaded up the truck, the sun had begun its slow descent, painting the sky in soft amber and stretching shadows long across the ground. The girls were winding down after a long day, their energy fading with the light.

Ivy handed out drinks while Grace tore into a loaf of fresh bread, passing pieces around. The warm scent mixed with the cool evening air, a quiet comfort after the day's chaos.

Beth sat beside Marge, her gaze fixed on the road ahead. The hum of the tires filled the quiet space between them.

After a while, she spoke. "Hey, Marge?"

"Yeah?"

"Thanks for bringing us."

Marge smiled. "Thanks for not setting anything on fire, and being ready to bail me out of jail if things go sideways."

Beth grinned. "Ron's job."

Marge just shook her head. "Never a dull moment."

CHAPTER 23

The steady hum of computers filled the dimly lit office, their glow casting sharp reflections on stacks of classified files. Agent Solomon sat at his desk, flipping through a manila folder stamped **CLASSIFIED** in bold red ink.

The label read:

He scanned the documents with practiced efficiency—foster

placements, financial arrangements, heavily redacted authorizations—and everything was in order.

Too much in order.

A knock at the door.

Without looking up, Solomon said, "Enter."

The door swung open, and Agent Bodhi Estrada stepped in. Dressed in a hoodie, ripped jeans, and a carefully chosen Rolling Stones T-shirt that looked thrifted but wasn't, he carried himself with the effortless slouch of an indifferent teenager.

But Bodhi wasn't a teenager.

He was twenty-seven, though no one would guess it. His lean frame, sharp features, and unnervingly youthful face made him a once-in-a-generation asset. Psychological testing, physical training, language proficiency—Bodhi had scored higher than anyone in the division's history.

And now, he was about to become the Trentons' newest foster kid.

Solomon tapped the file in front of him, studying Bodhi the way one might study a high-stakes chess piece. "You're sure you can pull this off?"

Bodhi scoffed and dropped into the chair across from him, slouching just enough to sell the act. "Please. This is cake."

Solomon didn't blink. "You'll have no backup. You'll be living with them for months—maybe longer. If anything feels off, we pull you immediately. You know the protocol."

Bodhi stretched, cracking his knuckles lazily. "Yeah, yeah. Blend in, act like a normal foster kid, don't set off alarms." He smirked. "You act like this is my first rodeo."

Solomon exhaled slowly. "It's your first long-term rodeo. We've had you in and out of situations, but this? This is deep cover."

For a split second, something flickered behind Bodhi's eyes.

Then the grin was back. "Good thing I got the 'orphaned street kid' routine down, huh?"

Solomon exhaled sharply. "Fucking kid. That arrogance only works so many times, and only with certain people. My job is to keep you alive and get this mission done, so take it down a notch. Understood?"

Bodhi held up his hands in mock surrender, but the smirk never fully faded. **"Loud and clear, boss."**

A decade ago, he'd been the real deal—a kid who fell through the cracks. His birth name wasn't even Bodhi Estrada. Unbelievably, a caseworker had given it to him, too short on time and resources to dig up and validate his real identity.

For all he knew, his real name had been lost in a bureaucratic void, buried under misplaced files and system failures.

He'd been raised in foster care, bouncing from home to home, sixteen to be exact, always too smart for his own good, watching, always calculating. By fifteen, he had learned that trust was a currency you could trade but never afford to spend. By sixteen, he had figured out how to survive in places that would chew up most adults.

And by seventeen, he had disappeared—no one noticed, and the system didn't care.

The system lost track of him, and that's how he wanted it. He spent a year off the grid, working for people who didn't ask questions, cash only. That's when they found him—someone high up, someone with connections. They gave him a choice: vanish forever, or work for them.

Bodhi didn't hesitate—he searched exhaustively for anything to be connected to.

From there, he was rebuilt. The agency sharpened his skills, honed his instincts, and trained him into something more than just a survivor. He became an infiltrator, an asset who could slip into places no adult operative could. He had posed as a runaway, a street kid, a rich brat gone rogue—whatever the mission required.

But this?

This was different. This was the long game.

Solomon forcefully slid another file across the desk.

"Damn, Chief." Bodhi raised an eyebrow as he flipped through it. "You don't trust them?"

Solomon's jaw tensed. "I trust that they're useful. Whether they know it or not."

Bodhi leaned back, eyes narrowing. He could read between the lines.

The Trentons weren't just some random foster parents plucked from the system. Someone had placed them in this position for a reason. And if specific scenarios played out, if options ran thin—they could become expendable.

And now, the government was embedding an asset in their home.

"Why?" That was the part Bodhi still didn't know.

But that was what made it fun.

A few doors down, in a separate monitoring room, a low-level analyst watched a bank of monitors—some displaying surveillance feeds.

One screen showed Ron Trenton, pacing through the junkyard, already scheming and planning his next big venture.

Another showed Marge Trenton, cigarette smoke curling above her head as she stared at the adoption papers.

And the last? A digital profile of Bodhi Estrada.

The analyst hesitated, then picked up the phone. "Estrada is in. The Trentons don't suspect a thing. No signs of questions or resistance."

A pause. Then a voice on the other end, cold and precise. "Good. Let's see how long they last."

CHAPTER 24

The old junkyard had never been this quiet. It was eerie and wonderful all at once. Marge and Ron sat at the kitchen table, lost in thought.

Usually, mornings were a symphony of chaos—Joey's dramatic speeches, everyone else doing their regular routine. But today? The silence was unnatural.

Ron stood in the middle of the Yard, hands on his hips, scowling as the school bus rumbled away in a cloud of dust and black diesel smoke. "Damn school system, stealing my best workers. Most of the kids are smart enough—smarter than most adults!"

Marge walked past, coffee in one hand and a grocery list in the other. "You mean our *children*? The ones who legally have to get an education?"

Ron waved a dismissive hand. "Semantics. Good work ethic will serve them a lifetime, education evaporates over time. Look at me." He regretted that before he finished saying. He hoped to his core, Marge wasn't listening.

Marge stopped, snorted, then burst into hysterical laughter. "Oh, sweetheart, that might be one of the worst examples you've ever used to make a point—straight from that unique mind running the Scarecrow. And I say that with both love and respect."

She wiped a tear from her eye, still chuckling. "And don't act like you didn't pray for this day every summer—when we had a house full of cranky kids and a fridge that emptied itself overnight."

Ron grumbled but said nothing. He had, in fact, counted down the days every summer, waiting for school to start again so the kids would burn their energy elsewhere. But this year?

This year, he was losing his workforce.

Grace, Danny, and Lewis were his mechanics-in-training. Ivy was the best at keeping inventory. Beth was sharp with numbers, which meant fewer 'accidental' budget miscalculations on Ron's part. Ivy handled marketing and inventory; even Joey and Max were decent at sorting scrap.

Now? He was left with… himself.

A terrifying thought.

"I can't believe I'm saying this, but I *miss them* already."

Marge patted his arm. "That's sweet." Then she smirked. "You know, if you want, I could homeschool them. Keep 'em here year-round."

Ron's eyes widened in horror. "Okay, now *that's* child abuse."

Marge barked a laugh and walked back toward the office. Ron sighed and turned back to the garage, where a single figure stood, kicking at a rusted pipe with the toe of his boot.

Max.

His only remaining "employee."

The eight-year-old looked up at Ron, expectant. "What now, Boss?"

Ron sighed. "Now, Max, we pretend I know how to run this place without a crew."

For the kids, school was a mixed bag.

Beth tolerated it—barely. The structure, the rules, the authority figures telling her what to do? Not her thing. But she liked the library and had a reputation to uphold as the girl who always had a sarcastic remark ready.

Danny loved it *only* because the school had a shop class.

Lewis? He was indifferent—he could blend in anywhere, school included.

Ivy kept to herself, drifting in and out of conversations without ever getting too attached.

Grace, despite her quiet nature, loved school. She liked knowing what to expect. There were rules. Systems. No surprises.

And then there was Joey.

Joey hated school the way most people hated root canals. He despised sitting still, following directions, and—worst of all—reading out loud. The first day of school was *the worst day of his life* every single year.

This was why Marge wasn't surprised when her phone rang at 10:47 AM—less than two hours after she had put him on the bus.

She answered with a sigh. "What did he do?"

The school secretary chuckled on the other end. "Good morning, Mrs. Trenton. We have Joey here in the office."

"Already?"

"He…tried to organize a labor strike against his teacher. Really got the class all wound up!"

Marge ran her finger back and forth across the top of her forehead. "Of course he did."

"To be fair, his argument was well-structured. He claimed recess should be doubled and that 'the people'—meaning his classmates—should rise against 'the oppressive regime of education.' Oddly articulate and thought-provoking for someone barely seven years old."

Marge couldn't help it—she laughed. "Tell him I said he's grounded from pirate movies and we'll talk when he gets home. Thank you for calling."

Ron was elbow-deep in an engine that afternoon when a very expensive-looking car pulled into the yard. The hum of the engine alone told him it didn't belong. Most of the vehicles that rolled through the junkyard had either been on their last legs for years or were held together by prayer and duct tape. This one? It purred.

Marge was the first to step out of the office, wiping her hands on a rag as she squinted against the sun. She was only on her third cigarette of the day—her attempt to cut back for health reasons still holding, more or less.

When she recognized the driver, her lips curled into a knowing smirk.

"Guess who's back?" she called.

Ron pushed himself up from under the hood, wiping sweat off his forehead with the back of his hand as Lillian "Lily" Harlow stepped out of her car, adjusting her blazer like she was about to walk into a boardroom instead of a place that smelled like rust and motor oil.

"Wow," Ron said. "I think your outfit just raised our property value."

Lily gave him a tight-lipped smile. "And yet, I'm still here. Lucky you."

She pulled out a folder and handed it to him.

"I looked into your… situation."

Ron raised an eyebrow as he took the folder, flipping through the crisp, neatly stacked documents. "Which one? I've got at least five."

Lily didn't smile. "The business. Licenses, ownership, liabilities. You're in decent shape, but there are gaps."

Ron exchanged a glance with Marge, who was already standing beside him, arms crossed, her expression unreadable.

"What kind of gaps?" Ron asked.

Lily adjusted her sleeves, ever the professional. "The kind that make you vulnerable to certain… predatory business deals."

Marge's gaze sharpened. "You mean people like Donahue."

Lily hesitated just a beat too long. "I mean people who know how to manipulate loopholes. If they ever decided they wanted a piece of this place—or all of it-you wouldn't have much standing to fight back."

Ron clenched his jaw. "Fan-fucking-tastic, just fantastic."

He knew the junkyard was a mess. Hell, half the time, he barely kept it running. But the idea that someone could swoop in and take it out from under them? That sent a different kind of unease curling in his gut.

Lily leaned against the desk. "I can help. We can tighten things up, make sure the Yard is protected."

Ron studied her carefully. "And you're really doing this for free?"

Lily smirked. "You think I need the money?"

"No, but I'm waiting for the part where you tell me you own my soul now."

Lily rolled her eyes. "You're family, Ron. Distant, sure, but family. And I like what you and Marge are doing here with the kids. So consider this my way of keeping you in business."

Ron exhaled, rubbing a hand over his stubble. He didn't trust free things. But he trusted Lily more than he trusted some sleazy developer sniffing around for an easy payday.

"Alright," he said finally. "Let's do it."

Lily nodded, already pulling out more forms. "Smart choice."

Marge exclaimed, "**A rare moment! Mark the calendar!** Can I get a hallelujah?"

Ron glared in her direction, but she just sipped her coffee, looking way too pleased with herself.

"I like Lily, I really do." Marge said.

By the time the sun set, Ron was back outside, staring at the two new trailers parked near the back of the lot.

He had five grand in his pocket. He had a lawyer covering his ass. That should have felt like a win.

But it didn't.

The junkyard was quiet in the evening, the kind of stillness that made everything feel heavier—like it was slowly slipping away into the darkness. The distant hum of the highway was barely audible over the wind, which rattled loose sheets of metal, whispering through the scattered scrap.

Ron ran a hand down his face.

What the hell had he just signed up for?

He glanced over his shoulder toward the packed house. The kids were inside, eating dinner. Laughing. Safe. For now.

A colder wind blew through the Yard, rattling the trailers and tarps and creaking the doors on everything.

Whatever was inside…those tarps, it wasn't leaving anytime soon.

Later that night, after the dishes were done and the kids had drifted off to bed one by one, Marge stepped outside and found Ron near the trailers, a cigar glowing cherry red as he took slow, intense drags.

She leaned against the truck beside him, pulling her coat tighter against the chill.

"You gonna tell me what's eating you, or do I have to start guessing?" Marge said.

Ron exhaled, watching the smoke curl into the night air. "We've got two new trailers, a solid family lawyer we trust, and more money in one place than we've had in months. This should be a good thing."

Marge took a slow drag of her own cigarette. "And yet?"

"And yet." He gestured toward the trailers. "I can't shake the feeling that we just put a target on our backs."

Marge nodded. "You're worried about Donahue, aren't you?"

"I'm worried about *everything*. The more we build this place up, the more eyes are gonna be on it. Eyes that aren't just looking for a scrap yard. They're looking for a payday."

Marge sighed. "That's always been the game, Ron. We're just finally playing it with better cards."

Ron scoffed. "Yeah? And what happens when someone decides they don't like the way we're holding onto those cards?"

Marge didn't have an easy answer for that. Instead, she flicked ash onto the ground and said, "We deal with it when it comes."

Ron huffed a laugh. "Great strategy."

Marge smirked. "Ain't it just?"

Silence stretched between them, filled only by the distant sound of Max talking in his sleep and the wind shifting through the junk piles.

"You think we're making a mistake?" Marge said. She was quieter and a bit concerned this time.

Ron hesitated. His confidence was wobbly at the moment.

"No," he said eventually. "I think we're doing what we have to. I don't like how many ways it can go wrong, but I believe in us and the family."

Marge nodded. "Well. Welcome to parenting and life."

Ron snorted. "We're not exactly conventional parents, and well, life that is a whole other story there."

Marge smirked. "Maybe not. But look at them, Ron. They're here. They're safe. And fairly happy, plus they're *ours*."

"Ron Trenton, I know the plan was to adopt and foster a workforce," Marge said, shaking her head. "Feels weird to say it now that we're so far down the road, but the truth is—we care about these kids. And if they happen to earn their keep along the way, so be it. We still care."

Ron exhaled slowly, glancing back at the house.

Yeah. They were.

And that scared him more than anything. Because now, he had something to lose.

"Time to call it a day, hon. A night's sleep will surely help me," Ron said.

The night seemed to pass in a blur. Beth was already up inside, making coffee like she was forty instead of sixteen. Ivy sat at the table, absentmindedly picking at the crust of her toast, lost in thought.

Ron watched them for a moment before stepping in. "Alright, gang. New day, New rules. New things!"

Beth raised an eyebrow. "Oh? Are we finally banning Max from inventing new ways to set things on fire?"

"Not yet," Ron said. "But today's about getting the new trailers cleaned up. We've got space now. Might as well use it."

Ivy glanced up. "Use it for what?"

Ron hesitated. "Storage. Maybe an office."

Beth's eyes narrowed. "Or…?"

Ron sighed. "Or emergency housing, if we need it."

Beth exchanged a look with Ivy, then turned back to Ron. "For us, or someone else?"

Ron didn't answer—on purpose. He glanced at her, then turned and walked the other way.

Beth exhaled through her nose. "Right."

Ron ran a hand through his hair. "It's just a backup plan."

Beth didn't argue. But she didn't look convinced, either.

Marge strolled in, sipping her own coffee. "Alright, people. Let's move. We've got work to do."

Ron watched as they all got up, stretching, grumbling, heading outside to start the day.

He took one last sip of his coffee and followed.

Whatever was coming, they'd handle it. One way or another, they always did.

CHAPTER 25

Our junkyard always felt different at night. The daytime clatter—Joey's shouting, Max's endless exploring, Beth's sharp sarcasm, and the crew's constant banter—faded into a heavy stillness. Under the pale wash of moonlight, the rusted metal cast long, jagged shadows. The whole place seemed to hold its breath. The atmosphere wasn't exactly good or bad—just strange, like the air was charged with something unspoken, waiting.

Ron stood near the back lot, hands shoved deep in his pockets, staring at the damn trailer. *I like the money. Don't like that shady bastard, Donahue,* he thought, a dry laugh escaping him.

Hell, who was he kidding? His own liberal interpretation of right and wrong was practically as shady.

That trailer had been sitting there for weeks, taking up space and crawling under his skin like a chigger bite. He had followed Donahue's rules—kept his mouth shut, kept his hands off. But that didn't mean he hadn't thought about it.

What was inside?

Drugs? Weapons? Something worse?

Not my problem, Ron told himself. Over and over. But the question lingered, gnawing at the edges of his resolve.

And then, late that night, two blacked-out SUVs slid into the yard, engines low, headlights off. Ron had no idea that one conversation was about to change everything.

The vehicles didn't bother with headlights as they rumbled through the open gate. Their engines were deep and controlled—like wolves growling in the dark. Ron glanced toward the office, where Marge was still awake, the glow of her desk lamp visible through the window. He had told her something was happening.

But five grand was five grand. More importantly, Donahue had hinted this was a test, opening up the bigger dollar deals for business and family.

Ron figured passing it was the better option.

A tall, broad-shouldered man stepped out of the lead SUV. He wore a black jacket, black gloves, and a face that looked carved from stone. His presence alone thickened the air, making the space between them feel smaller.

Ron sighed. "You the welcoming committee?"

The man ignored the question. "We're here for the trailer."

"Yeah, no shit, *James Bond*," Ron shot back, crossing his arms.

The man gave Ron a *fuck off* glare, then jerked his chin toward the second SUV.

The back door creaked open.

Donahue stepped out, smoothing the front of a sleek suit that looked like it belonged in a boardroom, not a junkyard. It was too clean, too polished, and too wrong.

"Ron Trenton! **My favorite businessman.**"

Ron folded his arms. "Yeah, yeah. You got new toys for the kiddos for me or what?"

Donahue grinned. "Toys for kids? What are you talking about?"

"I tell myself they're toys for underprivileged kids. At-risk youth." Ron shrugged. "It's how I look in the mirror and sleep at night."

Donahue chuckled. "That's what I like about you, Ron. No small talk. Straight to what *Ron* thinks about things."

He turned to the men behind him. "Get it done, quickly."

The switch happened fast. The first crew moved in like professionals, unhooking the trailer from its spot and rolling it out. They didn't speak. Didn't hesitate. Every movement was old hat, quiet, and efficient.

Ron watched as they latched it to one of their SUVs and drove it right the hell out of his life until the next time.

In its place, two new trailers arrived—the same size, with the same battered exteriors and the same mysterious silence about what was inside.

Ron felt a headache coming on. "Oh, come on. Two? That wasn't the deal."

Donahue tsked. "Consider it an expansion of opportunity."

"Consider it a pain in my ass, explaining to my wife."

Donahue smirked. "You're still getting paid, Ron Trenton. A lot more."

Ron kept his mouth shut. The money was the only thing that mattered. He forced himself to focus on that—*just the money*. Not the risks. Not the questions about what the trailers might bring.

Donahue reached into his coat, slow and deliberate, and pulled out an envelope.

"**Your bonus. Five grand**." He handed it over, his grin sharp. "Congrats—you passed the test."

Ron took the envelope but didn't move. "That a good thing? It is right, it's just goddamn toy."

Donahue smiled, slow and knowing. "That depends on you, and delivering on our agreements." He got into the remaining SUV and left, taking his silent men with him back into the darkness of the night.

Ron stood there, alone. *Really* alone.

The Yard stretched out in front of him, silent and still, the weight of the night pressing down. Had he just made the biggest mistake of his life?

Maybe.

But the five grand in his pocket felt real enough. Solid. *(He smiled at that.)*

The next morning, Ron finds Marge in the kitchen, making coffee as if she were preparing for battle.

She didn't look up as he walked in. "How bad is it?" she asked.

Ron hesitated. "It's... completely manageable, babe."

Marge finally turned, arms crossed. "You ever gonna tell me what's in those damn things?"

Ron sighed. "You know the rules."

"Yeah. And I also know rules are usually made to keep someone in the dark."

Ron slid the envelope onto the counter. "Five grand says I made the right call."

Marge stared at it. Then at him. "Are we ever gonna stop digging this hole? Trenton, seriously, how dirty and blood-covered is that cash?"

Ron flashed a lopsided grin. "Hey, let me know if you find a ladder—or maybe an elevator—to pull me out of this hole. Five grand for doing literally nothing. Not bad, right?"

Marge let out a loud, pointed sigh. She grabbed her coffee and stomped off, muttering, *"Fuck off. Stupid men and their stupid choices."*

Ron watched her go, the grin fading.

Yep. He wasn't sleeping in their bed tonight.

It had been an unforgiving stretch of heat—dry, relentless, and harsher than usual, even for Albuquerque. The sun baked the earth from dawn to dusk, turning dirt into dust and metal surfaces into scorching hazards. The air felt brittle, as if it might crack with one wrong move, and the faint scent of asphalt and sunburnt weeds clung to everything. People were on edge, tempers shorter than usual. Conversations that might've passed as harmless banter sparked into arguments.

The swamp coolers worked overtime but barely made a dent, and at night, the heat lingered like a bad memory. No breeze. No relief. Just the heavy, oppressive reminder that the desert didn't care how much anyone had to get done—or how close things might be to boiling over.

That afternoon, Ron was elbow-deep in an engine, grease staining his arms and the smell of oil thick in the air, when a very expensive-looking car rolled into the yard. The sleek, polished exterior looked almost out of place among the rust and scrap. Ron leaned back, wiping sweat from his brow with the back of his hand, and smirked. *Funny how the expensive rides get just as dirty as the jalopies.* Didn't matter how shiny they started—out here, everything collected dust, rust, and regret eventually.

Marge was the one who stepped out of the office first. "Guess who's back?" she called, smirking.

Ron wiped his hands on a rag as "Lily" Harlow stepped out of her car and adjusted her blazer.

"Wow," Ron said. "I think your outfit just increased our property value."

Lily gave him a tight-lipped smile. "And yet, I'm still here. Lucky you."

She pulled out a folder and handed it to him. "I looked into your… situation."

Ron raised an eyebrow, glancing around the yard. "Which one? I've got at least five—no, damn… six." He let the words hang in the air, smirking at his own mess. It was hard to keep track when half the junk looked the same under layers of dust and rust.

Lily didn't smile. "The business. Licenses, ownership, liabilities. You're in decent shape, but there are gaps."

Ron flipped through the paperwork. "What kind of gaps?"

Lily adjusted her sleeves. "The kind that make you vulnerable to certain… predatory business deals."

Marge's gaze sharpened. "You mean people like Donahue."

Lily hesitated. "I mean people who know how to manipulate loopholes. If they ever decided they wanted a piece of this place—or all of it-you wouldn't have much standing to fight back."

Ron clenched his jaw. "Fantastic, just fucking wonderful."

Lily leaned against the desk. "Relax, I can help. We can tighten things up, make sure the Yard is protected."

Ron studied her. "And you're really doing this for free?"

Lily smirked. "You think I need the money? Look at me, man."

"No, but I'm waiting for the part where you tell me you own my soul now."

Lily rolled her eyes. "You're family, Ron. Distant, sure, but family. And I like what you and Marge are doing here. So consider this my way of keeping you in business."

Ron exhaled, the weight of the decision settling on his shoulders. "Alright. Let's do it. And, seriously—thanks."

Lily nodded, momentarily caught off guard by the rare glimpse of sincerity in his voice. For a beat, Ron wasn't cracking jokes or sidestepping the moment. He was *serious*.

Recovering quickly, she pulled out more forms with a faint smile. "Smart choice."

Marge snorted. "*Rare moment*. Mark the calendar—Trenton made a smart choice *and* said thank you. *Wow.*"

She shook her head, grabbing her coffee with a dramatic sip, eyes glinting with sarcasm. "What's next? Hell freezing over? You picking up after yourself?"

Ron shot her a look but couldn't help the grin tugging at the corner of his mouth.

By the time the sun set, Ron was back outside, staring at the two new trailers. He had five grand in his pocket and a lawyer covering his ass. That should have felt like a damn good day, some wins for a change.

But it didn't feel as good as he hoped.

He glanced over his shoulder. The kids were inside, eating dinner. Laughing. Safe. For now.

Ron rubbed a hand down his face and muttered, "What the hell did I just sign up for?"

A cold wind swept through the yard, sharp and sudden, cutting against the lingering heat like a warning. It rattled loose sheets of metal, sent dust swirling, and made the trailers creak—a long, hollow sound that set Ron's teeth on edge. The breeze came from nowhere anyone could figure out, unnatural against the remaining warm air.

Whatever was inside those trailers...**It wasn't leaving anytime soon**.

CHAPTER 26

Barely holding itself together, the junkyard took a deep breath. Between the kids being back in school, Ron trying to keep things running with Max as his only remaining "short-term employee," and the two new mystery trailers sitting in the back lot, things felt... unsettled. The late January wind whistled through the stacks of cars, carrying with it the promise of another New Mexico winter storm.

The past had a way of creeping back, but it wasn't creeping this time—it was snarling. It started with a phone call.

The kind that made your stomach drop before you even picked up. The kind that didn't just bring trouble—it *promised* it.

Marge had just finished making lunch when the office phone rang. She answered, half-expecting it to be Joey's school again. The ancient phone's cord tangled around her coffee mug as she reached for it.

"Trenton's Salvage," she said, tucking the receiver between her shoulder and ear while rescuing her coffee.

A clipped, professional voice responded. "Mrs. Trenton, this is Emily Calloway from Sunrise Group Homes. We have a situation."

Marge knew that name. The group home was one of the places that often placed kids with them. Troubled kids. Hard-to-place kids. Kids who reminded her too much of herself at that age.

Marge sighed, already bracing herself. "What kind of situation?"

"His name is **Ezra Bishop**. Seventeen. Extremely intelligent. IQ tested at 160. Full scholarship to MIT lined up, but..."

Marge's eyebrows rose. "But?"

A pause. Through the phone, Marge could hear papers shuffling.

"He's difficult. Stubborn. And not great with authority figures. Being honest? Life's been tough on him—he's just getting through it daily. Three placements in six months."

The words hung in the air, heavier than they should've been. The kind of description said *handle with care*—or *don't bother at all.*

Marge rubbed her temple. "What'd he do?"

"Nothing criminal, if that's what you're asking. He just... doesn't fit in. He's smart, but he's also condescending. Doesn't respond well to rules he doesn't respect. His last foster father found him rewiring the house's electrical system at 3 AM because he thought it was just 'dumb.'"

Marge smirked. "Sounds like half, no most of the kids in my house today."

"Yes, well, the others adjusted. Ezra doesn't seem interested in that. He's... different. Most homes can't handle his combination of genius and attitude."

Marge tapped her fingers against the desk, watching through the office window as Ron argued with Max about proper tool organization. A kid who didn't respect authority? Didn't fit the mold? Maybe he'd do better somewhere without a mold.

"Fine," she said. "We'll take him."

Emily exhaled, like she'd been expecting Marge to say no. "Thank you. I'll bring him by this afternoon."

Marge hung up, grabbed her coffee, and muttered, "Ron's gonna *love* this."

Her smile flickered—more nervous than usual. The kind of smile that knew trouble was coming, and this time, it had a name.

The black government-issue SUV pulled into the junkyard just after 3:00 PM, its pristine exterior looking comically out of place among the rusted treasures Ron called gold and inventory.

Ron, who had been perfectly happy ignoring the world while fixing a carburetor, looked up at the vehicle and groaned. "Tell me that's not what I think it is."

Marge smirked. "New kid."

Ron wiped his hands on a rag that might have been white sometime during the Carter administration.

"Oh, thank God. And *Christ*, Marge—" he glanced up with a smirk, "you collecting them now? Going for an even dozen, maybe?"

He tossed the rag aside, but the grin didn't quite reach his eyes.

The SUV door opened, and Ezra Bishop stepped out.

First impression? He didn't belong here.

Everything about him—his stance, the guarded look in his eyes, the way he kept his hands shoved deep in his pockets—screamed *out of place.* The junkyard, with its rusted edges and rough voices, wasn't built for someone like him.

It was going to be an uphill climb for him to feel like he fit in.

Tall and lanky, Ezra looked more like a college professor than a foster kid. He wore a charcoal button-down shirt under a navy sweater, dark jeans, and a look of perpetual disappointment. His black hair was neatly trimmed, and his sharp blue eyes flicked over the junkyard like he was mentally cataloging everything wrong with it. The wind ruffled his carefully styled hair, and he reached up to smooth it back into place.

Then, he spoke.

"This place is a disaster." His voice carried the weight of someone used to being the smartest person in any room. "I count at least seven OSHA violations from here, and that's not including the obvious fire hazards."

Ron snorted. "You're off to a great start, kid—but at least you can count."

He tried to keep the grin on his face, but his mind was already spinning. *The kid's got skills. We'll use 'em.*

Opportunities always came wrapped in trouble around here—and Ron was already thinking about how to unwrap this one.

Ezra turned to him, expression unreadable. "Are you the owner, or just a guy who looks like he's about to lose an OSHA lawsuit?" Beth, who had just come outside with her ever-present notebook, choked on laughter.

Ron rolled his eyes. "Oh, fantastic. He's a comedian, we don't have enough of those under 18 here."

Marge stepped forward. "Ezra, this is Ron. My husband. I'm Marge. We run this place."

Ezra adjusted his sleeves with deliberate care, expression flat and clearly unimpressed.

"Noted. Though I question using the word *'run'* in this context."

Ron opened his mouth, but Marge beat him to it—with a grin he knew too well.

She already liked Ezra. Partly because the kid had a sharp tongue. Mostly because he annoyed Ron. A definite bonus.

Beth was the first to step forward, her dark hair pulled back in a messy bun, and the ink stains on her fingers matched the ones on her notebook. "I'm Beth. I'm already exhausted by your entire vibe."

Ezra eyed her notebook. "**You write?**"

Beth arched an eyebrow. "Why? You gonna critique me already?"

"That depends. Are you terrible?" His tone was flat, but there was something almost playful in his eyes.

Beth grinned. "Oh, you're gonna fit in just fine. We need someone else around here who appreciates the art of being insufferable."

Danny and Lewis wandered out next, both looking mildly curious. Danny had grease up to his elbows, and Lewis carried what looked like half a transmission.

Ezra turned to Danny first. "Let me guess. You're the mechanic?"

Danny crossed his arms. "How'd you guess?"

Ezra gestured to his grease-stained jeans, face and who vibe completely unreadable.

"Educated deduction, kid. Your stance suggests formal training—probably vocational school. And your hands? They indicate a preference for German engineering over domestic."

Danny blinked, staring at him like he'd grown a second head.

"Okay, that's just *creepy*. And all wrong, *Professor Doolittle*."

Danny's smile faded as quickly as it came. His posture stiffened, voice sharp.

"*Drop the kid thing. Now.*" he snapped, agitation bubbling just beneath the surface.

The yard went quiet for a beat—Ezra watching, calculating, while Ron raised an eyebrow, sensing there was more to that outburst than just pride.

Ron snorted from across the yard. "Kid's got jokes *and* attitude. He might survive here after all."

Lewis, who had been watching quietly, finally spoke. "You don't like it here, do you?"

Ezra hesitated, his carefully constructed facade cracking slightly. "I don't see the appeal, no. This place is... chaotic. Disorganized. Inefficient."

Lewis studied him with those quiet eyes that always seemed to see too much.

"You'll get used to it. Chaos has its own way of creating some weird rhythm."

Silence followed.

Ezra looked doubtful, arms crossed and expression unreadable. Meanwhile, everyone else just *stared* at Lewis—brows raised, mouths slightly open.

Ron was the first to break the silence.

"Did—did Lewis just get *deep* on us?"

Marge sipped her coffee, eyeing Lewis like he'd grown a second head. "Huh. Guess miracles do happen."

Lewis just shrugged, already turning back to his work like he hadn't just dropped the most insightful line of the day.

Emily Calloway cleared her throat. "Mrs. Trenton, can we handle the paperwork?"

"Right," Marge said. "Ezra, Beth can show you where to put your things."

Ezra turned to retrieve a single, pristine suitcase from the SUV. Beth eyed it suspiciously.

"That's all you brought?"

"I travel light," Ezra said. "Most material possessions are unnecessary encumbrances."

Beth rolled her eyes. "Oh god, you talk like a thesaurus threw up, plus I don't think you have a lot anyway, none of us did when get got here."

Eza didn't respond to Beth's observation or acknowledge its accuracy.

Once the paperwork was signed and Emily had departed, Marge decided Ezra needed a proper introduction to the junkyard.

Which meant—manual labor.

No danger, nothing extreme, but the same onboarding every kid before him had gone through. *Earn your keep, get your hands dirty.* Then, Ron stepped forward, a grin tugging at the corner of his mouth as he handed Ezra a wrench.

"Welcome to your new home. Hope you like hard work."

Ezra took the wrench, eyeing it like it might bite him.

"Charming," he muttered. "Truly, a warm welcome."

Marge smirked from the doorway. "If you're lucky, you'll hate it a little less by tomorrow."

Ezra glanced around at the rusted metal, creaking trailers, and sun-bleached scraps.

"Doubtful," he said flatly.

Ron laughed. "Yeah? You'll fit right in."

Ezra stared at the wrench like it was a foreign object. "I've built computers from scratch. Rewired a college network. Solved a Rubik's cube in fourteen seconds. And you want me to... turn bolts?"

Ron smirked. "Yep. Unless you'd rather clean the bathroom."

"This is beneath me." Ezra's fingers closed around the wrench anyway.

Beth strode up with a grin and clapped Ezra on the shoulder, leaving a greasy smudge—*on purpose.*

"Oh, buddy. You have *no idea* what's beneath you yet."

Ezra glanced down at the stain, frowning, but Beth wasn't done.

"Wait till you meet the possums, rats, and *killer squirrels* under the office."

"Killer squirrels?" Ezra repeated, deadpan, raising an eyebrow.

"Yep." Beth flashed a wicked smile. "Mean little bastards. Sharp teeth. Attitude problem. One nearly took Joey's finger last summer."

Ron snorted from across the yard. "Should've let it. Might've knocked some sense into him."

Ezra looked between them, expression unreadable.

"…You're joking."

Beth winked. "Sure. Keep telling yourself that."

From the corner, Joey chimed in, holding up his hand with a dramatic flourish. "Still got the scar!"

Ezra sighed, glancing at the wrench in his hand.

"Great. Hard labor *and* wildlife hazards. The full package."

Beth grinned wider. "Welcome to the family."

Danny led Ezra to a partially dismantled Ford F-150. "Alright, professor. Let's see how that genius IQ handles a stuck timing belt."

"The timing belt is a simple mechanical component," Ezra said, rolling up his sleeves with precise movements. "The real challenge would be optimizing the entire engine's efficiency matrix."

Danny stared at him, slowly shaking his head. "Just... just turn the wrench, man."

By the end of the afternoon, Ezra's neatly pressed clothes had streaks of oil, his hands were covered in three layers of grime, and his back ached in ways he didn't think were possible. But he'd also successfully removed the timing belt, even if he'd complained about the "primitive tools" the entire time.

When dinner rolled around, the kitchen erupted into its usual chaos. Joey was arguing with Max while simultaneously arguing with Ivy about who got the last pizza roll, Beth was writing in her notebook while fending off Lewis's garlic bread, and Danny was trying to explain carburetor theory to Grace and an unimpressed cat.

Ezra sat at the kitchen table, arms crossed, watching as the familiar dance of family dinner played out before him.

Laughter echoed, forks scraped against plates, and teasing jabs bounced across the room like a well-rehearsed play. Ron's loud jokes,

Marge's dry comebacks, Beth's snark, Lewis's attempts to steal extra portions—chaotic but comfortable, and safe.

Ezra didn't join in. He sat still, his gaze sharp, tracking every interaction. Every casual touch—a playful shove, a ruffle of hair. Every inside joke that passed without explanation.

His own plate sat untouched. The look on his face wasn't sour— just discerning. Studying.

Like he was trying to decide if this was something he could ever belong to—or just another scene he'd watch from the sidelines.

"You should eat," Marge said, sliding into the chair next to him with a fresh cup of coffee. "Ron's spaghetti might look like a dumpster fire, but it's actually pretty good."

Ezra poked at the pasta with his fork. "The protein-to-carbohydrate ratio isn't good."

"Everything here is likely more than not, "isn't good"," Beth called from across the table. "That's like, our whole aesthetic and vibe, dude."

"Speaking of isn't good," Ron said, dropping into his chair. Tomorrow, you're helping Danny with the computer system. Things have been acting up since it was designed, which was the beginning of the Internet."

Ezra's eyes lit up for a fraction of a second before he controlled his expression. "Your whole system is practically a legitimate antique. I noticed it when we were working on the pickup."

"Yeah, well, not all of us can afford *MIT*-level equipment," Ron grumbled. "In fact, we've got *SHIT*-level systems at the Yard!"

The room erupted.

Laughter bounced off the walls—loud, genuine, and unexpected. Marge nearly spit out her coffee, Beth doubled over, and Joey practically fell out of his chair.

Even Ezra cracked a smile. A real one.

A quiet chuckle slipped out before he could stop it.

Ron noticed, flashing a grin. *"Ha!* Got a laugh outta the new guy. Mark the calendar!"

Ezra shook his head, still smirking. "Guess even *SHIT*-level jokes can land sometimes."

The family roared even louder.

For a moment, just a moment, Ezra didn't feel like he was on the outside looking in.

"MIT," Lewis perked up. "You're going to MIT?"

"I have a full scholarship," Ezra said, his voice carefully neutral.

"Assuming I maintain stable placement until graduation."

The table went quiet for a moment. They all knew what that meant and what it cost to say it out loud.

Lewis broke the silence. "Pass the garlic bread."

Just like that, the spell was broken. The chaos resumed, but something had shifted. Ezra picked up his fork and took a bite of spaghetti.

"This is..." Ezra paused, considering his words carefully. "Not terrible."

Marge smiled into her coffee cup, eyes glinting with amusement.

"High praise, young man," she said. Then, after a long, dramatic pause, she added with a smirk, "*Especially* for the *old man's* cooking."

The room *exploded* with laughter.

Ron threw up his hands in mock offense. "Oh, come on! I slave over a hot stove—"

"Hot microwave, you mean," Beth cut in, wiping tears of laughter from her eyes.

Ezra shook his head, watching the scene unfold. The corner of his mouth twitched ever so slightly.

"Don't let it go to your head," he said, his voice steady—but that faint smile didn't go unnoticed.

It was a good evening for everyone.

After dinner, Ezra stood on the back porch, arms folded, staring at the two mystery trailers silhouetted against the fading glow of the evening sky.

They sat there, still and quiet but somehow watchful—as if waiting for the right moment to matter. The wind had picked up, carrying the sharp scent of creosote and the faint promise of rain. Rare for this time of year, it hung there, teasing the idea that something was about to break.

Ezra's gaze lingered on the trailers, expression unreadable.

The Yard was noisy by day—clattering metal, sharp voices, and rusted engines coughing back to life—but now, with the sun dipping low and shadows stretching wide, everything felt different.

Those trailers didn't just look out of place.

They *felt* wrong.

His tone wasn't accusing, just observant. Calculating.

Marge glanced at the covered items—neatly stacked crates and a tarp stretched too perfectly over something large. They seemed out of place in a yard where everything else was scattered and loud.

She nodded, a faint smile tugging at her lips. "Good eye."

Ezra turned to her, waiting for more.

But Marge just took a sip of her coffee and stepped back.

"That's a mystery for another day."

Ezra watched her walk off, his gaze drifting back to the crates. *Waiting.*

Yeah, he'd be coming back to that.

Ezra turned to her. "I don't see how this is supposed to help me."

"It's not," Marge shrugged, leaning against the doorframe with her coffee in hand. "You're not a problem we're trying to fix, kiddo."

She glanced at Ezra, giving him a look that was softer than usual—steady, no-nonsense, but with something else underneath.

"You're just part of the mess now."

Ezra looked away, his jaw tightening, but he didn't interrupt.

"We're in this together," Marge continued, voice quieter this time. "*If* you let us. Think about that."

The wind picked up again for a moment, rattling something loose in the yard. Ezra didn't say anything right away. His gaze drifted back toward the trailers, but his posture had shifted—just a fraction.

Maybe he was thinking about it after all.

Ezra stared at her. "That's... comforting. In a weird way."

"You'll get used to it." Marge headed back inside. "Oh, and Ezra? Wake Danny up the next time you decide to rewire anything at 3 AM. He could use the education."

And, for the first time since he'd arrived, Ezra actually *smiled*.

It wasn't big or showy—just a small curve of his lips, quick and almost cautious, like he wasn't quite used to the feeling. But it was real.

He glanced at Marge, then back toward the yard, and gave a slow, deliberate nod.

"Yeah," he said quietly. "Okay."

Marge smiled into her coffee, hiding her relief behind a sip. *Progress.*

Inside, he could hear Ivy and Joey arguing over whose turn it was to do the dishes, their voices overlapping in a mix of whining and defiance. Danny cursed at the ancient popcorn maker, its sputtering hum punctuated by metallic clanks. And, somewhere in the background, Grace hummed an off-key but steady tune.

The sounds drifted out to him, wrapping around him like an ill-fitting hoodie—uncomfortable, but warm and familiar.

Ezra stood there for a moment longer, listening.

Maybe this place wasn't home. Not yet. But it didn't feel quite as foreign as it had before.

CHAPTER 27

Today, on a Saturday morning, the junkyard had a rhythm to it.

Mornings were always loud—kids arguing over breakfast, Ron cursing at a pile of engines that stubbornly refused to cooperate and make him rich, and Marge yelling at Joey, "Get down from there before you break something important—like your skull! I swear to God, Joey."

The usual symphony of chaos. Predictable. Noisy. And somehow, it worked.

By midday, things settled into a familiar pattern: work, schoolwork, tinkering, *avoiding* work, and Ron scheming to find loopholes in the definition of "legal business practices."

The Yard buzzed with its usual brand of barely contained chaos, full of clattering metal, shouted warnings, and loads of near misses.

Engines sputtered, tools clanged, and somewhere in the distance, Ron was swearing about "perfectly good parts" refusing to cooperate.

And in the middle of it all, Ivy and Max had found their places—sort of.

Ivy had been in the junkyard for four months. She wasn't the newest anymore—Ezra had taken that title—but she still wasn't fully one of them either. She moved like a shadow, slipping in and out of conversations without getting too close. She helped when asked, but never too much.

Marge always paid attention, and noticed things.

Ivy never asked for anything, never said she was hungry, never complained, never made a fuss. She stayed out of fights, didn't argue, and didn't get attached.

It was the kind of behavior Marge had seen before, anytime in her whole life.

Kids who had learned the hard way that asking for things meant disappointment. That speaking up meant trouble. That getting attached meant losing something.

Marge wasn't about to push. But she wasn't about to ignore it either.

That evening, after dinner, Marge found Ivy sitting on the roof of an old truck, staring at the stars.

Marge lit a cigarette and leaned against the hood. "You planning an escape, or just enjoying the view?"

Ivy smirked. "Wouldn't tell you if I was."

Marge took a slow drag. "Fair enough, kiddo."

The night was cool, and the smell of rust and oil mixed with the faint aroma of leftover stew. The junkyard was never completely quiet. The wind rattled loose metal sheets, something small scurried between the wrecks, and inside, Joey was humming to himself as he tried (and failed) to fall asleep.

Marge sat on the hood of an old truck, cigarette dangling between her fingers, watching the smoke curl into the air. Ivy was beside her, knees pulled to her chest, staring at the sky.

For a few moments, they sat in silence. Then Ivy spoke.

"You know I don't plan on staying until I'm 18, right?"

Marge didn't look surprised. "I figured that could be the case."

Ivy glanced at her. "That doesn't bother you?"

Marge shrugged, leaning back with her coffee in hand. "Not my job to make you stay. My job's to make sure you land somewhere safe— whether that's here or not."

She paused, giving Ivy a steady look. "You're a smart young lady. That gives me confidence you'll make good decisions."

Ivy didn't answer right away. Her gaze dropped to her lap, fingers picking at the frayed hem of her jeans.

The yard noises drifted in from outside—Ron shouting about a stripped bolt, Joey laughing too loud, still not going to sleep. But for a moment, everything between them was quiet.

Ivy kept picking at the threads, thinking.

"You ever stay somewhere longer than you meant to?" she asked.

Marge exhaled smoke, watching it. "Once."

Ivy didn't press, and Marge didn't explain.

For a long time, they just sat there, listening to the distant creaks and groans of the junkyard settling into the night.

Then, quietly, Ivy said, "I don't know how to do this."

Marge glanced at her. "Do what?"

Ivy hesitated, staring at the ground like the words might be hidden in the dirt. "Be part of something. Be part of the family."

Marge took another drag of her cigarette, considering that.

"You don't have to force it," she said eventually. "It either happens or it doesn't."

Ivy nodded, though she didn't look entirely convinced.

But after that night, she started lingering a little longer in conversations and sitting at the dinner table just a bit later than before.

Marge noticed. And she was quietly encouraged by it.

Ivy had never been much for routines. Routines meant predictability, and predictability meant expectations—things Ivy had learned not to trust. But somehow, without meaning to, she had fallen into one here.

Mornings were the loudest.

The clatter of breakfast dishes, kids arguing over who got the last slice of toast, Ron cursing at engines that refused to make him rich, and Marge's voice cutting through it all—*"Joey, get down from there before you break something important—like your skull!"*

It was chaotic. Messy. Loud. But it was *predictable.*

And for Ivy, that was starting to feel like something close to comfort.

Max had more energy than should have been humanly possible, running circles around the junkyard before breakfast. Beth tried (and failed) to keep him in check, and Joey usually wandered around in a sleepy daze until someone handed him food.

Ivy always woke early, but she didn't join the chaos. She lingered near the back of the lot, taking her time before stepping into the fray. She liked to pretend no one noticed.

Marge and Beth did.

She didn't say anything about it, but every now and then, when Ivy finally wandered into the kitchen, there was already a plate waiting for her.

One afternoon, Beth caught Ivy just as she was about to disappear behind a pile of old tires.

"Hey."

Ivy paused. "Hey."

Beth crossed her arms. "You avoiding me?"

Ivy arched an eyebrow. "Would it work if I were?"

Beth smirked. "Not a chance."

"Then, no. Not avoiding you." Ivy sighed.

Beth studied her for a second, then said, "Wanna help me with something?"

"…What kind of something?"

Ivy hesitated. The plan had been to slip away for a few hours—find some quiet, breathe without all the noise and movement of the Yard.

But something in Beth's expression made her pause. It wasn't pushy, just… expectant. Like she wasn't asking for help so much as offering something else.

And Ivy *had* been working on getting more involved. Very slowly—but a little more each week.

"Yeah," Ivy said after a beat, shoving her hands into her pockets. "Sure. What do you need?"

Beth smiled—small, but genuine. "Come on. You'll see."

Ivy followed, still unsure, but less hesitant than before.

That was how Ivy ended up in the makeshift garage, watching Beth dig through an old toolbox.

Beth pulled out a wrench and tossed it to her. Ivy caught it instinctively.

Beth raised an eyebrow. "You ever change an alternator?"

Ivy snorted. "I don't know what an alternator is."

"Well, you're about to learn."

Beth crouched by the open hood of a battered old pickup truck, wiping grease onto her jeans without a second thought. Ivy watched for a second, then slowly crouched beside her.

"Alright," Beth said. "First lesson: don't break anything important."

Ivy smirked. "Well to start, define important."

Beth laughed out loud. "Guess we'll find out."

They worked side by side for the next hour, Beth explaining things in a way that actually made sense. Ivy listened, asked a few questions, and—much to her own surprise—picked up more than she expected. The steady rhythm of work wasn't so bad, especially with Beth's easy commentary filling the gaps.

When they were finally done, Beth leaned back against the workbench, stretching with a satisfied sigh.

"*Not bad,* new kid. **Apprentice mechanic material, even.**"

Ivy grimaced, wiping a streak of grease from her cheek. "Please. I barely did anything besides get in your way."

Beth shot her a grin, tossing a wrench onto the bench with a loud *clank*.

"Yeah, but you *could've* broken something. And you didn't."

Ivy rolled her eyes but couldn't quite suppress the small smile tugging at the corner of her mouth.

"Guess that's progress not perfection then."

"Damn right it is," Beth said, bumping Ivy's shoulder lightly. "Stick with me, you might actually get good at this."

Ivy didn't pull away. For once, she didn't feel like she had to.

Ivy didn't know what to say after that, mainly because Beth didn't push.

She just handed her a bottle of water, then stood and dusted off her hands.

"C'mon," she said. "Let's get food before Max eats everything."

Ivy hesitated only a second before following.

That night, Ivy found herself back on the hood of the old truck, staring at the sky.

She had always liked the night. It was quiet. Predictable.

But tonight, she felt like it was a good day. She heard the office door open, the soft scrape of boots on dirt. A moment later, Marge climbed up beside her.

They sat in silence for a while.

Then Marge said, "You getting comfortable?"

Ivy tensed slightly. "So what does that…."

Marge stopped. "I didn't mean anything. Just noticing you might have had a good day."

Ivy picked at a loose thread on her sleeve. "Maybe I'm just waiting."

"For what?" "You think staying distant makes it easier?" Marge asked.

Ivy didn't answer right away.

Then, quietly, "It's always been easier."

Marge took a slow drag of her cigarette. "Maybe. But 'easier' and 'better' ain't the same thing."

Ivy frowned. "It's better than getting attached and losing it all, again, and again."

Marge was quiet for a long moment. Then she said, "Or maybe it's worse, not sure, kiddo."

Ivy didn't know how to respond to that. She stared at the sky, letting the words settle.

Then Marge almost casually said, "No one's asking you to stay forever."

Ivy swallowed. "I know."

"But," Marge continued, "no one's kicking you out, either."

Ivy didn't look at her, but her fingers curled slightly against the metal hood. She wanted to say something. But she didn't know *what*.

So she just nodded.

Marge seemed to understand. She flicked ash from her cigarette and stood. "Get some sleep."

Ivy stayed there a while longer, staring at the stars. She still wasn't sure if she belonged here but did have a good day.

But, for the first time in a long time…She didn't feel like running.

Max was eight years old and had more energy than the entire junkyard combined. He was not like Ivy.

Where Ivy stayed in the background, Max made himself impossible to ignore.

Ron had accidentally taken him under his wing.

Not because he planned to. But because Max followed him around constantly asking questions.

"What's this?" "Can I touch it?" "What happens if I do this?" (*Insert the sound of something breaking.*)

Max had no fear. No hesitation. No sense of self-preservation.

"Kid, do you even know what patience is?" Ron asked one afternoon as Max poked at an old alternator with a screwdriver.

Max grinned. "Yeah! It's when you wait for something but really, really don't want to!"

Ron sighed. "Yeah, that checks out."

Max carried around a crumpled list titled **"Favorite Things To Do!"** scrawled in uneven handwriting:

Taking things apart. (*Putting them back together? Not so much.*)

Following Ron around like a duckling. (*Whether Ron liked it or not.*)

Climbing stuff he absolutely should *not* be climbing. (*Roofs, stacks of tires, unstable shelves—you name it.*)

Fixing random junk and calling it an "invention." (*Most of it barely worked, but Max swore each creation was "genius-level."*)

The list said a lot about Max—he was curious, fearless, and reckless enough to keep everyone on their toes.

His latest invention was a **"super awesome trap"** made out of scrap metal, rope, and three questionable-looking springs.

Beth found it first by falling into it.

"MAX!" she shrieked as the rope wrapped around her ankle and yanked her half a foot off the ground.

Max ran over, thrilled. "It works!"

Beth tried to murder him. But since she was upside down and tangled, all she could do was threaten his entire existence.

"I'm going to feed you to wild dogs, you little goblin!"

Max grinned. "You have to catch me first!"

Marge, watching from the office, just shook her head.

Another normal day.

Later that night, Ron found Ivy standing near the office, arms crossed, staring at the junk piles like she saw something no one else could.

"You good?" he asked, leaning against a rusted-out fridge.

Ivy didn't answer right away.

Then she said, "I used to be good at disappearing."

Ron frowned. "What do you mean?"

Ivy exhaled through her nose. "Before here. I was in three different foster homes in two years. None of them kept me long. I was 'too quiet.' 'Didn't participate enough.' 'Didn't bond.'"

Ron didn't interrupt.

"The last place before here?" Ivy continued, voice steady but distant. "I figured out if I stayed quiet enough, they forgot I was there."

The words hung in the air, heavier than anything Ron had expected.

His stomach twisted—a hollow, sinking feeling. A kind of sadness crept up on him, sharper because even *he* couldn't brush it off with a joke.

For a moment, the usual sounds of the Yard—clanking metal, distant voices—felt too far away.

Ron cleared his throat, glancing at Ivy, who fixed her gaze on the ground.

"Well," he said, voice rougher than usual, "guess you're outta luck here. Ain't exactly a quiet bunch."

Ivy didn't smile, not quite. But something in her shoulders eased.

Ivy smiled without humor. "It worked. They left me alone. I was just… part of the furniture."

Ron scratched his jaw. "That's why you don't talk much here?"

Ivy shrugged. "Habit."

Ron nodded slowly. "You know, you don't have to be part of the furniture here. Right?"

Ivy smirked. "Yeah. I figured that out when Joey tried to paint my nails with motor oil."

Ron snorted. "That tracks."

A pause. Then Ivy said, quieter, "I still don't know if I belong here."

Ron considered that.

Then he said, "Look, kiddo. You don't have to figure that out today. Or tomorrow. But if you ever decide you want to belong somewhere… You could do worse than here."

Ivy didn't respond. But she didn't leave either.

And Ron figured that was enough for now.

That night, Ivy lay awake in the old camper she shared with Beth. She could hear the sounds of the junkyard—the wind shifting metal, Marge's distant laugh as she teased Ron about something, and Max whispering to himself as he tinkered with a flashlight under his blanket.

She turned onto her side, staring at the ceiling. She had left without a second thought in every other place she'd been. It had been easy. Here, though… it felt different.

She wasn't sure if that scared her or comforted her. In the other bed, Beth snored softly. Outside, a dog howled.

Ivy closed her eyes. And, just for tonight, she let herself feel like she belonged.

CHAPTER 28

There was the time Joey had accidentally set a tire on fire while Ron was giving a "safety demonstration." Or the time Ivy, newly trained rewired a generator, causing the office lights to flicker then go out like a haunted house. Or, Marge's personal favorite, the time Ron had tried to rent out the junkyard as an event space and nearly got sued by an amateur wrestling group and Girl Scout troop, all in the same weekend.

But today?

Today might take the crown.

Because Donna Lujan had just pulled up at the end of the day, 5:30 pm, looking like she meant business, as usual.

And Michael Donahue arrived five minutes later.

And both of them looked pissed.

Marge took several deep breaths. Then muttered under her breath, "I need a damn drink, vacation, with more drinks."

Donna Lujan stepped out of her car first. Clipboard in hand, eyes sharp, hair in a no-nonsense bun that could deflect bullets.

Marge liked her, mostly. Donna was one of the few bureaucrats who actually gave a damn. She worked for the city, helping place at-risk kids in stable environments, and she had a reputation for not taking bullshit from anyone.

The problem was, she also had a reputation for showing up unannounced.

And judging by the well-dressed man stepping out of the passenger side, today's visit wasn't just social.

Watching from the garage, Beth muttered, "I smell trouble."

Lewis, wiping grease off his hands, nodded. "Same."

Ezra, who had only been here a few weeks but had already figured out how to read a situation, added, "Statistically speaking, this will not end well for the Trentons."

Ron groaned. "What now, it's been a long day already.?"

Marge looked at him. "Go inside. If this is school-related, I don't need your brand of problem-solving making it worse."

Ron threw up his hands. "I am *very* professional."

"Ron, last week you tried to bribe Joey's teacher with a case of beer."

Ron grinned. "And did it work?"

Beth shrieked. "It *absolutely* did not."

Ron groaned again but made himself scarce, which was good, because then Donahue pulled in.

Marge's stress level doubled the second the sleek black SUV rolled to a stop because Donahue had a habit of showing up exactly when she didn't want him to.

The back door opened, and Donahue stepped out, dressed like he had just walked off a yacht where he had probably been committing tax fraud. His expensive suit, perfectly styled hair, and that shit-eating grin made her want to throw something.

"Marge Trenton!" Donahue spread his arms like they were old friends and were not currently engaged in a questionable business arrangement.

Marge deadpanned. "You're unannounced."

Donahue smirked. "I like to keep people on their toes."

Donna Lujan, who had been ignoring the exchange up until this point, finally turned. She gave Donahue a once-over and immediately looked like she wanted him removed from existence.

"Who the hell is this?" she asked.

Donahue chuckled. "Ah, introductions! Always important. Michael Donahue, businessman, investor, and all-around charming individual."

Donna didn't blink. "I asked *who* you are, not for your damn resume, slick."

Marge liked Donna a little more at that moment, and she didn't suppress her grin.

Donahue grinned wider. "Just here for a quick chat with Mr. Trenton. Business matters. No big deal."

Donna crossed her arms. "Well, I'm here on school matters, so whatever dealing you're working on can wait."

Marge said. "Can we *not* do this in my damn driveway?"

Marge turned to Donna first. If she had to prioritize disasters, school problems would usually come before criminal activity.

"Alright, let's hear it."

Donna handed over a folder. "We need to talk about Ivy."

That made Beth's head snap up.

Marge frowned. "What about her?"

Donna sighed. "She's missed too many days. Teachers say she barely participates. Doesn't engage. And frankly, the school is worried she's not adjusting well."

Beth rolled her eyes. "Oh, so now they care? Where was all this 'concern' when she was bouncing between foster homes for years?"

Donna held up a hand. "I'm not here to argue. But Ivy's close to aging out of the system. If she doesn't finish school, she's got fewer options. And the school wants to know if she even wants to be there."

Marge exhaled. She knew this was important, and Donna wanted the best for Ivy.

She already knew Ivy didn't like school.

Marge also knew Ivy was smart as hell but hated being around people who didn't take her seriously.

Marge glanced toward the office, where Ivy was sitting on the porch, pretending not to watch but clearly was listening. Her arms were crossed tight over her chest, her expression blank in that way Marge had come to recognize as her armor.

"I'll talk to her," Marge said.

Donna nodded. "Good. But sooner rather than later, as in today."

Unfortunately, that meant it was now Donahue's turn.

Marge turned to him with zero patience left. "Make it fast."

Donahue chuckled. "You wound me, Marge."

"Not yet, but I'm tempted. Ron is messing with a new project around the office."

Beth snickered.

Donahue sighed dramatically, like a man carrying the world's weight. "Alright, fine. Just wanted to remind Ron that the… storage deal is still ongoing."

Marge clenched her jaw. It was uncharacteristic of Donahue to bring all that up with someone obviously of official standing here taking some interest.

She hated that Donahue had trailers in their yard, filled with God-knows-what. She definitely didn't like Donahue, now she had real concerns Donna Lujan would take an interest in the arrangements.

She hated that Ron had agreed to it and, most of all, that they needed the money.

"We know," she said flatly.

Donahue smirked. "Good. Because things might be moving soon. And I wouldn't want you to be unprepared."

Beth frowned, arms crossed. "That sounds ominous."

Marge's expression tightened. She was *done* with him.

"If that's all—go through and finish the conversation with Ron."

Donahue held up a hand, that smug smile still plastered on his face. "One last thing—"

But Marge cut him off, her tone dropping to ice.

"As I *asked* before, go through and talk with Ron. I won't ask you again."

The sharpness in her voice made even Donahue pause.

"Okay, okay," he said, throwing his hands up in mock surrender. "My apologies. Wasn't understanding the process. Around back, right?"

He turned, voice rising just loud enough for everyone to hear.

"Ron, Ron! Where you at? Don't wanna get in trouble again!"

Ron appeared from around the corner, wiping his hands on a grease-stained rag, looking thoroughly unimpressed.

Donahue didn't waste time with small talk.

"Hey, there may be a… ***special delivery*** in the next few weeks. I'll keep you posted."

Ron's throat got instantly dry. He hated *everything* about that sentence—except for the promise of more money.

But before Ron could push for details, Donahue was already heading back to his sleek SUV, looking entirely too pleased with himself.

Typical.

Ron never got answers in meetings like this. Only more questions— and the uncomfortable feeling that sooner or later, that "special delivery" was going to bring more trouble than it was worth.

As soon as Donahue was gone, Donna turned back to Marge.

"You want to explain why that man looks like a walking money-laundering scheme?"

Marge took a long, slow sip of coffee. "No, I do not."

Donna narrowed her eyes. "Trenton. What the hell are you involved in?"

Marge sighed. "Nothing you need to worry about."

Donna didn't look convinced. But she also didn't press.

Instead, she just handed Marge a business card. "Call me if you need help. And I mean real help."

Marge took the card. "Noted, and no worries I won't need it, but thank you."

Then Donna got into her car with the unintroduced co-pilot, and drove off, leaving Marge standing in the yard, wondering if it was too early for whiskey.

Marge didn't go straight inside after that. Instead, she leaned against the truck, running a hand over her face, and could feel Ivy watching her.

After a moment, Marge pushed off the truck and walked over to the office porch. Ivy didn't move. Didn't say a word. She just kept staring at the spot where Donahue's SUV was, her expression unreadable.

Marge sat down next to her, lighting a cigarette. "You heard all that, huh?"

Ivy shrugged. "Not like you were being subtle, and we hear everythinggggggg."

Marge exhaled smoke, watching it drift into the cooling evening air. "You wanna tell me why you're skipping school?"

Ivy's jaw tightened. "I'm not skipping. I'm just… not going."

Marge huffed a dry laugh. "You know that's the same thing, right?"

Ivy picked at the frayed hem of her sleeve. "School's a waste of time."

Marge gave her a side-eye. "School's a pain in the ass. But it ain't a waste of time if you want to make short-term life easier on yourself, kiddo."

Ivy's shoulders tensed. "What's the point? I already know how to take care of myself. A stupid diploma isn't gonna change anything. I will get a GED, some job, then work until I die."

Marge studied her, arms crossed, a thoughtful look settling on her face.

She was impressed—*and* a little saddened—by the level of cynicism in someone so young. This wasn't just teenage rebellion, the usual eye-rolls and backtalk.

No, this was deeper than that.

It was the kind of wariness that came from learning too early that trust had a price. From figuring out that people didn't always stick around, and promises didn't always mean much.

Marge took a slow sip of her coffee, keeping her expression neutral. "Smart kid," she murmured to herself. "Seen too much, though."

And with that, she decided—*this one might take some work.*

She tapped ash from her cigarette. "You're smart as hell, kid. But smarts won't always be enough."

Ivy let out a humorless laugh. "Worked fine so far."

Marge leaned back. "Yeah? And how's that been working out for you?"

Ivy's eyes flashed. "I'm still here, aren't I?"

Marge nodded. "Yeah. You are, and I am happy about that. But let me tell you something, Ivy—there's a difference between surviving and actually having options. And options? They matter."

Ivy crossed her arms, her voice quieter now. "I don't see any good ones."

Marge sighed. "That's 'cause you've never been given any."

Ivy didn't reply.

Marge flicked the cigarette away, then rested her elbows on her knees.

"Look. You don't have to like school. Hell, I didn't. But you do need to finish. Not for them. For you. Because once you turn eighteen, the world doesn't suddenly get easier. And if you don't have something solid under you, it'll knock you on your ass faster than you can blink."

Ivy swallowed but didn't say anything.

Marge softened her tone, leaning against the counter, overseeing Ivy. She hoped some of this conversation was sinking in.

"I'm not saying you gotta be a damn honor student," she said, her voice steady but gentler. "But you *gotta* show up. That's the deal."

Ivy fixed her gaze on the floor, fingers twitching at the hem of her sleeve.

Marge continued, taking a step closer.

"You stay here, you're part of this family. And in this family, we don't throw away our chances."

The conversation fell quiet.

Ivy didn't respond right away, but Marge could see it—*something* happening, even if just a little. A hesitation. A pause. The kind that meant the words had landed beneath the guarded silence.

Marge gave a small nod, letting the moment breathe.

Ivy's breath changed as if she were considering arguing. But then, slowly, she nodded again.

Marge leaned back, satisfied. "Good. Now get inside before Beth starts acting like your parole officer." Ivy huffed a quiet laugh. "She already does."

Marge grinned, a knowing glint in her eye.

"Yeah, well. That's Beth—tough as they come. But she loves you too."

She took a sip of her coffee, watching Ivy for a reaction.

"Not that she'd ever *say* it out loud, of course. She's got a whole reputation to protect."

A flicker of something—maybe a smile—crossed Ivy's face before she looked away.

Marge caught it, however. It was *Progress*.

Ivy hesitated only a moment before getting up and heading inside.

Marge sat there a little longer, watching the sky darken. She had a bad feeling about Donahue and what was coming. But for now, she had a kid inside who was choosing to stay.

And for tonight, that was enough.

CHAPTER 29

Sarcasm, bad decisions, and sheer force of will were honestly the engine and gas that ran the Yard.

And today? It was running on a little bit of all three, with high octane!

The day started normally enough—which meant impending doom.

Beth was already in a mood because someone (Joey) had used her notebook as a launchpad for his latest "flight test experiment." Danny was grumbling about school, muttering under his breath about pointless assignments and teachers who "didn't get it."

Max was missing a shoe—again—hopping around the yard like it was part of some personal scavenger hunt. Ezra had locked himself in the office, slamming the door shut after announcing, *"You're all too loud for me to think about anything good."*

And Ivy? She had sequestered herself to a small corner at the far end of the Yard, a spot she'd quietly arranged for herself. A makeshift sanctuary away from the noise, the chaos, and the endless voices.

Everyone searched for their rhythm in the mess—*or at least tried to today.*

Ron, wisely, was nowhere to be found.

Marge, coffee in one hand and zero patience in the other, stood in the middle of the chaos and announced.

"We're cleaning the yard today."

A collective groan filled the air.

Beth looked personally offended. "We *live* in a junkyard. What's the point?"

Marge sipped her coffee. "The point is, I don't want to trip over a rusted-out fender and get tetanus or bit by a junk rat."

Danny frowned. "Wait, what the hell is a junk rat?"

Marge did not elaborate.

Beth was the one who tracked down Ivy and Grace, one sitting behind an old shipping container and the other reading a book in her room.

Beth frowned. "You know, for someone who's supposed to be all mysterious and brooding, you suck at hiding, Ivy."

Ivy did not look up. "I was hoping you'd send Max instead. He'd get distracted and forget why he was looking for me."

"Yeah, well, Marge sent *me,* and I have the memory of a grudge-holding elephant. Let's go." Ivy said.

Ivy sighed but closed her book. "Fine. But I refuse to do *grunt work.*"

Beth smirked. "Oh, trust me, we're *all* doing grunt labor. Consider it character-building, young lady."

Ivy muttered something that sounded suspiciously like 'you're a young lady dictator' but followed Beth back to the group.

Meanwhile, Ron had returned from wherever he had been hiding or doing in his opinion. And, in typical Ron fashion, he had a terrible idea.

"Why don't we just set some of this on fire?" he suggested, gesturing to a particularly useless scrap pile.

Marge stared at him. "Ron, what did we say about fire in the yard?"

Ron blinked. "Only if it's *contained?*"

Marge blinked. "No goddamnit, you *jackass,* we said *no fires in the yard. Solid parenting Ron.*"

Ezra, who had finally emerged from the office, muttered, "Honestly, I feel like that should have been common sense."

Ron pointed at him. "You're new. You don't get a vote."

Ezra smirked. "I have an IQ of 160. **I *always* get a vote.**"

Beth snorted. "Yeah, welcome to our lives."

Marge turned back to Ron. "No fires. Do your job, keep the kids safe, and clean up the yard today."

Ron grumbled but started picking up things and gestured to the kids to get started. But Max, being eight years old and extremely determined, had taken it upon himself to drag a large wrench that was almost as big as he was across the yard to show off for Ron, his mentor.

Danny found him struggling with it.

"Kid, what the hell are you doing?"

Max gritted his teeth. "Being STRONG."

Danny smiled. "It's literally bigger than you."

Max stopped, dramatically wiped his forehead, and pointed at Danny. "Then you do it, help me!"

Danny grabbed the wrench and lifted it with one hand. He wanted to show off to his slightly younger sibling; he was extra strong for his age.

Max stared. "Okay, but like… you're *cheating* because you're *tall*."

Danny smirked. "Yeah, stronger, smarter, and funnier, let's go with that."

Max was not pleased with the inference of his capabilities versus the older Danny, but easily got distracted by another tin pile across the yard.

Ezra, watching from a distance, shook his head. "You know, the kid's going to take this as a personal challenge and come back with a forklift."

"Oh, God. *Not again.* He is so determined, to a fault, to prove himself," Marge muttered, watching Max scramble around the yard in his latest half-baked attempt at "inventing" something.

The words slipped out before she could stop them.

She winced, realizing Ezra was standing nearby, arms crossed, watching everything with his sharp, unreadable expression.

Marge sighed, rubbing her temple.

"Didn't mean to say that out loud. Forget you heard it, Ezra. *Please.*"

Ezra didn't respond right away. He just raised an eyebrow, the faintest hint of a smirk tugging at the corner of his mouth.

"No promises," he said, turning back toward the office.

Marge shook her head with a groan. "Great. Just great."

The day dragged on, and Ivy found herself actually working. This was not what she wanted, but she privately didn't mind because she was part of the group; everyone was working.

But then something weird happened.

Grace, of all people, came over and handed her a water bottle.

Ivy frowned. "What's this for?"

Grace shrugged. "You look hot."

Ivy blinked. "Excuse me?"

Beth snickered from across the yard. "Oh my God, Ivy. Take the damn water and calm down."

Ivy, who was not used to casual kindness, slowly took the bottle.

Grace nodded once, then walked away.

Beth smirked. "Congratulations. You've been *adopted into the chain gang*."

Ivy squinted. "I don't know how to feel about that."

Beth patted her shoulder with a loud laugh. "You'll get used to it. Or die trying."

Ivy wasn't sure which one was more likely, but hopefully, getting used to it. The Yard was finally starting to look organized when Marge's phone rang.

She glanced at the caller ID. "***Fucking Donahue.*** *said Marge.*

She exhaled sharply, narrowing her eyes at the glowing screen like it had personally offended her.

"Of course," she muttered, setting her coffee down with a little more force than necessary.

For a moment, she considered letting it ring. But Donahue wasn't the type to *go away.*

With a resigned sigh, she picked up the phone.

"What?" Marge had no intention of hiding her disdain for him.

Donahue chuckled, smooth and oily. "Mrs. Trenton, darling. Always a pleasure."

"You have thirty seconds."

"Straight to business. I respect that. Just calling to say—expect a visitor tomorrow. Someone… important."

Marge's stomach twisted. Important. That word rarely meant anything good in her world.

"Important how?" she asked, already regretting the question.

Donahue chuckled again, making her want to throw her phone into the nearest scrap heap or throw up, whichever was first. "The kind of important that could change things. Keep your calendar open."

The call ended before she could tell him exactly where to shove his important visitor.

Marge put the phone down and took a very long sip of coffee. Then she took another. It still wasn't enough.

"Ron. ROn. RON!"

Ron, who had just finished stacking a pile of tires, looked up. He took one look at Marge's face and immediately braced himself. "Yeah, babe?"

Marge took another slow sip. Then, in the calmest voice she could muster, she said, "I hate your business associates. I need to chat with you right now."

Ron sighed. "Yeah. Me too, babe."

Sitting on the steps with a wrench in one hand and a suspicious-looking sandwich in the other, Beth groaned. "Oh great. More Donahue bullshit incoming."

Ezra, who had been around long enough to sense trouble but not long enough to know its full extent, muttered, "Should we be concerned?"

Marge exhaled, flicking ash from her cigarette. "Always be concerned, unfortunately."

"RON, talk now!" Marge yelled.

And with that, the day officially shifted—from *anticipatory* to *complicated.*

The complication that settled in Marge's gut and refused to leave.

By the time night fell, the Yard had quieted. The usual sounds—Ron's snoring from the couch, the creak of old pipes, the distant hum of traffic—did little to settle her nerves.

Marge didn't sleep well.

She lay awake, staring at the ceiling, replaying Donahue's call over and over. His smug tone, the vague hints, the promises of something *coming.*

Something she knew wouldn't be good.

The wind picked up outside, rattling loose siding on the trailers.

Complicated, she thought, turning onto her side.

And tomorrow wasn't likely to be any easier.

At three in the morning, she got up, wrapped herself in a jacket, and stepped outside. The junkyard was quiet, but not in a peaceful way. It was the kind of quiet that sat heavy, as if the whole world was holding its breath.

The wind rattled loose metal, making the shadows stretch and shift. A pair of vultures perched on the old water tower, watching like they knew something she didn't.

"Expect a visitor tomorrow........"Marge clenched her jaw.

Whatever was coming, she doubted it was just a social call, and fraught with extra risk for the Trentons.

By sunrise, the junkyard was moving, heaving, and *alive*.

The familiar clang of metal echoed through the yard, mixing with the hum of engines and the sharp chatter of voices.

Ron was already up, cradling a mug of coffee that smelled strong enough to corrode metal. He took a long sip, grimaced, and muttered, "Perfect."

Marge leaned against the truck, watching the road. She didn't know what she was looking for. But she'd know it when she saw it.

At 10:17 AM, she saw it.

A sleek black car rolled up the dirt road, kicking up dust as it pulled into the lot. It was too clean and polished, a sharp contrast to the junkyard's rust and grit.

Marge stiffened, and Ron stopped. "Well, that's where we go, and it's never a good thing."

The car came to a slow stop, the engine humming. A moment later, the driver's door opened, and out stepped a man.

He was tall, sharp-looking, dressed in a charcoal suit that probably cost more than the entire junkyard. His shoes were too clean for someone who had any business being here. His expression was unreadable, the kind of face that didn't give anything away unless it wanted to.

Marge had met many men like that in her life. She had never liked one of them, 100% the rule; she'd never been proven wrong.

The man adjusted his cuffs, glanced around the junkyard like he was taking inventory, then finally met Marge's eyes.

"Mrs. Trenton," he said quickly.

Marge looked. Didn't blink. "Who are you?"

The man smiled, but it wasn't friendly. "Mr. Donahue sends his regards."

Beth, standing nearby with her arms crossed, thought, "Oh, this guy sucks."

Ron stepped up beside Marge. "What do you want......and what should we call you, your name?"

The man sighed, almost bored. " There's no need to be hostile. I'm just here to discuss a mutually beneficial opportunity. Call me Mr. White."

Marge's patience was already wearing thin. "We're not interested in more than we've agreed to already."

The man's smile widened. "You don't even know what it is yet, Mrs. Trenton."

"I don't need to. Donahue's involved, it's a bad deal for us and a great deal for him and whoever he works with."

The man chuckled. "He said you'd say that."

"Smarter man than I thought," Marge said.

The man took a slow step closer. "Here's the thing, Mrs. Trenton. This little… operation you've got going here? It's useful. But it could be more useful to several important people."

Ron tensed. "Meaning what, no reason to talk in code here, Mr. White?"

The man's gaze flicked toward the trailers. The ones Donahue had placed on their lot. The ones they never opened.

Marge's stomach turned to stone.

The hair on her arms, the back of her neck—*everywhere*—stood at full attention.

That deep, gnawing feeling hit her hard.

Intuition.

Not a passing worry. It's not the usual stress of managing the yard and its chaos.

This was different, her whole body was on *full alert.*

She set her coffee down slowly, eyes narrowing as she scanned the yard. The familiar noise—Ron's grumbling, Ezra and Joey's arguing, Lewis and Max's reckless climbing—faded into the background.

Something was going to get more complicated for them, she could feel it coming.

And Marge knew better than to ignore *this* feeling.

"You've been very accommodating," the man continued. "But there's a… bigger picture here. Donahue wants to make sure you understand your limited but essential role in it."

Marge exhaled. "You're talking a lot without saying a damn thing, Mr. White."

The man's smile sharpened. "You'll see soon enough, and I get to the punchline for you. We're not asking; it was a courtesy call to update you, so there are no surprises. Am I being more clear now?"

Beth muttered, "I really want to punch this guy."

Marge put a hand on her shoulder. "Not yet, honey. Please go start a late breakfast for the family."

Beth didn't question the tone and direction Marge gave her. She knew something important was happening, so she gathered Max, Joey, and Grace on the way to the house.

The man straightened his cuffs again, as if bored with them. "Just be ready, Mrs. Trenton. Things are going to move fast. And you don't want to be caught off guard; that would be an unnecessary complication."

That was the end of the conversation. He turned on his heel, walked back to his car, and slid into the driver's seat with the same eerie calm he'd arrived with.

A moment later, the car was gone.

Silence.

Then Beth let out a low whistle. "Well, that was unsettling as hell. And I will have breakfast ready in 15 minutes, Mom."

Ron exhaled, rubbing a hand down his face. "Jesus."

Marge didn't move, she was thinking about the conversation, and if Ron was praying or swearing, "Jesus," he might need to go higher in the organization at this point for that miracle.

She was staring at the empty road, her mind racing. This wasn't just about Donahue anymore.

This was something bigger, and she didn't like it, not one damn bit.

That night, Marge called a meeting.

The younger kids were inside. This wasn't for them.

Around the table sat Ron, Beth, Ezra, and Ivy, who had taken a seat but was doing a very good job pretending she wasn't involved.

Marge exhaled. "We got a problem. This isn't likely a surprise to some or any of you."

"Yeah," Beth said. "That guy looked like he eats expensive food and has people killed for sport."

Ezra, always the practical one, asked, "Get dark fast enough, Beth, so what do they want?"

Marge tapped the table. "I think more control. Donahue's got plans for this place. And I don't think we're gonna like them or be part of the decisions, down the road."

Ron grunted. "We have to be careful, Marge. We need this place, and sorta need them for the moment."

Beth crossed her arms. "And if they try to push us out, Pop?"

Marge's expression darkened, and she stood up quickly..

"Then they're going to find out we push back in more than one way, but we need more resources than we have access to."

Silence.

Then Ivy, still leaning in the corner, murmured, "Guess I picked an interesting place to land."

Marge smirked. "Kiddo, you have no idea. But you'll be safe, I promise that."

CHAPTER 30

It was amazing how all after-school activities could get 'bad exciting' at the end of the day. For the Trenton junkyard, this meant a crisis.

Beth was the first one to hear the scream. But it wasn't the usual Joey-being-dramatic scream or the Max-just-did-something-stupid-again scream.

No, this one was different.

Sharp. Real. Loud. Painful.

By the time Beth reached the garage, she found Danny curled on the ground, gripping his hand, blood dripping between his fingers. So much so, it was pooling on the ground.

Ron and Ezra were already there, and Ezra—who had exactly zero medical experience—looked vaguely horrified.

Ron took one look at Danny's hand and swore. "Well, that ain't good."

Beth, unhelpfully, added, "Oh, shit. Oh my god."

Danny hissed through his teeth. "No kidding. Goddamn it hurts."

Marge shoved her way in, took one look, and sighed—sharp, tight, all business.

"ER. NOW."

No hesitation. No questions.

She grabbed the keys and was behind the wheel before anyone could process what was happening.

Marge *drove*.

Fast.

Basic F1 fast. Tires screeched as the truck tore down the dirt road, kicking up a cloud of dust in its wake.

The passengers—Beth clutching the door handle, Joey wide-eyed and speechless, and Ezra gripping the seat like his life depended on it—were all collectively *freaking out.*

"Marge, slow down!" Beth yelled.

But Marge didn't flinch, eyes locked on the road ahead.

Not this time. Danny needed looking after, and nothing—*nothing*—was going to slow her down.

Beth was in the back seat, while Danny sat in the passenger seat, his hand wrapped in a rag already soaking through.

"It's not that bad," Danny grumbled.

Marge didn't even look at him. "You need stitches or stables. And possibly a tetanus shot."

"Oh, come on—"

Marge gave him a look that immediately shut him up.

At the hospital, things got worse.

First, the receptionist acted like they were trying to scam the system. The standard line came, flat and rehearsed: *"We need to verify your Medicaid coverage before proceeding."*

No urgency. No glance at Danny, who was pale and clutching his side.

Marge thought bitterly, " Don't worry about the bleeding or pain. Let's make sure the paperwork's perfect first." She clenched her jaw, fists tightening at her sides.

Breathe.

"It's in the system," she said, voice low and firm. The kind of tone that didn't ask—it *told.*

The woman gave her a look. Bored. Dismissive.

"It's not showing up."

Danny groaned, slumping further into the chair. His voice came out strained but laced with sarcasm. *"I'm literally bleeding onto your desk, lady."*

Still, the receptionist didn't flinch.

"Paperwork first. *It's the policy.*"

Marge leaned in, planting both hands on the counter.

Her voice dropped even lower—*dangerously* calm.

"Well, here's *my* policy. You get someone out here *now,* or you'll be mopping more than just my kid's blood off this floor."

The receptionist's smile faltered for the first time.

Danny gave a weak grin. "Knew you'd get their attention."

Marge didn't take her eyes off the woman.

"Oh, they're listening now."

Marge took a deep breath. "Okay. Listen. Either you check again and hurry up doing it, or I start quoting every federal regulation about patient stabilization and EMTALA laws while my kid bleeds all over your office. While simultaneously calling our lawyer."

Beth, who had tagged along, whispered to Danny. "She's about five seconds from climbing over the desk."

Danny smirked. "I'd pay to see that actually." It was a nice moment to distract from the blood and pain.

Finally, after a lot of glaring, they got a room. Danny sat on the hospital bed, looking bored. "I'm fine, really, I am feeling better."

The ER doctor, a tired-looking man in his fifties, glanced at the chart. "You nearly took your damn finger off, young man."

Danny shrugged. "Yeah, but like… it's *attached. I'll be fine.*"

The doctor looked at Marge. "Does he always have this attitude?"

Marge sighed. "I stopped hoping for basic survival instincts years ago, Doctor."

Danny grinned. "Thanks, Mom."

The doctor cleaned the wound, and Danny hissed. "Ow. Watch it, Doc, that hurts."

"Maybe don't stick your hand in sharp machinery next time."

Beth snorted. "See? The doctor has the common sense that Danny lacked; he gets it."

Danny smirked, he appreciated Beth trying to take his mind off the wound care at hand.

But then the billing discussion happened. "You're listed under Medicaid, but there's an issue with your coverage."

Marge rubbed her forehead right above her nose, a habit she acquired years ago, right after meeting Ron. "Let me guess. System error. Name wrong. What?"

"Probably. But we still need confirmation before we proceed with stitches." Doctor shrugged.

Danny, bleeding, blinked. "You can't just—y'know—fix it first, what is the deal with this place?"

The doctor sighed. "Look, I don't make the rules—"

Beth glared. "You *literally* do."

The doctor gave her a tired look, and Marge, at maximum stress, was about to tear the whole place down when the ABQ PD walked in.

Officer Javier Reyes was one of the few cops in Albuquerque that Marge liked; he was always calm and seemed to care.

He took one look at Danny, bleeding on the bed, and sighed. "Jesus. You people can't go a month without an ER visit?"

Marge crossed her arms. "It's been two months, thank you very much."

Reyes smirked. "Progress, not perfect, as they say." Let's go for three months, next time around, okay?

The doctor, not sure what was happening, frowned. "This is a hospital, not a police matter, Officer."

Reyes smiled. His tone was firm but not forceful. "Yeah, but I know these folks. They run a good place, take in a lot of kids, and don't have time for your normal system 'errors.' So maybe… patch him up?"

"I can get my Captain on the phone, then eventually the Deputy Mayor or the Mayor herself, to speed things up. We don't really have to do that do we?" Reyes said.

The doctor hesitated. "That's not how—"

Reyes leaned in. "Or, we can call the hospital administrator first, and I can ask them why a nine-year-old with a known Medicaid record is bleeding out while you argue over paperwork."

The doctor sighed heavily. Danny grinned. "I like this guy."

Beth smirked. *"Me too."*

With a grin, she lifted her hand for a high-five with the officer. But the officer had already turned away, missing the gesture entirely.

Beth stood there for a beat, hand still raised, before laughing it off with an exaggerated stretch, hoping no one noticed.

Danny, still pale but grinning, caught it immediately.

"Nice, Sis."

Beth shot him a glare, but the smile tugging at the corner of her mouth gave her away.

"Shut up. You're lucky I don't let you bleed on purpose next time."

Danny chuckled, wincing slightly. "Yeah, yeah. Still left you hanging, though."

Beth shook her head. "Next time, I'm charging for the rescue."

Marge, finally able to relax, just nodded. "Reyes, you are my favorite person today."

"That's what I'm here for." Reyes said.

While Marge was handling medical bureaucracy, Ron was handling customers.

Badly, even with Max acting as his '#1 assistant' for the day.

They decided since Marge left to the ER to start selling:

Random car parts.

Scrap metal.

Caffeine gum.

"Wait, you're actually selling this?" Ezra asked, holding up a pack.

Ron shrugged. "Why not? Keeps you awake, keeps your teeth busy. It's perfect."

Ezra squinted at the ingredients. "This has the caffeine equivalent of three cups of coffee."

Max grinned. "Yeah! One piece and you're READY TO FIGHT GOD."

Ron patted his shoulder. "Careful there but, that's my boy. He looked at Ezra quizzically to acknowledge that Max was a bit intense."

Ezra actually laughed loud at Ron's look.

A customer, an older man with grease-stained hands, eyed the gum. "Does it work?"

Max nodded way too fast and laughed hysterically. "Oh yeah. I ate two pieces once and thought I could see the future."

Ron grinned. "You want a pack or what, Sir?"

The man thought for a second. "Eh, goddamnit, screw it. Gimme two."

She was exhausted when Marge and the kids finally returned from the hospital.

She opened the office door to find Ron counting cash, Max buzzing with energy, and Ezra reading the caffeine gum package like it personally offended him.

Marge blinked.

Then said, "I'm too tired to ask."

Beth immediately pointed at Max. "He sold *caffeine gum* to strangers."

Marge exhaled. "Of course he did."

Still loopy from the pain meds, Danny held up his bandaged hand. "Look, Mom. I survived."

Marge sighed. "Barely. Let's not do that again, please."

"But hey, at least we made some cash while you all where off having fun at the ER, socializing." Ron said.

Marge walked past him, grabbed a pack of caffeine gum, and shoved two pieces in her mouth. The sarcastic comment didn't amuse her, but she let it go.

Beth watched in horror. "Mom, NO."

Marge chewed aggressively. "I have had a *day*."

Ezra, still reading the label, muttered, "We are all going to die."

Marge just leaned back in her chair, waiting for the gum to hit. Nothing complicated, just a rush of caffeine-fueled energy as the sun finished setting on another eventful day.

CHAPTER 31

Yard business was picking up. Which, for the Trentons, meant two things:

1. Money was coming in.
2. That meant more problems to solve.

The junkyard had always been functional, but lately, it was starting to feel like an actual business. Customers were coming in more often. People were talking. And most importantly?

They were making real money, not associated with Donahue, and illegal whatever they were intertwined with the last few months.

Marge leaned against the office doorway, arms crossed, watching Ron count cash.

"**$20,000 in a month**," she mused. "Never thought I'd see the day."

Ron grinned. "And it's all mostly legal."

Beth, sitting nearby, snorted. "Define 'mostly.'"

Ron did not elaborate. He was a little lost in thought about how to pay the least amount of taxes possible. The cash always helped, and the government couldn't track some of that.

The money coming in was good—more than good. But with more money came more people sniffing around, and that was the last thing they wanted. Success attracts opportunists; they want some or all of what you have, easy as that.

ABQ was full of hustlers for different reasons, mostly Americans but some Mexicans, Colombians, and Eastern Europeans. No one really had good theories about the Eastern Europeans; they seemed to like dealing in electronics.

Marge had made one thing crystal clear—they weren't taking any damn money, more than minimal necessary from the government (local, state or feds for the kids.

Government money meant extra oversight and justification for every breath they took—not exactly, but a significant administrative burden because they wanted to track the money.

Oversight meant more rules, people, and interference in their business.

And that? Absolutely fucking not. Marge thought.

Beth sat at the old junkyard computer, glowering at the screen like it had personally insulted her. She hated working with it because it was so old, slow, and frustrating.

Ezra, standing behind her, sighed. "Beth. You're trying to run an actual business on what is essentially a dinosaur held together by malware and stubbornness."

Seriously, the viruses likely on this from the Chinese are better code than whatever is left from Bill Gates' original computer. Ezra continued to squint and shake his head.

Beth threw up her hands. "I know that, *genius!* But we don't exactly have a brand-new computer budget."

Ivy, leaning against the desk, spoke up. "Actually… we kinda do now."

Beth blinked. "Wait. We *do?*"

Ezra smirked. "Twenty grand a month, remember? I think we can afford a new system that wasn't built before the internet had color."

Beth quickly responded, "Okay, fine. But we're getting something efficient and cheap *that works*. I refuse to be one of those idiots who spend five grand on a computer just to check emails."

Ezra nodded, getting all serious. "Agreed. But if you let me handle the setup, I promise I can streamline everything—inventory, customer files, repair logs, everything. I'll build it custom. In a week, it will be better and 25% of the cost of anything you'll find at a store."

Beth arched an eyebrow. "You *promise, you guarantee?*"

Ezra proudly said, "Beth. I built my first network when I was ten."

Beth sighed. "Fine. But if you turn this place into a sci-fi dystopia, I blame you if Terminator-thingy rises from the rubble."

Ezra grinned. "I can't believe you know the word, "dystopia", and I can live with those terms."

Across the yard, Grace stood with Marge, looking out over the junkyard.

"It looks like a mess," Grace said, arms crossed.

Marge took a slow sip of coffee. "That's because it *is* a mess."

Grace nodded. "We need a fence."

Marge sighed. "Yeah, we do, Gracey!"

Ron walked over, frowning. "Why the hell do we need a fence?"

Grace gestured toward the yard. "Because right now, it looks like an episode of 'Hoarders. Maybe can at least aspire to look as professional as the final season of Sanford and Sons.' If we divide it up, organize it, maybe even hide some of the… questionable sections…"

Marge smirked but serious. "Like the shady *trailers*."

Grace nodded. "Exactly. We separate the junk from the parts we sell, making us look more legit."

Ron scratched his chin. "Alright. That's actually… not a bad idea."

"Wait. You're agreeing with us? Just like that? No random other idea, WTF is happening." Marge blinked

Ron shrugged. "What? You expect me to argue with such a logical idea?"

Beth, walking by, snorting. "Yes, Yes, Yes. That is *exactly* what we expect."

Ron ignored her. "Alright. Fine. I'll figure out the fencing situation. But I'm not spending a fortune on it, and we'll have to do the work."

Grace yelled triumphantly. "Good thing we own a junkyard, huh?"

Ron grinned. "I like the way you think, kiddo."

Of course, the biggest reason for the fencing project wasn't organization.

It was hiding the damn trailers.

The ones that were making them over twenty grand a month.

Marge still didn't know exactly what was in them. And she honestly didn't want to.

She had rules:

No one looked inside.

No one asked questions.

If Donahue showed up with bad news, Ron handled it.

Simple.

Now, they just needed to make sure no one else started asking questions either.

By late afternoon, things were moving:

Ezra, Beth, and Ivy had found a solid, affordable computer setup that wasn't older than Joey—kind of state-of-the-art, in fact.

Ron and Grace were planning out the fencing sections.

Marge, Max, and Joey were handling customers.

Today, the group included a guy looking for a '92 Chevy alternator, a teenager determined to fix up a dirt bike with more enthusiasm than skill, and a woman who was *specifically* there for the caffeine gum.

She seemed *way* too eager about it—kind of jonesing, actually. A bit concerning. But hey, *sales are sales.*

Ron blinked, watching her practically snatch the gum from the counter.

"Wait. We have *repeat customers* for the gum?"

Beth smirked from behind the register.

"Apparently. Guess we're diversifying."

Ron shook his head, still baffled.

"Hell, I thought that box was a mistake when it showed up." The woman popped a piece in her mouth immediately, sighing like it was a lifeline.

"Not a mistake," Beth muttered. "Looks like we're fueling more than engines around here."

Ron rubbed his chin, glancing at the woman, buzzing with renewed energy as she walked off.

"Well, I'll be damned. Might be our most newly reliable product."

"Sadly true," Beth said, ringing up the next customer.

Max grinned, practically bouncing on his heels. "Yeah! She bought a pack last week and said it helped her finish her dissertation in one night! Whatever a disser-nation is…"

Ron shouted. "Well, damn. We're officially a supplier of performance-enhancing substances. All legal people, I want to point that out."

Marge, walking past with a clipboard in one hand and a cigarette in the other, whacked him on the arm without looking up. "Don't say that out loud, dumbass statements like 'all legal' invite bad spirits, Christ babe."

Ron chuckled, rubbing his arm. "Fine. But it's selling, and I'll continue to sell it."

Marge sighed, flipping through the pages. "Everything's selling. Which means we actually have to keep things organized."

Ron groaned, stretching like a man already exhausted by the thought. "I knew there'd be a downside to our success."

Beth, leaning against a stack of crates, crossed her arms. "Yeah, no kidding. You know Max keeps rearranging the inventory? I caught him putting the LED headlamps in the same box as the spark plugs."

Max huffed. "They fit! And they're both shiny!"

Beth shot him a look. "Yeah, and they have nothing to do with each other, you little gremlin."

Max stuck his tongue out, then scampered away before Beth could retaliate.

Marge pinched the bridge of her nose. "We need to start running this place like an actual business. Which means we need systems. An inventory. Some goddamn structure."

Ron exhaled, rubbing his chin. "Fine. But you're in charge of all that."

Beth raised a hand. "I'll help. If it means Max stops hiding things in random places."

Marge smirked. "Good. You're officially head of operations."

Beth blinked. "Wait, was that a joke or did I just get promoted?"

Marge walked off without answering.

Beth groaned. "Fantastic, but what will you do on Monday when all of your labor goes back to school?"

Marge sat on the porch, sipping whiskey instead of coffee for once. The bottle sat beside her, a quiet acknowledgment that today had been long.

Ron sat beside her, staring out at the Yard. The dim light from the trailer windows cast long shadows across the dirt, the distant hum of the highway filling the quiet.

"This place is changing," he said, voice low and contemplative.

Marge tipping back her glass. "Yeah. And for once, not for the worse."

Ron exhaled. "Feels weird."

Marge smirked. "What? Running a real business instead of just winging it every day?"

Ron chuckled. "I do like winging it."

Marge took another sip, whiskey burning. "Yeah, well… maybe having a plan isn't so bad either."

They sat in silence for a bit.

Then Ron muttered, "You really think we can pull this off? No government money, no outside help, just… us?"

Marge looked at him. They'd pulled off worse, under worse circumstances.

She thought of every time they'd barely scraped by. Every scheme, hustle, and time Ron had convinced her to take a risk that somehow worked out in their favor.

"We've pulled off worse working situations, Trenton," she said.

Ron thought about that. Then grinned. "Yeah. Yeah, we have. Love ya, Babelicious."

Marge looked up with surprise. Ron hadn't called her that in years. She might have requested he wait a few more minutes before using again, but she just smiled. It was not a decision she'd make today as the darkness got more intense.

Then again, the sun came up right on time. Marge had just started her second cup of coffee when she heard the commotion outside.

Beth's voice was sharp. "What the hell, Max? That's not funny!"

Marge sighed, already bracing herself. She stepped outside just in time to see Beth and Max facing off near the garage. Ivy and Ezra were watching, both tense, like they weren't sure if they needed to step in or let it play out.

Max crossed his arms. "I wasn't *trying* to be funny!"

Beth looked furious. "You gave Joey a goddamn switchblade."

Marge's stomach dropped.

She stalked forward. "Excuse me?"

Max flinched but stood his ground. "It wasn't *real!* It's one of those fake ones with a retractable blade! I found it in the scrap pile, and Joey wanted it, so I gave it to him."

Beth threw her hands up. "That's still not the point, Max! You don't just hand knives—fake or not—to a six-year-old!"

Joey, standing off to the side, shuffled his feet, suddenly realizing he was very much a part of this. "I wasn't gonna hurt anybody."

Marge rubbed her temples, feeling a headache creep in. "Jesus Christ. Alright, enough."

Max bristled. "I didn't do anything wrong."

Marge snapped her gaze to him. "Oh, really? Because from where I'm standing, you're acting like a kid who *really* wants to test my patience."

Max glared at her, his usual mischievousness replaced with something harder.

"Why do you care?" he said. "You're not my real mother." The silence that followed was sharp. Beth inhaled sharply. Ezra shifted uncomfortably. Ivy didn't move at all.

Marge's jaw tightened.

"Say that again," she said, voice deceptively calm.

Max crossed his arms, doubling down. "You're not my mother."

Marge exhaled extra slowly then she crouched slightly, leveling her gaze with his.

"No," she said, voice even. "I'm not. But you know what? I'm the one who puts food on your plate. I'm the one who keeps this place running. And I'm the one who keeps your ass from getting into trouble **every single damn day.** So, no, Max, I'm not your mother. But you *sure as hell* don't forget I give a damn about you. That's who I am."

Max's lip trembled, and for a second, Marge thought he might push back harder.

Instead, his shoulders slumped, and his voice dropped to a whisper.

"…I didn't mean it like that."

Marge softened, just a little. "Then don't say it."

Max swallowed, then, so quietly it almost didn't happen, he mumbled, "Sorry, Mom."

Marge took a deep breath.

Beth's eyes went wide. Ivy's fingers curled slightly against her jeans, like she wasn't sure how to process what had just happened.

Marge exhaled, slow and steady.

Then she reached out, ruffling Max's hair roughly. "Yeah, yeah. Just don't do it again. It does hurt my feelings, as well as make me angry, because it's not a nice thing to say."

Max nodded quickly, still looking slightly stunned at himself.

Beth cleared her throat. "So… we're just gonna pretend that didn't happen?"

Ezra smirked. "I think we all just agreed to a silent contract."

Marge rolled her eyes. "Beth, take Joey inside. Ivy, Ezra—clean up whatever mess Max made before this argument started."

Beth, still grinning, saluted. "Aye aye, *Mom.*"

Marge pointed a finger at her. "Do not start with me, young lady."

Beth cackled all the way inside, all back to as normal as it gets.

As Ivy and Ezra got to work, Max lingered.

Marge sighed, crouching again so they were at eye level. "You okay?"

Max nodded, but he still looked unsettled.

"…I just got mad," he admitted.

Marge nodded. "I know. But you don't gotta pick a fight with me when you do."

Max hesitated, then—to Marge's **absolute shock**—he stepped forward and hugged her. "Sorry, Mom."

It was quick, barely a second, and by the time Marge registered it happening, Max had already pulled away and bolted inside like he was afraid she'd call him out on it.

Marge sat there for a second, then let out a breath she didn't realize she was holding.

Ron walked up, hands in his pockets.

"Did Max just—?"

"Shut up," Marge muttered, taking another long breath.

Ron sighed. "You're getting soft and motherly."

Marge scowled. "I will end you, Trenton, we both know this to be true."

Ron just grinned. And with that, the day moved on.

CHAPTER 32

The junkyard was changing. More business, more customers, more *responsibility.*

And Ron? He was desperately trying to keep up.

The thing about change was that it never asked permission. It just happened. One day, the yard was a barely functioning scrap heap, a place where Ron and Marge scraped by, keeping a roof over their heads.

Now?

They had employees, regular customers, and eight kids.

Eight.

Ron still wasn't sure how that had happened.

With the school year in full swing, some kids had started making friends, which was a little weird. The small band of misfit toys was close, even if they annoyed each other.

Beth, for example, had never been a 'friendship' kind of person. Too sharp, too guarded. But lately, she'd been spending more time with a girl from school named Riley.

Riley was a nice kid. Her Mexican-American family moved to Albuquerque before she was born. Her parents, who were not divorced, one set of grandparents, and an older brother annoyed her. She lived about 15 minutes away, so she was close and loved the Yard.

Ron had once overheard them sitting in the yard, talking about "found family narratives."

Whatever the hell that meant, but he smiled when he heard it, because they were both smiling during the conversation.

Surprisingly, Danny had also made a friend—a kid named Milo, who was just as into cars and mechanical stuff as he was. They spent hours arguing over engine specs and fuel efficiency in the garage, betting with each other on who could put or pull something apart quicker.

Max had befriended a kid from school named Leo, a fellow "menace to society," as Ron liked to call them. Then he laughed; he just adored Max, his little shadow.

The boys spent most of their time "inventing" things, which usually ended in almost disaster.

And then there was Ivy.

Ivy, who had spent months keeping her distance, had finally let someone in.

Her friend was named Enina, but she went by Nina. She was quiet and had a dangerous intelligence that perfectly matched Ivy's sarcastic pragmatism.

Marge had watched them once, sitting on the hood of an old car, not talking, just existing in the same space.

And for Ivy?

That was huge.

Life was moving along quickly, and business was booming with the Yard.

Once barely making it, the yard was now getting a steady stream of customers, even several repeaters who like to come by and chat and look around for what is new and exciting.

People came looking for:

Used auto parts.

Scrap metal.

Old tools and machinery.

The infamous caffeine gum. (*their second-best-selling item*)

Reclaimed doors and windows (a new edition)

Rehomed furniture

Marge had even caught a group of college students trying to turn the junkyard into a "vintage aesthetic" backdrop for some photography project.

(*They had paid $150 to take pictures. Marge didn't question it.*)

Ron stood near the back of the lot, arms crossed, staring at the two mystery trailers.

They sat there like ghosts, heavy with whatever secrets Donahue had packed inside.

Ron didn't ask questions. Didn't look inside. Didn't search for answers, because some things were better left unknown.

But that didn't stop him thinking that $20,000 a month was a lot of money.

Enough to keep the business running. Enough to give the kids a stable home.

But also?

Enough to get them in real trouble if things went south. Ron exhaled, rubbing a hand over his face for an extended period of time.

He had eight kids, assembled in a non-traditional way, business that was actually working, and criminal shit sitting in his backyard. "Fucking unsettling." Ron said.

It was a lot.

And the worst part? He wasn't sure what he'd do if Donahue ever changed the rules.

Marge had developed a routine. Saturday mornings, Lily Harlow showed up.

Dressed casually for once, hair pulled back, sleeves rolled up, and looked less like a high-powered lawyer and more like someone who belonged in the yard.

The family had really come to like Lily. And visiting the Yard was apparently her "exercise."

"I sit behind a desk all week," she had explained. "Figured manual labor is cheaper than a gym membership."

So now, every Saturday, she helped sort inventory, organize paperwork, and occasionally tell Ron he was being an idiot, and get his shit together.

Marge liked her a lot.

She was no-nonsense, sharp, and not afraid to get her hands dirty. Which made her a rare breed.

Today, she was sorting through old paperwork, making notes, and occasionally sighing dramatically, and shaking her head.

"Ron," Marge called, hands on her hips, staring at the absolute disaster that was their **so-called filing system.** "Please tell me this is a joke."

Ron, from across the room, glanced up with a smirk.

"What filing system?"

The room went quiet for what felt like minutes, but it wasn't.

Beth froze mid-page flip, giving Ron a flat look.

"The one you *claimed* existed," she shot back. "You know, the one where you said, *'Everything's where I left it—organized with meaningful intention.'"*

Ron leaned back in his chair, arms behind his head.

Without looking up from his notebook, Ezra muttered, "Explains so much about why he feels this is a well-oiled machine."

Joey snorted. "Guess that's why we still haven't found the keys for the Dodge." He had heard Ron say that phrase repeatedly, the keys having been missing for about four wemonths.

Ron waved a hand dismissively. "Nah, I know where they are."

Beth raised an eyebrow, arms crossed. *"Oh, really?"*

"Yeah," Ron said with a grin. "Somewhere in the pile labeled *'Important stuff not to misplace under the penalty of flogging.'"*

He laughed at his own joke, clearly amused.

Beth didn't crack a smile.

"Oh, perfect. That narrows it down to *three* piles instead of five."

Ezra, still scribbling in his notebook, didn't look up. "Optimistic to think there's any system at all."

Ron pointed at him, still grinning. "Hey, *organized chaos* is a system."

Beth snorted. "Right. And Max climbing the scrap heap is *'a structural test.'*"

A distant clang echoed from the yard as if on cue, followed by Marge yelling, *"MAX! GET DOWN FROM THERE!"*

Ron shrugged. "See? Everything's running exactly as planned."

The collective groan that followed was almost loud enough to shake the filing cabinets—assuming anything in them was actually *filed*.

Lily, who had been flipping through a pile of paperwork that barely counted as "organized," slowly lifted her head. "I hate you, really do; not just the process I hate, you're included in the hate(ish)."

Marge snorted, crossing her arms. "Get in line, sweetheart."

Lily shook her head, but there was a hint of a smirk. "How the hell do you people actually run a business?"

Ron shrugged. "With grit, determination, and absolutely zero reliance on proper bookkeeping."

Lily rested her nose in her hand, shaking her head with a groan.

"I'm an officer of the court. I *should not* be enabling this kind of behavior. I must be broken—something's definitely wrong with me. Bleeding heart or optimist, maybe."

Marge patted her on the back with a grin.

"Then stop coming by."

Lily sighed dramatically, glancing around the chaotic yard—Ron yelling about something missing, Lewis chasing Max off the scrap heap, and Beth and Ivy pretending not to care.

"And miss *all this?*" She waved her hand at the scene like a game show host presenting a grand prize. *"No chance."*

Marge smirked. "Thought so."

Lily shook her head again, but this time there was a smile tugging at the corner of her mouth.

"Absolutely broken."

Later, as they sorted through a massive pile of scrap metal—because Ron had taken in more junk than they had space for—Lily asked, "You ever think about expanding?"

Marge raised an eyebrow, tossing a rusted pipe into the *usable* pile. "We just started getting things organized. Let's not get crazy, and for the love of god, don't say that around Trenton. I just can't."

Lily shrugged, wiping sweat from her brow. "Just saying. You've got land and business, and you're already running this place like an empire. Might as well make it official."

Marge sighed, wiping grease on her jeans. "More official means more eyes on us. I like keeping things simple, and as quiet as we can, dear."

Lily smirked. "Marge, nothing about you and the Yard is simple." Marge couldn't argue with that.

They worked in silence for a few minutes, the sounds of metal clanging and distant shouting from the kids filling the air.

Then Lily, never one to let something go, said, "Have you ever thought about what's next?"

Marge shot her a look. "Next for what?"

"For you. For this place."

Marge exhaled. "Right now, my only goal is to keep this place running, keep the kids fed, and not get arrested. Anything beyond that is ambitious."

Lily tilted her head. "Well, I am here to get you out of jail. And what if you could have more?"

Marge scoffed. "I don't have time for 'more. I don't know, I don't think like that, right or wrong."

Lily leaned against a stack of old hubcaps. "You're already doing more, Marge. You took in eight kids. You built a business from a literal scrapyard. You run this place like a goddamn general. Whether you like it or not, you've expanded."

Marge didn't respond right away. Because the truth was, Lily wasn't wrong.

That was terrifying to think about, plus Lily didn't know 100% about everything happening with the business.

As the sun started to set, Ron sat on the office porch, a beer in one hand, watching the Yard. He started to think about clearing part of the side lot for soccer. He didn't know why no one played, but it might burn off some of Max's energy. He would think about it.

The end of the day had become routine—this moment of quiet before the inevitable nighttime. At this time, the kids were always scattered across the lot, finding ways to entertain themselves.

Beth and Riley were sitting on a stack of tires, laughing about something—probably at someone's expense.

Danny and Milo were arguing over engine parts, both of them

gesturing wildly as if the world's fate depended on whether or not a carburetor needed to be cleaned *before* reassembly.

Max and Zeke?

Building something that can potentially be highly dangerous, thinking about pestering Beth and Riley. But at the last minute, they reconsidered that idea as not good.

Ivy and Nina were leaning against an old truck, watching the chaos unfold at the end of the day with identical unimpressed expressions.

Grace and Lewis both hadn't connected with many friends. Grace buried herself in a book; she liked to read and have her time alone to do it. Lewis was starting to experience art and being creative.

Ezra was in the office working on a laptop that Lily had bought him to help with his studies and lab work for school.

And Ron?

He just took it all in.

Eight kids.

A booming business.

A lawyer helping out on weekends.

Two trailers full of **God-knows-what-illegal-shit.**

And for some insane reason…

It was working, for now.

Marge was cleaning up in the kitchen when she heard a small voice behind her.

"Hey… Mom?"

She froze with the dish in her hand nearly slipping.

She turned slowly.

Max stood there, arms crossed tight, like he dared her to call attention to it.

For example, he'd take it back if she reacted too much.

Marge swallowed. Carefully.

"You need something, kiddo?"

Max shrugged. "Just… wondering what's for dinner."

Marge exhaled through her nose, turning back to the sink. "Whatever I find first in the icebox. Might be real food. Might be a science experiment."

Max snorted. "Sounds right. Do you know why they call it an icebox?"

And just like that, he was gone. Marge didn't get a chance to share a long story about what she felt was an interesting story about her grandparents' icebox.

Marge braced her hands against the sink, staring down at the water.

Mom. He'd never called her that before with an apology after a fight about something. It made her unusually emotional.

And now that he had?

She wasn't sure if it scared her… or warmed something she didn't want to acknowledge.

Beth, lurking just outside the kitchen, smirked as Marge walked out.

Marge narrowed her eyes. "Don't say a word."

Beth grinned. "I didn't say anything."

"You were loudly thinking it."

Beth leaned against the wall, looking way too pleased with herself. "You're getting attached and all emotional, Mom."

Marge scoffed. "I've always been attached. That's not the problem."

Beth asked. "Then what is?"

Marge exhaled, rubbing her forehead. "The problem is… attachment means there's something to lose. That is the other part of caring that I work to not think much about."

Beth's smirk faded.

Because that, more than anything, was the truth of it.

Marge didn't do half-measures. Not with the kids. Not the Yard.

And sure as hell not with family.

But the more this Yard felt like home, the more she realized…she wasn't sure what to do if she ever lost it.

That night, as Marge sat outside with one cigarette after another, stress smoking, staring at the sky, Ron sat down beside her.

"You okay?" he asked.

Marge took a long drag before answering. "Max called me 'Mom' today."

Ron blinked. "Oh yeah?"

Marge shot him a look. "Do not start."

Ron chuckled. "Nah, it's cute. He's never called me that."

Marge groaned. "I will strangle you. Right fucking here and now, Ron Trenton."

Ron just grinned.

Marge exhaled, tapping her cigarette against the railing. "They're getting comfortable, like they believe they're safe, and that we do care."

Ron nodded. "That's a good thing, and I agree, babe."

Marge didn't respond right away.

Then, quietly—

"Yeah. I know."

He draped an arm over the back of the chair, watching the stars. "You ever think about what comes next?"

Marge huffed a small laugh. "Lily asked me the same damn thing."

Ron smirked. "And what'd you tell her?"

Marge flicked her cigarette into the dirt.

"I told her I'm just trying to keep this place running, keep the kids fed, and not get arrested."

Ron snorted. "Sounds about completely right and simple."

Marge looked up at the sky. She let herself consider the idea of something more for the first time in a long time.

Maybe—just maybe—this wasn't just a junkyard. Perhaps it was a future.

CHAPTER 33

The Yard Family had an unspoken rule: They were full.

Eight kids. That was it. No more. Hard limit.

…Or at least, that's what Marge told herself.

But life? Life didn't give a shit about limits.

The phone rang, a ripple in the otherwise quiet morning.

Marge was knee-deep in paperwork, trying to make sense of Ron's disaster filing system (*which mostly consisted of putting things in piles labeled "important" and "eh, probably fine"*).

She answered it without looking up. "If this is another sales pitch, I swear to God, I will find where you live."

A pause. Then a familiar voice. "Marge. It's Emily Calloway."

Marge sat up. Emily worked for Sunrise Group Homes, the same place that had called about Ezra and Ivy.

This was not going to be a good call.

"Christ. What now?"

Emily hesitated. "I've got a kid. He needs a place. Temporary, maybe longer. But… you're the only people I trust for this one."

Marge exhaled.

They were already at capacity. But something about Emily's voice made her pause.

"What's the deal, Emily?"

Emily sighed. "His name's Ryder. He's seventeen. And he's… different."

Marge leaned back. "Different how?"

"Smart as hell, but weird. Doesn't do well in normal homes. Doesn't talk much. A little creepy, honestly. He got passed around so much he just stopped trying to connect to people." Emily hesitated. "Last placement went bad. Real bad. He needs out."

Marge didn't ask for details. She already knew.

Foster homes weren't always safe places.

"He's weird, huh? Here mind was racing, money, meals, space, shit….."

"Extremely."

Marge smirked. "Fuck it. Bring him over."

Ryder showed up the next day. He did not look impressed.

Tall, lanky as hell, with shaggy black hair and dark eyes that didn't blink enough. He wore an oversized hoodie in the middle of summer and had a stare that could make grown men nervous.

Beth looked at him and muttered, "Oh, fantastic. We adopted a haunted Victorian child."

Danny, arms crossed, eyed Ryder. "Dude, you… *speak?*"

Ryder blinked slowly. Then said, "Yes."

Silence.

Beth gestured vaguely. "…And?"

Ryder shrugged. "I just don't see the point most of the time. People yell and scream back."

Beth turned to Marge. "Marge. Mom, I can't. He's like if Ezra and Ivy created a cyborg, but it was possessed."

Ezra, who had been watching with mild curiosity, smirked. "What? What does that even mean, weirdo?"

Standing next to him, Ivy muttered, "I don't."

Ron, observing from a safe distance, rubbed his face. "Marge. Marge, Marge, why? We already have *eight*. That is *so many kids*."

Marge sipped her coffee, gazing steadily at the yard.

"Yeah, well. Now we have *nine*."

Her tone was flat, but the weight behind the words wasn't lost on anyone.

Ryder hadn't exactly *integrated* into the household.

He was a *lurker*.

Didn't cause trouble. Didn't pick fights. Didn't steal.

He just *existed*—hovering in the background like a ghost no one had the energy to get rid of, talk with, or even acknowledge for long.

Quiet. Forgettable.

Disappearing.

Like Ivy described before—stay quiet enough, and they'll forget you're there.

And Ryder seemed to be perfecting the art.

But Max?

Naturally, Max wasn't fazed in the slightest.

He'd already started dragging Ryder into his world of "inventions," bad ideas, and questionable climbing decisions.

"C'mon, you gotta see this! It's gonna be *awesome*—or explode. Either way, you don't wanna miss it."

Ryder didn't say much. Barely nodded.

But he didn't walk away either.

And in this place, sometimes that was enough.

Ryder hardly reacted at all.

Until Max pulled out a completely jacked, half-broken Game Boy.

Ryder's eyes actually flickered with interest. "You planning to fix that?"

Max shrugged. "Nah. Too complicated."

Ryder took it from him. "I'll do it."

Max beamed. "Oh, hell yeah. Creepy kid knows shit."

"Creepy?" Max said.

It was only a matter of time before Ryder freaked someone out.

The lucky winner? Lewis.

It happened when Lewis got up in the middle of the night to get water.

I found Ryder standing completely still in the kitchen, staring at nothing.

Lewis froze. "Dude. The fuck?"

Ryder slowly turned his head. "Couldn't sleep."

Lewis stared at him. "So you're just standing here? Menacingly?"

Ryder nodded. "Yes."

Lewis walked away. "Nope. Not dealing with this."

Marge caught Ryder picking apart an old radio one evening. "You break it, you buy it," she warned. Ryder didn't look up. "I'm fixing it."

Marge folded her arms, watching. The kid's hands were quick, precise, and careful.

"Where'd you learn to do that?"

"Trial and error." Marge asked, "You self-taught?"

Ryder shrugged. "Didn't have anyone to teach me."

Marge hated how normal he sounded when he said it. Like it was just another fact of life, no one is here for me, oh well.

She didn't press. Just nodded.

"You do good work. You wanna help out in the shop?"

Ryder paused. "For money?"

Marge smirked. "For food, water, and a bed?"

Ryder considered. "I could eat." Marge laughed then patted his shoulder. "You'll fit in just fine."

That night, Ron found Marge sitting outside, watching the yard.

"Nine kids, Marge."

Marge sighed, rubbing her temples before taking a long sip of coffee. "Yeah, yeah. I know." Her voice was tired, but not regretful.

Ron sat down beside her on the porch, stretching out his legs with a grunt. He didn't say anything at first—just watched the yard, where the kids were finishing up their usual nighttime chaos.

Danny and Milo were still arguing; they seriously never stopped and seemed to love it.

Beth was rolling her eyes and watching them all.

Ron let out a slow breath. "Think we can handle it?" Marge swirled the last of her coffee in her cup. "Guess we'll find out."

Ron burst out with a reactive laugh, head shaking. "You're a goddamn lunatic, women."

Marge turned to him with a smirk. "Yeah? Well, you married me, so who's the real idiot here? Women, really?"

Ron gave her a look, then let out a defeated chuckle. "Shit. You got me there. I fugured it might get you into the mood."

They sat in comfortable silence for a moment. The kind of silence that only came after years of surviving together.

"I'm in a mood, just not the one you're hoping for there player." Marge said.

Ron tapped his fingers against his knee, then said, almost thoughtfully, "Nine kids, huh?"

Marge snorted. "Don't say it out loud. Makes it feel extra real."

"Marge. It is real."

"Yeah, well. Denial is cheaper than therapy and cigarettes when I stress smoke.." Marge said.

Ron laughed, low and tired, but genuine. He looked back at the yard, where their misfit family had somehow come together, against all odds.

And then, across the way, standing alone on the porch, was Ryder.

The newest, strangest addition to their ever-growing chaos.

He stood there, arms crossed, staring out at the night like he was trying to make sense of it. Like he was still deciding whether or not he belonged.

Marge followed Ron's gaze and sighed. "Think he'll settle in?"

Ron shrugged. "Eh. Max adopted him, so he doesn't really have a choice."

Marge smirked. "That kid could bond with a brick wall."

Ron chuckled. "Yeah. Lucky for Ryder, I guess."

Marge watched Ryder for a moment longer, then muttered, more to herself than anyone, "He'll figure it out. They all have so far."

And Ryder might have a home now for the first time in a long time.

The next morning, Beth gathered the kids in the garage.

"Alright, listen up, idiots," she announced. "It's time for the official Junkyard Code."

Max perked up. "We have a code?"

Beth smirked. "We do now. And rule number one—**don't be a dumbass.**"

Milo raised a hand. "Gonna need a little more on that one."

Beth rolled her eyes. "It means if you're about to do something stupid, stop and think for two seconds. We don't want to make Pop and Mom's life harder."

Max sighed dramatically. "That's a lot of thinking."

Beth ignored him. "Rule number two—**we watch out for each other.** That means if you see someone screwing up, you stop them before Marge murders them in cold blood."

Ezra nodded solemnly. "That seems fair enough, Beth."

She briefly stared at Ezra. Moving on. "Rule three," Beth continued, "if we ever get arrested, we all agree to pin it on Max."

Max gasped. "HEY."

Zeke nodded.

Max flailed. "I HAVEN'T EVEN DONE ANYTHING!"

Danny smirked. "Yet."

Beth grinned. "Exactly."

Max crossed his arms, pouting. "You guys suck."

Beth clapped her hands together. "Anyway—rule number four. **If you run, we'll find you.**"

The joking stopped.

That was serious.

Max swallowed. "You mean…?"

Beth's voice softened. "I mean none of us are alone anymore. So if you ever think about leaving… we'll come get you. No matter what."

There was a long pause.

Then, Ryder—quiet, careful Ryder—muttered, "That's a stupid rule."

Beth raised an eyebrow. "Yeah?"

Ryder's voice was flat. "Because if I leave, I don't want you to find me."

The room went silent.

Then Marge's voice cut through the air like a knife.

"Tough shit, kid. It's the rule." Everyone turned as Marge stood in the doorway, arms crossed, expression unreadable.

Ryder held her gaze. "And what if I don't follow the rules?"

Marge shrugged. "Then you're an idiot. But always remember you're now our idiot."

Ryder swallowed. His fingers curled slightly into the hem of his hoodie.

Beth grinned. "See? That's the spirit."

Max hesitated. Then, slowly, he stepped closer to Ryder.

"You don't have to like it," Max said. "But they, I mean we mean it."

Ryder didn't say anything. But he didn't leave, either.

And that? That was enough.

Marge sat outside later than usual, staring at the night sky with Ron next to her, sipping a good beer today, Mexican lager, ice cold.

"You doing good?" he asked.

Marge exhaled. "Yeah. Just thinking about Ryder."

Ron nodded. "Thinking about what?"

Marge smirked. "Will he stay, run off, or murder us all in our sleep?"

Ron chuckled. "Eh. Worth the risk."

They sat in silence.

Then, softly—

"You really think they believe in all that 'we'll find you' stuff?"

Marge turned to him, dead serious.

"I don't give a damn if they believe it."

Ron raised an eyebrow. "No?"

Marge looked back at the yard, where nine kids had somehow found each other.

"I just give a damn that we mean it."

And with that, the night settled in. And a family that refused to fall apart.

CHAPTER 34

Lily pulled up to Marge's place early, honking twice before Marge finally stepped outside, sunglasses on and looking only halfway awake.

"Damn, Lily, it's too early for this," Marge muttered as she climbed into the passenger seat.

Lily smirked. "It's never too early for menudo. You'll thank me once you have coffee."

Twenty minutes later, they were settled at their favorite hole-in-the-wall Mexican diner, steam rising from their bowls of menudo. Lily stirred her broth, the deep red liquid swirling as the scent of hominy and spice filled the air. "You know, my grandma used to say menudo could cure anything—hangovers, heartbreak, even bad luck."

Marge snorted, sipping her coffee. "If that were true, Ron would be the luckiest man alive."

Lily laughed. "You don't think there's something special about it?"

"Oh, it's special alright," Marge admitted. "Takes half a day to make, and God help you if you screw up the tripe. But if you get it right? Yeah, it's magic."

Lily smiled, dipping her tortilla into the spicy broth. "Guess that's why we keep coming back to it."

After they finished eating, Lily dropped Marge back home and followed her inside, lingering in the doorway.

Marge raised an eyebrow. "You coming in or just gonna hover?"

Lily hesitated, then stepped inside, closing the door behind her. "Actually… there's something I wanted to talk to you about."

"Wow, sounds a bit serious, Ron, what did you do?" Marge shouted.

"No, nothing this time, Marge. Ron started smiling again, instantly. It is about how you might adopt the kids. The process, at least start the conversation."

The Yard had officially hit maximum capacity.

Nine kids. Nine all who were not adopted, all had similar but unique biological and legal situations, not to mention all the off-the-record placement activity with the Trentons.

And Ron wasn't up for this conversation this morning. Needless to say, he wasn't handling it well at all, so he left the discussion just hanging there.

Ron stood in the middle of the yard, hands on his hips, removed from a very serious conversation that needed to be started at some point.

Beth, being sixteen, was drinking coffee at the speed of light these days. Ezra was reprogramming the new office system like a cyberpunk supervillain, and the rest were either arguing or nowhere to be found.

Max and Zeke were building a "robot"

(*Attaching scrap metal to an old vacuum cleaner and hoping for the best.*)

Grace and Ivy were sorting inventory. Then there was Ryder.

Ron squinted. Where the hell was Ryder?

"Beth!" Ron called. "Where's the creepy one?"

Beth didn't even look up from her coffee. "Be more specific."

Ron sighed. "The *new* creepy one."

Beth pointed vaguely toward the fence. "He's over there. Being more ominous than creepy."

Ron turned, and sure enough, Ryder was standing by the farthest fence, arms crossed, staring at absolutely nothing like a horror movie extra. Then he pulled a phone from his pocket and sent a text message.

Ryder didn't cause problems.

He didn't argue, fight, or break shit.

He just… existed. Even Ron agreed with that assumption, but the phone was new, and Ryder didn't tell anyone about that.

Quiet. Unblinking. Always observing.

And the worst part? No one else seemed to notice.

Danny shrugged it off. Beth acted like she didn't care. Max had already adopted Ryder as his new science experiment, and Grace, Ivy, and Lewis left him alone.

Joey and Marge both weren't fazed. It was just another kid in the Yard.

Ron was alone in thinking that Ryder was probably one bad day away from scaring the shit out of all of them.

That is why, today, he is going to try something new.

Ron walked up to Ryder, clearing his throat. "So. What are you doing?"

Ryder didn't look at him. "Thinking."

Ron blinked. "…About sending another text message?"

Ryder stopped mid-sentence. "Various things, and just a text message to my only friend.."

Ron sighed. "Kid, you could have told us you had a phone and how you paid the bill."

Ryder turned slowly to face him. "Why?"

Ron hesitated. "Because it's important to share some things, you *share nothing*."

Ryder nodded once. "Okay, I hear what you're saying." Then turned back to staring into the abyss.

Ron ran a hand down his face. "Christ."

If talking wouldn't work, maybe throwing Ryder into social situations would.

Ron found Max, who was working on yet another "invention."

"Hey, Max. Ryder's your new project now."

Max looked up, grinning. "Sweet! You wanna see what I'm building?"

Ryder tilted his head. "Why.................what is it?"

Danny walked in, and then Max proudly gestured to what appeared to be a bicycle attached to a car battery.

"It's going to be a self-powering bike! No pedaling needed!"

Ryder blinked. "That seems incredibly dangerous."

Max grinned wider. "I know."

Ron ignored it all. Ryder was talking to someone, anyone.

That night, the family sat around the dinner table, eating a probably not FDA-approved meal.

Beth, poking at her plate, muttered, "What *is* this?"

Marge sipped her whiskey. "It's food. Eat it."

Ezra sniffed it suspiciously. "Define 'food.'"

Marge was borderline irritated. "If you don't know, you don't need to know."

"If you don't like, get your ass into the kitchen and cook for everyone." Marge got up abruptly and walked out of the room.

Sitting at the table's end, Ryder watched the chaos quietly.

Ron, kids you need to figure out what we're eating then eat it or stop talking about it. Something is up with Marge. I'll leave her be for a few minutes.

Lewis, trying to make him participate, nodded at Ryder. "So, Ryder. What's your deal?"

Ryder blinked. "I don't have a deal."

Beth leaned in. "Everyone has a deal. What's your weird talent? A good place to start?"

"I retain information easily."

Danny raised an eyebrow. "Like… photographic memory?"

"Something like that."

Beth smirked. "Cool. What's my middle name?"

"You don't have one."

Beth froze. "Okay, that was impressive and creepy."

Marge walked back in, laughing into her drink, and shook her head. "God, I love this kid."

The group stared at her, she just walked about pissed off at the group about dinner. Then Marge, tapped her glass like a toast. Hey, quiet, I am sorry, didn't mean to snap at everyone, okay.

But I was serious, you all can start helping cook, then complain about your own cooking. Marge smiled for about two seconds.

Ron just groaned.

Later that night, as everyone drifted off, Marge found Ryder outside, sitting on an old car hood.

She leaned against the truck, sipping her coffee, eyes steady on Ryder.

"You good, kiddo?"

Ryder was quiet momentarily, gaze fixed on some distant point in the yard.

Then, without looking at her:

"Why do you say *'kiddo*? This place is strange."

Marge smirked, pushing off the truck with a shrug.

"Yeah, well. *Kiddo* is a habit—means I like you more than I don't." She paused, giving him a side glance. "And so are you. Strange, that is."

Ryder didn't argue. Didn't smile either.

But he didn't walk away.

Marge figured that was as good an answer as she was gonna get.

A long pause. Then: "I don't understand why you took me in."

Marge paused. "Because you needed a place."

"I don't fit here," said Ryder.

Marge snorted. "Ryder, *none* of us fit here. That's why it works."

Ryder looked down at his hands. "I don't know how to do this."

Marge sighed. "Do what?"

"Be… normal."

Marge smirked. "Good news, kid. *We're not normal either.*"

Ryder actually laughed.

It was quiet, short, but it was real.

And for the first time, Marge saw something shift in him.

Maybe, just maybe…

He was starting to believe he belonged here, too.

Ryder was a good agent, he thought as he wrapped up his notes for the day. Off to bed in the shared room with Max.

CHAPTER 35

Ron woke up to the sound of an engine but not a normal engine. Not one of the kids' half-dead project cars or some customer showing up at an ungodly hour.

No, this was something bigger.

A truck. And it was leaving.

By the time Ron got outside—barefoot, pissed off, and very much undercaffeinated—all he saw were taillights disappearing down the road.

And one of the mystery trailers?

Gone.

Marge appeared behind him, arms crossed, gripping a coffee mug like a weapon. She squinted at the road.

"So… I guess Donahue forgot to send a memo."

Ron ran a hand down his face. "Jesus H. Christ."

Beth, now standing in the doorway, yawned. "Is this a 'we need to worry about being murdered' situation or just a 'Ron's gonna have an aneurysm' situation?"

Ron didn't answer, with a displeased look on his face.

Beth nodded. "Cool. I'll go make breakfast for school."

Fifteen minutes later, Ron and Marge were sitting at the kitchen table, both trying to process the $10,000 worth of illegal storage revenue that had just vanished with zero warning.

Ron stared at his coffee. "We need cameras."

Marge raised an eyebrow. "Are you finally admitting I was right about that?"

Ron scowled. "No. I'm admitting that our business partner is a shady as fuck, suit-wearing bastard who just took our trailer off our property in the middle of the night without so much as a goddamn text message."

Marge smirked. "So… I was right."

Ron groaned. "Yes, dear, correct again."

Across the room, Beth yelled, "Kiss already and buy the cameras!"

Marge laughed out loud. Ron threw a sugar packet at Beth's head.

Ezra, who had been silently eating toast, finally spoke. "If we are getting a system, let me handle it. No store-bought shit. I'll custom-build it."

Ron looked at him. "You know how to do that?"

Ezra shrugged. "I learned how to bypass most security systems when I was fourteen. Pretty sure I can build one from scratch for a junkyard."

Marge raised an eyebrow. "Should I be concerned that we have a child criminal in the house?"

Beth threw her hands in the air. *"Oh my God,* now you're concerned?"

Ezra didn't flinch. He calmly sipped his coffee, matching Beth's energy with a perfectly indifferent expression—like he was *way* above this conversation.

Ron rubbed his temples, letting out a groan.

"Fine. Build the system. … don't hack anything that'll get the FBI, CIA, or—hell—*the Cartels* involved."

Ezra shrugged, setting his coffee down with deliberate slowness. "No promises…"

He let the pause linger just long enough for Ron's eye to twitch.

"…Just kidding."

Beth narrowed her eyes. "Are you, though?"

Ezra gave her a faint smirk. "Guess we'll find out."

Ron sighed, muttering under his breath, "I'm too old for this shit, this early."

Later that night, after Ezra had started planning his sorta-illegal-but-definitely-good security system, Ron sat on the couch with half the kids.

And somehow, the conversation had devolved.

Beth, lounging across an old recliner, stretched and smirked. "Alright. What's your favorite movie?"

Ron blinked. "What? You're being silly."

Beth rolled her eyes, "Silly."

"We're stuck with you people. We should probably know if you have good taste or not."

Danny, sitting cross-legged on the floor, nodded. "Yeah. This is important."

Max leaned forward from his spot on the couch like this was a military interrogation.

Ron sighed. "The Godfather."

Max gasped. "Boooooring."

Beth squinted. "You sure about that? Feels like a safe answer. Too predictable."

Marge walked in, sipping coffee. "He's lying. His favorite movie is *Con Air*."

Beth's jaw dropped. "No. Fucking. Way. Pop, you're a Cager?"

Ron pointed at Marge. "Shut up, already."

"Oh my god. The movie where Nic Cage has long hair and punches a dude in the throat?" Max said.

Marge smirked. "Yep. No Academy Awards for it either, what a travesty."

Beth cackled. "That's worse than I thought."

Ron threw a pillow at her. "You little shits don't deserve my cinematic genius."

Danny, barely laughing, asked, "Alright, what about food? You at least have good taste there?"

Ron hesitated.

Marge smirked. "It's gas station burritos."

Beth lost it. Max fell off the couch laughing. Danny wheezed. "Pop. No. Joey, I love buttritos!" They all just lost it at Ron's expense.

Ezra, who had walked in halfway through the conversation, shook his head. "That's… honestly kind of impressive. How are you not dead?"

Ron threw his hands up. "I hate you all, good night."

Marge sat on the arm of the couch, still grinning. "Yeah, yeah. But you hate to miss us, you looooovvvvveeeee us."

Ron grumbled. "Jury's out. Night."

Beth wiped tears from her eyes. "Holy shit. I was expecting steak or barbecue or something manly. Gas station burritos?"

Ron crossed his arms. "Alright, Miss Judgmental. What's *your* favorite food?"

Beth didn't hesitate. "Nachos. But like, the really shitty ones from movie theaters."

Marge pointed at her. "And you're judging him?"

Beth shrugged. "Hey. Fake cheese is delicious."

Max grinned. "See? Beth gets it." He gets up and gives her a rare hug.

Marge sighed. "We're raising a bunch of gremlins."

Ron stopped as he was leaving the room. "Yeah, little goddamn, gremlins and gargoyles." He laughed. And despite everything—the missing trailer, the illegal business deals, and the general chaos of their lives—

He couldn't help but feel a little lighter.

For all their experiences…At least they weren't alone.

Ron woke up early and didn't sleep as well as he hoped after an enjoyable night with the kids and Marge. He was prepared to track down Donahue for answers.

Instead, Donahue called.

Ron answered, exhausted, "Hello, what happened to one trailer?"

Donahue chuckled. "Oh, Ronnie. No need for hostility."

Ron pinched the bridge of his nose. "If you're calling to explain why you stole our goddamn trailer in the middle of the night, I suggest you start explaining."

Donahue sighed dramatically. "Borrowed, Ron. We *borrowed* it. And you'll be happy to know everything's been taken care of, so relax alright."

Ron gritted his teeth. "Define *'taken care of'.*"

"Handled," Donahue said. "Nothing for you to worry about."

Ron exchanged a look with Marge, who had just walked up.

Donahue went on speaker; Marge shook her head. "That means 'worry more'."

Ron sharply. "Donahue, if this comes back to bite us—"

"It won't," Donahue interrupted. "Trust me."

Ron absolutely did not trust him. But Donahue hung up before he could argue.

Marge finished her coffee. "So. That's… basically bad, right?" Ron groaned. "Yeah. feels bad."

Beth, walking past, smirked, she started to comment.

"Get out, not this morning." Ron glared.

Beth didn't question, she noted he wasn't kidding around.

Marge clapped Ron on the shoulder. "Welp. Guess we'll find out what kind of bad soon enough."

Ron dropped his head onto the table. "I need stronger coffee."

Ezra rolled into the room walking quickly. "Ron. I *reprogrammed* the junkyard inventory system in three hours. Do you really think I *don't* know how to set up cameras?"

Ron sighed. "I never said you couldn't do it, but keep this simple, you struggle with that concept occasionally, and no AI nonsense. Last thing I need is a robot turning states evidence, and testifying against us"

Ezra smirked. "Okay, I can promise that."

As if things weren't already chaotic enough, Marge got a call later that day. By the time she hung up, she was smiling.

Ron, who had seen that expression before, immediately felt suspicious.

"What?"

Marge sipped her coffee. "We just got three new contracts."

Ron blinked. "From who?"

"Two from the city, good ole' ABQ, and one from the county."

Ron stared at her. "We're doing official *government work* now?"

Marge shrugged. "They need vehicle disposal and salvage work. We have a junkyard. Seems like a *you scratch our back, we make an obscene amount of money* situation."

Ron leaned back in his chair. "So… let me get this straight. We're running a *legal* business, making *illegal* money, and now the *government* is literally handing us contracts?"

Marge smirked. "Yep."

Ron groaned. "I need a drink but won't because we have work to do."

Beth walked by again. "Can I speak this time?" Ron ignored her.

Ron threw another sugar packet at her. He was getting better with his aim, he'd get here someday.

He'd forgot about the trailer being taken in the middle of the night. Now, Ron was back on edge, new contracts and all.

He kept checking the yard, pacing the office, and glaring at the empty space where the trailer used to be. He almost anticipated the police or someone to bust down the gate to get him and Marge.

At some point, he noticed something. Ryder was standing outside the fence.

Just standing there. Motionless. Staring into the distance like a damn robot.

"Kid. What the hell are you doing?" Ron frowned.

Ryder didn't look away. "Watching." Ron exhaled sharply. "For what?"

Ryder's head tilted slightly. "In case they come back."

Ron blinked. "Who? Donahue's guys?"

Ryder nodded.

Ron sighed. "Jesus, kid. You can't just stand out here like a haunted scarecrow."

Ryder finally turned, expression unreadable. "I don't sleep much."

Ron ran a hand down his face. "Yeah, well. You standing out here all night is gonna make *me* lose sleep, so get your ass inside, okay."

Ryder stared for another second. Then nodded. "Okay."

And just… walked away.

Ron stared after him.

Then muttered, "What the fuck is wrong with that kid?"

From behind him, Beth called out, "You're his Pop, genius, have to figure it out!"

Ron groaned.

The next day, Marge called for a "family meeting."

This meant everyone got dragged into the kitchen against their will.

Marge stood at the head of the table. "Alright, listen up, degenerates, and I mean that in a good way. We've got some changes happening."

Beth smirked. "We're getting a pay raise?"

Marge snorted. "We *aren't* getting arrested and you get food. That's your pay raise."

Joey, who was sitting on top of the fridge for no reason, raised a hand. "Can I get a sword? And it's almost time for the school bus."

Marge didn't even blink. "No. And I know."

Ron pointed at him. "Get down from there before you break your damn neck."

Joey sighed dramatically and flopped onto a chair.

Marge continued. "Number one: We're upgrading security. Ezra's handling it. No, it will not be hacked by Russians. No, you will not be allowed to tamper with it for 'science.'"

Max and Zeke both groaned. That's when everyone noticed that Zeke stayed the night. But Marge kept going in the meeting.

"Number two: We're getting more business. More business means more customers. More customers means y'all need to act *semi-professional* when they're here."

Beth snorted. "Define 'semi' and you're definitely talking about pay raise type of requirements for our working situation.'"

Marge blatantly ignored her. "Number three: We have *no idea* when Donahue's gonna pull another stunt, so stay out of his business."

Everyone nodded, except Ryder.

Ryder just tilted his head. "You don't trust him."

Marge laughed dryly. "Ryder, I don't even trust the *toaster.*"

Ryder accepted this answer.

That night, Ron sat outside, staring at the spot where the trailer used to be. Marge joined him, sitting down with a bottle of whiskey.

Ron sighed. "We have a security system now, and it's really good, and was cheap. We have *government contracts*. We have nine fucking kids."

Marge took a sip. "Yep."

Ron rubbed his face. "How did this happen? I am getting concerned we're able to do a good job. He got a bit serious for a minute."

Marge smirked. "You ever hear of 'found family narratives'?"

"Beth's been talking to you, hasn't she?" Ron said.

Marge just grinned. Then in the distance, Ryder stood by the fence again. Watching. Waiting. No one really understood what was going on with him at all.

Ron sighed. "That kid is gonna give me a goddamn heart attack."

Marge annoyingly patted his head. "Yeah. But you love every second of it."

Ron didn't respond. He shook his head, grabbed his chest, and coughed. But he didn't disagree.

CHAPTER 36

School had officially been in session for a couple of months, and by some miracle, no one had been expelled, arrested, or started a student rebellion.

Joey's anti-math uprising had lost steam (*probably because the other students still had the attention spans of goldfish at that age*).

Danny was *thriving* in shop class—tools in hand, grease on his sleeves, and a grin on his face. The rest of his classes? He was doing well *enough*. Passing, at least.

But his *favorite* saying, the one he slipped into conversation *annoyingly* often, was:

"C's get degrees."

He'd drop it with a smug grin whenever anyone mentioned school, grades, or effort—like it was the ultimate life hack.

Marge figured one of his older siblings at the Yard had armed him with that gem.

Beth denied it, though her smirk said otherwise.

Ron claimed it was "words of wisdom."

Ezra just rolled his eyes and muttered, "Aim higher."

Ivy had no opinion on that or much of anything these days.

But Danny?

Danny wore it like a badge of honor.

Ezra had already hacked the school's WiFi restrictions, but instead of getting in trouble, he'd been offered a part-time job helping the IT department.

Grace had somehow convinced his science teacher to let her "experiment" in class, which meant there were now three different banned substances in the school handbook because she is becoming quite the little scientist.

Lewis kept his head down and his grades up. Quiet, reliable, and sharp, he was the kind of student teachers liked because he didn't cause trouble and always turned in his work on time. He wasn't flashy about it—*Lewis never was*—but he had a knack for math and science that didn't go unnoticed. His teachers called him "focused." The truth was, Lewis had learned that staying busy and doing well left fewer questions for people to ask.

Ivy was... complicated.

When she showed up, she did *fine*. Smarter than she gave herself credit for, Ivy could ace a test without studying and write essays that left her teachers raising their eyebrows in surprise. But she didn't *care* much about the gold stars or the praise. School wasn't a place to stand out for her—it was a place to blend in. She wasn't failing, but she wasn't thriving either—she was surviving. And for Ivy, that was enough.

Max, on the other hand?

Max treated school like an extension of the Yard—*one big experiment*. His grades were a rollercoaster: straight A's in science when the lessons involved blowing things up or taking them apart, and barely passing in subjects that required him to sit still and *pay attention*. He was notorious for "fixing" broken electronics around campus—sometimes they worked better; other times, not so much.

His teachers called him "distracted." Marge called him "a handful."

But Max?

Max called himself an *"inventor in training."* And honestly, that wasn't too far from the truth.

Beth still *hated* everything—school included.

But despite her attitude, she managed to pass—usually with solid Bs and the occasional C, enough to keep teachers off her back but never enough to seem like she cared. Caring was vulnerability, and Beth didn't hand that out freely.

The one exception? *Writing.*

Writing came easily. It was the one thing she actually *enjoyed*—maybe even found a little therapeutic, though she'd never admit it out loud. She controlled writing in a life where so much had been unpredictable and unstable. Just her, a worn notebook, and a handful of pencils she could get free through a school or library program.

It was *hers.*

Beth never talked about the darker years growing up. Her sharp sarcasm, the snarky comments that kept people at arm's length? That wasn't just personality—it was defense. A coping mechanism she'd honed since she was seven.

Seven.

That was when everything *shifted.*

Life got volatile after the death of one of her parents. The other? They tried to cope—but ultimately, *they didn't.* The fallout hit Beth hard. She learned quickly that relying on people was dangerous, that sometimes the ones who were supposed to stay didn't.

So, she relied on herself.

Her notebooks were filled with stories, poems, half-thoughts—some light, most not. But they were hers. Words no one could take away.

The Yard?

It was the most stability Beth had known since that seven-year-old girl who once embraced life without hesitation. She wouldn't say it aloud—maybe not even admit it to herself—but a part of her was starting to believe that *maybe* this place, with all its chaos and noise, could be home.

Maybe.

So, all things considered?

Marge was calling this a win in providing stability for the kiddos.

The day never disappointed in how many twists and turns it could throw Trenton's way.

Ron hadn't taken a trip in years.

Between the junkyard, the kids, and the constant potential for criminal involvement, there just wasn't time. As a visionary, he always looked forward; as a grey-area crime boss (said dramatically), he spent the rest of his time looking over his shoulder for who might want something without asking for it.

But when a guy he knew from way back tipped him off about three train cars full of salvage up for auction in El Paso, Ron saw an opportunity. "We go, look, maybe buy, and turn a profit. Simple."

Marge grimaced. "You? Take a *business trip?* Without causing an incident? Trenton, El Paso is on the border, meaning you have the opportunity to piss off an entire other government, who have worse jails from our government."

Ron grinned. "I am *highly* professional, mostly at all times."

"Oh, that's hilarious. Are you taking that on tour?" Beth said. She kept on walking right by the actual conversation.

Ron ignored her. "I've decided to take Danny, Max, and Lewis."

"I am really anticipating hearing your plans, okay let's hear it." Marge waited.

Danny because he was actually good at picking out valuable salvage and keeping an eye on Max.

Max, because… well, Max needed to see more of the world beyond the junkyard.

Lewis is responsible and can help keep an eye on the boys. But even with Lewis helping out, I am not up for bringing Joey on this trip.

"*See?* I know my limits, *MargyPargy*," Ron said, flashing a grin and turning up the charm with that signature twinkle in his eye.

Marge didn't even look up from her coffee.

"Uh-huh. Your limits? Sure. News to me."

Ron leaned against the counter, still grinning. "C'mon, don't pretend you're not impressed."

"Oh, I'm impressed, all right—impressed you've survived this long *without* a clue."

Ron held a hand to his chest, mock-wounded. "*MargyPargy,* you wound me."

"Keep talking, Ron. You'll be feeling real wounds soon enough. Goddamnit, hard not to like you. For the record, your easy to love, but damn hard to like when you get into scheming mode." Marge said.

Ron just laughed, undeterred. "Admit it. You'd miss me."

Marge had one rule for this trip, and she wasn't kidding when she said it: "Don't let them get hurt, arrested, or die."

Ron sighed. "Jesus, Marge. Give me some credit."

Marge just looked at him, then handed him a first-aid kit.

Ron rented a big white minivan because they had to haul back potential purchases.

Danny took one look at it and immediately lost his shit, he was beside himself about the special van.

"Oh my *God*, Pop. This is a *mom van*."

Max gasped dramatically. "This is a *soccer mom* van."

Ron scowled. "It's *practical, and they gave me a huge discount because they had 50 off them sitting there.*"

Danny grinned. "Ron. My dude. My *guy*. You look like you should be driving a bunch of PTA moms to a brunch."

Max nodded. "Yeah. You should really be wearing yoga pants for this."

Ron glared. "Shut up both of you, enough of that chatter, or someone might stay home." They spent the rest of the morning loading up the van, calling the school with the excused absences, and keeping everyone out of trouble.

Max and Lewis climbed into the back and immediately started touching every button.

Danny sat in the passenger seat, grinning like an idiot. "Man, this thing has *cup holders everywhere*. You sure it doesn't come with free juice boxes?"

Ron seriously considered throwing him out.

The plan had been simple: roll into town and find a cheap motel— no reservations, of course. Money was always tight. We wanted something basic, no frills, and definitely not expensive—just a place with four walls, a locked door, and hopefully no obvious health code violations.

That plan went out the window when Lily Harlow called.

"Hey, Trenton. Heard you're taking a road trip to El Paso. Thought I'd help out."

Ron frowned. "You paying my gas bill?"

Lily snorted. "No, and better. You'll stay at the *Marriott in downtown El Paso. It is a nice property, I've stayed there a couple of times for work.*"

Ron blinked. "Excuse me?"

"I had some points to burn. Figured you could use an upgrade from the schemy and sleezy motorcoach inn you'd planned. This is mainly for the kids; they need something fun on the road trip."

Ron would have been insulted if it were coming from someone other than family, and Lily was right, yet he did hesitate. "…How nice of a Marriott are we talking?"

"Fancy as hell, Trenton. Pool, bar, two restaurants, cigar bar, and room service. Don't embarrass yourself or need a lawyer, please."

Ron was speechless, and smiling.

Danny, overhearing, smirked. "Wait. We're staying somewhere *fancy*? You're gonna have to wear a tie, old man?"

Ron hung up the phone and glared at them. "All of you. *Behave.*"

Lewis looked at Ron with a 'what did I do?' look. Max and Danny absolutely did not behave; it was way too big of an ask.

The drive to El Paso went fast, they didn't stop, and everyone was excited for the hotel. They almost forget about the scrap auction, the point of the trip to start. By the time Ron pulled up to the beautiful glass-and-steel hotel.

Danny whistled. "Damn, Pop. I didn't know you had this good *taste.*"

Max bounced in his seat. "Is there a *pool*? Or the gameroom or restaurants?"

Ron groaned. "Yes. There's a pool. No, we are not getting kicked out of this place. I *like* having a lawyer who doesn't think I'm a lost cause."

"Yes, I have good taste, but this is a gift from Lily to you boys to have an extra nice time on the road trip. I expect everyone to tell her thank you if we don't get kicked out," Ron said.

Danny grinned. "No promises but I am game to try."

Ron knew they might not fit in when they walked into the lobby.

Everything was crisp. People were wearing suits.

Max immediately pointed at the grand piano in the corner. "Can I touch that?"

Ron grabbed the back of his hoodie. "Absolutely *not.*"

Danny, spotting the bar area, smirked. "Yo, you think they'd serve me a margarita if I act confident enough when I order?"

Ron dragged the younger ones toward the elevator after check-in. Lewis looked around; he'd never been in a place like this before.

The second they got to the suite (*which had a freaking living room*), Danny collapsed onto the bed.

Max immediately found the hotel phone.

"I'M ORDERING ROOM SERVICE!"

Ron grabbed the phone away. "Like *hell* you are. It's not all free, we are not made of money? $22 hamburgers, not a goddamn chance, kid."

Danny rolled over, still laughing. "Ron. C'mon. Let the kid order *one* stupidly overpriced thing."

Ron sighed, muttering, "I'm gonna regret this." Then handed Max back the phone. "You can order up to $30 worth of stuff, that is it, no more".

All the boys were so excited. They ate room service, watched two huge TVs, and swam in the pool for hours. It was a good day for everyone.

The next morning, they arrived at the salvage yard with three train cars of junk. They were massive, which impressed the whole ragtag family.

Danny immediately started examining engine parts. "We could flip a lot of this to make some scratch."

Max was more excited about the weird stuff. "There's a *suit of armor* in here. Can we keep it? I can figure out how to make money with it, Pop!"

Ron answered quickly and consistently. "No, Max, we are not bringing home a damn suit of armor. You're not helping, keep your eye on the prize."

Danny, already deep in calculations, looked up. "Pop, we should bid."

Ron hesitated. The starting bid was $12,000, but the resale value could be triple that.

Ron nodded. He was also nervous. That was a lot more money than they usually worked with to buy things. "Alright. Let's make a deal. Spend money to make money."

They won the bid.

Which meant they now owned three train cars full of weird and potentially valuable crap. Ron then went into 'oh shit mode', how was he getting it back to the Yard, three hour and half hours away.

They returned to the hotel, ate way too much room service, again, and let Max and Danny burn off whatever chaotic energy they had left in the fancy-ass pool with Lewis in charge.

Ron wasn't about to admit it—not to the boys, Marge, or *anyone*—but he'd forgotten, or maybe never really *known*, what relaxing felt like.

While the boys splashed and yelled in the pool, Ron slipped away, quiet and unnoticed.

The hot tub wasn't far. Hidden just enough to be out of sight. Perfect.

He eased into the steaming water with a low sigh, sinking until only his head remained above the surface. The heat worked its way into his shoulders, kneading out knots he hadn't realized were there.

For a moment, *just a moment,* there was complete serenity.

He took a deep breath, letting it out slowly.

No one died on this trip.

Ron leaned his head back, staring at the ceiling with a half-smirk.

"I'll take that as an *incredible* milestone in my parenting," he muttered.

The distant sound of laughter echoed from the pool.

For once, everything felt… okay.

Max, who had commandeered an inflatable pool noodle, floated past, arms behind his head like he was sunbathing. "You think Mom will let us do this again?"

Danny snorted. "Not a damn chance, but reconsidered, maybe."

Max sighed dramatically and let himself drift. "Cool."

Danny smirked. "Bet if we tell her we learned some valuable life lessons, she might get on board with another trip! We did learn some things, right, like how to order room service." The boys laughed as loudly as possible at the comment.

Ron walked up. "Yeah? And what other valuable lessons did you learn?"

Danny thought. "Rich people really overcharge for burgers."

Ron chuckled. "Accurate, and our poor folks are dumb enough to order them for room service." Again, they all laughed, loud enough to have lights come on, several floors above them in the hotel.

Lews perked up. "Oh! And that I can totally do a backflip off the side of the pool."

Danny turned to him, eyes narrowing. "Wait. You can?"

Lewis grinned. "Wanna see?"

Ron sat up. "No. Absolutely not."

Lewis was already climbing out of the pool. Ron groaned and Danny cheered.

Ten minutes later, Ron had dragged Max out of the pool before the hotel staff could murder him, Danny was still laughing, and the fancy hotel pool had a very wet lifeguard who did not appreciate the boy's acrobatics.

Max pouted for a few minutes on the way back to their room, a towel draped over his head like a dejected ghost. "I almost stuck the landing."

Ron pointed at him. "If you try that shit again, I'm calling Marge."

Max gasped. "You wouldn't."

Ron grinned. "Try me."

Danny, still laughing, high-fived Max and Lewis anyway. "For the record, it was pretty badass boys, pretty epic."

Ron rubbed his temples. "The three of you will be the death of me, seriously, all of you." He was trying to hide how much fun he was having as well, trying not to encourage, but it showed through; the boys knew he was also having a good time.

That night, as Max snored loud enough to wake the dead in town and Mexico, and Danny scrolled on his new phone, and Lewis watched TV, Ron sat on the hotel balcony, staring out at the city.

It was quiet, for once.

The morning air in El Paso was unusually crisp, carrying just a hint of warmth that promised a hotter afternoon. Ron figured getting the boys out for a walk before the real work began—*hauling scrap back to the Yard*—wasn't the worst idea. Plus, he'd heard about something that might actually keep them entertained for more than five minutes.

"C'mon," Ron said, waving them along. "We're heading out. It's close. You'll like it."

Max groaned but followed without complaint, still half-asleep. Lewis perked up at the mention of *"you'll like it,"* convinced it meant something exciting. Danny trailed behind, earbuds in but paying attention, as always.

The walk was only a few blocks from the Marriott, and the city slowly woke up around them. The streets buzzed with quiet energy—coffee shops opened, early risers jogged past, and traffic was distant.

When they reached the San Jacinto Plaza, the boys slowed, curiosity taking over.

"*Whoa.*" Lewis stopped in his tracks. "Are those—*alligators?*"

Sure enough, there they were. The alligators. Right there in the middle of the city square.

Max pressed up against the railing. "That's… actually kinda cool."

"Told you," Ron said, smirking.

Danny pulled out one earbud, raising an eyebrow. "Seriously? Alligators. In the *middle* of the city?"

"Yep. Super unique, right?," Ron replied, crossing his arms as he watched the boys circle the enclosure.

Joey squinted at the alligators, whom he'd figured out aren't real, yet he was playing along. "They don't do much."

"They don't *have* to," Max said, tapping the rail. "They're alligators. Just being here makes them cool."

Ron chuckled. "Exactly. No effort needed. Kinda like me."

"Beth would've rolled her eyes at that one if she were here." Lewis said.

The boys spent longer than Ron expected watching the alligators until they all figured out they weren't real. They still thought it was cooler than any alligators in Albuquerque. There wasn't much action, but somehow, it held their attention. Maybe it was the novelty. Maybe it was the quiet.

For Ron, it was rare to see them relaxed, *together,* without the noise of the Yard or the weight of whatever came next.

Eventually, Ron clapped. "Alright, let's get moving. We've got scrap to haul and a long drive ahead."

"Back to the grind," Danny muttered, slipping his earbud back in.

"Yeah, yeah," Ron said, waving them forward. "But hey—y'all got to see some alligators this morning. Not a bad start to the day."

As they returned to the Marriott, the city came alive behind them. The boys waited outside the hotel where guests parked while Ron walked six blocks to the free on-street parking. He would never pay $25 a night for parking. The boys continued talking more than usual— mostly about who would win in a fight: an alligator, Marge, or Ron.

Ron just smiled as he pulled up to the ragtag bunch with their old country-looking pile of luggage. "Load it up, let's get out of here!" Ron said.

CHAPTER 37

The arrangements to get the three railcars of scrap trucked up from El Paso were not going smoothly, as much as Ron thought he had it all arranged. His shortcuts and deals were causing some issues. All still had to be worked out.

It felt like the Yard was fueled by chaos, sarcasm, nicotine, caffeine, and bad news.

But today?

Today, it ran on rage.

Beth and Ivy were supposed to be running errands—nothing complicated—just a quick trip downtown for some supplies.

And yet, somehow, that trip had ended in handcuffs.

When Marge's phone rang, she was halfway through inventory, and the last thing she expected was a call from Lily.

"Marge. We have a little problem."

Marge, immediately sighed. "Jesus. Who's in jail?"

"Beth and Ivy."

Marge paused. "Don't kid about them, Lily."

Lily assured Marge, she didn't kid about kids getting locked up, and the girls were alright. Then, Marge calmly said, "I'm going to kill them."

Annoyed but controlled, Lily muttered, "They didn't do anything."

Marge blinked. "…Then why are they in jail?"

Lily sighed. "Shoplifting charge. Total bullshit. I'm on my way to get them now. You might want to meet me there."

Marge massaged the sides of her head. "Yeah. Headed out now."

She turned to Ron. "Get in the truck. NOW."

Ron, who had been peacefully drinking his coffee. "What *now?*"

Marge grabbed the keys out of his hands. "Beth and Ivy are in fucking jail." Ron froze mid-sip, then, smoothly, "Goddammit, all before my first cup of coffee."

By the time they got to the precinct, Lily was already there, standing at the front desk, arms crossed, pissed off, and looking like she was about to sue or fight everyone in sight.

Next to her? Two familiar faces.

Officer Reyes and Munoz.

They were some of the only cops in Albuquerque that the Trentons actually trusted to listen and do all they could to help the situation out. Both Ron and Marge's growing-up experiences weren't great, and they left a bad taste in their mouths about the police.

Marge strode in like she owned the place. "Where are they?"

Munoz sighed. "Holding. We're getting them out, but the store's pressing charges."

Marge got louder, "What fucking store?" Ron scowled. "On *what grounds?*"

Reyes, looking deeply unimpressed, muttered, "None. The owner's a prick. I will talk to him after we get the girls out."

Lily, still furious, added, "And a racist, classist piece of shit, from what I'm hearing."

Ron gritted his teeth. "Fuck, of course he is."

Marge slammed a hand. "I want to see my kids. *Now.*"

Munoz nodded. "Please just calm down a little, and follow me."

When they stepped into the holding area, Beth paced like a caged animal, and Ivy sat on the bench, arms crossed, looking bored.

The moment Beth saw Marge, she exploded.

"We didn't fucking do anything!"

Marge held up a hand. "I *know*. Calm down a little, repeating instructions from Officer Munoz here."

Beth threw up her hands. "We were *browsing,* and the next thing I know, some asshole manager is accusing us of stealing and calling the cops!"

Ivy, deadpan, added, "I don't even like shopping, said I didn't want to stop."

Lily frowned. "They've done this before. Target poor or brown kids, call the cops, scare them into not coming back."

Ron clenched his jaw. "That's illegal as hell, why would a business do that? We run a business and sure as hell don't do that nonsense."

Reyes nodded. "Oh, trust me. We're working on it. You're not the first but it is hard to stop it."

Marge turned to Lily. "So what now?"

Lily smirked. "Now? We get them the fuck out of here. Grabbing both girls by the arm, encouraging them to hurry."

Minutes later, Beth and Ivy walked out free, but furious and upset once the adrenaline had worn off a bit.

Officer Munoz called a couple of hours later with an update, the store refused to apologize after the officers talked to them about the profiling pattern.

Ron, still fuming, muttered, "We should sue their asses. I fucking mean that."

Lily smirked. "Oh, I already filed the paperwork. We're going hate crime because of the profiling pattern and documentation through the police reports. All open records."

Beth turned to Ivy. "Hey. We'll start shopping *exclusively* from thrift stores to spite them."

Ivy nodded. "Obviously."

That night, Beth and Ivy were still tense.

But instead of ranting about it, they were quiet.

Marge noticed, "What's on your minds?" she asked.

Beth exhaled. "We need to do something else."

Marge paused. "What do you mean?"

Ivy answered plainly, arms crossed. "We need to get jobs."

Ron, walking into the room mid-conversation, *froze*. His eyes widened, and for a second, he almost looked *panicked*. "*Wait*. You want to *work?*"

Beth, sitting close, rolled her eyes so hard it was a wonder she didn't pull something.

"Yes, *Pop*. *Work*. You know—like a *real* job. Outside the junkyard."

Ron blinked, still trying to process.

"Hold on. *Voluntarily?* You *voluntarily* want to work? Not court-ordered? Not community service? No threats from Marge?"

Ivy raised an eyebrow. "You make it sound like we're criminals."

"*Hey,* I didn't say that," Ron said, holding up his hands. "But I distinctly remember the last time I suggested *work,* Grace tried to fake his own death, and Ezra claimed manual labor stifled his creativity."

Beth smirked. "Ezra's still sticking to that story."

Ron rubbed his temples. "And you're sure about this? Real jobs? Waking up early? Dealing with *people?*"

Ivy shrugged. "We need money."

"Yeah, Ron," Beth added with a grin. "Turns out, freedom and snacks aren't free."

Ron sighed dramatically. "Unbelievable. My own crew, betraying the family business."

Beth crossed her arms. "We can still work here sometimes. But face it—scrap metal and half-broken appliances aren't exactly a fast track to a future for the two of us."

Ivy nodded. "And we want more options."

Ron glanced toward the yard, then back at them, then slowly back at the yard.

"Alright, alright. I get you want more experiences than scrap, but if you all turn into a bunch of responsible adults, don't expect me to keep up with all that."

Beth snorted. "Trust me, we *don't.*" She was glad that Ron was smiling, but Marge wasn't saying much which didn't feel like a good sign.

Ron pointed at her. "*Rude.*" But the corner of his mouth tugged into a grin.

"Fine. Go get your real jobs, if and only if Marge gives the ok. Remember, don't come running back when you realize the Yard's the best gig in town."

Ivy exchanged a look with Beth.

"Deal," Ivy said.

And with that, Ron watched them walk over and grab Marge's arm to get the final decision.

"Kids these days. *Wanting to work.* What's next? Paying bills on time?"

Ivy nodded. "I want something else. Something that doesn't involve people I see 24/7."

Marge and Ron exchanged looks.

Finally, Ron sighed. "You're serious about this?" Beth nodded. "Yeah. I love the Yard, but… I want my own thing."

Marge nodded. "I respect how you girls are thinking about this; it's okay with me, but I want information about each place you both work. Do you understand?"

Both girls enthusiastically nodded in unison and agreement.

Two days later, Ryder announced that he also had a job. This surprised everyone mostly because no one remembered him applying for one.

Ron, arms crossed, narrowed his eyes. "Where?"

"Bookstore and electronics fixing place."

Beth blinked. "Wait. *You*? Working two jobs?"

Ryder nodded. "Both are quiet. They don't talk to me, I don't talk to them. I shelf books and fix electronics. It's perfect."

Max looked personally betrayed. "But you're *one of us, here at the Yard, working*."

Ryder shrugged. "I require funds to do stuff, pay isn't great here."

Beth grinned. "That's a *really* fancy way of saying 'I want money.'"

Ryder did not deny it, he needed to get time away from the Yard. The case he was working on recently got a lot bigger.

Ron sighed. "Fine. Just… don't get arrested, okay?"

Ryder blinked. "Why would I?"

Beth smirked. "Well, *we* didn't think *we'd* get arrested either, yet here we are."

Ryder thought about that. "…Fair point, Beth."

Meanwhile, Joey had his first friend over.

A girl, named Lily.

Not lawyer Lily. A six-year-old who was somehow as loud as Joey.

Ron stared in horror as they ran through the junkyard, screaming like feral gremlins. Ron turned to Marge. "Why are we allowing this?"

Marge smirked. "Because it's cute, albeit loud, still cute."

Beth, walking by, laughing. "What's the matter, Pop? Can't handle more *children*?"

Ron pointed at her. "Shut up, inmate 5097855."

Beth cackled, too soon, Pops, too soon.

That night, Marge and Ron sat on the porch, watching the stars, which they did a lot more of in the Yard.

Ron sighed. "They're all growing up."

Marge nodded. "Yeah. And they're figuring out who they want to be."

"The Yard," Ron said with a chuckle, glancing out at the familiar chaos.

Marge sipped her coffee, smoking a cigarette. She had started up again after months of doing well cutting back. "You'll still have Joey and Max to terrorize you for a few more years."

Ron groaned, rubbing his face. *"Christ. That's *not* comforting. Honestly, I'm thinking… maybe we get one or two more kids."

Marge choked on her coffee, then stared at him.

For a moment, the look on her face was unreadable.

Then she laughed—*hard.*

But just as quickly, her expression shifted to one of dramatic seriousness.

She stepped closer, pointing a finger right at Ron's chest.

"*You are out of your ever-loving-fucking-*mind,* Trenton."

Ron threw up his hands. "What? I'm serious!"

Marge narrowed her eyes. "No. No, no, no. You think *more* kids are the answer? We've already got a human demolition crew, a genius in training who doesn't believe in safety regulations, and enough emotional baggage to fill the damn yard."

Ron grinned. "Exactly. What's a little more chaos?"

Marge shook her head, muttering as she turned back toward the house.

"Out. Of. His. Damn. Mind."

Ron just chuckled, watching her go.

But the idea lingered.

Maybe one or two more wouldn't be so bad…

And in the distance, Ryder stood by the fence—watching the night, covertly engaging in a text conversation with his handler.

CHAPTER 38

The fallout from Beth and Ivy's wrongful arrest hit fast. Word spread quickly—faster than even Ron expected.

People talked. People had opinions. And for once? People were on their side.

It started with customers. More people came into the junkyard than usual, and not just to buy scrap.

"Heard about what happened," an older man said, flipping through a car parts bin. "Damn shame. Those girls didn't deserve that."

A woman buying some old fencing materials nodded. "That store's pulled this before. Maybe now something'll actually be done."

Even one of the mechanics from a shop down the road stopped by, slapping a twenty on the counter even though he wasn't buying anything.

"For the legal fund," he said.

Marge, taking the bill, blushed a little. "We've got a lawyer working for free."

The guy shrugged. "Then buy 'em a beer or three."

Of course, with all the noise, it was only a matter of time before someone from the city showed up. That someone?

Councilwoman Dolores Vega.

A name Marge recognized. Vega was new to the local government scene, but she'd made a name for herself by being involved.

Sometimes that was a good thing, othertimes a pain in the ass.

Today?

It was definitely the second one.

Vega pulled up in a clean, city-issued SUV. Stepped out in a crisp blazer and heels that were definitely not meant for walking around on junkyard gravel.

She smiled politely, but the kind of smile said, *I'm here to ask questions you won't want to answer.*

Standing by the office, Marge exhaled slowly, then yelled something familiar. "RON."

Ron, leaning against a pile of tires, muttered, "Goddamn it. What now?"

Marge nodded toward the car. Ron looked. Saw the city seal on the license plate.

Then groaned. "Jesus. What do they want now? We *paid our taxes, and no one got arrested this week.*"

"Guess we're about to find out."

Vega approached with a perfectly rehearsed politician's smile.

"Mr. and Mrs. Trenton. A pleasure to meet you."

Marge shook her hand, offering not much of a smile. Vega's smile didn't falter. "I understand there's been… some controversy involving your family recently."

Ron snorted. "That's one way to put it."

Vega clasped her hands. "I wanted to come by personally. I've heard a lot about your business. About the kids you take in. It's… unique."

Marge folded her arms. "Uh-huh. And?"

Vega hesitated. "I wanted to see it for myself. Understand what you're doing here."

Ron frowned. "Why are we interesting to you?"

"Because you're providing a service this city sorely lacks." Vega replied with something that caught them off guard.

Marge stunned. "You sure you're a politician? That almost sounded like a compliment."

Vega smirked slightly. "I call it like I see it, like it or not."

Ron scratched his chin. "And what do you *see here with us at the Yard?*"

Vega looked around at the piles of chaos. The kids were working in the shop, the junkyard that was somehow a business, a home, and a second chance for kids nobody else wanted.

Finally, she said, "Something the system isn't built to handle. It's working, god knows how, but these kids are happy, mostly out of trouble, and you run a small business."

Marge and Ron gave Vega a full tour, skipping the trailer area, of course, against their better judgment.

Vega saw Danny working on an engine, Grace helping Ezra install even more security cameras, and Joey explaining—at full volume—to his friend Lily how metal recycling might work.

She asked polite and honest questions.

Marge and Ron gave short, concise answers, still skeptical about what game was here with Councilwoman Vega.

The kids? The kids were not helpful.

Seeing Vega in her polished blazer, Max immediately asked, "Are you here to arrest us?" Beth overhears the comment. "Nah, Max. *We* already did our time in County."

Vega looked mildly taken aback. She might not have been fully immersed in the Albuquerque experiences when she grew up.

Marge sighed. "They're joking. Mostly."

Finally, back at the office, Vega got to her real reason for coming.

"I'm considering pushing for more city and county cooperative programs to help kids in unstable and, candidly, unsafe home situations," Lily said, her tone thoughtful but firm.

Ron grizzled from his spot at the table, arms crossed and face twisted into a scowl.

"You mean foster care? *That's* already a joke. That shit program hurts half the kids and helps the other half—*maybe.* Those are horrible numbers."

Vega paused, expecting this reaction.

"It's not just foster care, Mr. Trenton. I'm talking about programs that actually *work*—community support, mentorships, wrap-around care, and real resources—things that don't just shuffle kids from one broken place to another."

Ron shook his head, not believing it would happen that way.

"Doesn't matter what they *call* it. The system's still broken. You've seen it. Hell, we've all *lived* it. Paper-pushers sitting in offices deciding where kids should go, like they're picking lottery numbers."

Vega met his gaze, unflinching.

"That's why it needs to change. And people like you—people who *actually* step up—you're part of the proof that different outcomes are possible."

Ron laughed. "Oh, please. I'm no poster child for good decision-making. I'm just stubborn enough to stick around when things get messy."

"Exactly," Vega said with a small smile. "Sometimes that's all it takes."

Ron went quiet for a moment, his fingers drumming against the table.

"Still don't like the odds," he muttered. "But I guess half saved is better than none."

Vega nodded. "It's a start."

Ron sighed, glancing toward Marge, and out the window toward the Yard, where the kids' laughter echoed faintly.

"Yeah," he said quietly. "It's a start, I suppose."

Vega tilted her head. "Which is why I want to know what works. And despite... your unconventional methods, it seems *this* works."

Marge frowned. "Are you asking us to be part of some city program?"

"I need to use the bathroom. I'll be back in a few minutes," Marge said, pushing back her chair. She needed a break from the Councilwoman's bullshit and endless doublespeak. She could feel her temper rising fast; if she didn't step away now, she might say something *very* regrettable.

Vega hesitated, then continued as if Marge were invisible. "Not officially. Not yet. I just... wanted to understand it better."

Ron leaned back. "Well. Now you understand. What happens next?"

Vega was silent for a moment. Then, with a small, almost amused smile, she said, "Nothing. Not yet."

Ron didn't know what to say, so he stayed silent, letting the weight of the pause settle between them until Marge returned.

Marge narrowed her eyes, glancing between them. "So this was just... a visit?"

Vega nodded. "For now."

Ron exhaled. "God. Bureaucrats are exhausting."

Vega laughed. "Tell me about it, hard to stand myself most days."

As Vega left, Marge turned to Ron. "Well. That was... weird."

Ron nodded. "I don't like people in suits showing up unannounced. Makes me nervous. I think commandos, dogs, and helicopters are showing up next!"

Beth, walking by, muttered, "You *should* be nervous. You run a mostly....yes, mostly legal business."

Beth grinned, and never stopped walking.

Marge rubbed the back of her neck, although it was hard to reach, forcing her to contort to finish it. "I don't know if that was a good or bad visit."

Ron shrugged. "Nothing came of it. That's *probably* the best we could hope for."

Marge nodded slowly. But deep down? She felt this wasn't the last time they'd be seeing Vega.

CHAPTER 39

If there was one thing Ron liked, it was money.

And if there was one thing Marge liked, it was making people pay what they actually owed. There was a sense of class justice in the world when this happened.

So when a film studio reached out about using their junk for a sci-fi and country farm set, the entire yard was buzzing with excitement.

Well, except for Ron. He was already suspicious yet the dollar signs eased his discomfort.

Because Hollywood people meant negotiations. And negotiations meant bullshit to deal with, yet, Ron did like some hardcore negotiating.

Two shiny, black cliché SUVs glided to a stop next to the rusted-out trucks, their polished surfaces gleaming in the morning sun. They looked *painfully* out of place—sleek, expensive, and silent, like wolves among stray rez dogs.

Then the doors opened—slow, deliberate. Out stepped three people.

A producer, mid-40s, expensive sunglasses, fake smile.

A production designer, thin, twitchy, already taking notes.

Holding a clipboard, some assistant was the only one looking reasonably normal.

Ron leaned toward Marge. "They look like they drink overpriced lattes and don't know anything about even changing light bulbs. I don't like them."

Marge smirked. "Calm down. That means we can charge them extra."

Beth, standing nearby, muttered with excitement, "I'm going to enjoy this; I can feel it."

Lily Harlow, their part-time lawyer and part-time enabler, had also shown up—just in case the business got serious.

She leaned against the office doorway, watching with amusement.

"You think they're gonna try and lowball you, get some deal from the ABQ bumpkins?" she asked.

Marge scoffed. "Obviously. Then laughed loudly, amused with herself."

Ron cracked his knuckles. "Then let's show them why that's a bad idea."

The lead producer, Mark, smiled as if he wasn't about to be the most irritating person Ron had met all week. "Good morning, Mr. and Mrs. Trenton, and you are, turning to Lily."

"Ms. Harlow, the family attorney." Lily said.

"Okay! We're really excited about this collaboration. We're looking for authentic, distressed, and unique pieces for two different sets—one for a *gritty sci-fi colony,* and one for a *classic American farmstead.*"

Ron, arms crossed, nodded slowly. "Uh-huh. Right. Acting like he was listening intently, taking all the information in before offering wisdom back."

The production designer, Karen, clutched her notes like they were her lifeline. "We need things that look real. Weathered. Aged. Like they've been through something. We want *character.*"

Beth grinned. "Congratulations. You've come to the most character-filled scrap pile in Albuquerque, maybe Central New Mexico."

Mark chuckled, thinking she was joking.

Ron didn't smile. "Show us your budget, and let's discuss the economics of this whole conversation, please."

Mark hesitated. "Well, we hoped to discuss pricing after seeing what you have."

Marge, equally unimpressed, gestured toward the yard. "Look all you want. But nothing leaves until we have a deal. If you break it, you buy it. We clear?"

They ignored the last comment. Mark, Karen, and Clipboard Assistant wandered the junkyard for the next hour, pointing at things.

An old tractor? Perfect for the farm.

A rusted-out shipping container? Sci-fi colony material.

Broken satellite dishes? "Yes, we'll take all of them."

Crumbling neon signs? "Incredible aesthetic."

Even a pile of old vending machines got way more attention than Ron thought necessary. He thought, what a load of horseshit all this was, we'll never make any money.

At one point, Max tried to sell them his latest "invention," which looked suspiciously like a blender attached to a car battery.

"This could be futuristic! Movie quality." Max insisted.

Karen stared. "What… does it do?"

Max shrugged. "Good question, we don't know yet!"

Beth dragged him away. "Max. For the love of God. No science experiments during negotiations with these people."

Max pouted. "But they like weird stuff!"

Ron shook his head. "Jesus Christ."

Once the tour was over, they sat down to talk numbers. Mark smiled. "Alright. We love what we've seen. So let's talk pricing."

Ron leaned back. "Let's."

Mark cleared his throat. "So, here's our offer. For the things we've selected, we're willing to pay… $10,000."

Silence. Then Marge laughed.

Lily grinned. "Oh, that's adorable. You're joking, right?"

Mark looked mildly concerned. "Uh… no?"

Ron smirked. "I have to be so direct, Mark, Mark right? You're an idiot if you think that's all it's worth."

Karen fidgeted. "We *do* have a budget limit—"

Beth stepped in to cut her off. "You guys are making a multi-million-dollar movie, and you think we're gonna let you buy prime vintage scrap for the price of a used car?"

Marge folded her arms. "This is all specialty material. It's real, not Hollywood fake. If you want authentic, you pay authentic prices."

Mark shifted uncomfortably. "We just assumed there'd be room to negotiate."

Lily smiled sweetly. "Oh, there is. We'll negotiate *up*."

Mark sighed. "What were you thinking?"

Ron glanced at Marge. Then at Beth.

Then said, "$30,000."

Karen gasped. Mark blinked rapidly. "That's… quite a jump from $10,000 per week to $30,000."

Marge froze, then eeked out in a softened voice. "We know what it's worth."

Beth leaned forward. "Also? You guys already spent twenty minutes gushing about how *perfect* all this was. So we know you love what the Yard has to offer."

Mark sighed heavily. "Twelve five hundred.."

Ron raised an eyebrow. "Mark, I like you. Let me know, talk to my partners."

Karen shook her head. "Okay."

Lily, poke face activated, politely smiled, and leaned in. "Let's go into the office for a few minutes."

Marge nodded and grabbed Ron and Beth both. She turned and stared at all three of the movie team, "Look. We don't *need* this deal. We're doing just fine. But you *need* this inventory. Some Hollywood prop house will give the same crap everyone else uses, seems like a big waste of time to go that route for *fake* junk."

Mark hesitated. Clearly doing some quick thinking as Marge herded everyone to the office.

Finally, he yelled. "Seventeen. That is the final offer, today only."

Marge paused then kept walking. Then nodded.

Beth closed the door, only party ajar, grinning the whole time. "Holy shit, that is a lot of money."

The office meeting ended quickly, and they landed the first big legitimate deal. After signing the paperwork, the studio folks shook hands and left, looking mildly exhausted.

Mark from the production studio shifted awkwardly before clearing his throat. "Mind if I use your restroom?"

Marge gestured down the hall. "Go for it. Second door on the left."

A few minutes later, he returned, brushing his hands on his jeans. "Wow," he said, glancing around. "That's, uh… an *old-school* setup you've got in there. Small. Quaint."

Ron raised an eyebrow. "That's a polite way of saying *rundown?*"

Mark chuckled. "Let's just say it has *character.*"

Marge smirked. "That's one way to put it."

Once they were gone, Ron stretched out his arms. "That, my friends, is unfuckingbelievable! I love Hollywood and it's golden bullshit."

Beth yelled. "Damn, Pop. We almost looked *competent.*"

Ron ruffled her hair. "Shut up, we did a good job, even if we were confused 95% of the time."

Beth laughed, screaming, "$17,000 weekly for some junkyard treasures!" Marge came from the kitchen with beer and soda. It was celebration time for the whole family.

Still sad about not selling his invention, Max muttered, "Next time, I'm bringing *blueprints and more pictures.*"

Marge patted his shoulder. "We'll work on your pitch, kiddo."

Lily chuckled. "Well. That was fun. I may become a professional negotiator. But for tonight, how about I order pizza for everyone, New York style? "

The group smiled. "YES, PIZZA!"

Ron leaned back, satisfied with more ways to not be tied to Donahue financially. $68,000 a month for literal junk. Yeah. That was a damn good day by anyone's yardstick.

CHAPTER 40

Today it all started at a gas station.

Ron had stopped for coffee—because Marge's rule was no talking before caffeine—when an old guy in line squinted at him and said, "You run that junkyard, don't you?"

Ron, used to random people recognizing him, grunted. "Yeah."

The guy nodded slowly, like he was considering something important.

Then, as if making a formal decree, he said, "You oughta start a coffee club."

Ron blinked. "A what?"

The guy sipped his coffee, eyeing the Yard with a lazy grin.

"Coffee club or corner. You know—a place for old bastards like me to sit, drink something hot, complain about the world. You got space. You got people. Hell, I bet you even got a coffee pot older than my second wife."

Ron chuckled but didn't immediately brush the idea off.

He *should've*. But for some stupid reason, it *stuck*.

The thought of a few old sorts hanging around the Yard—shooting the breeze, talking nonsense, adding some background noise that wasn't kids arguing or engines sputtering—it had *appeal*.

What's wrong with me? he thought, rubbing the back of his neck. *Maybe I didn't sleep well. That's gotta be it.*

But still, the idea lingered. A *coffee corner*.

Ron had an Uncle Phil who spent half of his life sitting in a cafe or gas station with coffee and tables, shooting the shit, tell'n lies about life in general, and always complaining while poking fun at each other. Maybe the idea was just comfortable, familiar.

Hell, it might not be the worst thing.

A week later, Ron converted an old storage room in one of the outbuildings. Definitely nothing fancy. Just a couple of tables, mismatched chairs, a coffee machine that looked like it had survived the Cold War, a fancy blue Porta John with hand sanitizer inside, and a hand-painted sign compliments of Lewis, outside that read:

Old Cogers COFFEE & BULLSHIT Corner: 7AM – 10PM
***Invite only. Clean up after yourselves.**

Marge took one look at it and sighed. "You're really doing this?"

Ron shrugged. "Seemed like a good idea, I just couldn't shake it, don't know why."

Ezra, passing by, laughed. "You're opening an extra shitty Waffle Hut"

Ron flipped him off, smiling, and then waved like it wasn't meant, but they both knew it was.

But the next morning, the old men started showing up.

Meet the Codgers. By the end of the first week, the "Coffee & Bullshit Club" had five regulars.

And these weren't just any old men.

These were the kind of old men who had been through some shit, seen some things, and had opinions about everything.

Manny Rodriguez (74) – Hispanic – Former mechanic. Always smelled like motor oil. Had strong opinions on carburetors, politicians, and the proper way to grill steak.

Luis Castillo (79) – Hispanic – Retired truck driver. Smoked like he was training for the Olympics. Called everyone "kid," including Ron.

Earl Two Rivers (82) – Native American (Navajo/Diné) – Army vet. Quiet, observant, and only spoke when necessary. When he did, it was either deep wisdom or a devastating insult. Nicknamed, Cherokee Earl.

Reggie Parker (85) – Black – Former jazz musician. Wore a leather jacket no matter the weather, and was fluent in French. Knew everyone's secrets and held grudges like a dragon hoarding gold.

Hamish McDougal (71) – Scottish – Unknown background, maybe prison. Nobody actually knew what he did for a living. Claimed he had "escaped" Scotland but never explained why. Thick accent, swore constantly, loved whiskey more than breathing.

The Rules:

Coffee is free.

Cigars & cigarettes welcome.

No politics unless you're prepared to be yelled at.

You'd better have a good reason if you complain about your wife.

If someone doesn't show up for two days, we go looking.

At first, Ron didn't intend to hang out. But then he sat down one morning, made the mistake of saying something, and got sucked into the vortex.

"So, what's the deal with that councilwoman sniffing around?" Manny asked, stirring his coffee like it had personally offended him.

Ron shrugged. "She wanted to see how we run things."

Luis snorted. "Means she's either gonna help or get in your damn way. Probably the second one. Might be the end of the club, when she closes you down."

Earl took a slow drag of his cigarette. "People don't look into things unless they want something."

Reggie nodded. "Watch your back, kid. Government types ain't never done folks like us no favors."

Ron blinked. "Jesus guys, nothing encouraging from you lot. Why do I feel like y'all know something I don't?"

Hamish cackled. "Because we *do*, ye dense bastard."

And just like that? Ron was officially a member. The biggest surprise was how much these old bastards knew. They had connections everywhere.

Need a part for an engine? Manny knew a guy. Need a truck repaired? Luis had a nephew. Need something handled *quietly*? Reggie would make a call. Want to disappear? Hamish had "ideas."

And Earl?

Earl knew every single damn thing happening in town before the local news did.

One morning, he casually said, "That retail store that got Beth and Ivy arrested? The manager's getting fired next week. The owner is a 'Family Trust', allegedly clueless about how it is managed or the bad things they were doing. We'll see about that."

Marge walked into this shoot-the-shit-shack, poured herself a coffee, and paused. "How the hell do you know that?"

Earl exhaled smoke. "I know things."

Hamish grinned. "Earl's a damn wizard."

Manny nodded. "Or a demon. Not sure yet."

Ma'am, don't forget to pay for the coffee, that's the rule. That got a big laugh from everyone.

Ron, still processing, just sipped his coffee.

They might have been old bastards, but they looked after each other. If someone didn't show up, they checked in. When Reggie had a bad week, Luis picked him up for coffee.

Manny's hip started acting up, so Hamish forced him to take a break to get better so he wouldn't die. Then one morning, Earl showed up late.

Sat down slower than usual. Didn't say much.

Everyone noticed.

After pouring more coffee, Ron finally asked, "You good, Earl?"

Earl sighed. "Got some bad news yesterday."

That was all he had to say. Nobody pried.

Luis glanced over. "What's your problem?"

Manny grunted and pushed himself up with an exaggerated groan. "Damn coffee goes straight through me. Gotta take another piss."

Reggie snorted. "Again? Manny, you spend more time in the can than in your chair."

"Blame the coffee, not me," Manny muttered, already shuffling toward the rickety bathroom out back.

Ron shook his head. "Man's got a bladder like a busted radiator."

Hamish snorted. "Aye, but at least a busted radiator doesnae piss an' moan every time it leaks."

The table erupted in laughter just as the shack's screen door slammed behind Manny.

But the next day, Manny brought his favorite cigars.

Reggie brought a bottle of whiskey.

Hamish slapped a bottle of aspirin on the table. "For the hangover ye'll have after in the morning."

And just like that? No one sat alone with their bad days.

One night, Marge found Ron leaning back in a chair, laughing with the old guys. She smirked. "You adopted grandpa."

Ron took a sip of coffee. "Seems that way."

Marge leaned against the door. "Good group?"

Ron nodded. "The best kind of troublemakers."

Marge chuckled. "God help us all." Ron just grinned, but after a very short period of time, neither could see the yard without the club. They just fit.

For the first time in a long time, he had found something unexpected—Not just a business. Not just a family. But a place where even the oldest troublemakers could belong.

CHAPTER 41

Marge had just finished yelling at Joey for trying to make a slingshot out of bungee cords, all before school, and an old car battery when a shiny blue Ford truck pulled into the yard.

Two familiar faces stepped out. And for a second, Ron didn't recognize them. Then it hit him.

Hector and Paloma Morales.

Hector and Paloma had owned this junkyard for nearly 40 years before selling it to the Trentons.

They had been semi-retired for years, living on a small ranch outside of Las Cruces, that was Paloma's wish, and every now and then, they popped up to Albuquerque for supplies, business, or to stir up shit for fun.

Hector, mid-70s, was built like he could still throw someone through a wall. The sun carved his face, and his mustache rivaled that of a 1970s cop show.

Paloma, early 70s, sharp as a blade, with dark, knowing eyes, had always been the real boss of the junkyard.

Ron grinned, the corners of his mouth tugging up in genuine surprise.

"Well, I'll be damned. The *Moraleses.*"

Hector eyed the place like a suspicious landlord inspecting a rental. "Heard you were still kicking. Wanted to see it with our own eyes."

Paloma snorted. "More like we *bet money* on whether or not you'd run this place into the ground by now."

Marge appeared out of the office with crossed arms. "And?"

Hector rubbed his chin. "Well, you ain't bankrupt yet, so I just lost twenty bucks."

Paloma grinned. "You keep up on the payments?" Ron rolled his eyes. "Every goddamn month, on time."

Beth, walking by, popped her head in. "Ron *did* suggest arson once."

Ron pointed at her. "Inmates don't speak until spoken to."

Hector and Paloma burst out laughing.

After an hour of catching up, Ron had an idea.

"Y'all wanna stay for dinner?"

Hector and Paloma exchanged looks. "Depends. Y'all still eat like hobos?" Hector asked.

Marge smirked. "Nah, we upgraded. We got plates now."

Paloma snorted. "Alright, then. We'll clear our busy calendars."

Dinner was loud. It was a mess. And it was fucking hilarious, truly enjoyable by everyone at the table. A full table it was, fifteen in total, with the extra friends staying over, a usual occurrence.

At some point, Hector and Paloma started telling old junkyard stories.

"Had a guy once try to trade us *goats* for a transmission," Hector said, shaking his head.

Danny paused mid-bite. "Did you take it?" Paloma grinned. "Hell yeah, we did. Those goats cleared out the weeds for years. Ended up liking them more than Hector at times."

Max, eyes wide, whispered, "We need goats."

Marge shot Ron a look. "No. Absolutely not."

Everyone rolled with laughter. The night was going strong when a black SUV pulled into the yard.

The mood shifted instantly. Ron felt it first: that subtle tightening in the air, the way people got quiet.

And then Michael Donahue stepped out. *(still a prick)*

His expensive-ass suit was out of place, yet still charming, with a dangerous and shady smile.

Only this time? His smile disappeared quickly as he walked up to the porch and opened the door.

Donahue's eyes flicked over the scene. The dinner table, the kids, Hector and Paloma watching like they smelled bullshit on the wind.

Finally, he spoke. "Got a minute, Trenton?"

Ron leaned back in his chair. "We're eating."

Donahue exhaled sharply. "Didn't realize this was a full-blown *family reunion*."

Marge, calm, sipped her whiskey. "What do you want, Donahue?"

His jaw tightened. "We have a problem."

"The *movie people* are a problem."

Ron shrugged. "They paid us good money. What's the issue and why do you care?"

Donahue gave him a flat look. "You don't get to be *seen* that much, Ron. Not when you have associated *certain business interests*."

Marge set down her glass. "You mean *your* business interests."

Donahue's gaze darkened.

Upon picking up on the tension, Beth muttered, "Should I grab dessert, or are we skipping straight to the yelling?"

Ron jumped up, let's go to the office to finish the conversation.

Donahue ignored Beth and Ron. "This was a low-profile arrangement. Now, between the city, country, politicians, and a goddamn Hollywood production snooping around, this place is on people's radar."

Hector, watching from the sidelines, frowned. "What the hell is he talking about?"

Paloma's smirk faded. "Marge?"

Ron didn't move, then he moved quickly from the table, grabbing Donahue's arm escorting him to the office, and out of this conversation.

Donahue, still pissed, ran a hand through his hair. "If people start *asking questions* about what's been stored here, it's not just *your* ass on the line."

Marge followed Donahue to the office. As she walked in, she asked, "Are you *threatening* us, Donahue?"

Donahue exhaled. "I'm warning you."

Silence.

Then, Hector came walking into the office, inviting himself. The old man was over seventy, but the way he squared his shoulders? He might as well have been twenty again.

"Ron." His voice was steady. "What's in those trailers?"

Ron didn't answer.

Because for the first time in a long time? He didn't know what to say.

Donahue watched. Waited. Let the silence do its work. Finally, he shook his head. "Figure this all out, Trenton. Before someone else does."

He turned on his heel and left as quickly as he arrived. Leaving behind a dinner that didn't feel so fun anymore.

As soon as the SUV was gone, Hector turned back to Ron.

"What the hell was *that*?"

Paloma frowned. "Who exactly are you in business with?"

Marge sighed. "It's complicated."

Hector scoffed. "That's what people say when they've stepped in shit and don't know how to scrape it off."

Ron, for once, didn't have a snappy comeback.

Because deep down? He knew Hector was right.

Beth, arms crossed, finally broke the silence. "So. Are we completely screwed, or just *mostly* screwed?"

Ron exhaled. "I don't know yet."

And for the first time since buying the junkyard, he felt something he hadn't before.

Fear and doubt.

CHAPTER 42

After Michael Donahue's little performance, Ron didn't sleep much that night; things at the Yard felt different.

Not immediately. Not obviously. But there was a shift. A sense of waiting.

For what?

Hell if Ron knew. But it wasn't good.

And judging by how Hector and Paloma stayed behind after dinner, sitting on the porch long after the kids had gone inside, they felt it too.

Ron was about halfway through his third beer when Hector finally broke the silence.

"You're in deep shit, aren't you?"

Ron exhaled. "That depends. How good are you at ignoring

things?"

Hector smirked, but it didn't reach his eyes. "Not as good as you seem to think."

Paloma, who had been watching the Yard like she expected something to jump out of the shadows, finally turned to Marge.

"That man—Donahue. He doesn't talk like someone making a suggestion. He talks like someone issuing orders."

Marge nodded. "Yeah, well. That's the problem, isn't it?"

Paloma tapped her fingers against her glass. "What exactly is being stored in those trailers?" Ron froze. "We don't ask."

Hector gave him a long, disappointed look. "Bullshit."

Ron frowned. "I mean it. That was the deal. We don't look, we don't ask, and we get paid."

Paloma inhaled sharply. "Ronald Trenton, goddamnit."

Ron winced. Everyone only used his full name when he was about to be scolded or divorced. Paloma leaned forward, voice sharp. "That's the kind of arrangement that gets people killed. What about your family?"

She continued, "Getting yourself killed because you deal with bad people, that shit is on you, but it's not just you, it's a wife and nine kids. Goddamnit. That sonofabitch is dangerous, I can tell that a mile away."

Ron forced a smirk. "Now you sound like Marge."

Marge kicked his chair.

Hector sighed and his voice softened. "Look, kids. You're handling yourself better than we thought, but this? This is a mistake. It's really bad."

Ron rubbed his face. "You think I don't know that?"

Paloma's eyes narrowed. "Then why are you still involved?"

Ron didn't answer right away because the truth was complicated.

The money was too good, and the risk seemed lower in the beginning. For a long time, it had felt like they were actually winning at growing the business.

But now?

Now, *Donahue* was worried.

Which meant *Ron* should be too.

Hector leaned back in his chair, arms crossed, gaze steady.

"Alright. If you're not gonna cut ties, what's your next move? Let's get serious here. You've got a problem—what are the options for solutions?"

Ron let out a long sigh, running a hand through his hair.

We're upping security. Keep our heads down. Hope Donahue gets bored."

Hector raised an eyebrow. "*Hope?* That's your plan?"

Ron shrugged, forcing a grin. "Hey, it's worked before."

Hector shook his head slowly. "Donahue doesn't seem like the type to get bored. He seems like the type to get *even.*"

The grin faded from Ron's face.

Yeah, that was exactly what worried him.

Hector's eyes widened. "That's a shitty plan, goddamn distaster in fact." Ron subdued. "Yeah, well, it's the only one I've got."

Paloma wasn't convinced. "We know people, Ron. People who can help."

Marge frowned. "What kind of people?"

Hector hesitated. "The kind who don't like guys like Donahue." Ron stared at him. "You mean cops?"

Paloma laughed once, dry and sharp. "No, mijo. We mean the *other kind* of people."

Ron blinked. "Oh. Shit. Mmm."

That was… an interesting development.

Marge smirked. "How illegal are these people?"

Hector chuckled. "Depends on your definition, illegal in the US or when they break the law? It is a complicated question, young lady."

The tension eased for a minute.

Beth had been "casually" loitering by the window for the last ten minutes. Finally, she stepped out onto the porch where everyone had migrated, arms crossed.

"So, just to summarize: We're keeping the Yard, keeping the shady business arrangement, *and* possibly getting involved with some off-the-books enforcers?"

Ron said in a very serious tone. "Beth, go to bed."

Beth grinned. "Nah, this is way more fun."

Hector chuckled. "She's smart."

Beth beamed. "See? Someone appreciates me."

Ron grumbled to Marge. "Help me please."

Beth ignored him. "Look. We all know this Donahue guy isn't gonna *go away.* So why don't we stop pretending we're not in a shitstorm and start planning for it?"

Paloma nodded approvingly. "I like this one."

Marge turned around. "Beth. Enough, I am not repeating myself. Gone."

Beth saluted. "Aye aye, Captain Denial, " she then pointed at Ron because she didn't want Marge to think she was being smart."

After another hour of arguing, plotting, and considering their extremely limited options, Hector and Paloma finally stood.

Paloma looked at Ron. "We're going to make some calls. See what we can find out about Donahue that might help or not."

Ron hesitated. "I don't want you two caught up in this."

Hector smirked, leaning forward with that familiar glint in his eye.

"*Kid,* we ran this place for four decades. You think we don't know how to handle trouble? *Please.* We used to eat trouble for breakfast and piss solutions for dinner."

The room went quiet for a beat.

Then Marge burst out laughing, nearly spilling her drink.

"*Did you make that up, Hector?*"

Hector grinned, shrugging.

"Eh… might've borrowed it from a movie we saw last month. But I liked it. *Pretty good, huh?*"

Ron laughed slowly. "Yeah, yeah. Real poetic. Next, you'll tell me you bleed motor oil and sweat success?"

Hector leaned back with a wink. "Only on Thursdays."

Marge shook her head, still smiling. "Jesus. You old timers and your lines."

Hector pointed at her, still grinning. "Hey, don't knock it. Kept this place running for *years.*"

Ron sighed, glancing toward the Yard.

"Well, let's hope that tough-gal and guy wisdom still works. We're gonna need it."

Hector raised his drink in a mock toast.

"To eating trouble and pissing solutions."

Marge and Paloma groaned but clinked glasses anyway.

"*Unbelievable.*"

Ron exhaled. "I just don't want to owe more people favors."

Paloma patted his shoulder. "Too late, mijo. You're family."

Ron swallowed hard. And just like that, Hector and Paloma were in.

Ron woke up the next morning feeling like a truck had run him over. Not because he'd been drinking.

Just… everything.

Beth had been right. This was a shitstorm. And pretending it wasn't wasn't gonna help.

As he walked out onto the porch, coffee in hand, he found Hector and Paloma's truck already gone.

But on the porch table? A note.

"We'll be in touch. In the meantime, keep your doors locked, and cameras pointed toward the trailers."

Marge walked out, coffee in hand. "They gone?"

Ron nodded. "Yeah."

Marge took a sip. "Good. Now we wait." Ron exhaled. "I hate waiting."

Marge smirked. "Then you're gonna *really* hate today."

Ron frowned. "Why?"

And then, from inside, Joey screamed.

"THE TOASTER'S ON FIRE!"

Ron groaned. "Jesus *Christ.*" Marge snorted. "Told you."

And just like that? Another day at the Yard began. Only this time, they weren't just surviving or underestimating. They were preparing for a local war of sorts.

CHAPTER 43

Ron was trying to drink his coffee in peace. Key word: trying.

He was desperate after Donahue's last visit and the conversation with Hector and Polamo, he shared some of what was going on with the trailers. He also regretted it as soon as he finished.

The old men were already well into their morning routine.

Manny and Luis were arguing about whether real trucks had automatic transmissions. Reggie was reading the newspaper and making judgmental noises. Earl was watching everything in silence, like a goddamn hawk. And Hamish?

Hamish was laughing his ass off.

"Well, well, well," he wheezed, slapping the table. "Look at you, Ronnie-boy. Finally knee-deep in the kinda mess that makes life *interesting.*"

Ron sighed. "I don't want life to be interesting, Hamish. I want life to be *predictable* and *profitable.*"

Manny snorted. "Then you should've opened a goddamn grocery store instead of a junkyard."

Earl, who had been sipping his coffee slowly, finally spoke.

"You boy got a problem."

Ron exhaled. "No shit."

Earl nodded, tapping his cigarette against the ashtray. "We know some things. Might be time to share 'em."

Ron blinked. Then stared at Luis.

"What?"

Luis took a long drag of his cigarette. "Councilwoman Dolores Vega. She's my niece."

Ron set his coffee down. "And you're just now telling me this?"

Luis shrugged. "You didn't ask me, and it didn't seem important until now."

Reggie laughed. "Kid, you should know by now—everybody's connected in this town. Ain't nobody six degrees from anything in either Albuquerque or New Mexico."

Ron groaned. "Jesus Christ."

Luis leaned back in his chair. "I ain't saying she's dirty. But I *am* saying she knows more than she lets on."

Earl nodded. "Wouldn't surprise me, she knows about Donahue. Woman like her? She doesn't like shadows in her city."

Flipping through an old car magazine, Manny muttered, "Then she sure as hell ain't gonna like Donahue."

Reggie grinned.

"Funny thing, boys. Y'all ever wonder how I know so much?"

Ron raised an eyebrow. "Because you're nosy as hell?"

Reggie laughed. "That, and because I've been in AA for twenty years. And lemme tell you something—drunks? They talk."

Ron stared. "Are you telling me you have dirt on half the politicians in this state because of *AA meetings*?"

Reggie grinned wider. "Kid. I know things that'd make your *hair curl*."

Hamish cackled. "And they know yours, aye?"

Reggie nodded, still laughing. "Hell yeah, they do. Keeps the balance and peace, putting your secrets into the light."

Earl, who had been watching quietly, muttered, "So what do we do with that information?"

Reggie tapped his fingers on the table.

"We do what we do best. We bullshit."

Luis started waving his hands around. "Stop, stop. I forgot to talk about something the other day."

Earl what tribe are you a member? Earl's expression never changed,

"Navajo/Diné."

"You're Not Cherokee?"

Earl sighed. "Ain't never said I was."

Ron blinked. "Wait. So you're *not* Cherokee?"

Earl smiled. "Hell no. Always been Diné."

Hamish choked on his coffee. "Wait a bloody minute. Ye mean to tell me we've been callin' ye 'Cherokee Earl' all these years and ye never corrected us?!"

Earl shrugged. "Wasn't worth the argument."

Ron rubbed his temples. "Jesus Christ. You guys are something."

Walking past as she seems to do a lot, Beth overheard and immediately yelled, "CULTURAL APPROPRIATION, EARL!"

Earl grinned. "Nah. Just letting idiots be idiots."

Earl stretched out his legs. "Now, I ain't Cherokee. But I *do* know some people."

Ron turned his head more, interested and piqued. "What kind of people?"

Earl, deadpan. "The kind who run half the damn military installations in this state."

Ron paused. "...What do you mean?"

Earl took another slow sip of coffee. "I mean, I know some folks in the Air Force. And a couple even in the Space Force. High-ranking types. The kind Donahue wouldn't want sniffing around."

Manny whistled. "Well, ain't that interestin'."

Ron leaned forward. "You think you could make some calls?"

Earl shrugged. "Don't gotta call. I got a poker game next week with two of 'em."

Reggie laughed. "Donahue, you done fucked up. You pissed off the old men's network."

Ron confused. "I don't even know how this happened, you all are involved."

Hamish grinned. "Aye, lad. But it's happenin'."

The old men talked and plotted. They had connections, dirt, and a willingness to use them to help Ron and Marge.

And most importantly? They had nothing to lose.

Ron leaned back in his chair, rubbing his face.

This was either the best plan they'd ever come up with…

Or the dumbest.

Marge walked in, took one look at the group, and sighed.

"Do I even want to know?"

Ron smirked. "Probably not."

And for the first time in a while? Ron actually felt hopeful.

Because Donahue had money and power.

But the Trentons had something better. They had old men with relationships, willingness, and a belief in justice.

And that was *way* more dangerous.

CHAPTER 44

Ron had officially lost control. Not that he'd ever really had control, but at least before, it had been the illusion of control.

Now?

Now he had:

Hector and Paloma are asking dangerous questions.

Old bastards in the Bullshit Club plotting like a rogue intelligence agency.

Local politicians are sniffing around the operation.

And, apparently, the goddamn U.S. military getting involved.

The Bullshit Coffee Club, Hector, and Paloma all gathered at the Yard after dark.

Because nothing good ever started with, "Meet me at the junkyard at 9 PM."

Marge poured a drink. "Alright, let's hear it."

Earl, who somehow always looked like he knew something you didn't, leaned back in his chair. "Made a call. Got some ears pointed in Donahue's direction."

Ron sighed. "Earl. Who exactly did you call?"

Earl smirked. "A friend."

Hamish cackled. "A friend who happens to be a *four-star general* in the Air Force."

Ron stared. "WHAT?"

Earl shrugged. "We served together back in the day. Guy owes me several favors."

Hector whistled. "Shit, Earl. You're really calling in favors."

Paloma, who had been watching Earl closely, finally asked, "And what exactly does your general friend think about Donahue?"

Earl took a slow drag of his cigarette.

"He thinks Donahue is into something *big, way bigger than a trailer in an Albuquerque junkyard."*

Earl continued. "Donahue's name has been floating around certain circles. Not just business. Government circles."

Ron felt his stomach drop.

"Federal? Like what type of agencies?"

Earl nodded. "FBI's poking around. So is the DoD."

Reggie chuckled. "Kid, you pissed off a guy who's on the government's shit list. This keeps gettin' better, not in a good way."

Ron groaned. "I hate this. I hate all of this."

Hector crossed his arms. "So what's our next move?"

Paloma had been quiet up until this point. Then, without saying a word, she pulled out her phone and dialed a number.

Everyone watched.

Who the hell was *she* calling?

"Matias, it's me," she said, her voice low.

Ron blinked. "Who the hell is Matias?"

Paloma held up a finger, silencing him. "Yeah, I need a favor. No, not that kind. I need information."

Pause. Then she smirked. "You owe me, cabrón. Start talking." Paloma hung up a few minutes later, looking unusually smug.

Ron folded his arms. "Well?"

Paloma sipped her whiskey. "Matias knows things."

Hector shook his head. "That man is a goddamn problem solver, a Wolf."

Ron frowned. "Define 'problem solver,' and explain what a "Wolf" means.'"

Manny grinned. "The kind of guy you call when your *other* guy fucks up."

Ron sighed heavily. "Jesus Christ."

Paloma finally explained. "Donahue's got more than just shady business deals. He's been moving money around. Big money. Someone's funding him."

Marge raised an eyebrow. "How big?"

Paloma exhaled. "Millions."

Silence.

Ron finally muttered, "Well, that's fucking terrifying. How did you find this out in five minutes, Paloma?"

"I ask the right person, the right questions with enough favors in the bank to get an honest answer." Simple as that, kid.

Ron ran a hand hard through his hair. "Okay. So we've got the military sniffing around, the feds looking into Donahue, and now some 'fixer' in Paloma's back pocket feeding us intel. What the hell are we supposed to do with this?"

Earl smirked. "Simple. We wait. See what shakes loose."

Ron scowled. "I hate waiting."

Marge patted his back. "Sucks to be you, unless you have a better plan, babe."

As everyone left the meeting, Ron sat on the porch, watching the night, trying to disappear into the darkness.

The junkyard felt different now.

Not just a business. Not just a home. A battleground.

And Ron?

He wasn't sure if he was ready for war. But it was coming.

CHAPTER 45

He was losing his goddamn mind. Not in the usual, business-is-a-nightmare, kids-are-too-loud, Donahue-is-gonna-get-us-killed kind of way.

No.

This time?

It was because, somehow, everything with the kids was actually going well, while other parts of the business were not so much.

Danny would've been at the top of the list if you'd asked Ron six months ago which kid was most likely to burn down a building in a failed science experiment.

The kid was about ten years old. Loved taking things apart. Hated rules.

But now?

Danny was thriving. Not just doing fine. Not just getting by.

Really Thriving.

His teachers had started sending home actual praise, which Ron hadn't even known was a thing teachers did.

One even wrote:

"Danny has an incredible mechanical mind. His problem-solving skills are years ahead of his age. With guidance, he could have a real future in engineering."

Ron read that note five times. Then checked the name.

Then asked Marge, "Did Danny bribe or hypnotize his teacher?"

Marge laughed. "No, Ron. That boy is actually smart." Ron grumbled. "Well, now I have to rethink my entire worldview."

Marge just patted his shoulder. "Tough break, babe."

Beth and Ivy had both gotten jobs away from the Yard.

Beth was working at a small independent (indie) bookstore, surrounded by old paperbacks and judgmental silence.

She loved it.

Ivy? She was doing even better.

She'd gotten a job at a local bakery and—shocking absolutely everyone—she was good at it. Like, really good.

One day, Ron had stopped by to see how she was doing. And he had never been more terrified in his life. Ivy had been smiling.

Actually smiling.

Not her usual dry smirk. A real, actual, human smile. It had freaked Ron out so bad he had to leave. Marge had found him sitting in the truck, staring blankly at the dashboard.

"What's wrong with you?" she asked.

Ron exhaled. "Ivy was smiling."

Marge frowned. "So?"

Ron turned to her, haunted. "She was smiling because she was *happy.*"

Marge laughed. "Jesus, Ron. Kids are allowed to be happy."

Ron shook his head. "No. Something's wrong. The universe is setting us up. This is a *trap. A parent trap. He smirked.*"

Marge rolled her eyes. "You're an idiot."

Ryder had somehow kept his jobs at the bookstore and electronics place. They weren't allowed to stop by for a visit, he said they both had problems in the past with employee friends, so they just banned visiting.

Beth had bet against him lasting more than two weeks.

She had lost.

His boss? Loved him per what little Ryder shared, and did show a performance review. "He doesn't bother customers, organizes shelves perfectly, and never complains."

Beth, mildly horrified, muttered, "They hired a psychopath and called it good customer service."

Ron, equally horrified, muttered, "I think that's just retail, kid."

Max was still making weird science projects in the garage. He had not blown anything up yet. But he was probably going to.

Meanwhile, Marge, Grace, and Lewis were completely unfazed by everything, as it was their superpower.

While Ron was having a slow-moving nervous breakdown, Marge just kept going.

Paying bills. Running the business. Raising kids.

The usual. Mostly happy, except for Donahue.

One night, Ron finally cracked.

"How the hell are you so calm?!" he demanded.

Marge sipped her whiskey. "Because someone has to be."

Ron groaned. "Jesus. The kids are doing fine. Business is running smoothly. Donahue hasn't shown up in weeks. This is *too much peace.* Something *terrible* is coming."

Marge shrugged. "Probably but no update, and quiet is our best right now."

Ron gaped at her. "That's it?! *Probably??*"

Marge grinned. "Yeah. But we'll handle it."

Ron rubbed his face. "I hate you so much when you're calm, reasonable, and opposite of me losing my shit.."

Marge patted his cheek. "No, you don't."

And annoyingly, she was right.

Despite everything…

The kids were doing well.

Marge was steady.

And Ron?

Ron was trying to survive, because peace never lasted.

CHAPTER 46

The Bullshit Club was in session, spread out in their usual spots in the garage with the kids in toe—Joey, Beth, Danny, Lewis, Max, Manny, and Luis. The table was covered in snack wrappers, half-drunk sodas, an ashtray, and a deck of cards no one actually played with.

Joey held up the tin of biscochitos, peered inside, and let out a horrified gasp. "Who ate the last one?"

Reclining with her boots on the toolbox, Beth casually popped the last bite into her mouth and shrugged. "You snooze, you lose."

Lewis clutched his chest like he'd been shot. "That's *treason*, Beth. *Actual* betrayal."

Danny snorted, flipping through an old car magazine. "First rule of the Old People Club—if you leave food unguarded, it's free game."

Manny, leaning back in his chair, grinned. "Harsh, young man. We are old but can still whoop you if need be. But you gotta protect what's yours."

Joey groaned. "You don't even like biscochitos like I do. You eat them."

Beth dusted off her hands, smirking. "And yet, here we are."

Max shook his head. "Tough break, lil dude. But I saw her eyeing that tin for like an hour. You had time."

Luis, barely awake in the corner, muttered, "Or at least licked it first."

Manny laughed. "Yeah, but then you risk someone calling your bluff."

Luis opened one eye. "True. *Very* high-stakes move kids, let that be a lesson."

Ray, one of the old codgers who just arrived suddenly chimed in. "You know, back in the day, we settled things like this with fists."

Beth grinned. "You wanna take this outside, Joey?"

Joey sighed dramatically, shaking his head. "Unforgivable."

Beth grinned wider, reaching over and stealing the last sip of his soda for good measure.

Manny snorted. "Damn, she's cold. I knew I liked her." He then awkwardly raised his hand for a high-five.

Beth stared at it for a second, then gave him a half-hearted slap before going back to her drink.

Manny nodded approvingly. "Good enough."

Luis finally sat up and stretched. "This is why you always gotta have a backup snack." He pulled a churro from a brown paper bag and took a slow, smug bite.

Joey stared at him in betrayal. "*You had that the whole time?*"

Luis grinned. "And I *guard* my snacks."

Joey muttered something under his breath, already planning his revenge.

Outside, past the sound of laughter and good-natured insults, Ron sat alone on the back steps, staring out into the dark. The warm glow from the garage barely reached him, flickering against the dirt and gravel like an afterthought.

He could still hear them—Beth, Joey, Manny, the whole bunch of them, laughing about something stupid. It was good. It meant things were *normal*, at least for now.

Ron had spent weeks waiting for disaster to strike.

Instead? Everything kept getting better, and it was unnerving.

Marge had just finished tallying the monthly numbers when the office phone rang.

Still skeptical about their last movie deal, Ron didn't bother answering.

Marge did.

"Trenton Salvage."

Pause.

Marge smirked. "Oh? You need more junk? Sorry, *vintage* scrap."

Ron froze mid-coffee sip.

Marge held up a finger to silence him. "Uh-huh. Yeah. We can work something out."

Another pause.

Marge raised an eyebrow. "Wait. Did you say *three* productions?"

Ron choked on his coffee. "THREE?!"

Marge ignored him.

"Send over a list. We'll see what we've got."

She hung up and turned to Ron, looking far too pleased with herself.

"Congratulations. We're officially Hollywood's favorite junkyard."

Ron groaned. "Oh, for fuck's sake."

By the end of the week, they had three separate film crews coming to the Yard for props.

One was for another sci-fi project. One was for a modern Western. And the third? A full-blown post-apocalyptic series.

Beth read the email and smirked. "We're basically selling the end of the world. Fitting."

Ron sighed. "They're gonna try to lowball us again."

Marge grinned. "Good thing we like negotiations."

Ron rubbed his temples. "I hate negotiations."

With so much money coming in, Marge made a decision.

The kids were getting a share.

Beth and Ivy? Got raises for their jobs. Danny? Got a full set of professional tools.

Ryder? Got noise-canceling headphones and a gift card to the bookstore.

Max? Got a small science lab setup (with strict safety rules). Grace, got a new microscope, she was loving science, with Lewis, got a 3-day art camp at the University for kids. Joey? Got… well, Marge still hadn't decided.

Ron, watching all of this, muttered, "You're spoiling them."

Marge shrugged. "They work hard."

Ron sighed. "I know they work hard. So fine. But no goats. I draw the line there."

Max, overhearing, groaned. "Ugh, Ron, c'mon!"

Ron laughed.

"We'll wear him down." Beth grinned.

Ron pointed at her. "Over my dead body, kiddo."

The *real* surprise came a few days later. A black SUV pulled into the Yard.

Ron groaned. "If that's Donahue, I swear to God—"

Then the door opened. And out stepped one of the actresses from the sci-fi movie.

Ron blinked.

Beth squinted. "Wait. Is that—?"

Marge raised an eyebrow, arms crossed. "*The* lead actress. Huh."

Ron sighed, rubbing his face. "*Great.* More Hollywood nonsense."

He wasn't impressed by stars of any kind. The only ones that caught his attention were the rough-and-tumble types from *Junkyard Kings* or those treasure hunters on *Gold Digging: Global.* At least *they* got their hands dirty.

But *this?*

Annika Wells.

Famous as hell. Probably too rich for her own good. The kind of celebrity whose face was plastered on magazines Marge flipped through at the grocery store but never bought.

And here she was.

Striding across the Yard in designer boots that had no business touching dirt, sunglasses still on, looking around with curious eyes like she'd stepped onto another planet.

Ron muttered under his breath, "This place better not end up on some home makeover show."

Marge smirked, glancing sideways at him. "What? Afraid she's gonna redecorate the Yard?"

"She's welcome to try," Ron grumbled. "But if she touches my wrenches, we'll have a problem."

Annika paused near a rusted-out Chevy, pushing her sunglasses up just enough to get a better look. "*Interesting,*" she murmured.

Marge leaned toward Ron.

"Looks like someone's about to get real interested in 'Hollywood nonsense.'"

Ron crossed his arms. "Not a chance."

But the way his gaze followed Annika's every step?

Marge wasn't convinced.

She met her first. "You lost, sweetheart?"

Annika smiled slightly. "No. Just wanted to see the place for myself."

Ron grunted. "It's a junkyard."

Annika laughed. "Yeah, but it's a *good* junkyard."

Beth whispered to Marge, "Did she just compliment the trash?"

Marge elbowed her. "You mean the Yard or Ron?" Beth contained her laugh.

Annika glanced at Ron. "You don't seem impressed."

Ron crossed his arms. "Lady, we sell rusted-out cars and appliance parts for a living. I'm not gonna lose my shit over a movie star in my junkyard."

Annika grinned. "See, that's why I like you guys."

Ron raised an eyebrow. "Uh-huh."

Annika stuck around longer than expected.

She asked about the business. Talked to Marge about running things. Even sat with the Bullshit Club for coffee, which terrified Ron.

At one point, Reggie pointed at her.

"You ever met any politicians, sweetheart?"

Annika smirked. "Too many."

Reggie grinned. "They as full of shit as they seem?"

Annika sipped her coffee. "Worse."

Hamish cackled. "Aye, I like this one."

By the time Annika left, Ron had to admit…She wasn't bad.

Even if she did make Beth insufferable for the rest of the day.

"I'm just saying, we should leverage this! Maybe start selling celebrity-approved junk!" Beth mused.

Ron groaned. "No."

Beth grinned. "Just hear me out—"

Ron walked away. Because at this point? Saying *no* was just a formality.

CHAPTER 47

Three rules for dealing with Hollywood people, Ron lived by them.

1. Don't trust them.
2. Make them pay up front.
3. Avoid unnecessary conversations.

So far, two out of three have already been broken.

The film company had sent another email. Then another. Then an actual human person showed up at the office—some poor production assistant who looked like he hadn't slept in three days.

Marge welcomed him in with coffee.

"Ron?" He asked.

Ron just leaned against the counter, arms crossed, waiting for the bullshit.

The guy—Chris, late 20s, deeply overworked— pulled out a list.

"So, uh… we need a few more things." Ron grunted. "Of course you do."

Chris looked at Marge instead. "A few… specialty items."

Beth, sitting in the corner, smirked. "Specialty? What, like a spaceship?"

Chris hesitated.

Marge raised an eyebrow. "Wait. Do you *actually* need a spaceship?"

Chris laughed nervously. "Not a *real* one. But we need parts that *look* real."

Ron sighed. "Kid, this is a junkyard. Not Area 51."

Chris rechecked his list. "Do you have any, uh… weird-looking mechanical panels? Control boards? Anything industrial but vaguely futuristic?"

Marge looked at Ron.

Ron looked at Marge.

Then they both looked at Ezra.

Ezra, standing in the doorway, grinned. "Oh, I can make something."

Ron groaned. "Jesus Christ."

Chris, still looking exhausted, ran through a ridiculous list of requests.

Old CRT monitors. Rusty chain-link fencing. Strange metal pipes. Barbed wire.

Beth, still smirking, whispered to Ron. "Basically, they want trash. Premium-priced trash." Ron sighed. "Yep."

Marge folded her arms. "Alright. Here's the deal. We'll pull what we have; if you need custom work, it costs extra."

Chris blinked. "Custom work?"

Ezra grinned. "I can make you a spaceship console that looks like it actually *does* something."

Chris's eyes lit up. "How fast?"

Ezra tilted his head. "How much are you paying?"

Marge smirked. "We'll send over an estimate."

Chris looked relieved. "Great. I'll tell the production team."

Ron ran a hand over his face. "God help me."

The next morning, the first payment hit their account. **$25,000.** For literal junk. Marge, holding up the bank statement, grinned. "You still hate them?"

Ron didn't even hesitate. "Yes."

Beth rolled past in an office chair. "Then you'll *really* hate what I did."

Ron's stomach sank. "Beth. No."

Beth, grinning too much, pulled out her phone. "I set up a website."

"Jesus *Christ.*" Ron groaned.

Marge leaned over. "'Trenton Salvage: Hollywood's Premier Junkyard'? Beth, that's *genius.*"

Beth spun in her chair. "I *know.*"

Ron rubbed his temples. "This is my nightmare."

Two days later, another black SUV pulled up. Ron braced himself.

Out stepped Annika Wells. Again.

Wearing perfectly casual sunglasses, as if it were normal for an A-list actress to show up at a junkyard twice in one week.

Beth, barely containing her glee, leaned over to Ivy and Lewis. "If she shows up a *third* time, we have to kidnap her."

Ivy sipped her coffee. "Agreed."

Annika walked over, hands in her pockets. "Hey."

Marge, unfazed, nodded. "Back for more?" Annika smiled. "Honestly? Just wanted to hang out for a bit."

Ron blinked. "Why?" He never asked a more sincere question.

Annika laughed. "Because I like it here. You all treat me normally."

Beth grinned. "Because we don't give a shit about celebrity status?"

Annika pointed at her. "Exactly."

Ron muttered, "We should be charging for this."

Beth perked up. "Oh! Should we sell celebrity junkyard tours?"

Marge smacked the back of her head. "No. Knock it off."

Beth pouted. "You never..........."

Annika, to Ron's complete horror, wandered back over to the Bullshit Club.

The old men stared at her. Annika stared back. Then she grabbed a cup of coffee and sat down like she belonged there.

"Does anyone have a cigar? Cover me this time. I'll bring a box of Cubans back next time," Annika said.

Hamish leaned forward. "So, lass. Whit's yer joab again?"

Annika smirked. "I pretend to be other people for a living."

Reggie grinned. "So a politician in this city."

The table erupted in loud uncontrollable laughter.

Annika just sipped her coffee, completely at home. She seemed excited that they had decent cigars. She clipped the end, and lit it a blaze like a pro.

Ron watched from a distance.

Beth elbowed him. "You're jealous."

Ron scowled. "Of what?"

Beth grinned. "She fit right into the Bullshit Club faster than you did."

Ron groaned. "I *hate* everything about this place today, except for the money we make. And not jealous." He then walked away to another part of the Yard not my the Bullshit Club.

CHAPTER 48

Business was booming. Hollywood was paying them obscene amounts of money. The kids were thriving, doing beyond expectations.

And Ron? Ron was waiting for the universe to kick him in the teeth. They needed help at the Yard, so interviewing potential employees wasn't helping his mood.

Instead of doing the healthy thing—like talking to Marge, taking a day off, or accepting that things were actually going well—Ron did what he always did when life got too good.

He started making bad financial decisions.

Not *illegal* ones. Not *dangerous* ones. Just... deeply questionable business ideas.

Ron had read a stupid article about how people were buying up "authentic" items from movie sets for thousands of dollars.

So, naturally, he had a brilliant idea. "We should start selling junk as 'movie memorabilia.'"

Marge looked up from the books. "Ron, that's literally just lying."

Ron shrugged. "Hollywood does it all the time."

Beth, overhearing. "Ohhh, I *love* this. Let's list some stuff online. 'Post-Apocalyptic Scrap—As Seen in [Insert Movie Here]!'"

Marge rubbed her temples. "Jesus Christ, not you too."

Beth grinned. "Ron, if this works, I want a cut. And help."

Ron pointed at her. "Fine. But if we get sued, you're taking the fall." Beth saluted. "Obviously, but my cut goes up, more risk, mo-money!"

Annika Wells—the A-list actress who wouldn't leave—had mentioned how "peaceful" the junkyard was.

Ron, desperate for more cash flow, latched onto that idea like a drowning man grabbing a life raft.

"What if we sell the 'junkyard aesthetic' as an *experience*?" Ron suggested.

Marge gave him a long, unimpressed stare. "Are you suggesting we turn this place into a B&B-like place?"

Ron grinned. "People *pay* for 'gritty, rustic getaways.'"

Marge leaned back. "You mean they pay to sleep in trash."

Ron shrugged. "Rich people are weird."

Beth, who had been typing something on her laptop, suddenly muttered, "Shit."

Marge narrowed her eyes. "What?"

Beth spun the screen around.

She had found two separate listings for junkyards that had been turned into "gritty luxury camping retreats." One was charging $300 a night.

Marge sighed heavily. "I hate the world. No way, I am wrong about the level of bad idea this really is…."

Beth grinned at Ron. "So… we're doing this?"

Ron grinned back. "Oh, absolutely."

Marge groaned. This one wasn't really illegal. Mostly.

Ron had discovered that some collectors paid ridiculous prices for "one-of-a-kind" industrial salvage, so he had started secretly organizing an invite-only junk auction.

Marge walked in on the first one just as Ron described an old rusted sign as a "rare mid-century piece, rich with industrial history."

Marge folded her arms. "Ron. That's literally from a gas station that went out of business five years ago."

Ron did not flinch. "It's *vintage*."

Marge stared at him.

Ron sipped his beer.

Beth, standing nearby, whispered, "Holy shit, I think he's getting away with it."

Marge sighed. "You're all going to hell. Ron, you're the worst example for the kids, I am no better, because I stick around with the madness."

The week got more interesting. Ezra finally got his MIT offer letter. While Ron was spiraling into a capitalist fever dream, Ezra was quietly dealing with something way bigger.

He had applied to MIT on a whim.

Not because he *wanted* to leave. But because that's what smart people were supposed to do, right?

He didn't tell anyone. Not until the letter arrived.

Ezra sat at the kitchen table, envelope in hand, staring at it like it was a bomb.

Sitting across from him, Ryder finally muttered, "You gonna open it or set it on fire?"

Ezra exhaled. "Not sure yet."

Ryder shrugged. "Either way, we will support you."

Ezra rolled his eyes but smiled slightly.

Finally, he ripped it open.

Beth, walking by, saw the letter. "Holy shit. MIT letter?"

Ezra nodded. "Yeah."

Beth grinned. "Damn, man. That's huge!" Then she proceeded to shout at the top of her lungs, **come to the kitchen**, even rang the new dinner bell, Lewis and Ron installed on the lowest roof off the back steps.

Ezra wasn't happy about all the extra attention he received at his moment of indecision about MIT.

Beth frowned. "Wait. You don't sound happy."

Ezra sighed.

Because how the hell was he supposed to explain this? MIT was MIT. It was everything a kid like him was supposed to want.

But…

It wasn't the Yard. It wasn't this family.

Beth, ever perceptive, leaned against the counter. "You don't wanna go, do you?"

Ezra hesitated. "...I don't know."

Beth crossed her arms. "Alright. Say MIT didn't exist. What would you do?"

Ezra thought about it.

He liked fixing things. He liked building things. And, despite himself, he liked being part of this chaotic mess.

"...I'd stay."

Beth nodded. "Then maybe that's your answer."

Ezra ran a hand across his face. "Everyone's gonna say I'm crazy if I don't go."

Beth smirked. "Ron comes up with high-risk money schemes for *fun*. You think *you're* the crazy one?"

Ezra laughed despite himself.

Beth clapped him on the shoulder. "Whatever you choose, it's gotta be *your* choice. Not what people expect. Got it?"

Ezra nodded slowly. "...Yeah, thanks." But he still wasn't sure.

Ron found the MIT letter the next morning.

"MIT?!" he bellowed from the kitchen. "WHY DID NO ONE TELL ME?!"

Ezra groaned. "Jesus, Ron. It's early."

Ron stormed in, waving the letter. "THIS IS A BIG DEAL."

Ezra rubbed his eyes. "I *know*."

Ron paused, then frowned.

"...Why don't you look happy?"

Ezra stayed quiet.

Marge, standing behind Ron, already knew.

She placed a hand on Ron's shoulder.

"Because he doesn't know if he wants to go."

Ron blinked.

Then sat down.

"...Oh. I'm sorry kid, I just assumed."

Ezra exhaled. "I don't wanna leave, Ron. This place—this *family*—it's… I don't know. It's home. My first actual home in my life."

Ron nodded slowly. "...Yeah. It is."

Silence. Then Ron grinned.

"So you're telling me I don't have to deal with fancy MIT people judging me?"

Ezra smirked. "That's one way to look at it."

Ron slapped the table. "Fucking *great*. We keep the genius, and I don't have to pretend to be impressed by nerds in ties."

Marge sighed. "Ron. He still has a decision to make. And we support you no matter what, kiddo."

Ron waved her off. "Eh. He'll figure it out. Either way, he's family."

Ezra looked at Ron.

And for the first time, he felt completely sure.

CHAPTER 49

Marge had decided: The girls **needed a break.**

Hell, *she* needed a break.

And thanks to Lily—their overly competent, slightly terrifying, and increasingly attached lawyer— they were about to get one.

The Plan: Denver, Baby

Lily had pulled some strings, flexed her absurd stockpile of hotel points, and booked them a super classy Westin by Cherry Creek Mall.

She had also pre-paid for a full spa day, meals, and drinks (of course).

Because, as she put it:

"You people live like feral animals. It's time you remember what civilization feels like."

Beth, reading the itinerary, grinned.

"So, just to be clear—we get a bougie-ass hotel, overpriced shopping, and *someone else* is paying for us to be covered in mud and massaged by professionals?"

Lily smirked. "Yes."

Ivy, deadpan: "Sounds fake. But okay."

Grace, actually excited for once: "I call first turn picking music in the minivan."

Beth groaned. "Goddamn it, Grace."

Marge clapped her hands. "Load up, girls. We're getting out of the Yard before Ron can dampen or sabotage this trip."

Renting a minivan was already a point of contention.

Beth refused to let it go.

"Marge. *Marge.* You could've picked *anything* else. A Tahoe. A Jeep. *A horse-drawn carriage.* But no. You picked—"

Marge cut her off. "A vehicle that fits all our crap, gets good mileage, and doesn't scream 'please pull me over, I'm reckless.'"

Beth groaned. "You're killing me."

Grace, from the backseat: "I like the minivan."

Beth whipped around. "Traitor."

Marge, deadpan: "You can walk."

Beth sulked for about 60 miles, then gave it up.

The moment they checked in, Ivy stared at the lobby. "Why does this place smell expensive?"

Beth threw herself onto one of the lobby chairs.

"Lily. I think it might be our sugar mama."

Grace examined the complimentary fruit-infused water. "Do rich people just… drink cucumbers?"

Marge took a deep breath. "Jesus Christ. We haven't even gotten to the rooms yet."

The spa employees were not prepared.

Beth refused to shut up during her massage.

"Listen. I don't mean to brag, but I have *the* most stress out of all of us. Can I get, like, *bonus* relaxation?"

Ivy, half-asleep already: "Shut up, Beth."

In the facial treatment room, Grace is staring at herself covered in a charcoal mask: "I look like I'm about to rob a bank."

Marge was starting to enjoy herself.

Then her phone rang. She almost ignored it.

But the caller ID?

"FBI - Denver Field Office."

Her entire mood shifted. She stood up, walked outside, and answered. "This better be fucking good."

A pause.

Then a calm, professional voice.

"Mrs. Trenton, we need to speak with you. In person." Marge gritted her teeth. "I'm on *vacation*."

The agent didn't miss a beat.

"Then it's convenient you're already in Denver."

Beth took one look at her face and immediately said, "Ah, shit. What happened?"

Marge grabbed her drink, downed it in one gulp, and scowled. "The FBI wants to talk."

Silence.

Then Ivy, completely unbothered: "Cool. Before or after we go shopping?"

Beth grinned. "I vote after. If Marge is going to be interrogated, she should at least look rich as hell." This was one of those magical ideas that was ridiculous on the surface, but due to the situation, everyone was onboard and thought it brilliant.

Grace, nodding: "Strategic intimidation."

Lily called: "Marge. You want me there?"

Marge exhaled.

Then cracked her neck.

"No. Then, there was a long pause. Yes, if you can come up, Lily. Thank you," Marge said.

If they wanna waste my fucking vacation, they're gonna deal with me at full force." Marge grabbed the car keys. "Let's go spend Lily's money before I end up on a goddamn nofly watchlist."

CHAPTER 50

Marge had one rule for dealing with law enforcement. Never let them control the conversation. So when the FBI decided to ruin her vacation, she decided to ruin their day right back.

Beth had insisted that if Marge was going to war with the feds, she had to look like she owned Denver.

Which meant purchase, thanks to Lily:

A black designer blazer.

A pair of absurdly expensive sunglasses.

Boots that could stomp a man's soul into dust.

When Marge stepped out of the hotel lobby, the girls paused.

Beth whistled. "Holy shit. You look like you're about to fire someone *just for breathing wrong*."

Ivy nodded. "I'd be afraid of you in a boardroom."

Grace, dead serious: "I'm a little afraid of you right now."

Marge adjusted her sunglasses.

"Good."

Lily had caught the first flight out of Albuquerque.

By the time she stepped out of her Uber at the Denver FBI field office, she looked just as deadly as Marge.

Her heels clicked on the pavement. "Marge. You ready?"

Marge cracked her neck. "Always."

Lily smirked. "Let's make their day hell."

The FBI had two agents waiting. Both mid-40s, suits that were too stiff, expressions that screamed 'I take myself too seriously.'

The lead agent, Special Agent Carter, gestured for Marge to sit.

She did—sprawling out like she owned the damn place.

Lily sat beside her, crossing her legs elegantly, pulling out a notepad she probably wouldn't even use to make them nervous.

Agent Carter cleared his throat. "Mrs. Trenton, do you know why we asked to speak with you?"

Marge smirked. "Because you love wasting taxpayer money?"

Carter paused.

Lily hid a smile.

The second agent, Agent Mills, tried again. "We're looking into Michael Donahue."

Marge tilted her head. "Oh. That asshole."

Carter narrowed his eyes. "So you admit you've worked with him?"

Marge sighed dramatically. "I admit that he occasionally pays us for storage. Everything beyond that? Not my problem."

Lily nodded. "My client has been running a legitimate salvage and storage business. Any criminal activity on Donahue's end is his own burden."

Carter leaned forward. "But you *have* noticed unusual activity."

Marge grinned. "I notice a lot of things, Agent Carter. Some of them are important. Some of them are just dumbasses in expensive suits trying to intimidate me."

Carter's jaw tightened.

Mills sighed. "Mrs. Trenton, we're not here to antagonize you."

Marge leaned forward. "Then do your fucking job and go after Donahue. Because I guarantee you—*he's* the problem. Not me."

Silence.

Then Carter exhaled sharply. "So you're saying you don't know what's in the trailers."

Marge's expression didn't change. "Not a damn thing."

Carter studied her.

Lily clicked her pen. "Unless you have an actual charge against my client, I believe we're done here."

Mills hesitated. "Mrs. Trenton, if you ever—"

Marge stood up.

"We're done here."

Lily smiled, leading her toward the door like a goddamn queen escorting another queen out of a peasant's home.

The moment Marge and Lily stepped out of the FBI office, Beth was waiting in the minivan.

She rolled down the window.

"So… did you get arrested or are we good?"

Marge smirked. "We're good."

Beth fist-pumped. "Hell yeah. Now get in. We're going to lunch on Lily's tab."

Lily groaned. "Jesus Christ, Beth."

Grace, poking her head out of the backseat: "Wait. Can we get room service *and* charge it to Lily?"

Ivy, flatly: "Obviously."

Lily laughed. "I need better friends and family. Or less quality for less money." She was glad to help, and had incredible resources at her disposal.

Marge, grinning for the first time all day, climbed into the minivan.

"Let's go, girls. Denver isn't ready for us."

CHAPTER 51

The girls had barely made it back to the hotel before Ron called.

And by "called," what actually happened was:

Marge picked up her phone, saw 18 missed calls from Ron, and muttered, "Goddamn it. What is so important, you blow my phone up."

Beth smirked, eating a stolen macaron from the fancy hotel gift basket. "Oooh. Someone's in trouble."

Marge sighed. "Someone's *always* in trouble. Might as well get it over with."

She put Ron on speaker. "WHAT THE FUCK, MARGE?!"

Already pouring herself a drink, Lily muttered, "Oh boy."

Marge exhaled. "Ron. Breathe."

"BREATHE?! THE FUCKING FBI JUST CALLED ME!"

Beth, amused: "Oooooh, they called *you* too? We should start a fan club."

Ron ignored her. "Why the *hell* are you talking to the Feds while *on vacation*?!"

Marge, calm as ever: "Because they asked nicely." Beth laughed. "That is *not* what happened."

Ron groaned so loudly it sounded like he was dying.

"Marge. You know what happens when the FBI starts poking around, right? They don't just *stop* because you gave them your best 'fuck off' face."

Marge smirked. "It was a *very* good 'fuck off' face, everyone said so."

Lily, sipping her whiskey, almost spit it out: "It really was. I'd rate it a solid nine out of ten."

Ron was not amused. "For fuck's sake, Marge! This isn't a joke!"

Marge sighed. "I know."

Silence.

Beth, not understanding the concept of "reading the room," whispered, "So… are we still doing room service on Lily's card, or—"

Marge hung up on Ron before he could start yelling again.

Lily downed the rest of her drink. "I swear to God, Beth."

Ron was not handling this well. He was pacing the porch, whiskey in hand, muttering curses like a lunatic. Ezra sat on the steps, watching him. "You okay?"

Ron snapped. "No, I'm fucking NOT okay. The FBI is up our asses, and Marge is out there *shopping* like she's not on a goddamn watchlist already!"

Ezra nodded. "So, regular Tuesday then?"

Ron took a deep breath. "You know what? Fuck it. I need another drink."

He poured himself another glass of decent tequila and sat down.

"This is fine. This is all fine. We'll move to Mexico. Maybe open a taco stand. Well, learn to cook, cook tacos well, and then finally open one."

Ezra, raising an eyebrow: "Ron. We literally can't even keep track of Joey. You think we can run an international business, running from the FBI?"

Ron sighed. "Good point. Canada, then. No new language to learn." He was starting to legitimately spiral into a dark place with a bit of paranoia. Ezra thought, get some food into him to help chill him out, or the Bullshit Club might need called for help.

Marge, Beth, Ivy, Grace, and Lily were absolutely having a ball, compartmentalizing how wound up Ron might be! Ron's meltdown? Not their problem.

The adults were slightly drunk on expensive cocktails, shopping in stores where no one expected them to buy anything, and thoroughly enjoying themselves.

Beth held up a $700 designer bag. "This costs more than my *soul*."

Ivy, eying a display of overpriced jeans: "Who pays $400 to look homeless? No disrespect meant to the homeless of course."

Grace, frowning at a pair of heels: "These don't even *look* comfortable."

Lily, completely unbothered, sipping champagne: "Ah. Capitalism at its finest."

Marge, holding her cocktail: "To crime."

They all clinked glasses.

Beth smirked. "You're so cool, Mom."

Marge grinned. "I know." Then the group laughed, it was an odd and good day with just the gals in Denver.

Marge was halfway through a $19 cocktail when her phone rang. Again.

She checked the caller ID. FBI. Again.

She sighed. "Fucking *really?*"

Beth grabbed a fry. "If you get arrested, can I have your boots?"

Marge answered the call. "What."

Agent Carter's voice was irritatingly calm.

"Mrs. Trenton, we need to continue this conversation."

Marge took a deep, slow breath.

"Oh, do you? Because I seem to remember telling you to fuck off."

Carter ignored that. "We believe you have more information than you let on."

Marge gritted her teeth, voice dropping to a low, dangerous tone.

"*Listen, Fed.* If you think I'm lying, *charge me with something*—or get the fuck off my phone."

She was *done* with the half-accusations and veiled threats. The liquor she'd been sipping wasn't helping either—if anything, it was kicking in, sharpening her edges.

And a *spicy* Marge was *never* easy to deal with.

There was a pause on the other end of the line.

Marge didn't wait.

"Thought so." *Click.*

She tossed the phone on the counter, muttering, "*Bureaucratic bastards.*"

Lily, watching from across the table, grinned. "She's handling it well."

Grace, deadpan: "Is she?"

Beth, whispering: "I love this."

Carter sounded unfazed.

"Mrs. Trenton, we're not accusing you of anything. Yet."

Marge scoffed. "Oh, how generous of you."

Pause.

Then, Carter said something that actually made her blood run cold.

"We have reason to believe Michael Donahue's operations aren't just illegal. They're dangerous." Marge's grip tightened on her drink.

"Define 'dangerous.'"

Carter hesitated. "We can't disclose that."

Marge leaned forward.

"Then fuck off until you can."

She hung up.

Lily, setting down her drink, exhaled.

"Alright. It's time we talk about this a bit more in-depth, please." Lily went into complete attorney mode.

Marge leaned her head into her hand. "God, I hate when you say that."

Lily leaned forward. "They're not going away, Marge. They think we know something, and Donahue? Are the Feds actually afraid of him? That means *we* need to be, too."

Beth, for once, looked serious.

"So… what do we do?"

Marge sighed. Then downed the rest of her drink.

CHAPTER 52

By the time the minivan rolled back into Albuquerque, the girls were equally exhausted and victorious.

They had eaten food that didn't come from a dented can.

They had messed with rich people in high-end stores.

They had not had to force Lily to finance their nonsense.

All in all? A perfect trip.

Marge pulled into the junkyard at 9:42 PM, just late enough that the night air smelled like cooling metal and motor oil.

The moment she put the van in park, Joey sprinted outside in his pajamas, waving his arms like a lunatic.

"YOU'RE BACK, MOM! MAX SET SOMETHING ON FIRE!"

Marge closed her eyes. "Jesus fucking Christ." Then hugged the little man.

Hacking a bag of overpriced clothes out of the trunk, Beth muttered, "I was gone for *three days*."

Ezra leaned against the porch railing, smirking. "Technically, it was more of a *small* fire, not that big of a deal really."

Ron, standing beside him with a beer, scowled. "A fire is a fucking fire, Ezra."

Max, poking his head out the door: "It was *contained*!"

Marge exhaled slowly. "I'm too tired for this shit." She went to bed, no conversation had with her and Ron. That can got kicked down the road for the night.

Ivy, dragging her suitcase, smirked. "Welcome home, Marge."

The next morning, Marge found Ron sitting with the Bullshit Club in their usual corner, drinking coffee like he was bracing himself for bad news.

Hector and Paloma had also stopped by, which meant this meeting was actually serious.

Marge grabbed a cup, sat down, and sighed. "Alright. What did we miss?"

Earl, always one to cut the bullshit, exhaled. "Donahue's moving fast."

Manny nodded. "He's got people watching the Yard."

Marge stiffened. "What kind of people?"

Hamish, smirking slightly: "The kind who have guns, and sit in cars too long and think they're bein' subtle."

Ron groaned. "Fucking *great, give all the good news first.*"

Paloma leaned forward, her sharp eyes calculating. "We need more options here, folks. These are not great ways to deal with any of this."

Hector grunted. "Problem is, Donahue's got too many people in his pocket. We can't just push him out. It's a big problem."

Earl took a slow sip of coffee. "Then we make it expensive for him to stay."

Marge raised an eyebrow. "How do we do that?"

Earl smirked. "Pressure. From above, below, and sideways."

Luis tapped his cigarette against the table. "My niece— Councilwoman Vega? She's looking for an excuse to go after people like Donahue. We give her enough breadcrumbs, she'll make his life hell."

Ron frowned. "You think she'll actually take him on? And keep our name out of it?"

Luis chuckled. "She's young, ambitious, and thinks she can fix the world. That's dangerous for a guy like Donahue."

Ever the quiet strategist, Earl muttered, "I've been talking to some old friends. Higher-ranking ones."

Ron narrowed his eyes. "And?"

Earl smirked. "They don't like Donahue either. The second they have an excuse to move in? They will. But it is weird, they've left him alone this long, can't figure why."

Marge sat up. "Are we talking 'official investigation' or 'off-the-books problem-solving'?"

Earl grinned. "Depends on how much we push and their interest align with ours."

Paloma, ever practical, leaned forward. "We go after his money and supply chain once we know what he sells. That we still don't know. We might need to look under those tarps."

Manny nodded. "Donahue's power ain't just about muscle. It's about *funding*. You squeeze his cash flow? He starts making mistakes. If we can figure out what is going on, there seems to be a veil of protection around him and his operations."

Ron exhaled. "Alright. So we have government pressure, military pressure, and financial pressure. Maybe, if we figure out what he is doing."

Ron sighed. "Yeah. We need to sorta piss some people off. But if we don't? He's just gonna keep squeezing *us*."

Marge stared at the table, thinking. They were cornered, and being helpful.

For the first time? They actually had a strategy coming together to deal with this whole situation.

She looked at Ron. "We doing this?" Ron took a deep breath. "Yeah. We're doing this." And just like that? The war against Donahue had officially begun.

CHAPTER 53

Raising nine kids who were basically feral(ish). Running a junkyard that somehow became a Hollywood supplier. Getting tangled up with a shady asshole like Donahue.

It was a full year.

But nothing, not a single goddamn thing, prepared him for this particular brand of stress.

The Bullshit Club, Hector, and Paloma had laid out their three-pronged plan to make Donahue's life hell. Ron had agreed.

Which was why, at 10 AM on a Monday, he was sitting at the kitchen table, drinking whiskey like it was coffee.

Ezra, passing by with a bowl of cereal, paused. "Isn't it a little early for that?"

Ron took another sip. "Not if your life is a goddamn nightmare."

Ezra nodded. "Fair enough, Ron. Don't make it a habit."

Luis's niece, Councilwoman Vega, had agreed to meet with Marge and Hector.

Reading up on city zoning laws, Marge muttered, "If we do this right, we can make every business Donahue owns a bureaucratic nightmare."

Ron grunted. "You're saying we drown him in paperwork?"

Hector grinned. "Like a motherfucker."

Beth, walking by, smirked. Dang Hector, colorful language. "You *weaponized* government inefficiency? I'm so proud of you guys."

Earl had been making calls. The kind of calls that didn't get logged anywhere.

He sat at the Bullshit Club table, smirking. "Got confirmation. The right people are interested in Donahue."

Ron narrowed his eyes. "'Interested' how?"

Earl chuckled. "The 'let's see if we can ruin his life' kind of interested."

Reggie, laughing into his coffee, added, "You know how these old military types are. They *love* taking down smug little pricks."

Ron sighed. "Jesus. This is either gonna save us or get us killed."

Hamish patted his shoulder. "Aye, lad. That's *life*."

Ron took another sip of whiskey. "I fucking hate life."

Paloma had been quietly digging. And what she found? Was delicious. She dropped a stack of papers on the table.

"Donahue's been moving money through shell companies. A lot of it, and extra hard to find."

Marge leaned forward. "Illegal?"

Paloma grinned. "Most definitely."

Ron rubbed his face. "Jesus Christ. How do you even find this shit?"

Paloma smirked. "Sweetheart, I ran a business for forty years. I know how criminals hide their money." She continued to laugh, she knew what she was doing, an experienced businesswoman.

Ron exhaled. "Alright. So what do we *do* with this?"

Paloma grinned wider. "We expose it. Quietly. Anonymously. And make sure the right people notice."

Manny chuckled. "By the time Donahue figures out what's happening, half his money's gonna be frozen enough to be complicated."

Beth appeared from nowhere, grinning like a little demon: "Ohhh, I *love* this plan."

Ron just drank more whiskey, he could handle a lot. While all the scheming was happening, the kids were being absolute menaces.

Max and Danny? Had decided to "rebuild" a motorcycle.

Which sounded great in theory. Except they had entirely disassembled it and seemed to have no fucking idea how to put it back together.

Ron found them covered in grease, surrounded by parts, staring at the mess they'd made. Max scratched his head. "Sooo… I think we lost track of what went where."

Danny, completely unbothered: "We'll figure it out."

Ron sighed. "Jesus Christ. If I step on a fucking spark plug, one of you is *dead*."

Joey? Was trying to build a catapult.

Ryder? Was watching him, sipping a Coke, and not stopping him.

Ron rubbed his temples. "Ryder. Buddy. Pal. Why are you letting this happen?"

Ryder shrugged. "Social experiment?"

Ron groaned. "I hate science."

By 6 PM, Ron had reached his limit. Between the FBI watching them, the kids being insane, and the active conspiracy to ruin Donahue, he needed a goddamn break.

So he did the only logical thing. He walked to the Bullshit Club's corner, sat down, and poured himself a very large drink, and lit a cigar.

Marge, watching from the porch, yelled. "Rough day, old man?"

Ron glared at her. "We're committing *high-level* fuckery, Marge."

Marge sat down next to him. "Yeah. And, we can do this, we'll handle it then not get involved with this shit again."

Ron took a deep breath. Then exhaled. Then drank.

Then muttered, "Fuck it. Let's burn his empire down."

Marge grinned. "That's the spirit. And you're done drinking, I mean it."

Beth, passing by, smirked. "Ron, you've gone full villain arc. I love it."

Hamish raised his glass. "Then drink, lad. It doesn't get better."

And for the first time in weeks, Ron laughed, finished off his last glass of whatever booze made it over the ice cubes. Then went to bed early, stumbled a little to the house.

Because this was his life now. And if he was gonna be in a shitstorm? He was gonna own the goddamn storm. He was going to continue to tell himself that, over and over again.

CHAPTER 54

Not the FBI, not Donahue, not even the goddamn Hollywood nonsense, could have prepared him for this.

Because today?

Beth brought home a boy.

And the entire goddamn family lost its mind. It started innocently enough.

Beth walked into the Yard after work, bag slung over her shoulder, sipping an overpriced iced coffee, with some random guy walking beside her.

Ron was sitting with the Bullshit Club at their usual table, half-listening to Hamish bitch about property taxes.

Then he saw Beth and the boy.

He did a double-take. Then a triple-take. Then he stood up so fast his chair nearly tipped over.

"WHO THE FUCK IS THAT?"

Beth sighed loudly. "Oh my god, Pop. Chill."

The boy—tall, dark-haired, vaguely terrified—looking—awkwardly lifted a hand. "Uh. Hi?"

In under 30 seconds, the entire goddamn junkyard mobilized.

Marge stepped out of the office, arms crossed, immediately

analyzing the situation like a drill sergeant.

Ivy and Grace came running from the house, exchanging excited looks.

Joey actually climbed onto a stack of tires for a better view.

Danny and Max appeared, whispering like the nosy little shits they were.

Lewis, not home or he wouldn't of been in the middle of it.

Ezra was working, likely would got the story later anyway.

Ryder? Stood in the background, sipping a Coke, fully enjoying the chaos.

Beth groaned. "Oh my god, you people are insane."

Ron, completely ignoring her, pointed at the boy. "STATE YOUR BUSINESS."

The guy blinked. "...What?"

Beth rolled her eyes. "Ron. Stop interrogating him like he's a fucking spy."

Ron crossed his arms. "That language. I'll stop when I get some goddamn answers." He couldn't help but laugh at himself. Nevertheless, he was in character at that point.

Marge, amused but pretending to be neutral, smirked. "Beth. Introduce your friend before Ron has a stroke."

Beth sighed. "This is Nick. He works at the bookstore with me. He's a *friend*."

Still looking vaguely like he might die at any moment, Nick managed a weak smile. "Nice to meet you, Sir."

Ron squinted. "A *friend*?"

Beth groaned. "YES. JUST A FRIEND. CALM YOUR SHIT."

Grace, smirking: "But is he cute tho?"

Beth threw a pen at her.

Ron was still glaring. "How old are you?"

Nick shifted uncomfortably. "Uh. Seventeen?"

Ron, to Marge: "That's a grown man."

Beth facepalmed. She was holding in the hysterical laughter.

Joey, from the tire stack: "Do we like him, or are we chasing him off?"

Ron was considering all the options, staying in his character!

Marge sighed. "Jesus Christ. Nick, do you want dinner?"

Nick was visibly shaken. "Uh. Yeah. Sure."

Beth muttered to Nick as they walked inside. "You're gonna need a goddamn drink after this."

"I'm only seventeen, Beth" Nick said.

"That was a test, Nick, you passed, but I do need a drink now." Beth nodded.

Nick whispered back. "Do they usually act like this?"

Beth deadpanned: "No. This is better than usual."

While Ron was having a full-blown scripted crisis, Ezra and the tech crew were launching their new online retail and auction site. He didn't know what fun he was missing at the Yard.

Ezra had built the commerce site from scratch, with Ivy and Beth handling the marketing and inventory for the Yard.

Their goal? To sell high-end salvage and rare junk directly to collectors, movie people, and weird rich people.

They had barely gone live when the first order hit. Then another, and another.

By the end of the first day?

$1,129 in sales.

Ron and Marge were dumbfounded.

"$1,100? From selling old shit online?" Ron muttered, staring at a screen of the stats.

Ezra smirked. "Technically, it's *high-value industrial salvage*."

Beth, grinning: "And now? We're a *luxury brand*."

Ron just stared. "Jesus Christ. I don't even know what's real anymore."

Their lawyer, family, and friend, Lily, showed up the next morning already stressed.

"Why did you launch already? I need to review your terms of service before someone sues you. More success means more litigation."

Beth shrugged. "Ezra wrote them. We're good."

Lily pinched the bridge of her nose. "Ezra. How *legally sound* are they?"

Ezra paused and muttered, "They're… functional. I copied the edit from a big brand for us."

Lily groaned. "Oh my god, plagiarism, and they're garbage. Please send them to me. I need them in the next hour or sooner."

Ron clapped Ezra on the back. "Welcome to running a real business, kid. Where lawyers ruin all the fun."

Lily pointed at him. "I *heard that*, and keep you out of the debtor's prison and general jail"

Ron grinned. "I *wanted* you to hear, and thanks, Lily."

By the time Sunday night rolled around, things had finally settled.

Beth's male friend had survived dinner without a nervous breakdown.

The online store had made its first five thousand dollars.

Ron had survived yet another emotional rollercoaster week.

And despite all the insanity hanging over their heads, the Yard was still running along quite smoothly.

Marge clinked rocks glasses with Ron on the porch. "Not bad for a weekend."

Ron sighed. "I hate how well things are going. Makes me nervous."

Marge smirked. "Relax, Ron. The next disaster will be here soon enough."

Ron muttered into his drink. "That's what I'm afraid of."

And somewhere out there, Donahue was plotting.

But for tonight? The Trenton family had won this round.

CHAPTER 55

Marge and Ron needed a break. Not the "quick beer on the porch while the kids break something" kind of break.

Not the "locking the office door and pretending not to hear Joey screaming" kind of break. A real break.

So, with Lily promising to keep the kids from burning down the Yard and Hector and Paloma watching for Donahue-related issues, Marge booked them a suite at a fancy-ass casino hotel, 20 minutes outside of town, for the

For one night, they were gonna drink, eat, and have tons of sex like they did when they were younger.

It did not go 100% according to plan. But it was still a damn good night.

They arrived at the hotel just after sunset.

Giant chandeliers in the lobby.

A front desk clerk who looked vaguely terrified of them, which was weird.

A bar that actually served decent whiskey.

Ron, sipping his drink at the bar, sighed happily. "God, I forgot what it's like to be somewhere that doesn't smell like motor oil and charred tires."

Marge smirked. "I don't know, Ron. You still smell like both."

Ron grinned. "That's just my natural essence, baby."

Marge picked the restaurant.

It was one of those places where the plates were too big and the portions were too small.

Ron stared at his "artfully plated" steak and muttered, "This costs more than a car battery."

Marge, cutting into hers, smirked. "Just eat, Ron. Dessert will be worth it, I can promise you that."

Ron, grumbling but still eating: "Swear to God, if I'm still hungry, I'm getting a burger from room service."

Marge laughed. "If you can still walk by the time we get to the room, I'm doing something wrong."

Ron nearly choked on his steak.

Marge, pleased with herself, took another sip of her drink.

They were fairly drunk, laughing, and feeling twenty years younger when they stumbled back to the room.

Marge pushed Ron against the hotel door, kissing him hard.

Ron, grinning against her lips, muttered, "You keep this up, I might not even need that burger."

Marge smirked. "Oh, you're still gonna need it. Just *after*."

Ron groaned. "Jesus Christ, I love you."

They barely made it inside before things started heating up.

Shirts off. Hands everywhere. Marge straddled him on the fancy hotel bed.

And then—

Ron's goddamn phone rang.

Ron ignored it. For exactly three rings.

Then Marge's phone rang. Then the hotel room phone.

Marge stopped, breathless. "That's not good."

Ron groaned, grabbing his cell. "If this isn't an emergency, someone is fucking *dead*."

It was Earl.

The Bad News (Because There's Always Bad News) Earl didn't waste time.

"Donahue's moving."

Ron's buzz evaporated instantly. "What do you mean, *moving*?"

"He's got people shifting assets. Accounts closing. Trailers are being relocated. He knows something's coming. He got tipped off somehow."

Marge, already throwing her shirt back on, muttered, "Goddamn it."

Earl sighed. "You two better enjoy whatever the hell you're doing, 'cause when you get back? It's gonna be a shitshow."

Ron exhaled. "It's *always* a shitshow."

Click. Call ended.

Ron looked at Marge. Marge looked at Ron. Both frustrated. Both half-dressed.

Both knowing they had a goddamn mess waiting for them back home.

Marge sighed. "Well. That killed the mood."

Ron, rubbing his face: "Not completely. We still got, like… thirty minutes before I start panicking again."

Marge laughed. "Make it count, Trenton."

And despite everything? They did.

By the time they checked out the next morning, they were:

Slightly hungover, and mentally bracing for disaster.

Aware that Donahue was onto them.

Wondering how dangerous it was going to get.

Not ready to go home.

Ron pulled Marge in for one last kiss before they got in the truck.

"Next time? We turn our fucking phones off."

Marge smirked. "Next time, we leave the country."

Ron sighed. "Honestly? Not a bad idea."

And with that, they drove back to Albuquerque, knowing full well:

Their little vacation was over. And shit was about to hit the fan.

Ryder got a text and rushed back to the electronics place to work. He entered the side door, slid his badge, and entered a room that had four others talking and watching monitors. He opened a locked box, pulling a badge, 9mm, and five extra clips.

CHAPTER 56

Ryder wasn't the type to get sentimental, but lately, something about the junkyard felt… different.

Maybe it was the way Marge looked at him sometimes, like she was trying to figure out how to keep him from leaving without actually saying it.

Or maybe it was because Ezra had started talking about the future.

And Ryder?

Ryder didn't have a goddamn plan. He worked daily on not getting attached to the who Trenton family.

"So, what's next for you?" Ezra asked.

They were sitting on the roof of the old RV, watching the sun set over the junkyard. Ryder had spent years avoiding conversations like this, but Ezra had a way of making them happen anyway.

Ryder shrugged. "Not dying?"

Ezra smirked. "Solid plan. Very ambitious."

Ryder rolled his eyes. "What about you?"

Ezra tossed a screwdriver in the air and caught it without looking. "Got accepted to a couple of places, MIT. Mainly tech programs. Engineering stuff."

Ryder glanced at him. "MIT, and?"

Ezra hesitated. "And I don't know."

That was new.

Ezra always had a plan. The fact that he wasn't jumping at the chance to leave meant something.

"You're hesitating," Ryder said. He had noticed consistent changes with Ezra the last month or two; he actually liked it here.

Ezra exhaled. "Yeah, well. It's complicated."

Ryder smirked. "So, your whole *I'm better than you idiots'* thing was just an act?"

Ezra frowned. "Shut up."

But Ryder knew the truth now.

Ezra wasn't sure if he wanted to leave either.

And that? That was dangerous.

Because it meant Ryder would have to start thinking about what came next.

And Ryder hated that. He was mission-oriented for a reason—focusing on the job meant he didn't have to think about anything else. The future was messy, uncertain. He preferred the clarity of now.

While Ryder wrestled with his creeping thoughts, the rest of the kids, as usual, were busy causing chaos.

Beth, Danny, and Ivy had somehow convinced Ron to let them "reorganize" the storage yard.

Which, in Ron's head, meant sorting parts and labeling shelves.

What did it actually mean? Building a goddamn racetrack for go-kart demolition derby.

Standing on top of a stack of tires, Max raised his arms. "LADIES

AND GENTLEMEN! WELCOME TO THE FIRST ANNUAL JUNKYARD DEATH RACE!"

Ron, walking outside with a fresh cup of coffee, took one look at the makeshift racetrack, saw Beth tightening a homemade seatbelt out of duct tape, and just turned around.

"Nope. Not dealing with this. Whatever happened to the soccer pitch I talked about?"

Marge, stepping out of the office, immediately squinted.

"What the hell are you idiots doing?" Beth grinned. "Team bonding!"

Danny, tightening a motorized leaf blower to the back of his kart for extra speed, gave a thumbs-up. "Science!"

Max cackled. "VIOLENCE!"

Marge sighed and rubbed her face. "I need stronger coffee, super black and 100 proof. Damn kids."

Ezra, watching from a safe distance, leaned over to Ryder. "This is why we can't have nice things."

Ryder smirked. "It's impressive, honestly."

Ezra nodded. "Yeah. They're definitely gonna die."

Marge screamed. "I'm giving you all five minutes before I shut this down."

Beth grinned. "Five minutes is all we need."

And then? Then everything went straight to hell.

The first fifteen seconds were glorious, epic almost.

Danny took an early lead, his leaf-blower-powered go-kart screaming around the first turn. Beth was right behind him, steering with one hand and holding a literal wrench as a weapon in the other.

Max?

Max wasn't steering at all. He was standing on his go-kart, surfing it like a psychopath.

Marge immediately regretted everything. "MAXWELL JAMES, SIT YOUR ASS DOWN!" Max, grinning like a lunatic, yelled, "I CAN'T HEAR YOU OVER THE SOUND OF MY FREEDOM!"

Then Joey, the smallest and most dangerous of the bunch, took a shortcut through a pile of scrap metal, hit a bump, went airborne, and cackled like a demon.

Ron, stepping outside just in time to see this, blinked.

He took a sip of coffee. Waved to Ivy, who was smart enough to keep her distance.

Then, very calmly, said, "Marge. The children are feral, and I blame you, Trenton. All your ideas from the beginning."

Beth and Danny slammed into each other at full speed, spun out, and took Max with them.

Still standing, Max backflipped off the kart, landed in a pile of cushions, and yelled, "I AM A ICARUS!"

Ryder and Ezra exchanged glances. Ezra nodded. "That was impressive." Ryder shrugged. "Yeah, it was."

The race ended when Beth's duct-tape seatbelt failed, sending her tumbling into a pile of tires. Max declared himself the winner. Beth threw a wrench at him.

Marge finally snapped. "THAT'S IT! THIS IS WHY WE I CAN'T SLEEP AT NIGHT!"

The kids scattered with the faint, yelling, " Sorry Mom, Love you.

Marge rubbed her temples. "I swear to god, you're all going to be the reason I end up in prison."

Ron patted her shoulder. "Yeah. But at least it'd be quiet there."

Marge wasn't impressed by the observation.

After the Great Death Race disaster, Ryder found himself back on the RV roof, thinking about the future again. He got another text: "Deliver the TV to this address this afternoon. Watch your step, steep steps."

Ryder thought through the carefully phrased instructions. He now carried a weapon with 24/7.

Ezra sat next to him, messing with a circuit board.

"Who keeps texting you?" Ezra asked, staring at his phone.

Ryder showed him the text, it's work, I need to deliver a TV this afternoon. That satisfied Ezra's curiosity.

"Marge isn't gonna kick us out." Ryder said.

Ezra surprised. "No. Where did that come from?" Ryder didn't know why he said that.

Ryder didn't answer. He quickly crawled down off the RV and headed to his room to answer a more message on a secure text platform.

Later that night, Ryder was avoiding everyone when Marge found him.

It wasn't hard to find him. The kid had a routine. Anytime something remotely emotional happened, he disappeared to his designated pondering spot, which tonight happened to be the roof of the old RV at the edge of the Yard.

No one knew that the RV roof was the ideal spot for surveillance of the trailers, the exits, and the only entrance to the Yard.

Marge climbed up without asking, cigarette in hand, and just… waited.

She was good at waiting. She could out-silence anyone.

Ryder sighed, staring at the sky like it had personally offended him. "I know you're about to say something meaningful and parent-y, so just do it and get it over with."

Marge smirked. "I was just gonna say you're an idiot."

Ryder paused. "Wow. So wise. Why did you share that golden nugget?"

Marge took a drag of her cigarette. "Look, kid. You don't have to figure everything out right now."

Ryder hated that that actually made him feel better.

"But," Marge continued, "you have to figure out what you want."

Ryder exhaled, dragging a hand through his hair. "I don't know what I want."

Marge nodded. "That's fine. Just don't assume you have to leave to find it."

Ryder didn't answer. Because fuck, what if she was right? Except there were extenuating circumstances she may never know about.

Marge flicked her cigarette away, stretched, and stood up. "Come inside when you're done pouting or thinking, whatever you call it."

Ryder smirked. "I don't brood." Marge smiled. "Kid, you invented brooding."

Then she climbed down and walked off, leaving Ryder with too many thoughts and no desire to deal with them. He had to stay focused, which is one of the big challenges in deep cover jobs.

He sat there a while. Not thinking. Just watching.

Marge's silhouette moved across the yard, stepping into the house with that same unshakeable presence she always had.

And it hit Ryder, really hit him, that she never stopped.

Marge never fucking stopped. If something broke, she fixed it. If someone was hungry, she fed them. If someone was too damn proud to admit they needed help—she helped anyway.

And she never asked for a goddamn thing in return.

She just did it.

And Ryder? Ryder had spent months acting like this was all temporary. Like Marge was just another adult who would eventually shove him into the following shitty situation and be done with it. He was excellent at his job.

She wouldn't. Because she was Marge. And she wasn't going anywhere. Ryder thought, Fuck, just fuck.

He finally climbed down from the RV and went inside.

The house was quiet, mostly. Ezra was still awake, tapping away at some probably-complex, possibly illegal project on his laptop, but everyone else was passed out.

Ryder went to the kitchen and opened the fridge.

He didn't know what he wanted, but standing there, staring at discount milk and questionable leftovers, seemed like a metaphor for his life at this point.

The light flicked on. It was Marge, of course.

"You gonna stand there until the food organizes itself, or you actually looking for something?"

Ryder sighed and grabbed a soda. "Just thinking."

Marge raised an eyebrow. "Dangerous hobby, and expensive cooling the room while you think, kiddo."

Ryder popped the can open. "Tell me about it."

Marge grabbed a glass and poured herself a very large whiskey. She leaned against the counter and just… looked at him.

Ryder shifted uncomfortably. "What?"

Marge took a sip. "You're thinking about leaving."

Ryder stiffened. "I—"

Marge cut him off. "Look, kid. If you wanna go, that's up to you. But if you're thinking about leaving just because you think you're supposed to, that's fucking stupid. We're your family, like it or not, chosen family, sweetheart."

Ryder blinked. "You swear when you give pep talks to only me?" He was fighting off the tears, and couldn't believe he was getting so emotional.

Marge smirked. "You respond better to it."

Ryder hesitated. "I just… I don't know. I've never stayed anywhere this long."

Marge took another sip of whiskey. "Then maybe it's about time you did."

Ryder didn't know what to say. Marge didn't push, which was part of her magic with people.

She just downed the rest of her drink, coughed a bit, and she had more than she thought in that last drink. She patted him on the shoulder, and muttered, "Don't wake me up if you decide to dramatically pack your shit and leave in the middle of the night. I am tired, kiddo."

She smiled. And with that, she left. Because that's who Marge was.

She didn't do big emotional speeches. She just told you the truth, handed you a way out, and let you decide what to do with it.

The following sunrise, came what felt like almost immediately.

The kids were in rare form, almost from the beginning bell. Lewis had somehow superglued his fingers together.

Beth threatened to shave half of Danny's head if he didn't admit she was right about carburetor placement. Joey and Grace were attempting to ride a bicycle off the roof. I always thought Grace knew better than to do that, but Joey is convincing.

Marge, standing in the middle of the drama, just sighed.

"Why do I even try?"

Ryder, watching from the doorway, smirked. "So you're saying if I leave, I don't have to deal with this bullshit?"

Marge looked at him. "If you leave, I'll mail you Max and Joey in a box."

Max perked up. "Ooooh, field trip!"

Ryder laughed. "Noted, Marge."

Marge pointed at him with her coffee mug. "You're staying."

It wasn't a question. It wasn't a demand. It was a fact.

Ryder exhaled and leaned against the doorway.

"Yeah," he muttered. "I think I am for awhile."

Marge just nodded.

Like she already knew.

Like she had been waiting for him to figure it out on his own.

And Ryder? Ryder finally let himself believe it. Was any of it real, no, it couldn't be but for the sake of the assignment, it had to be real enough to believe.

The evening air had cooled a bit, but the conversation around the yard lingered, stretching out like the last rays of sunlight. Marge leaned back in her chair, listening to the familiar rhythm of laughter and easy banter.

It was a good night. A rare, quiet one.

Ron stretched, cracking his back. "Alright, we need anything before we shut down for the night?"

Marge tapped the ash off her cigarette, thinking. "We're low on propane."

Ron nodded. "Gas too."

Manny, sprawled in the chair next to them before gathering himself to go home, gestured lazily toward the road. "Tamale señora, Mrs. Estrada was at the gas station earlier. You might get lucky."

Marge and Ron exchanged a glance.

"Well," Marge said, standing and dusting off her jeans, "wouldn't want to risk missing out."

Ron grinned as he grabbed his keys. "Priorities."

They headed for the truck, leaving behind the hum of family conversation for the glow of gas station lights—and hopefully, a trunk full of tamales.

Marge rolled down the window as the older woman in the beat-up Honda Civic lifted the lid of a massive cooler in her backseat. The rich scent of fresh masa and red chile filled the air.

"How many you want, mija?" the woman asked, her voice warm but all business.

Marge glanced at Ron. "A dozen?"

Ron scoffed. "What are we, amateurs? Two dozen." Marge nodded. "Two dozen."

The woman gave them a knowing smile. "Good choice. You'll regret not buying more." She scooped out carefully wrapped tamales, stacking them in a plastic bag. "Ten bucks a dozen."

Ron handed over the cash without hesitation. "If I had a dollar for every time a homemade tamale changed my life, I could retire."

Marge smirked as she took the bag. "If you had a dollar for every tamale you've eaten, you'd be a millionaire."

Ron unwrapped one immediately, steam rising into the cold air. He took a bite and groaned. "Damn, that's good."

The woman grinned. "Of course, it is."

As Marge drove off, Ron sighed happily. "See, this is why I never trust restaurant tamales. If they're not sold out of a trunk or a backseat, they're not the real deal."

CHAPTER 57

He could handle a lot of things.

Business schemes? Sure. Junkyard disasters? Easy.

Nine chaotic kids constantly testing the limits of his patience? Every damn day.

But teenage relationships?

Absolutely not. It was the worst, the absolute worst. He thought, was he ever a teenager? No way, but he knew the truth: He was likely worse than them all.

And yet, here he was—sitting at the kitchen table, rubbing his head, while Marge and Lily tried to make sense of the absolute catastrophe unfolding before them.

It all started when Beth got caught sneaking back in through her bedroom window at 2 AM.

Marge—who had perfected the skill of knowing when kids were up to something—had been waiting in the dark.

Beth nearly screamed when she turned on the light.

Marge just smiled. "You wanna tell me why you're breaking into your own goddamn house?"

Beth, mid-heart attack, swallowed hard. "I... went for a walk?"

Marge just stared. Beth sighed. "Fine. I was with Riley."

Marge crossed her arms. "Doing what?"

Beth did not like that question.

"Talking," she said.

Marge didn't blink. "In the middle of the night?"

Beth hesitated. "...Among other things?"

Marge took a long, slow breath. "Beth. What things."

Beth groaned, dragging her hands down her face. "Oh my god, please don't make me say it."

Marge stared. "For fuck's sake, Beth, you're fifteen. You even—"

Beth's entire soul left her body. "MARGE. STOP TALKING."

Marge scowled. "I'm just saying—"

"DO NOT SAY IT."

Marge sighed. "We're talking about this in the morning."

Beth groaned. "Fantastic. Can't wait."

Beth was not the only problem.

Because Ezra had a girlfriend now.

And Ryder?

Ryder had a boyfriend.

Which meant Marge and Ron were about to have a truly spectacular meltdown.

Ron sat at the kitchen table, staring into his coffee like it had personally betrayed him.

"You okay?" Marge asked.

"No," Ron muttered. "I am not okay."

Marge sighed. "We knew this would happen eventually."

"Did we?" Ron said. "Because I feel deeply unprepared."

Lily, sitting across from them with her own coffee, smirked. "You two look like you just found out your kids joined a cult."

Marge gave her a flat look. "Lily. Shut the fuck up."

Lily laughed. She took Marge's suggestion in stride.

Ron took a deep breath. "Alright, let's lay it out. We got Beth sneaking out to mess around with Riley, Ezra acting like a goddamn lovesick idiot over some girl, and Ryder—"

"—who has a boyfriend," Marge finished.

Ron blinked. "Wait. What?"

Marge raised an eyebrow. "Did you not know?"

Ron's entire brain short-circuited. " I-no! I did not fucking know!"

Marge exhaled. "Well, now you do."

Ron opened his mouth. Closed it. Took a deep sip of coffee.

Lily watched with pure amusement. "You look like you're about to pass out."

"I might," Ron muttered.

Marge rolled her eyes. "Look, it's not a big deal."

Ron pointed at her. "Not a big—Marge. Beth was sneaking out in the middle of the goddamn night. Ezra is suddenly romantic? And Ryder—Jesus Christ, when did he even start dating other guys?"

Marge exhaled. "We'll talk to them. Like rational adults."

Lily snorted. "You two? Rational? This I gotta see."

Marge flipped her off, not smiling.

Ron took another sip of coffee. Then another. Then another, not saying a word. Then, suddenly, he looked at Marge and blurted, "Were we this fucking bad?"

Marge snorted. "Ron. We were worse."

Lily perked up. "Oh, this. I have to hear about this. I always assumed, but to hear it firsthand is worth the weight."

Ron groaned. "No, you do not."

Marge smirked, leaning back in her chair. "Oh, no, we're doing this. I need you to fully remember what kind of dumbass you and I were before you start freaking out about the kids."

Ron grumbled something unintelligible and took another sip of coffee.

Marge turned to Lily. "Alright, picture this: 1996. Mullets were still in fashion for some people."

Lily snorted. "Jesus. You guys are old but interesting."

"Shut up," Marge said and laughed.

"Anyway," she continued, "Ron was an overconfident idiot who thought he was invincible, and I was a very bored seventeen-year-old with nothing better to do. Well, other than likely masturbation constantly."

Lily's eyes widened. "I don't ever want to hear Ron's name and that word used in the same sentence, I can't, just can't.

"Wait. You were seventeen when you two got together?" Lily said.

Marge smirked. "Yep. I was working in a little diner. Ron was nineteen. And an absolute fucking disaster. Hustling even back then.

Ron groaned. "Can we not?"

Lily grinned. "Oh no, we're absolutely doing this. Please continue."

Marge smiled, "First time Ron ever asked me out, he did it by— Ron, do you wanna tell her?"

Ron dropped his head onto the table. "I will set myself on fire."

Marge cackled. "Fine, I'll do it. This genius—"

Ron cut in, groaning, "—I was young and ambitious."

"—broke into a county fair after hours because he thought it'd be romantic to take me on a 'private' Ferris wheel ride."

Lily's jaw dropped. "You committed a felony on the first date?"

Ron sighed. "It wasn't technically a felony, and it was a second date."

Marge laughed. "He bribed the guy running the ride with twenty bucks and a six-pack."

Ron grumbled, "I was working with what I had, okay?"

Lily wheezed. "Holy shit, that's kind of amazing."

"Oh, it gets better," Marge said. "Because halfway through the ride, the guy left. And guess what? The goddamn ride got stuck."

Lily clapped her hands over her mouth. "No fucking way."

Ron, miserable, muttered, "We were stuck up there for three hours."

Marge grinned. "And he was so goddamn nervous, he dropped the big speech he had planned and just blurted out, 'So, are we doing this or what?'"

Lily fell out of her chair.

Ron groaned. "I hate this conversation."

Marge smirked. "You loved it when I said yes."

Ron sighed. "Yeah. I did."

Lily, recovering from laughter, wiped a tear from her eye. "Okay, but like… what did your families think?"

Marge snorted. "Oh, they fucking hated us."

Ron muttered, "Understatement."

Lily leaned in. "No, no, I need details."

Marge exhaled. "Alright. My mom? Thought Ron was a 'bad influence' and said, and I quote, 'That boy is going to land you in jail or worse—marriage.'"

Lily cackled. "She was right about one of those so far."

Marge nodded. "Yeah, well. She wasn't wrong but, her voice softened, also not right."

Ron sighed. "Meanwhile, my dad took one look at Marge and said, 'That girl's gonna eat you alive.'"

Lily grinned. "Was he wrong?"

Ron exhaled sharply. "Not even a little bit. She is the buzzsaw I met the very first time, still today."

Marge smirked. "He told Ron to 'find a nice, normal girl' instead."

Ron chuckled. "Yeah. And I told him 'normal is fucking boring, and I love this girl.'"

Lily raised her coffee cup. "Respect, Sir."

Marge stretched. "Point is, Ron—we were a fucking disaster. We made every bad decision possible and somehow turned out okay."

Ron grumbled and smiled. "Debatable and true."

Marge nudged him. "So maybe, just maybe, we can chill the fuck out about Beth, Ezra, and Ryder."

Ron sighed, rubbing his face. "Fine. Fine. But I swear to god, if any of them try to pull a stunt like I did—"

Marge smirked. "Then we get to make fun of them for it forever."

Ron thought about it. Then, slowly, grinned. "Okay. Yeah. That's fair."

"We do need to get Beth on birth control, soon." Marge said.

Beth already looked done with life when she sat across from Marge.

"Before you say anything," Beth said, "I already know what you're gonna say."

Marge arched an eyebrow. "Do you?"

Beth nodded. "Don't be dumb, don't get pregnant, and don't think for a second that you can get away with sneaking out without you knowing."

Marge smirked. "Smart girl."

Beth crossed her arms. "Look, I like Riley. And yeah, we… do things. But I'm not stupid."

Marge exhaled. "I know you're not. But you're also fifteen, and I'm still gonna worry."

Beth sighed. "Can I go now?"

She smiled. "You want the condoms talk now or later?"

Beth's soul ascended. "I WILL WALK INTO TRAFFIC. Stop please."

Marge laughed her ass off, then got serious, Beth, it is important, not something to be ashamed, scared or embarrassed about, Okay.

Ezra was not in the mood.

Ron, arms crossed, sat across from him. "So. Girlfriend, huh?"

Ezra blinked. "Yeah?"

Ron narrowed his eyes. "You actually like her, or is this some kind of nerd experiment?"

Ezra rolled his eyes. "Yes, Ron. I am *testing* the human condition."

Ron sighed. "Look, I'm not gonna make a big deal out of this."

Ezra smirked. "That's good, because I wouldn't listen."

"I fucking hate teenagers." Ron groaned.

Ezra grinned. "You will have nine of them. Sucks to be you."

Ron threw a sugar packet at his head. He was getting good at hucking those quickly and accurately.

Marge, Ron, and Lily sat across from him.

Ryder was 100% ready to fight.

"Okay," Ron started, clearly still adjusting. "So. Boyfriend."

Ryder stared. "Yes. Want me to draw you a diagram?"

Ron glared. "Watch it, kid."

Marge sighed. "We're not mad."

Ryder snorted. "Could've fooled me."

Lily smirked. "Relax, moody broody. We're just making sure you're not being an idiot."

Ryder crossed his arms. "I'm always an idiot."

Marge smirked. "And a smartass, just try and listen for 5 minutes."

Ron exhaled. "Look. We're not gonna be those assholes who pretend we get to control your life. But don't think for a goddamn second we won't step in if someone treats you like shit or you them. Not to mention, safe sex, boyfriend or girlfriend, you have to be smart. If you don't it could change your life."

Ryder hesitated but was impressed Ron got serious with a talk.

And Marge saw it. This was new for him. Having adults who gave a shit.

"...Thanks," Ryder muttered.

Ron grunted. "Yeah, yeah. Now get outta here before I start thinking too hard about all this."

Ryder escaped slowly but immediately.

Lily laughed. "You two suck at this but are getting better with each conversation"

Marge groaned. "I need a drink."

Ron grabbed the whiskey. "Pour me one too."

Lily smirked. "Man, you two are soft. It's kinda adorable."

By the night's end, Marge and Ron sat outside, watching the kids wreak havoc as usual." That sucked but needed to be done." Ron muttered.

"Yeah. But we handled it." Marge said.

Ron grumbled. "Barely."

Did we do alright, babe?

Marge nudged him. "They know we care. That's what matters."

Ron sighed. "Yeah. I guess that's true."

CHAPTER 58

Earl Two Rivers had lived through plenty of bad mornings.

The kind that started with an ambush, a missing informant, or a coded message that sent a chill down his spine.

But this morning?

This morning, I started to feel a lot like those.

Which was why, at exactly 6:30 AM, he was sitting in his usual booth at The Diner, sipping black coffee and eating eggs, chorizo, and green chili that tasted like fire and regret—seriously, the cook must've been in a mood today—when someone slid into the seat across from him.

Someone he didn't know. Someone who didn't belong here.

Clean suit. Perfect smile. The kind of man who thought he was forgettable but stood out like a sore thumb in a place like this.

Earl didn't like that.

Didn't like it one fucking bit.

"Morning, Earl," the guy said, smiling like this was totally normal.

Earl barely looked up from his plate. "Know you?"

The guy ignored that. "Heard you've been asking around about a certain storage situation."

Earl's stomach went tight.

But his face?

Goofy old man mode: activated.

He let out an exaggerated sigh and scratched at his graying stubble like this was just another morning of too-hot chili and aching joints.

"Son," Earl said, lowering his voice like he was about to share a real deep secret, "at my age, I ask a lot of questions. Sometimes I even forget why I asked 'em in the first place. You ever walk into a room and forget why? It's tragic, really. Ain't what it used to be up here." He tapped the side of his head. "Cranial decay. Or maybe too much bad coffee over the years."

The guy's too-practiced smile did not waver.

"That so?" he said.

"Sure is," Earl said, nodding enthusiastically, like a grandpa giving useless life advice. "Y'know, a man of my age should be at home, watching reruns of *Matlock*, maybe complaining about the kids these days. Instead, I get up, eat my damn breakfast, and suddenly I got young men in fancy suits sittin' across from me, tryin' to talk all serious-like."

He leaned forward, grinning.

"Now, me?" he said, voice lowering conspiratorially. "I got no clue what storage situation you're referrin' to, but—oh! You mean that thing with Donahue's trailer?"

The guy blinked.

Earl watched closely.

Not a flinch. Not even the tiniest reaction.

Which meant two things: either the guy already knew what was in that trailer, or he'd been trained not to react. And either way, that was very fucking interesting.

"Lot of things moving these days," Earl said casually, spearing another bite of eggs. "Sometimes stuff gets lost. Sometimes folks get real curious about what's in those misplaced things."

The guy nodded, as if indulging a fool. "Sure. But some things? Better left alone."

Earl set his fork down.

There it was. That friendly, casual, perfectly normal little warning.

The kind that wasn't actually friendly at all.

He leaned back, chewing slowly, thoughtfully, as if he were weighing the words.

Then he let out a wheezing, smoker's laugh. "Boy, you sound just like my second ex-wife."

The guy's smile didn't change, but Earl caught the slightest shift in his posture.

Annoyance.

Which meant the guy wasn't used to being laughed at. Even better.

Earl picked up his coffee and took a long sip, forcing himself to act like a harmless old bastard who had nothing but time.

"You ever been married, son?" Earl asked.

The guy did not answer.

Earl smirked. "Didn't think so. You got that 'I work too much and go home to an empty fridge' look about you."

The guy finally exhaled, his patience clearly wearing thin. "Just be careful where you go digging, Mr. Two Rivers."

Earl sighed dramatically. "Now, that's the thing. See, I'm not even diggin'." He waved a hand. "I'm just an old man with too much time and not enough sense. If I were smart, I'd shut up and enjoy my eggs. But me?"

He leaned forward again, voice dropping into something just a little sharper.

"I'm a stubborn old bastard. And the thing about stubborn old bastards? We don't like being told what to do."

The guy's jaw ticked.

That was the best reaction Earl had gotten all morning.

Earl grinned. "But hey, I'll take your advice under consideration."

Earl sat there, staring at his plate like it might hold the answers to whatever the hell he just stepped into.

He wasn't new to being warned off something. He'd been given friendly advice before.

Back in Kabul, when a certain warlord had politely suggested he stop asking about missing supply shipments.

Back in D.C., when a government spook in an even better suit than this asshole had implied that his career might go a whole lot smoother if he stopped digging into a classified op gone wrong.

And now?

Now he was getting the same goddamn message over a plate of spicy eggs and burnt coffee in a nowhere diner in New Mexico.

Whatever Donahue was mixed up in, it wasn't just business.

It was bigger.

He exhaled slowly and waved down the waitress.

"Another coffee, sweetheart" he said.

She nodded, pouring him a fresh cup, and gave him a look. "You okay, Earl? You got that 'about to do something stupid' face."

He huffed a laugh. "That obvious?"

"Only every damn time," she said, shaking her head.

Earl picked up the coffee, took a long sip, and muttered, "Shit."

This wasn't over. Not even close.

Because now?

Now he had even more questions. And if there was one thing Earl Two Rivers had never been good at?

It was letting things go.

CHAPTER 59

Earl saw the flashing red and blue in his rearview mirror and knew.

This wasn't a routine stop.

He wasn't speeding. His tags were up to date. He hadn't so much as rolled through a stop sign in twenty years.

And yet, here he was. Getting pulled over on a long, empty stretch of Route 66 with nowhere to go and no one to witness.

His fingers flexed on the steering wheel, gut already tight.

This was about the trailer. It had to be.

Earl sighed through his nose. "Dumb bastard. Should've left it alone."

But he hadn't.

And now? Now someone was making sure he understood just how badly he'd fucked up.

The trooper who approached the window was clean-cut, professional, and polite.

Which meant he was probably not actually a trooper.

"License and registration, sir."

Earl handed them over, face blank. "What's the problem, Officer?"

The trooper studied his ID for a beat, then glanced toward the road behind them.

Empty. Not a single car in sight.

Earl caught that.

And that's when his pulse really started pounding.

"I need you to step out of the vehicle," the trooper said, voice too calm.

Earl's fingers tightened on the wheel.

"That so?"

The trooper didn't blink. "Step out, sir."

Earl let out a slow breath. Then, like a man with nothing better to do, he opened the door, climbed out, and stretched.

"Man, getting old sucks," he said, rolling his shoulder like this was just another Tuesday. "What are we doin' here, fellas? You guys finally get sick of my dumb questions?"

The trooper didn't answer.

Just gestured to the unmarked black SUV parked fifty yards ahead.

Yeah. That figured.

They drove him thirty minutes in silence. Didn't take him to a station.

Didn't take him to anywhere with cameras or witnesses. Just a small, quiet State Patrol outpost.

The kind that wasn't used for much anymore.

Earl recognized the move. Classic rendition of "We're Not Arresting You, But We Are About to Fuck Up Your Day."

The second they took him inside, Earl knew exactly how bad this was about to get.

The room was bare. There were no windows. There was just a table, two chairs, and the kind of emptiness that made sure people left more scared than when they walked in.

They took his phone.

They didn't cuff him. Didn't have to. The door opened.

And the man who walked in wasn't a trooper.

He was something worse.

Feds. Three-letter agency, Earl guessed.

Or the private sector. Didn't really matter. Trouble wore the same suit either way.

The military was high and tight, wearing a sharp suit, and the way he carried himself made it seem like he owned the room.

Yeah. Earl recognized that type.

And he hated them.

The man sat down across from him. Didn't say anything at first.

The man flipped the folder open. "Former military intelligence. Discharged 1999. Worked private security, some consulting, and now you mostly… drink coffee and play old man at a junkyard."

"Except lately, you've been busy, Mr. Two Rivers."

Earl smirked. "You should see me on my productive days."

The man's face didn't move.

"You've been asking about a trailer."

Earl shrugged. "Not really. Just making conversation."

The man flipped a page. "You asked a retired logistics officer about a missing shipment."

"Yeah, over beers. We also talked about baseball. You guys gonna haul me in for that too?"

"You spoke to two different truckers about transport routes."

"Like I just said. Only conversation, I'm a bored old man."

"You showed interest in Donahue's finances."

Earl snorted. "If you've ever met Donahue, you'd know there ain't a man alive who trusts that bastard with money."

The man finally looked at him. "Mr. Two Rivers."

His voice was calm.

Flat. Not a threat. Not yet.

"You've rattled a lot of cages."

Earl leaned back. "I do that."

"You don't want to keep doing it."

Earl didn't answer.

Because of that? That wasn't a warning.

That was a promise.

The man set down his folder. Crossed his fingers.

"Let's talk about Donahue."

Earl raised an eyebrow.

"Go on," he said.

The man tilted his head. "Tell me what you think you know."

Earl laughed. "Nice try."

The man exhaled through his nose.

"Michael Donahue is a middleman," he said.

Earl didn't blink. Didn't flinch.

But his gut?

His gut was screaming.

The man continued. "He's not important. He's not powerful. He's just useful."

Earl didn't answer.

Because of the fact that they were saying this?

That meant Donahue was a loose end. A pawn. A man who had outlived his usefulness. But what does that mean about the Trentons?

Which meant whatever was in that trailer? It was several levels above Donahue.

And that?

That was very fucking bad.

The man leaned forward, voice just a little softer now.

"You're poking at something you don't understand."

Earl let out a slow breath. He'd heard that line before.

Last time it had been whispered to him in a bunker in Kandahar.

Time before that? A dark alley in Bogotá.

The difference now? Now he was just an old guy in a goddamn junkyard. Or at least, that's what he was supposed to be.

"And you're telling me to walk away," Earl said.

"Yes."

Earl tilted his head. "And if I don't?"

The man was silent for a moment.

Then, without emotion, he said, *"We can make things difficult for you, Mr. Two Rivers."*

Earl's jaw tightened.

We're not in the business of kicking the shit out of you, or torture, no we just questions like, "You like your pension?"

Earl stayed still.

"You like your freedom?"

His fingers curled under the table.

"Then let this go."

Earl exhaled. Sat back. Forced himself to relax.

It was an old trick that had kept him alive more times than he cared to count. Act calm. Make them believe you were considering their offer. Let them think you were folding.

"Well," he said, "you sure make a good case."

The man studied him.

Didn't say anything.

Then stood, straightened his tie, and nodded.

"We'll be in touch."

Then he walked out. The door clicked shut, the sound far too final.

Earl let out a slow breath and finally let the tension go.

He wasn't scared.

He'd been threatened before.

But this? This wasn't a threat. This was a decision.

They had made their play.

Now it was his move.

Earl drummed his fingers on the table, running through the conversation in his head.

Every detail. Every pause. Every flicker of expression.

These guys?

They were used to control. Used to giving orders and watching people scramble.

And the second they realized Earl wasn't scrambling?

That's when they'd get dangerous.

So now, he had to make a choice.

He could stop. Play the dumb, washed-up old man. Forget Donahue. Forget the trailer.

Live out his years in peace, collecting his pension, fixing cars, watching the sun set over the junkyard.

Or—

He could push forward. And find out exactly what had Donahue tangled up so high above his pay grade.

Earl sighed.

He knew which choice he was going to make.

Had probably known it since the moment that smiling bastard sat down at his table back at the diner.

He rubbed the inside thumb, another technique he didn't need to consider.

Then muttered to himself. *"Guess I'm gonna do something stupid."*

Yeah.

Yeah, he was.

And now?

Now he had to figure out who else to drag into it. And that? That was the real question.

CHAPTER 60

Earl spent a lifetime being the type of man who didn't cut and run.

But sometimes, when the world started pressing in—when the questions outnumbered the answers, when old instincts kicked in and whispered *time to disappear for a bit*—he listened.

Which was why, one week after getting politely threatened by a nameless suit in an unnamed building, he threw a bag in his truck, told no one a damn thing, and drove out of town.

Not far.

Just far enough to think.

This was a big fucking decision—one that kept looping through his mind, over and over. He could be putting almost every friend he had at risk. Not just of losing everything, but possibly even their freedom.

"Where the hell is Earl?" Randall muttered, stirring his coffee with the aggression of a man who'd been left out of the scratch-off ticket split.

"Didn't say," Frank grunted, flipping through a newspaper like he might find an answer there.

"He didn't show up for poker night," Gus added, frowning. "That bastard never misses poker night. Even when he's losing." They all sat in silence for a second, processing the strange, unsettling fact that their resident ex-spook had just up and vanished.

Randall sighed. "You think it's got to do with that trailer mess?"

"No idea, but that goddamn trailer," Frank said. "I told him to let it go."

"You tell Earl to let something go?" Gus snorted. "Might as well tell a dog to stop sniffing another dog's ass." Randall rubbed his hair. "We should probably check on him."

"How?" Frank said. "The man's like a fucking ghost when he doesn't want to be found." They all stewed in that unfortunate truth for a moment.

Then Gus leaned back in his chair.

"Well," he said, "if he ain't back in a week, we flip a coin on who calls Marge. Loser has to tell her he's missing."

The table went dead silent. Randall winced. Frank shuddered. Gus looked suddenly like he regretted speaking.

Nobody wanted to call Marge with bad news. Nobody.

While Earl was off contemplating life and death, next steps, and avoiding gov suits, Ron and Marge had too much shit to deal with.

Because of the junkyard? It was outgrowing them.

The online business was booming—movie production companies, random collectors, and shady bastards that Ron had no intention of asking questions about. Orders were coming in every day.

This meant they needed space, and two shipping containers were about to be dropped in the yard.

Marge sighed, watching as the trucks rolled in. "I can't believe this is our life now."

Ron crossed his arms. "What? Organized crime through junk sales?"

Marge smirked. "You call it crime, I call it capitalism with some elevated risk. Plus I wouldn't joke outload about organizing your crime."

Ron shook his head. "You're just talking dirty now, babe. They both laughed out loud."

Ezra stood in front of the newly delivered shipping containers, looking too pleased with himself.

Ivy and Grace, standing beside him, looked much less pleased.

"This is stupid," Ivy muttered, crossing her arms.

Ezra grinned. "Nah. This is *genius*. *Wait, why stupid?*"

Marge, half-listening, raised an eyebrow. "I'm afraid to ask."

Ezra moved on from Ivy's comment and clapped his hands together. "Alright, here's the deal. These containers? Office space. But not just any office space. A high-functioning, fully equipped, badass headquarters for Trenton Junk Worldwide!."

Ron rubbed his face. "Christ. International laws getting broken is all that hear, Ezra."

Ezra looked confused and continued, undeterred. "We got funding from the new movie contracts, so we're doing it *right*. Insulation, electrical, water, and a real security system, make it a war-room—"

Ivy rolled her eyes. "Translation: He wants a hacker lair for all the shit, he doesn't tell anyone he is doing."

Ezra smirked. "Not hacking, I want a *functional workspace*. That happens to look *really cool* in moody lighting."

Marge pointed a cigarette at him. "You get shit done, and I don't care what kind of *nerd fortress* you build. Just hurry, we need the space like yesterday." She also outlined some requirements, such as a good ventilation system to clean the smoke out and two automated coffee machines.

Ezra grinned. "Perfect. I'll handle wiring and security, Ivy's in charge of logistics."

Ivy glared at him. "How the hell did I get roped into this?"

Ezra smirked. "Because I told Marge you'd be good at it."

Ivy turned to Marge. "Did you agree to that?"

Marge took a long sip of coffee. "I plead the Fifth. Ivy, I am sure you'll do a wonderful job with whatever Ezra said, and why not make Grace your assistant!"

Ron just watched in horror as their two most competent and undeterred kids teamed up for an absolute mayhem of a project, moving fast and already paid for!

Beth: *"If you had to kill someone, how would you do it?"*

Marge: *"What the fuck, Beth?"*
Beth: *"What? It's hypothetical."*
Ron: *"And deeply concerning."*
Beth: *"Okay, fine. How would you dispose of a body?"*
Ezra: *"Industrial acid. Quick, clean, no evidence."*
Ivy: *"You had that answer way too fast."*
Ezra: *"Google exists."*
Ron: *"Ezra, what the fuck."*

Danny: *"If I get bit by a radioactive raccoon, do I become a superhero?"*
Max: *"No, you get rabies."*
Danny: *"Shit."*

Joey (walking into the office): *"I have a very important question."*
Marge: *"If this is about murder, radioactive animals, or body disposal, just don't ask me, not today, bud."*
Joey: *"...Never mind."*

A week passed. And no one had heard a damn thing from Earl. This was not normal, something was definitely going on.

Earl wasn't exactly a social butterfly, but he always checked in. A text, a phone call, something. Even when he was off running errands, even when he was pissed off about something, he never just vanished.

Which meant this? This wasn't good.

Randall, Frank, and Gus sat at the club, staring at a coin like it might hold the answers.

It didn't. It just sat there mocking them.

"...So who's walking over to tell Marge?" Randall asked.

Nobody moved.

Gus took a slow sip of his beer, not looking at anyone.

Frank scratched his jaw. "We flip."

Randall grabbed the coin. Flipped it. Watched it land.

Frank sighed, staring at the result like it had personally betrayed him.

Then sighed again. "Fuck."

He got up and grabbed his phone. "Maybe I can call Marge? That was worse than calling the cops." The group protested Frank's alternate plan.

Marge looked as Frank strolled slowly toward her, asking the Yard. "Tell me you found Earl," she said, no greeting, just down to the point.

Frank swallowed hard. "Not exactly."

A pause. Then: "…So you called me instead of a funeral home. That's something."

Frank grimaced. "Jesus, Marge."

She was not amused.

"Where the hell is he, Frank?" Frank scratched the back of his neck. "We don't know. He didn't say shit to anyone before he left. Just up and disappeared."

Marge exhaled sharply. That was not a good sign. Frank could practically hear her calculating what they all needed to do.

Earl wasn't the type to run.

It meant one of two things if he left town without a word.

He was figuring out how deep in the shit he really was.

He was already dead.

Neither option was comforting.

Marge's voice came back, low and sharp. "He's not dead."

Frank hesitated. "How do you know?"

"Because I'm hopeful. That guy is tough as they come—but I don't know. And if he were running, he would've left us a way to follow."

Frank frowned. "…So what the hell is he doing?"

A pause.

Then: "Thinking."

Because Earl never took a whole week to think.

Which meant, when he came back? Something was gonna break. And it sure as hell wasn't gonna be him.

Meanwhile, Ron and Marge were out of space back at the Yard. Not metaphorically. Literally. Nine kids. Three Airstreams.

A growing business that had gone from barely scraping by to multiple daily orders—and now?

Now they had movie production companies throwing money at them like they were some legitimate operation.

Which meant they had to expand. Marge stood in the middle of the yard, arms crossed, staring at the mess. Two rail shipping containers sat on flatbeds, waiting to be moved into place.

Beside her, Ezra held a clipboard, ready to oversee the most chaotic construction project in history.

Ron squinted at the setup. "So let me get this straight—we're trusting the future of our business to a seventeen-year-old and an ex-criminal?"

Ezra didn't look up. **"I prefer 'problem solver.'"**

Ivy, standing next to him, smirked. **"I prefer 'alleged thief.'"**

Ron rubbed his face. "Christ. You two......."

Marge clapped her hands together. "Alright, shut up. Ezra, Ivy—you're in charge. Get the containers set up, get the new office wired, and whatever else we decided. PLEASE."

Ezra nodded seriously. "We'll do our best."

Ivy grinned. "No promises, but we're smart, so we'll do a good job."

Ron groaned, not convinced at all.

"Okay," Ezra said, looking at the containers. "We'll need to cut out windows, install insulation, and—"

Max interrupted. "Can we make a secret tunnel between them?"

Ezra blinked. "What?"

Max grinned. "Y'know. A tunnel. For tactical reasons."

Beth showed up and immediately scoffed. "What tactical reasons?"

Max's grin widened. "Sneaky shit."

Ezra sighed. "No, Max. No secret tunnels."

Max pouted but didn't argue, already moving on to his next idea.

Lewis raised a hand. "Can we put in a fire pole?" Ezra stared at him. "...For what purpose?"

Lewis shrugged. "For vibes, make it really cool."

Ezra rubbed his hat. "You people are insane and not helping." Beth smirked. "And yet, we're the ones running the show."

Step 1: Move the containers into place.

Simple, right? Except Max "accidentally" started operating the forklift before Ezra was ready. Ezra dove out of the way, shouting, "MAX, STOP TOUCHING THINGS!" Max grinned. "I'M HELPING!"

Watching from the roof of one of the Airstreams, Grace called down. "If he dies, I want his stuff!"

Ron, hearing the chaos, muttered, "I'm gonna have a stroke, and where is Ryder? I thought it was his day off to help us."

By day three, the containers were in place. Day five, they had windows, insulation, and half the electrical done. Day six, Ezra was threatening to electrocute Max if he touched another goddamn power tool.

By day seven, the office was almost functional. Marge stood back, arms crossed, actually impressed. Ezra, covered in dust and sweat, wiped his forehead. "Not bad for a bunch of idiots."

Ivy grinned. "You say that like you're not one of us." Ezra sighed. "...Fair point, PARTNER."

Looking at the finished setup, Ron muttered, "I can't believe this actually worked."

Marge smirked. "Shows what you know.................Again!"

CHAPTER 61

A week away. A week of thinking, watching, and putting together the pieces.

And Earl Two Rivers didn't like the picture forming in front of him.

Because something wasn't adding up. Not just the missing trailer. Not just Donahue's usual brand of sleaze.

No, this was bigger.

The Feds—NSA, FBI, maybe even CIA—were sniffing around the Yard.

That was a fact. It became increasingly apparent that Earl had stepped into something important to many people. The Trentons were part of the plot but never got invited to the movie.

Earl had spent his life spotting patterns from the shadows. Seeing what's up before anyone else even realized they were part of the plot.

And the way these agencies were moving? It wasn't random.

Donahue was small-time, but the heat on him? Too big. Which meant he wasn't the real target. Which meant the Feds were watching someone else.

And now?

Now Earl had a thought he really didn't want to have. The idea had wormed into his brain halfway through his trip.

"And now? Now, he couldn't let it go—but maybe, just maybe, he needed to."

Because something about this whole thing stank. Donahue was a piece of shit, sure. A crook, a liar, a scumbag. But maybe this was a national security level problem?

No way. Not unless he was part of something bigger than even he realized.

Or—**and this was a longshot—**not unless someone in the Yard was feeding information to the people who wanted him out of the picture because of something way more serious.

Earl rubbed his jaw, staring out at the desert highway. "Nah, no way, Marge or Ron, not a chance."

He didn't want to suspect anyone. The Yard was family. But he also wasn't about to let loyalty make him blind. So he started replaying everything.

The timeline didn't make sense. Donahue had always been dirty, but he'd never had this kind of heat before.

So why now? Why did the Feds start sniffing right after Donahue's trailer disappeared? And how the hell did they even know to start looking?

"Earl thought about the people in the Yard, his old codgers. The ones close enough to notice when things started to shift."

Marge and Ron were too deep in this. Too busy trying to hold everything together. They would've burned the whole thing down if they'd known what Donahue was up to before it got this far.

The kids? The lawyer? Earl needed to consider any possible combination to eliminate it from the table.

Ezra? No. The kid had zero poker face, and he was a kid.

Ivy? Doubtful. If she wanted to burn this place to the ground, she would've done it already, and again a kid.

The Bullshit Club? Not a chance. Those old bastards had more loyalty in their bones than most people had in their whole damn family trees.

Which meant…

Whoever was talking was just close enough to keep an eye on things without anyone noticing.

Earl hated the thought.

But now? Now he had to be sure. Which meant it was time to stop running theories. And start getting some goddamn answers.

Rule #1: Never let them know you're suspicious.

The second someone realized they were being hunted? They got sloppy. Or they disappeared.

Rule #2: Have an exit plan if you're gonna poke the bear.

Earl had stepped in some deep shit already, and he had no doubt it would get deeper. Which meant he needed leverage. Which meant he needed proof.

Rule #3: Find the crack. No one kept their story straight forever. All he had to do was push in the right place.

Earl turned his truck around and headed back to Albuquerque. The second he pulled onto the Yard, Marge was already walking toward him.

Arms crossed. Pissed. Yeah, that figured.

He barely had the truck in park before she ripped into him. "The fuck was that, Earl?"

He sighed. "Took a trip."

Marge narrowed her eyes. "Without a word, do you not give a shit about everyone here?"

"Needed to think." Ron crossed his arms. "You've been thinking for over a week, huh?" Earl exhaled. "Yeah. And I don't like what I'm thinking."

That shut them up. Because Earl didn't rattle easily.

And right now? He looked rattled. Marge folded her arms. "Spit it out."

Earl scanned the yard, eyes sharp. Too many ears. That wasn't good.

He gathered the Bullshit Club in the break room.

Manny, Luis, Reggie, Hamish, Randall, Frank, Gus, Ron, and Marge.

Earl didn't waste time.

"Alright," he started. "Something's really wrong. Bigger than Donahue, bigger than some stolen goods. The Feds are sniffing around the Yard, and it ain't just the FBI. NSA. Maybe CIA, who fucking knows, but it's serious."

Randall swore. "Jesus."

Reggie leaned back. "Why the hell would they care about some missing trailer?"

Earl shook his head. "That's what I'm trying to figure out."

Luis tapped the table. "You thinking arms? Drugs?"

Earl shook his head. "No. That'd be DEA, maybe ATF. This is what appears to be national security-level heat."

The room went dead silent. Because of that? That meant nasty shit.

Manny frowned. "No, no, you think someone's talking to them?"

Earl let that hang in the air. Because he didn't want to say it. But he had to.

"It's a possibility."

Silence.

Then, finally, Marge got fired up and defensive. "What are the fuck are talking about Earl, stop beating around the bush. Say it already."

Earl nodded. "That's exactly what I intend to do."

"Someone at the Yard might be an inside for the Feds." Earl didn't have hard proof yet, but raised an interesting and what felt like far-fetched suggestion.

That meant it was time to start watching. Who was isolated enough to take calls? Who lingered a little too long in the wrong conversations? Who knew just a little too much? And most of all, who got nervous now that he was back?

The shipping container office was almost done.

Ezra, Ivy, and the rest of the kids had turned absolute chaos into something that actually worked.

Movie production orders were rolling in, it felt like each day was getting busier, and the money was increasing. And if you didn't know better? You'd think everything was fine.

CHAPTER 62

But the truth? Most of the Yard was too distracted or chaotic to be a government mole.

Marge? Ron? Not a chance. The Feds would've had to sedate them before they'd ever consider cooperating.

Lewis? Max? Joey? Grace? Danny? Jesus Christ, no, all children.

The kids were many things—stubborn, reckless, prone to violence—but spies? No.

That narrows down to five people: Ivy, Beth, and Ezra. Ryder. Lily.

Lily was smart, a lawyer, and could have government connections, but Earl's gut said she wasn't the type to hide something this big in the way she had consistently acted.

Ezra? Kid was sharp as hell. Quiet. Smart. Knew how to keep things to himself. If anyone was running a long con, it could be him.

And Ryder? Ryder had always been a wildcard.

Kept to himself. Never said too much. Observed more than he spoke. The kind of kid who noticed things. And Earl knew from experience—the ones who noticed things were the ones to watch.

Beth? She was always writing things down in her notebook. But one of the old covers said that her family's childhood wasn't pretty, so maybe not.

And Ivy. Maybe, she was hard to read, kept to herself more than not, and was smart.

So if Ryder, Ezra, Ivy or Lily was the leak?

Earl needed to find out, so he eliminated four options. And he was going to do it old-school.

Earl started with Ryder.

Invited him over for dinner. Nothing fancy—just some computer problem he needed help with. Easy excuse.

Earl set everything up before the kid arrived. The house looked normal—mostly.

But he left things out. Bait. Old spook tools—disassembled listening device, and burner phone.

He printed A folded-up classified-looking document from the internet—total nonsense, but it looked real enough.

If Ryder wasn't trained? He wouldn't notice. If he was? He'd react. And Earl would know.

Earl had one more surprise waiting when Ryder showed up.

Dinner was simple: fried chicken, mashed potatoes, green beans.

Earl wasn't a gourmet chef, but good country cook, he could feed a kid.

Ryder ate without complaint. They made small talk about normal shit.

Music, new railcar office project, school, and movie company sending a lot of orders.

Nothing that set off alarms.

But then—

Ryder's eyes flicked, and Earl caught it with a quick glance at the burner phone, just for a second. Then—a glance at the listening device.

Ryder didn't say anything, didn't even react much.

Earl stretched, setting down his fork. "You ever think about doing something different?" he asked casually.

Ryder blinked. "Different how?"

Earl shrugged. "You know. Something bigger. Something more… official for a career."

Ryder went still, not a flinch. Not obvious.

But Earl saw something.

Finally, Ryder shrugged.

"Not really," he said. "I like it here."

Earl nodded slowly. "Yeah. I bet you do."

A pause. Then Ryder asked, casual as anything—"What's with all the gear?"

And there it was.

Earl smirked.

"Old habits," he said. Ryder picked up the burner phone and turned it over. "You were military intelligence?"

"Something like that." Earl said.

Ryder set it back down. "You keep these around for fun, or are you expecting company?"

Earl leaned forward.

"I think you don't trust people very much." Ryder said.

Earl chuckled. "Smart kid."

Ryder finished his drink, stood up, and stretched. "Well," he said, "computer's fixed."

Earl nodded, watched him put on his jacket, watched how he didn't rush, watched how he didn't seem rattled.

That? That was interesting.

"Thanks for dinner," Ryder said.

"Yeah. Any time, kid."

Ryder nodded, opened the door—

And hesitated, just for a second.

Good nights were given, and Ryder went back to the Yard.

Tomorrow, Earl was setting the next trap.

And this time? It was Ezra's turn.

CHAPTER 63

He was sure about Ryder. Kid was sharp, sure. Observant. But not trained.

Ryder had been suspicious because he was used to watching his back, not because he had something to hide. Okay, not Ryder, one down.

But Lily?

Lily made that decision for him.

At 3 AM, Earl woke up to a presence in his room. And the first thing he realized? His gun was gone.

The second? Lily was sitting right beside his bed, watching. A knife in his hand. Not threatening. Not panicked. Just there.

Waiting. Like she'd been there a while.

Earl's stomach went tight. He'd been compromised before—ambushed, cornered—but never at home. Never like this.

Lily's voice was calm.

"You move slow when you wake up."

Earl exhaled. Swung his legs over the bed, sitting up.

"Yeah," he muttered. "That's called being old as hell."

Lily flipped the knife in her hand. Not threatening—just thinking.

"You don't stop, do you?"

Earl rubbed his face. "Whatcha talkn about?"

Lily sighed.

Then, finally, she spoke clearly not acknowledging the lack of agreement, they both knew what Lily was talking about.

"You need to walk away, Earl. It is not going to end up good."

Earl snorted. "You really think that's gonna work?"

Lily didn't smile. "That wasn't a request."

Earl felt his stomach twist.

This wasn't some two-bit arms deal. Wasn't cartel shit, wrong agency involved. This was bigger confirming his theory. The big one that got people a case of the 'disappeared'. Big that made phone records vanish and bodies get written off as freak accidents.

And now? Now he was neck-deep in it. All because he couldn't keep his curiosity in check. Oh well. He sighed through his nose, watching Lily sit there, calm as ever.

"Earl had met people like her before—he remembered his dealings with Eastern European types. The kind who could look you in the eye, shake your hand, and decide right then and there if you lived or died, all without their heartbeat rising a single beat."

Lily was one of them. That meant she wasn't some low-level informant. She wasn't just passing notes up the chain.

Earl had been in classified shit before, most of the last part of his career. Hell, he'd seen what happened to people who asked too many questions, he was what happened to those people, more than once.

Removing people from their lives wasn't Earl's favorite part of the job, but it was part of the job at different levels of his career. It came with the job.

"There was one op—decades ago, back when he was still playing spy games. Somewhere in the Middle East. Not Syria, Jordan, or Iraq."

The target was a scientist. A guy who'd defected to the wrong side.

Officially, he didn't exist. Unofficially, the U.S. had a bullet waiting for him. He knew more about nuclear technology than anyone not employed by the U.S. could be allowed to understand.

Earl's job had been intel gathering.

Find the guy. Mark the location. Get out before it all happens. Simple. Until it wasn't.

Because the second he got too close, the agency cut the cord and burned the entire mission to the ground. Pulled every operative except him, he'd been expendable. And what was the only reason he made it out? Sheer fucking luck, nothing more or less. Earl always phrased it. "My god was working overtime that day."

The same agency that had trained him would bury him alive if it meant keeping their national secrets safe. That was the day he learned the true weight of his job—the last time he ever took a high-security operation.

Earl rubbed his jaw, feeling those old feelings of expendability, the weight of it.

Lily was giving him the same warning the agency had given him years ago.

Except this time? It wasn't just his own ass on the line.

Lily was right—this wasn't about the Trenton family.

Yet.

But if Earl kept pushing, if he didn't shut up, his pension would be wiped; Ron and Marge's lives would be burned down. Because the government didn't make threats, they made examples.

And if Earl wasn't careful? He'd become one.

Lily tilted her head, watching the old man process it all.

"You get it now?"

Earl exhaled. "You really gonna freeze my pension over this?"

Lily's voice was flat. "I won't, that is horrible. But they will, in maybe minutes, never giving it a second thought."

Earl ran a hand down his face. "Christ."

He wasn't scared of dying, he lost that fear 50 years ago. But fucking over his friends? That was a different kind of weight, one he took very seriously.

Lily stood. "You need to let this go," she said. "Or the next conversation won't be this friendly. And of course this discussion never happened, friend."

Then, like a ghost, she was gone.

Earl sat in the dark. Alone. Listening to the weight of a fight he couldn't win, and making sure she was actually gone.

He couldn't help but keep running through the conversation over and over.

"You keep pulling at this," Lily said, voice flat, "and the next conversation will be in an interrogation room not in the lower 48, get me, friend?"

Lily leaned forward. "And if that happens?" Her voice dropped.

"Your pension? Gone. Your bank account? Frozen. The Bullshit Club? Every single one of your friends loses their pensions, Social Security, and their damn retirement—if we can get to it."

Earl's pulse jumped a little, this was real. Lily wasn't talking about threats.

"All because you couldn't let go of a trailer," Lily finished.

Lily shook her head.

"You think you're the first person to dig too deep, not having a clue what you stepped into? I've seen brilliant men disappear for knowing less than you do right now."

Earl stared at her. And finally understood.

This wasn't some sting operation. This was real fucking intelligence work. Earl swallowed. "Is this the part where you kill me?"

Lily actually genuinely laughed.

"If I were here to kill you, Earl," he said, "you wouldn't have woken up."

Lily stood. Set Earl's gun on the nightstand, pointed directly at him. Smiled, then evaporated.

Ryder looked down at his phone. A notification flashed across the screen—a secure app request for agency communication.

Frowning, he tapped it open. The system prompted him for authentication. Thumbprint. Passcode.

He entered both. A message popped up.

"I know. We're on the same team. **Password: Blue Raven**. – Lily"

Ryder's pulse kicked up. Shock hit first, then calculation.

He stared at the message, his brain cycling through possibilities. Why now?

For fifteen seconds, he sat frozen, processing. She could've told him before. She should've told him before.

So why did she tell him now? His grip on the phone tightened.

Something was about to happen, or there was a problem.

CHAPTER 64

"The week leading up to Balloon Fest was always chaotic in Albuquerque. It was still weird that they'd moved it later in the year—everyone was still getting used to it.

The Yard had become a hotspot during the festival—vendors, visitors, and tourists hunting for 'hidden gems.' A damn nightmare for people who thrived on peace and quiet, like the Bullshit Club."

For the Feds? It was worse.

Because thousands of people flooded into Albuquerque, trying to run surveillance in that mess?

Their mission was to make the impossible not only possible but expected. Which meant this was the perfect cover for shit to go sideways.

And Earl knew it. Like a storm on the horizon, waiting to break. Something was coming, and it was gonna be big.

Marge had exactly zero patience for bullshit, she was consistent as the day was long.

So when she got a very polite request for a meeting from some unnamed federal agency, she almost ignored it.

Until she saw the name attached—Michael Donahue.

And just like that, she figured it was important to respond to the meeting, with Lily Harlow in tow.

They met in a coffee shop, a casual spot. Lily's idea—public enough to keep things civil. The suggestion was as much for Marge as it was for the party they were meeting.

Marge and Lily sat across from a very well-dressed man with a very neutral face.

The government was involved, not the FBI, but probably the NSA or something even more serious. It wasn't clear what was going on, but everything pointed to the Trentons being in trouble.

"Ms. Harlow," the man said. "Thank you for joining Mrs. Trenton and me for the meeting."

"Yeah, yeah," Lily said, stirring her espresso. "Being extra direct, because she really wanted this meeting to end quickly. Let's cut the foreplay. What do you want? We're at a bit of a loss as to why my client was dragged in today."

The man didn't react, and Lily kept her face neutral.

"Do either of you know Mr. Earl Two Rivers?"

She exhaled. "He's… around, sure we know who he is."

The man nodded and asked Marge the same question again. She answered the same as Lily, word for word.

"I'm not going to mix words. You're going to help us manage Earl," he said.

Lily blinked. "Excuse me?"

"Things are escalating with issues around Michael Donahue," he said smoothly. "We'd prefer it if you keep Earl out of all this business. We are comfortable that your company and you are not involved with Donahue more than storing sensitive information at a trailer in your junkyard for money."

The man across the table barely touched his coffee. His suit was expensive and didn't look flashy—well-fitted, well-pressed, and meant to blend into any room without drawing attention. His voice, however, was cold enough to send a chill up Marge's spine.

"Ms. Harlow. We're not asking. It goes forward the way we're talking about. More instructions to follow." He slid a folded piece of paper across the table, pressing it down with two fingers. "Or the other option is Federal prison under the Espionage Act."

And there it was. The part where it wasn't a request.

Marge stared at the paper, but she didn't touch it. Instead, her fingers curled around her coffee cup, gripping the ceramic like an anchor.

"You're kidding." Her voice came out flat.

The man didn't blink. "Do I look like I'm kidding?"

Lily shifted beside her, the only sign of tension in her posture—the slight tightening of her jaw. Marge glanced at her, looking for some sign that this was all a misunderstanding. That this wasn't as serious as it sounded. But Lily wasn't meeting her eyes.

Marge let out a short, humorless laugh, leaning back. "You think you can just sit down at a coffee shop and throw legal jargon at me, and what? I nod along and say, 'Sure, sounds great, let's commit some light treason'?"

The man exhaled sharply, not quite a sigh, but close. "Ms. Harlow, I don't think you understand the gravity of the situation."

Marge leaned forward, elbows on the table. "Oh, I get it just fine. You think you can scare me into playing along. I've been threatened before."

He tilted his head slightly. "Not by me."

Something about how he said it—calm, matter-of-fact, no need for bravado—made Marge's face tighten.

Lily finally spoke, voice measured. "This isn't the time, Marge."

Marge turned her head sharply. "Not the time to push back? Lily, what the hell is this? Who the hell is this?"

Lily didn't answer.

The man stood up, buttoning his jacket with slow precision. "You'll do the right thing."

It wasn't a suggestion.

Marge crossed her arms. "And if I don't?"

The man looked at her, something like disappointment flickering in his eyes before disappearing. "Then we'll see how long your little club of friends can hold out when their pensions, homes, and freedom are on the line."

Marge's heart raced.

The man nodded to Lily, then turned and walked out, leaving the piece of paper sitting untouched on the table.

Marge stared at it for a long moment, then exhaled, running a hand over her face.

"Lily," she said finally, voice low and tight, "tell me what the hell that was. And who the hell was that?"

She couldn't wait to get out of there.

By the time Lily and Marge stormed back into the Yard, the place was a madhouse.

Vendors are setting up, kids are running around, Ron is arguing with a man selling funnel cakes about "criminally high prices," and Beth is negotiating bulk beer deliveries, which is wrong on many levels.

It was not organized chaos, it was pure chaos.

And Lily who didn't talk to Marge on the way home, despite the laundry list of questions, didn't have any desire to answer the questions.

She found Earl first, grabbed him by the sleeve.

"Start talking, goddamnit" she hissed.

Earl sighed. "What now?"

Lily shoved him toward the office. Once they were inside, she slammed the door.

"You dragged us all into a mess you don't understand, old man," she snapped. "Did you not understand our conversation? It's rhetorical by the way. The fucking government just told me I have to 'manage' you, during a meeting with myself and Marge or—"

She cut herself off. Earl raised an eyebrow. "Or what?"

Lily exhaled sharply.

"Or they start treating you and the Trentons like the bigger problem instead of the part of the solution."

Earl rubbed his jaw. "Well. Ain't that a bitch."

"You think this is funny?" Lily snapped. Her level of anger was racing to an explosive level.

Lily leaned forward, furious. This is very fucking bad, I'm using smaller words so I don't have to repeat myself.

Outside, the Yard was alive. Marge was catching every third word or so, all the more confusing, partly because she'd never heard Lily that angry.

Inside? The walls were closing in.

Lily wasn't wrong. This was escalating fast. And with Balloon Fest in full swing, the perfect storm was brewing.

Ron walked into the office, took one look at their faces, and sighed. "Who's tryin' to kill who in here?"

Lily stopped talking, immediately. Earl just muttered, "We're about to find out."

Because the pieces were moving. And the explosion? Was coming.

Ryder had always been an enigma. He'd come to the Yard quiet, self-sufficient, and way too competent for a kid his age. Didn't talk about where he came from. Didn't complain about anything, and no flinching when shit got real.

The first time Jen James walked into the Yard, she looked around like she already knew every corner of the place, then walked straight over to Ryder at the side of the junkyard.

Sharp-eyed. Mid-40s, pretty but serious-looking expression on her face. Wore a suit like it was armor and had the kind of posture that never showed weakness.

She wasn't here for tourist bullshit. And she was here for answers, but what questions did she want to get answered?

Right behind her? Leon Smith. That probably wasn't his real name. But it was what he was using today. He looked like he belonged behind a desk, but his move was purposeful and commanded respect.

He looked straightaway like a man who'd spent years doing things that weren't written down.

Between the two of them? They weren't here to ask questions nicely. Jen and Leon weren't here for Ryder.

Not directly.

They were here for whatever foreign threat was circling Donahue and the trailers.

Which meant they needed to control the Yard.

Fast.

Jen stood in the middle of the chaos—vendors setting up, kids running past, Ron taking over the arguing about beer prices from Beth—and took it all in without blinking.

Then she turned to Leon.

"Go back and talk to that Ryder kid, and figure out the best way to start locking it down quickly."

Leon nodded.

And just like that? The Trentons were starting to get informed, with more than anyone wanted to share, but time had run out for finesse.

The final pieces were moving.

And Lily?

Lily was watching all of it because she knew. This was the beginning of the government's dealing with a current national security issue.

CHAPTER 65

The tension in the Yard had become tangible. You could feel it in the way people moved—quicker, sharper, looking over their shoulders. Conversations were shorter, and eyes darted toward exits.

Lily leaned against the hood of her car, scanning the crowd. "They've got eyes everywhere now."

Marge crossed her arms. "Yeah? Well, I'd rather have the devil I know watching than the one hiding in the dark."

Lily sighed. "That's the problem. There's more than one devil."

Inside the office, Ron and Earl were locked in a hushed conversation.

"I don't like this," Earl muttered, tapping his fingers on the desk. "We've got too many unknown and known players moving at once. Feels like someone's starting something. But what?"

Ron exhaled. "You're the expert here. What do you think, old man?"

It was apparent—his stress had moved into uncharted territory.

Ron had seen plenty of trouble in his time, but this? This was different. He wasn't used to feeling this far out of his comfort zone.

And right now? He didn't know how the hell to handle any of it.

Across the yard, Ryder sat on an overturned crate, typing furiously on his laptop. His connection bounced through three different locations, but even that felt like a weak defense.

Jen and Leon had made their presence known, their suits and no-nonsense attitudes cutting through the usual Yard chaos. They didn't belong here, and they didn't care.

Jen's sharp gaze tracked every movement, missing nothing.

Leon stepped closer, voice low. "Ryder's good. Really good. He's poking around, he's finding things."

He hesitated, then added, "You think he'll break his cover and warn anyone?"

Jen didn't look away, her expression unreadable. "We better make sure we know what he's finding—before he makes a decision he isn't permitted to make."

CHAPTER 66

There was always the hum of conversation, the clanking of metal, and the occasional laughter from some vendor trying to haggle with a tourist over junk they didn't need.

Marge felt it in her chest, in the way her shoulders stayed tight no matter how many deep breaths she took. She leaned against the office doorway, arms crossed, watching the crowd.

Lily stood beside her, expression unreadable.

"They've got eyes everywhere now."

Marge didn't bother asking who *they* were.

She scanned the lot—tourists, vendors, a few Yard regulars—but it wasn't the usual chaos. Something about it felt... off. Like a bad song playing on a loop in the back of her mind.

"Yeah? Well, I'd rather have the devil I know watching than the one hiding in the dark."

Lily sighed, shifting her weight. "That's the problem. There's more than one devil."

Ron and Earl stood over the desk, a map spread between them. Earl traced his finger along a route, brow furrowed.

"I don't like this," he muttered, tapping the paper. "Too much is going on simultaneously, doesn't feel right."

Ron exhaled, rubbing the back of his head. "What doesn't feel right?"

Earl didn't respond. He just stared at the map like it could somehow give him answers.

Across the Yard, Ryder stood, tablet in hand. His fingers flew over the screen, bouncing his connection through three different locations. He had to find out what was going on; something was happening.

Someone was watching him. He could feel it, he didn't have to look up or wonder.

His firewalls were good. His backdoors were better. But something was *pressing* against them, testing the edges. Someone on the other side wasn't just looking for him—they already knew he was there.

His phone buzzed.

UNKNOWN NUMBER: Move now. Too late if you wait.

Ryder's stomach flushed with nausea. Trained or not, he needed to respond. Now.

He glanced up. Across the lot, Lily was watching him. She saw the shift in his posture, the tension in his fingers. Her expression hardened.

Without hesitation, she ran to him.

"What are you doing?" she demanded.

Ryder didn't answer.

Because that's when Ezra ran up—eyes wide, out of breath, and looking like he'd just seen a ghost.

Ezra wasn't a paranoid guy. He didn't get spooked easily. But when he noticed the same damn black sedan parked a block away for the third time today, he started paying attention more to the neighborhood.

And now? Now there was a second car. Different make, same tinted windows.

He jogged up to Ryder and Lily, out of breath. "Something's wrong."

Lily straightened. "What?"

"Two cars. Unmarked, all black. Been circling the Yard all day."

Lily cursed under her breath. "They're getting ready."

Lily looked toward the office where Ron and Earl were still deeply discussing. Toward Ryder, who was now staring at his phone like he'd just seen a ghost.

And then—

CHAPTER 67

It started with a sound. Not the deep, echoing roar of an explosion. Not the high-pitched whine of sirens.

No.

It started with a pop.

A quiet, unnatural burst of air and pressure, like a seal breaking on something that should have never been opened.

And then, in the space of a single breath—

Hell broke loose at the Yard.

Flames didn't just rise. They erupted.

A sudden, blinding flash of orange and yellow, like a living thing—angry, hungry, and spreading fast.

The first explosion rattled people's attention. The second one shattered glass.

The heat hit like a sledgehammer, rolling through the yard in thick, suffocating waves.

One second, the world was whole.

The next?

It was fire and the smoke—It wasn't black, it was yellow.

Time stopped.

The first explosion rattled people's attention. The second one shattered glass.

The heat hit like a sledgehammer, rolling through the Yard in thick, suffocating waves.

One second, the world was whole.

It curled through the air like something alive, thick and toxic, twisting into every open space, grabbing everything and everyone in its path.

People coughed and staggered before they even knew what hit them, their eyes watering, their lungs seizing. Some tried to run, others dropped where they stood, choking on air that wasn't air anymore.

Earl knew that smell.

No doubt about it—chemical fire.

The kind that didn't just burn things down.

It evaporated them.

It crawled into your lungs, your clothes, your fucking bones—and worse than that, it stayed there. Forever.

And—

The body.

At first, it was just a shape in the haze, a silhouette against the inferno, barely human. But as the firelight flickered, Earl saw it clearly.

It looked as bad as it smelled.

But, if you could call it luck, the chemical stench masked the worst of it.

Who was it?

Family? Visitor? Bullshit Club?

Or just some poor bastard in the wrong place, wrong time?

Allegedly—Michael Donahue.

Or what was left of him.

Burned. Charred beyond recognition.

A blackened husk still gripping the handle of a trailer door.

Like he'd been trying to get inside.

Or trying to get something out.

Didn't matter now. Didn't matter at all.

Because nothing was getting out of there now. Nothing.

Ron's voice cut through the chaos and mayhem. What just happened, what was that? Ron screamed.

"Get the kids clear, get them out of here! NOW! Goddamnit."

Marge was already moving, grabbing kids and people, moving them in the opposite direction of the trailer, and a mess was happening on that side of the junkyard.

Beth and Ivy grabbed the little ones, and it didn't matter if they recognized them or not; they were dragging them toward the trucks. Ezra and Grace were hauling more people past the office.

Max was coughing, trying to run back, but Marge yanked him by the collar.

"NO, kid! You stay the hell back!"

"But—!"

"NOW!"

And then came the worst part. The panic check.

Marge's eyes snapped to Ivy and Grace first. "Head count! Where the fuck is everyone? NOW!"

Ivy grabbed Beth. "Where's Joey and Danny?!"

"Here, pointing to the left!" Max yelled, still struggling against Marge's grip.

"Riley?" Marge screamed. Where is Riley? He was nowhere to be found, at least with quick scans of the junkyard.

"Milo and Danny?"

"Over here, Mom!" The boys were both scared but kept it together to help.

"Joey?"

Silence.

Marge's stomach dropped. Her heart slammed into her throat.

"JOEY?! JOEY?! JOEY?!"

Nothing.

"JOEY!"

Grace spun in place, eyes wild, scanning the chaos.

"HE WAS RIGHT HERE I THOUGHT!"

"FIND HIM!" Marge screamed. Panic overtook everything.

The kids were yelling, crying, and coughing, searching, but the smoke was too thick, and the fire was too loud.

Marge felt her chest tighten like a fist had closed around her ribs.

Not Joey. Not now. She couldn't lose him.

"JOEY!" Ivy and Beth shouted.

"WHERE IS HE?!"

"THERE!"

Grace pointed..

A tiny, shadowed figure curled up behind a half-melted metal stack, coughing his lungs out, then Riley leaned down and picked him up at a full sprint toward the office. He didn't stop until he could safely drop him for help.

Marge moved before she could think.

Ron grabbed her. **"MARGE—!"**

She yanked free. Lungs burning. Vision blurring from the smoke.

But Joey? Joey was right there.

She dropped to her knees, scooped him up where Riley dropped him, and hauled him back toward the group.

Joey clung to her, shaking, face streaked with soot and tears.

"Gotcha, baby," Marge whispered into his hair. "You're safe."

She didn't even realize she was crying until she reached the others.

Ron helped her up, took Joey from her arms.

Everyone was there. Everyone was alive. Shaking. Terrified. But alive.

Marge exhaled like her lungs had been caged shut for hours. She looked at Ivy and Grace, their eyes wide and wild, their hands shaking.

They weren't okay. None of them were. But at least they had each other, and everyone was alive.

All that happened next was a blur—sirens, lights, and people in yellow and blue suits everywhere in minutes, at least it seemed like almost immediately. **Time was standing still.**

Ryder and Marge, at the same time, screamed: let's get everyone to the hospital to make sure you're alright, okay. The smell was overwhelming, not identifiable by anyone who'd never smelled a burned body.

Lastly, Earl and other Bullshit clubbers appeared and starting asking who needed help, then started getting people into ambulances, and trucks the ER and medical centers.

Marge looked up, she saw Lily with no expression, on the phone screaming at someone, it was fuck this, what the fuck, and not many other words. She saw Lily hang up, then walk into the edge of the yellow and blue hazmat suits, where she was talking to someone in charge.

The Feds ordered the city, county, and state to immediately lock down, guard, and fence off the damage from the explosion.

The official story?

"Chemical storage incident."

The real story? Whatever the hell was inside that trailer—

Nobody was allowed to look for it.

Lily overheard the orders. **NSA, FBI, CIA**, all the alphabets were barking orders at the local officials like their were teenagers not paying attention.

We were all coordinating to keep this quiet, but then the Air Force and Space Force showed up from somewhere. A lot of weapons and bigger perimeters were set up to keep people away; no one could get close to what used to be the trailer.

She heard one of them mutter—

"Paperwork will say the city paid them to store those chemicals. Makes cleanup easier and everything more manageable."

There was no press anywhere.

She glanced around, scanning the crowd. Civilians were still dazed, some coughing, others clutching their phones like they weren't sure whether to call someone or keep recording. But no reporters. No news vans. No cameras.

That was wrong.

"No press," she muttered, more to herself than anyone else. "Why?"

Standing beside her, still coughing, Ezra wiped his sleeve across his mouth. "Probably still at Balloon Park. You know how it is. Biggest event in the state."

Lily barely heard him.

She clenched her fists, fighting the need to punch something, anything. The adrenaline was still surging, the last few minutes playing on a loop in her head. The fire. The explosion. The body. The silence.

Whoever ultimately owned this event and mission they were burying it.

That much was crystal clear.

Lily was paid to know things. She stayed two steps ahead, predicting outcomes before they even existed.

And guess what—

She hadn't heard a whisper about any planned event, no chatter, no warnings.

That meant this wasn't a mistake.

Someone wanted this to happen. Someone made sure it happened without interference.

Lily's jaw tightened.

"This wasn't just an accident," she murmured. "This was cleaned up before it even started."

Whatever Donahue had been selling? Gone, along with him as a witness.

By the time the fire was under control, Marge had had enough.

"We're leaving," she said. Ron blinked. "What?"

Marge looked at the wreckage. At the burned-out trailers. At the fence already going up. At the men in suits talking in low voices.

"We're going," she repeated. "The kids need to be away from this."

Lily, still feeling exposed in the situation didn't argue.

She grabbed her phone and then stepped away to book a floor at the Marriott. There were no points or discounts. It was a special phone number requiring a passcode.

"Dark horizon, 98zulu33tango." Lily said. The rooms were paid for with a special government contract, and only the General Manager, along with one federal agent, could book them and check the Trentons into the hotel.

Marge gripped the wheel too tightly.

Lily was silent.

Ivy kept staring out the window.

Ryder? He disappeared again, Marge decided not to wait, and left it with Ron.

Beth had barely said a word.

Grace scowled, and even Max was quiet.

The phone rang, and it was Ron. "Christ, Marge. What a mess."

Marge didn't trust herself to speak. She handed the phone to Lily. "Ron, it's Lily, what is happening with Joey, you at the hospital?"

Ron talked slowly, it was hard to hear even for Lily, who has listened to a lot.

"Because of the fire?" Lily said. Most of the kids started to hold back their tears, thinking the worst about Joey, and the shock started to wear off.

"Okay, good. I will tell them. Bye." Lily put the phone on her lap. Then, she updated the car so everyone could hear: Joey is stable. He'll need to stay at the hospital for a little while. They're taking care of him, okay?

The blast had taken a third of the Yard, and upended a family made up of kids who were getting used to not having their lives blow up.

"Lily, the Yard would have been gone, but the emergency services got there extra quickly. They had extra units available during Ballon Week, which helped a lot." Ron coughed.

CHAPTER 68

The next morning felt wrong in every single way. Things had changed.

Not because of the smoke still hanging in the air. Not because of the charred ruins of a third of the Yard. Not even because the Feds were still hovering like vultures, controlling every cleanup detail.

It felt wrong because everything was quite literally deathly quiet.

No Ron shouting about coffee. No kids arguing over who got the last pancake. No, Marge threatened bodily harm if someone didn't clean up their mess.

The Marriott was comfortable, safe, and the staff went to extra lengths to make everyone feel welcome—but it wasn't home. Everyone thought it was odd that they had a whole floor to themselves—it's a big hotel. Plus, they had armed guards keeping them safe, Lily told Marge. Then they both talked to all the kids.

Ryder was still missing, which Ron was well aware, and searching with the Bullshit Club trying to find him before Marge had that stress to deal with.

And a bigger theme, maybe, just maybe, was that home wasn't the same anymore.

A joint meeting with the City and Country was scheduled for an official explanation. Marge sat across from a stone-faced city official, arms crossed, a coffee going cold in front of her. She was a bit numb but ready to deal with whatever at this point.

"So," she said, voice sharp. "You wanna tell me what the hell we were 'storing' for you?" The man didn't blink.

"Chemical compounds," he said smoothly. "Nothing hazardous. Just some outdated materials the city was holding for disposal."

Marge snorted. "Bullshit."

"We have paperwork." The representative from the city shared.

"Then let me see it." Marge shouted.

"That's unfortunately classified. Ma'am". The tension was growing by the minute.

Marge leaned forward, wishing Lily had come to the meeting, but she wasn't allowed. "Let me get this straight," she said. "You're saying the city paid us to store chemicals, didn't tell us what they were, and now that they've burned up in a mystery fire, we're just supposed to accept that and move on?"

The man smiled like a politician or psychopath. "That's exactly what I'm saying."

Marge wanted to flip the table, and bitchslap that smile off his face. Instead, she exhaled. "And the money?"

The man shrugged. "That agreement is now void."

Marge felt her blood pressure spike and heart rate rise, and she was about 15 seconds from going what they used to call "postal."

"Let me finish, Mrs. Trenton, please."

He proceeded to share that, yes, the agreement was void, but the damage would be covered under a combination of local, state, and federal government policy for this type of event.

That trailer storage deal had been a financial lifeline more times than not. It had kept them afloat even when things got tight. So, it was momentary relief to know the Yard would get rebuilt. Marge decided, she wasn't going to fight about this today.

"Have a nice day, Ms. Trenton. I am sorry this happened to you and your family."

Ron was pacing when she got back. "Tell me we're not totally screwed," he said.

Marge tossed her keys onto the hotel rooms desk. "Well, we're not totally screwed."

Ron groaned. "Son of a—"

"What, wait, what did you just say? My hearing is a little messed up since the blast." Ron said.

Marge explained the conversation with the City guy. They will get paid for the damages through a special policy that parties have with the Federal government. She said the details were a bit vague.

Marge continued, "We also picked up a new contract, if you can believe the roller coaster this week has been." Ron blinked.

Marge handed him the paperwork.

"Space Force?" he read out loud.

"Yep."

"For… salvage recovery and specialty metalwork?"

"Yep."

Ron rubbed his face. "This is two times the trailer deal."

"Yep."

"Why?"

Marge exhaled.

"Because someone wants us to survive all this," she said. "Which means someone in the government still wants us around, which I take as both good and bad. I don't know what is up and down at this point."

Ron stared at the contract. And for the first time in days, he laughed.

"This is the weirdest fucking business in the world."

"Yep."

"We need to get to the hospital," both Trentons said at the same time.

The kids, at least, got one thing out of the chaos—a full week off school.

Not because they wanted a break—because they needed it, and each day they went and visited Joey. He ended up being in the hospital for ten days but would make a full recovery. He ended up being more wild than ever.

The fire had rattled them. Max and Grace barely slept.

Danny wouldn't talk about it. Even Beth, who usually treated life like one big shrug, was restless.

Ryder showed up almost a full day later—disheveled, tired, but otherwise in one piece.

He strolled into the temporary housing like nothing had happened, hands in his pockets, yawning like he'd just woken up from a nap instead of disappearing after an explosion.

Marge crossed her arms. "You better have a damn good excuse."

Ryder pulled out his phone, waving it lazily. "I texted Ron."

Marge narrowed her eyes. "And?"

"Told him I crashed at a co-worker's parents' place. Figured I'd let the chaos die down before coming back."

Marge didn't respond right away. Something about it didn't sit right.

Not just what he was saying—but how easily Ron had accepted it.

Because, of course, Ron never called to check.

He was already on a plane to Denver, heading straight into a debrief. A go/no-go meeting about whether he'd even be allowed to return to the Yard after the explosion.

And right now? That answer wasn't looking great.

Lily didn't waste time. She and Marge got them counselors working through the school district. No questions asked, no paperwork nightmares, just help.

And slowly—very slowly—things started to settle.

Until Beth threw a grenade into the middle of it.

Beth waited until breakfast.

Because she was a little shit, and she knew that was when Marge and Ron were least prepared for bad news.

"So," she said, stabbing a piece of bacon, "I'm not going back to school." Marge froze mid-coffee sip. Ron choked on his toast. The entire table went silent.

"Excuse me?" Marge said.

Beth smiled. "I'm getting my GED."

"You're sixteen," Ron said, voice strangled.

"And?"

"And?!"

Marge rubbed her temples. She had been doing this a lot lately to cope. "Beth, you can't just decide to drop out."

Beth grinned. "Actually, I can."

Marge closed her eyes.

"You've been waiting for this fight, haven't you?" Beth's grin widened. "Oh yeah."

Ron sighed, looking at Marge. "Can we legally stop her?"

Marge clenched her jaw. "No. But I can make her life a bit more miserable."

Beth leaned back in her chair.

"You could. Or… you could just let me do what I want and not fight a losing battle."

Marge wanted to strangle her.

Ron sighed. "Beth, everyone, you included have been through some heavy stuff the last month, make sense why you want control back. A big decision, you get that control, short-term anyway." He then proceeded to ask a good question: What are you going to do?

Ivy and Grace were watching like it was the best show on TV.

Finally, Marge exhaled.

"I'm tired, kiddo. Fine," she said. "What's your plan?"

Beth straightened. "GED program, part-time work at the Yard, and I'm gonna start writing seriously."

Ron blinked. "Writing? You write?"

Beth scowled. "Not funny, Pop." She shared a couple of contests and competitions in which she entered her short stories. "I want to be an author and write novels."

Silence. It seemed to stay that way for an extended period.

Then Ron muttered, "God help us."

Beth beamed.

That same day, while Marge was still mentally processing Beth's choices, Lily walked in holding an official envelope.

"Sign this," she said, dropping it on the table. Marge frowned. "What—"

And then she saw the heading. State of New Mexico Adoption Records. Her stomach flipped.

She looked at Beth. Beth was grinning, but she was nervous. Marge's hands shook as she opened it.

Ron leaned over. "Holy shit." Marge blinked at the words.

Ms. Beth Trenton.

Not a foster kid. Not a temporary ward of the state. Not just some tough-as-nails kid who wormed her way into their lives.

Beth was theirs. Officially.

Marge didn't realize she was crying until Beth nudged her. "You gonna sign it, or you gonna sit there like an idiot?" Marge laughed, wiping her face. "Shut up, you little weasel."

She grabbed a pen. Signed the damn thing. Ron signed next, looking suspiciously like he was holding back tears.

And Beth?

Beth looked at the paper. And for the first time ever, she looked like she belonged.

Like she had a real, undeniable place in the world. It was happy. It was frustrating.

It was confusing as hell. But it was theirs.

Ron squinted, tapping his chin as if the next question weighed heavily on him. "So, you still quitting school, Beth?"

Laughter erupted around the table and grew louder when Pop's face stayed serious.

"NO, you goofball," Beth said, shoving his shoulder with a grin.

The Yard wasn't the same. The world wasn't the same. But they were still here.

And for now? That was enough.

Or at least, it should have been. But things didn't just go back to normal after something like this. You didn't just rebuild and pretend that an explosion and death in your home and business never happened.

Damn hard to ignore when a third of your property with home was still a burned-out wreck behind a government-ordered fence with armed guards.

Not when men in suits were still hanging around, taking notes, and making sure no one asked too many questions, not when the kids woke up screaming in the middle of the night.

Marge heard it first. A sharp, choked gasp from one of the rooms at the Marriott. She was halfway out of bed before realizing what she was doing.

In the hallway, she nearly ran into Lily. They exchanged a look. Not the first time. Not the last. They found Joey curled up in the corner of his bed, shaking, eyes wide.

His little chest rose and fell too fast.

"Hey, sweetheart," Marge murmured, sitting on the edge of his bed. "You're okay."

Joey shook his head. "It was still burning," he whispered. "The smoke—I couldn't breathe."

Lily sat on the other side of him, her voice low, steady. "You're not there, Joey. You're safe. You are at the hotel, with room service, a pool, and two TVs."

It took a long time for him to calm down. And it wasn't just him.

Grace had stopped talking as much. Max—loud, fearless Max—was suddenly too quiet at night. Even Danny looked worn down, like something had cracked beneath his usual mask of fix-everything.

Marge had been through some hellish times before as a kid and adult, but watching these kids struggle?

It was a different kind of hell.

So the next morning, she made a call. By the afternoon, the counselors were arranged to expand when there were available.

The kids and whole family just needed help and support, when they needed it, not 9-5, Monday through Friday, minus holidays. The trauma didn't stop, it was shaking and rattling their lives.

The family was learning how to carry the weight of what they'd experienced and survived. And that? That wasn't weakness. That was fucking courage.

The next few days passed in a strange limbo. The Space Force contract was signed. Salvage teams would be coming soon to the Yard. The Federal government made sure Trenton Salvage wasn't hurting for revenue—*too* sure.

The latest bank transfer made no sense. Marge and Ron had tried talking to Lily about it three times since the last deposit notification, but they only got vague reassurances and subject changes.

Ron didn't like it. Not one bit.

He brought it up over coffee at the Bullshit Club's temporary meeting spot—a dim, cluttered garage that smelled like oil and stale cigarettes. The Yard was off-limits for now, so this would have to do.

Earl sat on a piss bucket as he called it, nursing a chipped mug, guarded with his words. "Government don't give money for free, Ron. **There's always strings.** Probably steel cables in this case."

"You're damn right." Ron leaned against the rusted hood of a beat-up Ford, arms crossed. "They wired us more cash than I've seen in my whole damn life. For what? Some salvage contract? I've been doing this business game long enough to know scrap doesn't pay *that* well."

Benny, the youngest of the Club—a wiry guy with permanent grease stains on his hands—blew out a breath, smoke, and shook his head. "Could be hush money. Y'know, keep y'all quiet about whatever they're really looking for at the Yard."

"Yeah, or hazard pay." Mannyl took a slow sip of coffee. "What if that 'salvage' ain't just scrap? What if it's some experimental government shit? Military don't show up for old car parts."

Ron looked at Marge, who sat on a stool with her arms folded, her eyes narrowed in thought. "What are you thinking, Marge?" Ron asked.

Marge tapped her cigarette against a coffee can she was using as an ashtray. "I'm thinking the government doesn't make mistakes like this. If they're throwing money at us, they're either covering their ass or setting us up."

The room went quiet for a moment.

"You think Lily knows something?" Luis asked, glancing between them.

Ron rubbed the back of his neck. "If she does, she ain't telling. Not one damn word, that isn't her, however. I don't think she…….."

Benny snorted. "Maybe it's alien junk. Like from Roswell or something."

Earl shot him a glare. "Really? You're younger but didn't see you as having a child's mind, don't be an idiot."

"Well, fuck me running, Earl." Benny howled.

"No, wait, Benny might not be as dumb as he sounds." Marge said, holding up a hand. "It sounds far-fetched even stupid, but Space Force contracts don't come with regular scrap jobs. What if there's *something* out there they don't want the public seeing? Something they need cleaned up quietly."

"Wow, wow, wow." Benny proceeded to pout as his feelings were now officially bruised.

Ron sighed, dropping onto a battered folding chair. "I dunno. But whatever it is, I don't like being kept in the dark. We're at the end of the tail getting wagged."

Luis leaned forward, voice dropping. "If I were you, I'd keep out it. Please don't ask questions they don't want answered. Government money comes easily when it's meant to buy silence. You don't want any visitors."

"Maybe." Ron exhaled. He looked down at his coffee, feeling a bit at a loss. "But we've got kids to think about. A home and business to rebuild."

"For now," Marge said, standing and crushing her cigarette in the can, "we do what we always do. Nothing more or less."

"Yeah? And what's that?" Ron asked.

"One minute at a time. Keep the business running, and family together." She looked at each of them in turn. "But we keep our eyes and ears open. Because this?"—she gestured vaguely toward the Yard—"this ain't over. Not by a long shot."

The room fell silent again. The only sound was the soft hum of a fan spinning lazily overhead. And outside, somewhere beyond the quiet streets of Albuquerque, the government's salvage teams were likely on the way to get started.

CHAPTER 69

The Yard was still a fucking disaster. A complete wreck.

A third of it lay burned out, fenced off with shiny new chain-link and **"OFF-LIMITS"** signs posted every six feet like some warning chant. Big, bold letters—like the Feds thought Ron Trenton couldn't read. It was as if the message wasn't already clear.

Stay *out.*
Don't *ask* *questions.*
Forget what you saw.

Government vehicles still came and went, their tinted windows reflecting the New Mexico sun. There were no logos or plates that meant anything. Black SUVs, white vans, uniforms without names.

And the trailer? The one that had started all this? Gone. Reduced to ash, twisted metal, and rumors.

Ron stood at the edge of the fence, arms crossed over his chest. He stared at the burned-out section of his Yard, jaw clenched so tight it hurt. The salvage teams—if that's what they really were—had brought in excavators last week. Dug deep. Buried or dug *something up.*

Something they didn't want anyone finding.

The fire had knocked the wind out of everyone, but as Marge had always said—

"Out of shit, you make shit sandwiches and keep going."

So, when Lily called Ron one afternoon with a business opportunity, he expected he might get another scaped out mall.

What Ron didn't expect—a movie production company fire sale.

Of all the schemes, half-baked plans, and questionable opportunities that had crossed his path, this one? This one felt like it came straight out of left field.

The phone rang. Once. Twice. Three times.

Ron sighed, leaning back in his favorite old office chair. The Yard outside still looked like hell—fenced off, burned out, and crawling with secrets about god knows what. His half-warm coffee sat forgotten on the desk beside him.

Ring. "Yeah, yeah, I'm coming."

He picked up on the fourth ring.

"He saw the caller ID, what, Lily? I'm *so* busy, can't you tell? Just drowning in work here."

On the other end, Lily didn't waste a second.

"Not now, Trenton." Her tone cut through his nonsense. "I've got something you're going to want to hear. How would you like to buy a warehouse full of movie props and art—for pennies on the dollar?"

Ron froze. Squinted at the phone like he hadn't heard right.

"*…What?*"

A beat of silence stretched between them.

"Movie props?" Ron repeated, dragging the words out. "Like... fake swords and alien heads and shit like that?"

"Yes." Lily's tone had that *you idiot* edge to it. "Set pieces. Costumes. Art. Furniture. The whole lot. Some production company pulled out of Albuquerque at the last minute—liquidating everything."

"Pennies on the dollar, huh?"

"Dirt cheap. But there's a catch."

"There's always a catch, I swear, a lifetime of more catches," Ron muttered, rubbing his jaw.

Standing in the doorway with a fresh cigarette, Marge raised an eyebrow.

"What now?"

Ron covered the phone. "Lily's trying to sell us movie props. Whole warehouse. Cheap."

Marge snorted. "Sounds like a scam, let me talk to her."

"Or an opportunity," Ron shot back, waving her off. "Hang on—Lily, what kind of catch we talkin' here?"

Marge grabbed the phone. "Lily, where you been, we've seen or heard from you in days." Lily didn't hesitate. "I've been catching up and working on all the paperwork and insurance issues for the Yard.

Changing back to the topic at hand. "Marge, the warehouse is rough. And you'd have to haul everything *immediately*. They want it *gone*—72 hours, so this week. No questions asked."

Marge was holding the phone out, so she didn't have to repeat the conversation. Ron blinked. "No questions asked?"

"That's what *they* said."

Ron leaned back, tapping the desk.

A warehouse full of movie props? In *New Mexico*, in Albuquerque? The state had been crawling with production crews lately. Big-budget sci-fi flicks. TV dramas.

But *why* would they abandon a whole warehouse?

No questions asked. Those three words gnawed at him. He was a lot more suspicious after the issues they had at the Yard and with the new contracts.

Lily sounded way too pleased with herself. "Some big production wrapped, and they don't want to store a ton of art. They're selling everything for ten cents on the dollar. The highest bid takes the whole lot."

Ron ran a hand down his face. *"Jesus Christ.* What kind of art?"

"Paintings. Sculptures. Weird modern stuff—no clue. But it's real.

And it's *cheap*."

Ron leaned back in his chair, the old wood creaking under his weight. *Art*. What the hell did he know about art?

But then his mind drifted to Lewis, Ivy, and Ezra—the creative ones—always sketching, building things out of scrap, or arguing about some artsy movie nobody understood.

They could figure out if this junk art were worth something.

He glanced across the room. Marge stood there, arms crossed, watching him like she already knew he was cooking up something dumb.

"What?" Ron asked, feigning innocence.

Marge narrowed her eyes. "Lily's offering us a ratty warehouse and a *truckload* of random-ass art?"

"That's the deal."

Marge blinked. "The *fuck* are we gonna do with a truckload of art?"

"WAIT. BACK UP." Grace nearly knocked over her chair. "You're saying we could buy a massive lot of production art for dirt cheap?"

Ron nodded slowly. "Yeah?"

Ivy and Lewis looked at each other like it was Christmas morning.

"WE HAVE TO DO THIS," Ivy said.

"Do you know how much art goes to waste after films wrap?!" Lewis added. "It just sits in storage forever!"

Ron sighed. "Yeah, but what the hell do we do with it?"

The kids immediately bolted to their respective computers, diving headfirst into research.

Old art, new art, movie props, installations—*ad nauseam*.

Ivy rattled off facts about famous lost paintings. Lewis mumbled about "potential black-market value" like he was planning a heist. Grace bookmarked auction sites and art history databases, her fingers flying across the keyboard.

Ron watched them, wide-eyed.

"Jesus Christ," he muttered to Marge. "It's like I lit a fuse."

Marge didn't look up from her cigarette. "Yeah. A fuse strapped to a truckload of art we don't know jack about."

And that's when Marge had her epiphany.

She straightened.

"Wait, what if we… pawn it?"

Silence.

Then Ron blinked. "Pawn art?"

Marge nodded. "An art pawn shop. We sell it online, auction it off—hell, half our online business is booming because of Ezra and the kids already." I think Ryder knows someone in the pawn business because of the electronics shop.

Grace gasped. "HOLY SHIT, THAT COULD WORK."

The whole room busted out laughing, Grace didn't really cuss that much.

Ivy was already making a list. "We could do direct sales, consignment, pop-up shows—"

Lewis had walked in, heard that they were perma-grinning. "Oh my God. This is insane."

Marge smirked. "Yeah. But it's our kind of insane."

Ron groaned. "I can't believe I'm saying this, but… fine. Let's do it."

And just like that—

They were in the art business.

The following week, the truckloads started arriving.

And panic set in.

Ron lost sleep because the sheer amount of art was fucking overwhelming. He couldn't get his head around why they got all this. It wasn't because they were that smart.

Sculptures, paintings, weird-ass modern art pieces that looked like someone glued trash together and called it genius.

Ivy stood in the middle of it all, hands on her head. "Holy fucking shit, we're gonna die under an avalanche of art."

Beth was grinning like a manic lunatic. "We need a strategy. Storage first, inventory second, then valuation."

Ron sighed, dragging a hand down his face.

"Marge, this was *your* idea. Fix it."

Marge shot him a look, arms crossed.

Ron held up his hands, backpedaling with a grin. **"I mean—*we'll* fix it. Together."**

Marge narrowed her eyes. "Uh-huh. That's what I thought."

Marge smirked. "Lily suggested we look for a place in Santa Fe, a better market for what we're doing. She did a bunch of research, some art pawn market assessment."

Lewis's eyes lit up. "YES. SANTA FE. WE HAVE TO GO."

Ron threw his hands up. "Jesus Christ, this just became a full-time business."

Ezra had returned from a month-long trip to visit and work at MIT.

He luckily missed the explosion and all that came after. He almost came home, but Marge insisted he stay in Boston. "This is some rich people's nonsense. An art pawn shop sounds like it might really be unique and work. I researched that Santa Fe has demographics, tourism traffic, and affluence."

Ryder, who was off work for the day, added, "I fully support it. I can help a couple of days a week up there."

People suddenly started showing up in the middle of this fast-paced, random, and interesting new whiteboard-like session.

Sam is from the city. The county commissioner. The police chief.

All checking in making sure the Yard was still standing.

Even weeks after the incident, local vendors still stop by to drop off food. Folks still show up, offering to help rebuild—not for money, not for favors, just volunteering.

New Mexico was called the **Land of Enchantment** for a reason. And it wasn't the landscapes. It was the people.

And then—

The movie stars who had worked with the production company?

They *donated*. A huge, anonymous check.

Enough to rebuild what they lost, 5x over.

Ron stared at it.

"…I don't even know how to process this."

Marge smirked, arms crossed, cigarette dangling from her fingers.

"Take the money, genius. They want to help. We'll use part of it to help others—greedy we're not, capitalist we are."

So they did.

And for the first time in a long time…

It felt like things—*life, people*—were finally getting back to some normal.

Even with the big donations still rolling in, it felt *better* than a few weeks ago. Better than when Joey was waking up screaming from nightmares *every single night*.

For a moment, they thought—

Maybe we're moving on.

CHAPTER 70

A few months after the fire, life at the **Yard** had started to get chaotic. There was so much activity, so much noise, and so much normality again.

The burned-out section of the Yard was fenced off, officially a "Federal Cleanup Zone".

The Space Force contract was moving faster than expected—new money flowing in, new clients sniffing around, and most surprising of all?

They were officially planning to be in the art business.

The Trenton clan rolling into Santa Fe was like pirates docking in Monaco.

They were too loud, fast, and obviously from Albuquerque or Española.

"We're gonna get stopped at the county line," Ron muttered as they passed the exit for Bernalillo, eyeing the rearview mirror like a cop would materialize any second.

Marge smirked from the passenger seat. "Santa Fe's not gonna know what hit 'em."

Lily, hands steady on the wheel, flashed a grin. "I'm fully expecting some hipster or old retiree to take one look at us and call the cops."

"We can sic the old codgers on them if that happens." Marge laughed.

"We're too rough for their delicate energy," Beth added from the backseat, leaning forward with a smirk.

Ivy snorted. "We should get shirts made: *Too Rough for Santa Fe.*"

Scrolling on her phone without looking up, Grace said, "Already designing it, thanks."

Ryder, staring out the window, let out a low chuckle. "You all act like we're invaders. It's just Santa Fe."

Ron gave him a side-eye. "Just wait until some dude in expensive linen pants asks if your aura is aligned."

A pause.

"…Whatever, Ron."

They pulled off Cerrillos Road into a small, old smaller stand-alone adobe building with a second-floor apartment.

The building wasn't much to look at—aged stucco, faded signage—bars on the window, but it had potential. Big enough for storage. Close enough to constant driving traffic, walking distance to restaurants, and the art scene to matter. And, most importantly, the rent especially for Santa Fe, didn't make Marge's soul leave her body.

The second they stepped inside, Lewis lit up like a Christmas tree.

"This is it," he breathed, his voice filled with unfiltered art-nerd joy. "We can actually do this."

Ron glanced around at the exposed brick walls, creaky floorboards, and half-broken fixtures.

"Jesus Christ," he muttered. "We're really doing this, huh?"

Marge clapped him on the shoulder. "You'll live, remember the junkyard on day one, and well, today still."

Beth ran her hand along the rough brick and grinned. "So when do we open?"

All eyes turned to Lily, who was already scrolling through a stack of legal paperwork. "Depends," Lily said without looking up, smirking. "How fast can you get a pawn license?"

Ron groaned.

"Christ. Do they give white-collar criminals a **pawn license**?" The whole family laughed at "white collar."

Marge laughed, blowing smoke out the side of her mouth.

"Ron. We've always been *opportunistic*—for the *right* reasons. Not *per se* criminals."

Lewis pulled out his phone and found a café a few minutes away— Counter Culture Café—supposedly a local favorite. They piled into the truck, shoulders aching, stomachs growling.

The place was busy, a steady trickle of people coming and going, with one person even standing in the doorway waiting for a spot. The building was low-slung and a little worn, like Santa Fe, the kind of place you might miss if you weren't looking. Out front, the patio buzzed with life—tables crammed close together, aluminum chairs, and dogs sprawled underfoot, lapping up water from battered metal bowls. It wasn't fancy, but it had that easy, sunbaked charm that made you want to stay awhile.

Inside, it was packed with people: students hunched over sketchbooks, workers still in boots and dust, clusters of tourists with maps folded on their laps, and local retirees nursing mugs of coffee. Everyone seemed to belong, like it was normal to cram strangers together at long tables and act like old friends. It had the casual hum of a Manhattan deli, only soaked in sunlight and New Mexico charm. It was easy to see why the regulars leaned on it—places like this didn't just serve food; they gave you a soft place to land.

They ordered hibiscus tea, coffee, Asian plates, banh mi sandwiches, fried egg sandwiches, and split two head-sized cinnamon rolls. For the first time that day, the world felt a little less overwhelming.

Back in Albuquerque, things had *mostly* settled.

Ezra had officially deferred MIT, but unfinished business at the Yard kept him grounded. It wouldn't be for at least another year.

Ryder had enrolled at UNM part-time but still spent his days at the Yard, helping, watching, always watching, and *doing his job.*

Beth was still fighting about school, but between Marge and Lily, she'd been convinced to do *one more semester, so Ron wasn't wrong after all.*

The other kids—Danny, Max, Joey, Ivy, Grace, and Lewis—were getting back to normal. Or at least, *as normal as the Trentons ever got.*

Joey's nightmares weren't as frequent anymore. The therapy sessions, courtesy of the federal government, had helped indefinitely. Ignore what happened, money disguised as care. But it worked. The kids were healing.

The Bullshit Club showed up in full force: Randall, Frank, Gus, Earl, Benny, Manny, Luis, Reggie, and Hamish.

They said it was for *"one last job."*

Except—this wasn't a job.

It was a *thank you.*

The movie stars—the ones connected to the production company—had sent a donation.

Another *huge*, anonymous check.

Enough to rebuild *everything* they lost but it was already covered many times over. The Trenton's voted with the Bullshit Club, they used the donation to build a community center with an invite only separate building, only for old codgers to resume bullshiting. It would all be on the Yard's property, compliments of the Yard (Feds, and Movie stars) for the community.

The whole crew sat outside. The fire pit burned low, casting flickering shadows across tired but content faces.

A cooler full of beer and soda sat between them. Cigars and cigarettes were blazing away.

Beth was already outlining a novel in a battered notebook, head bent in concentration. Ezra and Ryder were arguing over the best way to run online sales.

Ivy and Grace deeply discussed paint storage solutions and gallery lighting. Lewis paced, still buzzing with ideas.

And Max, Joey, and Danny ran around yelling, and causing a bit of chaos with every cover they turned. Thankfully.

Ron sipped his beer, watching them all with a mixture of pride and disbelief.

"You know this is insane, right?"

Marge didn't even look up. "Yeah. But it's *our* insanity. Thank god, we have it."

Beth glanced up from her notebook, a grin spreading across her face.

"One last ride?"

Ron shook his head, laughing as he looked around at the people who somehow, against all odds, had built something new from the ashes.

"Nah," he said, raising his bottle. "More like the *next* damn chapter."

And for the first time in a long time—

Everything felt right.

For now.

[The End – Book One]

3/18/2025

ABOUT THE AUTHOR

Bryan Wempen is an author and entrepreneur living in Santa Fe, New Mexico, whose work captures the messy, beautiful complexity of the human experience. His writing, grounded in sharp observation and unflinching honesty, draws from a life lived across the stark contrasts of rural cattle farms, bustling cities, and the diverse cultures of America's Indigenous peoples, mainstream America, and international communities.

Following the critical success of his debut political suspense series *Ambition Unbound*, which traces a near-future U.S. presidential campaign rife with moral ambiguity and power plays, Bryan has taken a bold leap into literary fiction with ***Adoption, Inc. A Family Affair***. This gritty, character-driven novel peels back the rusted layers of a junkyard-turned-foster-home scheme, told with sharp wit and emotional depth. It's a raw, satirical look at family, survival, and the sometimes-questionable pursuit of the American dream.

Bryan's writing reflects a patchwork of experiences—from cattle farm roots and political fascination to corporate life and cross-border observations. He continues to write stories that balance dark humor, social reflection, and the humanity found in even the most flawed characters.

When he's not writing, Bryan enjoys hiking the high desert trails with his wife, Michella, a modern tinwork artist whose creativity and eye for detail inspire his work. He also savors mild cigars and debates the merits of red vs. green chile. A lifelong passion for different cultures, first kindled by childhood family stories, cherished books, and timeless films, weaves itself through every corner of his storytelling, lending it depth, color, and resonance.

ACKNOWLEDGMENTS

To my buddy, my friend, my partner, and my wife — you keep my nuttiness in check while inspiring me daily with your common sense, creativity, and kindness. You're my sounding board, my anchor, and one of my greatest sources of strength. I'm so lucky to be on your team. Please don't ever change much, sweetheart — I love you exactly as you are.

To the many stories, people, and places that have left their mark on me — thank you for providing the foundation upon which my imagination is built, grows, and thrives. From a small-town rural upbringing to the broader lessons learned in life's unexpected moments, each experience has shaped and enriched my storytelling. To my family: I am eternally grateful, even if I don't say it enough.

While the characters, geography, and events may evoke familiar places or people, they are purely products of my imagination. As they say, life can be considerably stranger than fiction at times, and that truth often finds its way into the pages of a story.